Praise for *To Sleep in a Sea of Stars*

Instant *New York Times, USA To...* ...seller
Winner of the 2020 Goodreads (...ction

"Breathes new life into the classic fi... ...ni makes the experiences of his well-shaded explorers vivid and gripping through smart world-building and believable stakes. James S. A. Corey fans will be especially riveted." —*Publishers Weekly* (starred review)

"This pulse-pounding science fiction novel pits human curiosity and technology against alien tech deep in the cosmos. . . . An excellent starting point for the series as a whole." —*Library Journal*

"Paolini understands that in the best character-driven science fiction stories, the alien tech is never as interesting as the human relationships. Tense and gripping." —*Kirkus Reviews*

"Mounting tension, danger, and uncertainty . . . Shows Paolini's range as a storyteller." —*Booklist*

"Books are doorways out of the reality we occupy. Good stories take us not just outside of ourselves, but beyond what we can even begin to imagine. Science fiction affords us the ability to escape into possibility, and *To Sleep in a Sea of Stars* explores those possibilities with an engaging plot that steadily builds momentum across its pages." —*Den of Geek*

FRACTAL NOISE

CHRISTOPHER PAOLINI

TOR PUBLISHING GROUP · NEW YORK

FRACTAL NOISE

Fractal Galaxy endpaper illustration by Immanuela Meijer
Interior illustrations by Christopher Paolini

"'Tis a Fearful Thing" by Rabbi Chaim Stern from *Gates of Prayer: The New Union Prayerbook*, copyright © 1975 by the Central Conference of American Rabbis. Used by permission of the CCAR. All rights reserved.

A Tor Book
Published by Tom Doherty Associates / Tor Publishing Group
120 Broadway
New York, NY 10271

www.tor-forge.com

Tor® is a registered trademark of Macmillan Publishing Group, LLC.

The Library of Congress has cataloged the hardcover edition as follows:

Names: Paolini, Christopher, author.
Title: Fractal noise : Christopher Paolini.
Description: First edition. | New York : Tor, Tor Publishing Group, 2023.
Identifiers: LCCN 2023007591 (print) | LCCN 2023007592 (ebook) |
    ISBN 9781250862488 (hardcover) | ISBN 9781250909770 (international edition) |
    ISBN 9781250870162 (ebook)
Subjects: LCGFT: Science fiction. | Novels.
Classification: LCC PS3616.A55 F73 2023 (print) | LCC PS3616.A55 (ebook) |
    DDC 813/.6—dc23
LC record available at https://lccn.loc.gov/2023007591
LC ebook record available at https://lccn.loc.gov/2023007592

ISBN 978-1-250-29210-0 (trade paperback)

Our books may be purchased in bulk for promotional, educational, or business use. Please contact your local bookseller or the Macmillan Corporate and Premium Sales Department at 1-800-221-7945, extension 5442, or by email at MacmillanSpecialMarkets@macmillan.com.

First Tor Paperback Edition: 2024

Printed in the United States of America

0 9 8 7 6 5 4 3 2 1

AS ALWAYS, THIS IS FOR MY FAMILY.

And also for those who have stared into the abyss during the small hours of the night.

CONTENTS

A FRACTALVERSE NOVEL

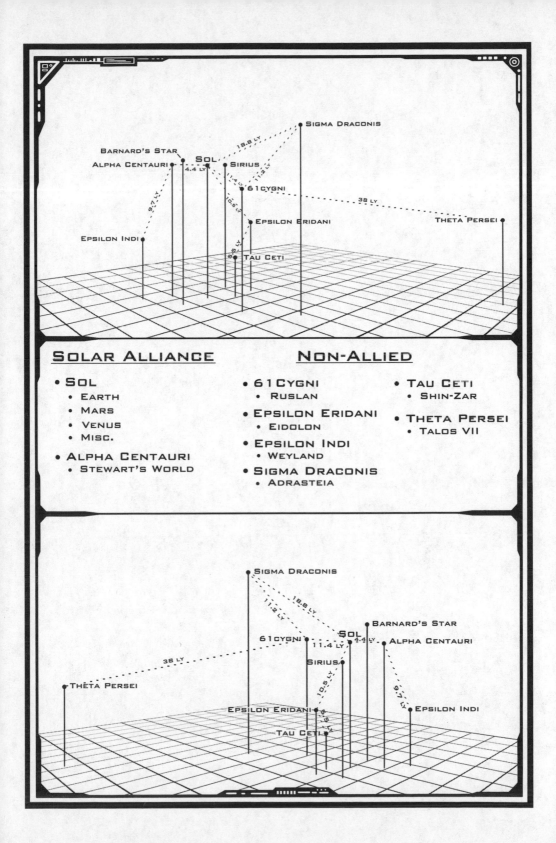

SOLAR ALLIANCE

- **SOL**
  - EARTH
  - MARS
  - VENUS
  - MISC.

- **ALPHA CENTAURI**
  - STEWART'S WORLD

NON-ALLIED

- **61 CYGNI**
  - RUSLAN

- **EPSILON ERIDANI**
  - EIDOLON

- **EPSILON INDI**
  - WEYLAND

- **SIGMA DRACONIS**
  - ADRASTEIA

- **TAU CETI**
  - SHIN-ZAR

- **THETA PERSEI**
  - TALOS VII

APPREHENSION

★   ★   ★   ★   ★   ★   ★

'Tis a fearful thing
to love what death can touch.

—CHAIM STERN

CHAPTER I

* * * * * * *

PERSPECTIVE SHIFT

1.

On July 25, 2234, they discovered the anomaly.

It was ship-night inside the SLV *Adamura,* and all the lights were off or else dimmed and set to red to avoid disrupting the crew's circadian rhythm. The halls and rooms of the vessel were hushed . . . but not silent. Life-support fans provided a constant background hum: lulling white noise that soon faded from notice.

Outside the *Adamura,* the sand-colored gas giant Samson receded into the black backdrop of space.

2.

The ship's lab was cramped. Equipment encroached from the walls, filled the center, leaving narrow walkways in between. Here it was warm from the computers, and the air had a thick, stifling quality. Numerous tiny indicators gave the impression of constellations scattered across the dark pieces of machinery.

Alex Crichton sat at the holo-display crammed into one corner, trying to read the results from the probe they'd dropped into Samson's atmosphere the previous day. Carbon, ammonia, methane . . . The list blurred before his eyes. It was well past midnight. But he still hadn't written his report, and the captain was expecting it first thing in the morning.

The smart thing would have been to write the report that afternoon, when he was still somewhat alert. That would have been the smart thing. Alex knew it. But he hadn't been able to bring himself to type a single word. Like most days, he felt little to no motivation during waking hours. It wasn't much better at night: an occasional spurt of panic would result in a brief run of productivity, but even then, the work he produced wasn't very good. He was too sleep-deprived, and Alex didn't want to take a wake-me-up pill like StimWare. What was the point? To feel better? That wasn't going to happen. As long as he could keep Captain Idris from chewing him out again, he didn't care to do more. None of it really mattered, after all. Not to Alex.

The holo swam before him, numbers floating disconnected from their background.

Alex blinked. It didn't help. Frustrated, and not having the strength to deal with the frustration, he crossed his arms on the plastic desk and rested his head on them. A shock of black hair fell across his forehead, cutting off his vision.

How long had it been since he got it trimmed? Three months? Four? It had been sometime *before*. That much he was sure of.

He buried his face in the crook of his elbow, and for a long while, the hum of the fans was the only sound in the lab.

3.

Before.

Never had a word so haunted Alex. Before leaving Eidolon. Before signing up for the survey expedition. Before the funeral.

Before . . .

It had been bright and sunny at the spare, A-frame remembrance center. The sort of bright and sunny that only occurred in nightmares. All their friends had attended the service, his and *hers*. Family too. That had been the worst of it. Her father with his heavy, shaggy head, murmuring advice and condolences that meant nothing to Alex. Her mother, a tiny, thin-boned woman who clung to his arm, weeping in such an effusive display, Alex found it actively off-putting. They both meant well, of course. How could they not? Their only daughter was dead, and there he was, a living link to the child they'd lost.

But he found their goodwill unbearable. Every moment of it had been a torment. He found himself staring past them at the pews of dark *yaccamé* wood; they seemed razor-edged in the clear, glass-like light streaming through the east-facing windows. Everything did, a world carved into being with the sharpest, most painful of instruments: grief.

At the front of the center was a bare concrete altar, and on the altar, the one thing he did not, *could* not, look at. The polished titanium urn he'd picked out three days earlier, barely paying attention while the funeral director guided him through a series of options. Like all the colonists who died on Eidolon, Layla had been cremated. Dust to dust, ashes to ashes. . . . Imagining the burner flames wrapping around her body caused Alex physical pain. It seemed obscene that her flesh had been subjected to such an ordeal, that her cells—still alive by most biological measures—should have been left to boil, wither, and char in the funeral home's ovens.

The Memorialist was an earnest, somber-faced woman who treated the proceedings with what seemed like appropriate gravitas. She spoke at length in a deliberate tone. None of what she said registered with Alex.

Afterward, the Memorialist brought him the urn. Her plain grey uniform was neat and clean, but she smelled of preservatives, as if *she'd* been embalmed. The scent nearly made Alex run.

He'd noticed the weight of the urn. It rested heavily in his hands, pulling him toward the floor, toward the ground and the end of all things. He didn't mind. A life should have weight. Old or young, it would have seemed wrong for a person's ashes to be too light.

Even when he accepted the urn, Alex still didn't look at it. Nor when he brought it back to the dome he and Layla had shared. Nor when he put it on the shelf at the back of her closet. Nor when—four weeks later—he packed his one bag, locked the pressure door, and left. The urn and the ashes it contained hadn't been *her.* They were something else, dull and inanimate, drained of color.

But even though he hadn't looked at it, Alex could still see the urn, could still see its polished curves, could *feel* it sitting at home with the weight of a truth that couldn't be denied.

And he hated it.

4.

A soft *beep* woke Alex.

He started and looked around, confused. The lab was as dark as before. Nothing had changed.

He scraped a crust of dried spittle from the corner of his mouth and checked his overlays: 0214. He should have been in bed hours ago. A message alert blinked in the corner of his overlays. He tapped it.

<Hey, come see me. You're not going to believe this. – Jonah>

Alex frowned. What was Jonah doing still up? The cartographer wasn't a night owl. No one on the survey team was, aside from Alex. And why ask to talk? The others didn't usually bother to interact with him, which was fine as far as Alex was concerned. Talking took too much energy.

For a long minute, he debated whether it was worth getting up. He didn't want to, but even in his exhausted state, he was tired of being alone, and a latent curiosity pricked him.

At last he pushed himself out of the tiny chair wedged in front of the desk. The muscles in his back protested as he stood, and his left knee throbbed; the old skiing injury being its usual asshole self. For all the miracles of modern medicine, there were still some things that couldn't be fixed. The doctors claimed nothing was wrong with the joint. It just . . . hurt. Like so much in life.

Alex took his mug of chell—now cold but still smelling of the spiced flavor— and made his way out of the dim, red-lit lab.

The main corridor was empty. His steps echoed off the grey metal, hollow and lonely, as if he were the only one left on the *Adamura*.

He didn't bother buzzing when he reached the survey station; he just hit the button next to the door, and it slid open with a loud clank.

Jonah looked over from his display. The light from the holo painted his gaunt face a sickly yellow. Faint wrinkles radiated from his eyes, like the deltas of dried-out rivers. They reminded Alex of the rivers of Eidolon. He wished they didn't.

"So you *are* up," said Jonah. His voice had a tense rasp. "Computer said you were."

"What about you?"

"Been busy. Couldn't sleep; doesn't matter. Come look. Got a whopper this time." His eyes gleamed with feverish intensity.

Alex sipped the chell as he went to stand by Jonah's shoulder. The tea stung his lips and mouth and left behind a warm glow.

Suspended in the display was an image of a flat, brown plain. Somewhere on the northern hemisphere of Talos VII, the second planet in the system, he guessed. A small dark spot lay like a drop of ink in the center of the otherwise empty landscape.

"That?" Alex asked. He pointed at the spot.

"That," Jonah confirmed. He reached into the image and spread his hands, enlarging until the spot filled the display.

A spike of adrenaline started to cut the haze in Alex's mind. *"Shit."*

"Yeah."

The spot wasn't a spot. It was a hole. A perfectly circular hole.

The burning in Alex's eyes worsened as he stared. "Are you sure it's real? Could it be a shadow of some kind . . . a trick of the light?"

Jonah grasped the edges of the hologram and turned it, showing the landscape from all sides. The black area was definitely a hole. "I spotted it right after dinner, but I had to wait to get pictures from a different angle to be a hundred percent."

"Could it be a sinkhole?"

Jonah snorted. "That big?"

"What's the scale?"

"Fifty kilometers from here to *here*." Jonah indicated points on opposite sides of the hole.

"*Shit!*"

"You said that already."

For once, his tone didn't irritate Alex. A hole. A *circular* hole. On an uninhabited planet located almost forty light-years from the nearest colony. At least, they thought it was uninhabited. All signs had indicated Talos VII was a dead, dry planet. Unless the life was buried. Or so different as to be unrecognizable.

His armpits grew damp.

"What did Sharah say?"

"Haven't told her yet. Ship minds need their sleep too, you know."

"Don't regs state—"

"I'll report it in the morning. No point in jumping the gun until I've got more data." Jonah glanced between him and the display. "Couldn't keep it to myself, though. Had to tell *someone,* and you're our resident xenobiologist. So whaddya think?"

"I . . . I don't know."

If the hole was an artificial structure, it would be the first concrete proof of intelligent, self-aware aliens. Oh, there had been rumors and hints, even going back before the Hutterite Expansion, but never anything substantial. Never anything obvious.

Alex swallowed as he stared into the center of the abyss. It was too large. Too perfectly symmetrical. Even with all the advances of the past few hundred years, he didn't think humans could make a hole like that. They just didn't have enough spare time or energy. And for what? Perfection implied seriousness of purpose, and there were only a few purposes that seemed likely: to pursue scientific research, to help fend off some existential threat, to fulfill a religious

need, or to serve as a piece of art. The last two options were the most frightening. Any species that could afford to expend that amount of resources on what
amounted to a nonessential project would be able to destroy every human settlement with ease, Earth included.

Perfection, then, was a warning to heed.

Vertigo unbalanced him as Jonah tilted the image. Alex clutched the edge
of the display to steady himself and reassure himself he was still standing in
the *Adamura*.

The hole terrified him. And yet he couldn't stop looking at it. "Why didn't
we notice it sooner?"

"Too far away, and Yesha and I didn't have the time. We've been swamped
mapping all the moons around Samson."

"Are you *sure* it's not a sinkhole?"

"Impossible. The curve of the edge varies by less than half a meter. Won't
know the exact amount until we're closer and we can get a better scan, but it's
not natural, I can tell you that much."

"How deep is it?"

"Again, can't tell. Not yet. Deep. Might be kilometers."

The sweat under Alex's arms increased. "Kilometers."

"Yeah . . . If this is what it looks like—"

"Whatever the hell that is."

Jonah persisted. "If this is what it looks like, we're talking about one of the
most important discoveries in history. Right up there with FTL. Hell, even if it
is just a big hole, we'll still get mentioned in every journal from here to Earth."

"Mmh."

"What? Don't think so?"

"No, it's just . . . If that was built, then where the fuck are the ones who
built it?"

5.

Alex sat on the bunk in his cabin, staring at his hands. With a sense of dread,
he opened the drawer by his pillow and pulled out the holocube.

He hadn't looked at it for almost two weeks, the longest stretch so far. He
might have made it another few days if not for Jonah's discovery . . . if not for
the impossible hole.

But now Alex had to see *her*. Even though he knew it would hurt. Even though he knew it would leave him worse off than before. He felt like an addict craving a fix; just one more hit, yes please. Stick the needle into the wound, dig deep into the ache, and let the fire fill his veins. He hated himself for it, and yet he couldn't stop.

The ghost of Layla's face looked out at him from within the cube. As always, it was her expression that struck him: a bright, flirty look, as if she were teasing him. Which she had been when he'd taken the picture. They'd gone on a hike behind their dome, out along the perimeter fence. The sun had been warm, the glitterbugs loud and sparkly—gemlike chips of color darting through the air—and her smile . . . oh, her smile. When she turned it on him, he'd felt the luckiest, handsomest man in the galaxy, and she the kindest, most beautiful woman. Truthfully, neither of them were, but he'd felt it, and the feeling had been enough.

I should have gone with her. I should have— He tried to ignore the thought, but it refused to leave: an evil mantra repeating on an endless loop.

He twisted the cube between his hands, forcing the points and edges into his palms, as if to split the skin. The pain was its own form of relief.

His head dropped lower. Again he could feel the weight of the urn dragging him down.

Sometimes the universe decided to rip apart your life and stomp on the pieces, and there wasn't a damn thing you could do about it except say, "Now what?"

He'd been asking himself that a lot over the past four months, ever since the accident. How was he supposed to move on? How was he supposed to act as if there weren't a giant gaping chasm inside him where everything he'd considered solid and dependable had crumbled away? How was he supposed to pretend to be normal again?

Alex didn't know. Often he wondered what would happen if he just *stopped*. Who would give a shit? Not his parents, that was for damn sure. They hadn't shown the slightest interest in his life after he left Stewart's World. He doubted that his death would be any different. As far as they were concerned, he was already gone. Out of sight, out of mind. They were practical like that.

Two weeks after the memorial at the remembrance center, his in-laws had insisted on taking him to church. Even under normal circumstances, he would have found it a strange experience; he'd never so much as stepped inside a place of worship—much less one as official as a church—before meeting Layla, and it wasn't something he'd gotten used to, despite her dragging him along for services every holiday (he'd drawn the line at regular Sunday attendance, not that work would have allowed for such frequency).

The church belonged to the Reform Hutterites, and the preacher was one of those relics with wrinkles and a beard who insisted on abstaining from STEM shots out of a belief that aging naturally brought you closer to God. He'd gone on about the usual Hutterite topics, which meant a lot of talk about sparseness and spareness and the benefits of self-denial.

It hadn't been what Alex needed to hear. If God existed, Alex figured he wasn't much for self-denial. No sir. If anything, God seemed to be a malicious prankster determined to make Jobs of them all.

He'd gone straight home after the service and signed up for the next available expedition. Anything to take him away from Eidolon and the hopes, dreams, and memories cremated there.

Leaving hadn't helped. No matter how hard he focused, no matter how many hours he pulled, the chasm still yawned inside him. And at the bottom of it was a gibbering, mindless version of himself. It wouldn't take much to push him into that darkness; he felt as if he were already halfway down the slope. Mostly though, he just felt tired. Exhausted.

The presence of an alien artifact on Talos did nothing to change that.

It scared him, of course. How could it not? But he felt no great desire to study the hole. His curiosity was a wet ember, guttering and smoking, fading to ash. Even *before,* he'd never been motivated by lofty ideals. He wasn't the sort to dream about discovering sentient aliens or of somehow learning deep secrets of the universe by examining strange new forms of life. Xenobiology was a job for him and little more. He enjoyed the puzzle-solving aspect of the work, but for the most part, it was just a means to pay the bills. And that had been enough.

Only now . . . it wasn't. Nothing was. Not work, and certainly not the hole. Were it up to him, he would take a few more readings and then leave. Let the folks who cared study the hole. He just wanted to stop thinking and feeling. Somehow. *Any*how.

Layla would have cared. All of the high-minded concepts that eluded him— and that he so often looked down upon as unrealistic and impractical—had lived within her. She spent hours talking about the possibility of finding intelligent life, about the philosophy of exploration, and what it would mean for humanity to finally know that they weren't alone. She'd burned with the power of her passion, and he'd admired her for it, even if he never really understood.

Oh, he could explain her beliefs in a rational, intellectual way, but he didn't *feel* them the way she did, which made it hard for him to embrace the positions she held. Most of the time that hadn't caused conflict between them, but when it did . . .

He pressed his lips together, and his breathing grew ragged.

The holo shimmered as he tilted the cube from side to side.

"Aliens," he whispered. "Sentient aliens."

The news would have delighted her . . . no, more than delighted—*transformed* her. The hole was everything she'd dreamed about finding. He could see how she would have smiled with excitement, and he knew there was nothing he or anyone else could have done to stop her from studying the structure.

Her smile . . . Tears filled his eyes. He wrapped both hands around the holo-cube, gripping it as hard as he could, and bent over, feeling the emptiness in the world where she ought to have been.

He fell asleep still holding the cube and tears drying on his cheeks. His last conscious thought was her name:

Layla . . .

CHAPTER II

* * * * * * *

QUESTIONS

1.

A loud hammering woke Alex. Someone pounding on the cabin door, the sound painful as a headache.

"Yo! Move your ass, Crichton! You're late. Briefing in the mess hall. Hurry it up!" Yesha, her voice the usual mixture of annoyance, impatience, and scorn.

Footsteps receded, and silence followed. Blessed silence.

Alex stared at the dark wall across from him. The lights were still off. His teeth hurt: a dull pulse of pain. He'd been grinding them while asleep. Again. If he kept it up, it wouldn't be long before he'd have to get them fixed.

. . . if *he* kept up.

An image of the hole filled his mind, black, huge, perfectly round. It felt immense enough to swallow all his thoughts—all his fears and torments—to swallow them and leave nothing behind.

It would be nice to be free.

He pushed himself upright, sat on the edge of the bunk. He felt thick and slow. Wrung out. A large part of him wanted to ignore the meeting in the mess hall and go back to bed, even if it would mean losing his contract with the expedition.

But he knew Layla would have gone to the briefing. *She* would have looked at all the data and asked all the questions that needed asking. And since she couldn't . . . He would do it for her, in honor of her memory. It was all he had.

He felt behind himself until he found the holocube under the tangled blankets. He put it in the drawer without looking.

Then he forced himself to stand.

2.

A confusion of overlapping voices struck Alex as he entered the mess hall. He winced, feeling assaulted by the noise. That and the harsh, full-spectrum lights of ship-day made him want to about-face and retreat to the dark comfort of his cabin. But he pushed forward, ignoring the throb of his knee.

The mess hall was the largest open space in the *Adamura,* which meant it was small, cramped, and bordering on claustrophobic. The whole crew was packed in around the white-topped table in the center, all twelve of them. Five women, seven men. They were a motley group: different colored hair. Different colored skin. Different accents. Only three of them—Alex included—came from the same planet: Stewart's World. For some reason, Stewart's produced more than its fair share of scientists and explorers.

And none of them originated from Eidolon. Not even Alex; he'd been a rare transplant. His lips twisted in a bitter smile. After all, who wanted to live in paradise when paradise could so easily kill you? If only he could have talked Layla into leaving. . . .

The hole on Talos VII hung projected above the table. Seeing the yawning abyss again did nothing to ease Alex's disquiet. There was something *wrong* about the hole. Artificial objects weren't supposed to be that big or precise. Stars, yes. Planets, yes. But not a goddamn *excavation* out on the edge of known space.

Pushkin, their geologist, sat pressed against one wall, wedged between his chair and the table. He was twice as wide as everyone else in the room and more than twice as thick—normal adaptations for anyone who grew up on the high-g planet of Shin-Zar, but in Pushkin's case, his size was as much fat as muscle. He kept complaining that he was wasting away on the *Adamura,* but if he had gotten any smaller, Alex couldn't tell.

The geologist wore an ornate silk dressing gown open to reveal an expanse of hairy chest that was tanned nut brown. The outfit was against regs—they were supposed to wear the company uniforms while on duty; navy blue jumpsuits with the Hasthoth Conglomerate logo sewn over the left breast—but arguing with Pushkin was an exercise in futility. He would happily debate from morning to night, or until he overwhelmed his opposition with a tide of disjointed words.

At the moment, he was slapping his palm against the tabletop and saying,

"—and I not understand why ship hasn't turned around. We already collect enough data to—"

"You're just a coward," said Talia in her snapping voice. She was their astrophysicist: a woman thin as a blade with a look of fervent intensity to her gaze. It wasn't a mistaken impression; the whole trip, she'd been focused, militant, and brittle as a bar of ice.

An indulgent smile split Pushkin's face, revealing his shovel-like teeth. "No, my dear. Quite to contrary. Only, I have well-developed sense of—how you say?—self-preservation. Something *you* appear to lack. Smart thing is leave system. Probable we been under observation since we dropped out of FTL. For all we know, aliens could attack any moment. We have responsibility here, responsibility *not* get blown up and warn everyone." His lips quirked. "Even *Alliance*." The mocking tone of his voice didn't surprise Alex. Citizens of Shin-Zar weren't particularly fond of the Solar Alliance, which was why their planet had (to date) insisted on maintaining its independence.

An expression of disgust formed on Talia's face, and she crumpled up her used napkin and threw it on the deck.

"Hey!" cried Jonah, and hopped back. His jumpsuit was rumpled, his hair a mess, and there were dark hollows under his eyes; Alex guessed he'd been up the whole night. No surprise there.

Talia leveled a finger at Pushkin. "As I said, *coward*." The word burned like a hot coal. "We do have a responsibility—to investigate this structure. If aliens are going to attack, then they attack. We need to find out what we can *now*, before it's too late."

"Screw responsibilities," said Yesha from where she sat by Jonah. Her appearance was as abrasive as her voice: long, spiked hair; blue tattoos that glowed with annoying brightness; and a seemingly permanent sneer. "What about our pay? If we bail early, is the company going to cancel our contracts?"

"Enough," said Captain Idris from where he sat at the head of the table. His voice cut through the commotion, like a razor through string. Silence fell in the mess hall.

Idris was built along the same lines as most of the starship COs Alex had met: tall, broad-shouldered, smart, good-looking, and gene-hacked to the legal limit, if not beyond. It was as if captains got stamped out of an identical mold, and each one emerged ready to climb the ranks of status and power. Was nature responsible for their sameness? Nurture? Societal stereotypes? Or was it just the gene-hacking? Whatever the answer, Idris's appearance and attitude did nothing to improve Alex's mood.

He was sure the feeling was mutual.

The captain leaned back in his chair and tugged on his gold-embroidered cuffs. His gaze flicked toward Alex, acknowledging his late arrival. *Dammit.*

Idris said, "Jonah, finish your report."

"Yessir." Jonah bobbed his head. "Uh, infrared shows the bottom of the hole is nearly seven hundred and seventy degrees Celsius. Could be geothermal, but if so, the hole is deep. Really deep. If not . . ." He shrugged. "Then there's some sort of reactor down there."

"Did you pick up any radiation?" asked Riedemann. The machine boss had been keeping notes on a pad in front of him; he was old-fashioned that way.

Jonah hesitated. "Sorta." He glanced at the ceiling. "Sharah, you want to tell them?"

From the speakers above came the synthesized voice of the ship mind, dry and somewhat amused: "As you wish."

The *Adamura* was lucky to have Sharah. A lot of research vessels had to make due with pseudo-intelligences, which were a poor substitute. Even so, Alex didn't care for the ship mind. The whole trip she'd kept trying to get him to move more, socialize more, visit the doctor more. More, more, more, *more.* Worried about his mental state, no doubt. Didn't mean Alex liked her butting in. Ship minds always thought they knew best, and maybe with good reason, but if he wanted to be miserable that was his own business.

The holo in the middle of the table flickered, and a simulated image of Sharah's head replaced that of the alien artifact. Short black hair, broad cheeks, square jaw, and eyes so blue they couldn't possibly be their original color.

Sharah opened her mouth, then frowned. An instant later, her head vanished and her whole body appeared: a foot tall and dressed in grey fatigues.

"Sorry. I hate being disembodied," she said, her too-smooth voice continuing to issue from the speakers.

Shouldn't have become a ship mind then, Alex thought.

Sharah clasped her hands behind her back, standing as if at inspection. "Per Jonah's request, I scanned Talos and went over every reading we've taken of the planet. Except for the hole itself, I found no evidence of a space-faring or even a postindustrial civilization. No thermal signatures, no electromagnetic emissions, and no unusual spectral readings. There *are* some hints of life on the surface: oxygen, ammonia, methane, carbon dioxide. It's not much, though—

more in line with low-level plants like algae rather than vertebrates or other complex organisms. But then we knew that already from our astronomical surveys."

While she talked, Alex edged his way to the back of the mess hall and made himself a cup of instant coffee. He took a sip and tried to ignore the metallic tang; the freeze-dried stuff never tasted right.

"Any gravitational anomalies?" Talia asked.

"Gravimetric readings are consistent with a planet of the size and density of Talos Seven."

"Maybe we ought to send—"

"The one strange thing I *did* find," said Sharah, "is the burst of static—high-frequency radio waves, three hundred and four megahertz to be precise—that emanates from the hole every ten point six seconds. Duration, point five two of a second. Energy approximately fifty-eight point seven terajoules, or five point five four terawatts, if you prefer."

The mood in the mess hall grew increasingly tense.

"That's a *hell* of a lot of energy," said Riedemann. He chewed on his lower lip, thick brow wrinkling. Alex could see him doing the math in his head. Alex wasn't sure exactly how much five point five four terawatts was, but if Riedemann—the man whose job it was to oversee the engines and other systems of the *Adamura*—was impressed, then so was Alex.

"It's spread over a fairly large area," said Sharah. "But yes, it's a lot of energy."

"Why didn't we detect it earlier?" asked Chen. Alex always forgot that he was part of the crew. Unlike Talia or Pushkin—or even Riedemann—the chemist seemed thoroughly unremarkable. His face was bland and indistinct, and he lacked the physicality of the others. Even his accent was impossible to identify. It was as if he were an anonymous placeholder, waiting to be supplanted by the actual article. . . .

Idris was the one who answered: "Too much interference from Samson and its moons. Also Theta P. was between us and Talos until the day before yesterday."

Theta Persei was the local star, yellow-white and boring.

"Not only that, but the pulse is more focused than you might think," said Sharah. "If I hadn't gone looking, it would have taken another few days to pick up."

"Three hundred and four megahertz," said Talia. "That's just about one meter exactly. A good wavelength for broadcasting through the atmosphere."

"The hole might be emitting other frequencies as well," said Sharah. "We won't be able to tell until we're closer." Her diminutive form started to pace on the table. Where her feet extended past the boundary of the projector, they vanished into thin air. "There's more. I went over the pulse with all the programs and algorithms in my memory banks. Despite first appearances, the EM *does* have an underlying structure. It was a bit difficult to suss out, as it's in trinary code—not the sort of thing that's immediately obvious. But I did find it. The sound is fractal. In fact, it's a highly developed representation of none other than the Mandelbrot set."

For a moment no one spoke.

Then Riedemann said, "It's not a hole, it's a *speaker*!"

3.

An odd mixture of fear, relief, and disappointment formed within Alex. The fear . . . well, it was nothing new. But he felt relieved that the hole might have a perfectly understandable purpose. And disappointment that the purpose was so mundane. A speaker, even a monstrously large one, was hardly very special.

The disappointment surprised him. He hadn't realized that he was so interested in the hole and that he'd been hoping for something more from it. *What* exactly, he couldn't say. Maybe an answer. Or even a question worth asking. Anything that would cut through the grey torment of existence.

"How many iterations?" asked Talia. "How deep does the set go?"

"I'm not sure yet," said Sharah. "I haven't figured out where in the set the signal is. The sequence is clear enough, but the exact position in the Mandelbrot set . . . I don't know. It's deep, though, deeper than I've been able to calculate. The signal might cycle for days. Years. Maybe it never stops."

Alex lifted the cup to take another sip and then put it back down when he saw his hand was shaking.

Across the table, Korith cleared his throat. Alex had barely talked with the doctor since boarding the *Adamura,* but he seemed like a good enough sort. Young, though, in a way that had nothing to do with age. He lacked the tinge of sadness that Alex had come to recognize in those who had survived a major loss.

Survived. . . . Endured was more like it. And to what end?

Korith said, "Why the Mandelbrot set? What could they be trying to communicate?"

"That they understand higher math?" said Talia. She shrugged.

Foil wrinkled, loud and annoying, as Pushkin unwrapped one of their limited number of dessert bars. Cheesecake, by the looks of it. "More likely explanation, signal is warning. Giant shout say *Stay Away!* to rest of galaxy. Trespass here and you find only death." He took a bite.

"Can you play it for us?" asked Jonah.

Sharah seemed surprised. Then she nodded and an eerie, shifting wail emanated from the speakers in the walls. It sounded like a synthesized whale song, or recordings of the kilometric radiation produced by the rings around gas giants.

The nape of Alex's neck prickled as he listened to the uncanny warble. Around the room, people's eyes gleamed; everyone knew it was a historic moment. The first time they or anyone else had heard a signal from another species.

After half a minute, the sound vanished. "That's enough of that," said Sharah.

For a while, no one spoke.

Captain Idris stirred. "When Sharah found this, I asked her to broadcast a short greeting in English, Mandarin, and ConLang Seven, followed by a mathematical progression in both binary *and* trinary on all reasonable frequencies. So far, there's been no response."

A flicker of alarm crossed Pushkin's face. "That not seem wise . . . *sir.*"

"If the aliens are watching, they've already spotted us," said Idris. "Might as well be friendly."

Pushkin opened his mouth as if to object and then subsided.

Yesha raised a hand. Her nails were rough and jagged. She had a nasty habit of gnawing on them while reading; Alex was always finding scraps of her nails in the lab. "Sharah, what about the planets that we haven't surveyed? Could there be artifacts on them also?"

The ship mind hesitated. "Possibly, but if so, they're inactive. After I finished looking at Talos Seven, I reviewed every bit of data we've collected since entering the system. So far I haven't discovered anything new. If other structures exist—holes, space stations, space*ships,* settlements—they're either abandoned or buried too deep to detect."

Chen looked at Alex with his weak, affectless eyes. "Could . . . I don't know, could the hole be some sort of emergent phenomena? Like a termite mound?"

A bark of laugher escaped Pushkin. "Why bother ask him? *Everything* is emergent phenomenon, Chen. Even you, and if you not know that, then your education was even greater failure than I thought."

"Hey now," said the chemist.

Talia made a dismissive noise. "The random action of the universe can't produce something as complex as a human, much less that hole."

Pushkin gave her a condescending smile and used his fingers to comb crumbs out of the beard that covered his double chin. "My dear zealot, just because faith blinds you to obvious realities of entropic action doesn't mean that—"

"You can debate this later," said Idris in a tone that precluded dissent. He was the only one who could shut down Pushkin's bullshit. Probably, Alex suspected, because the captain was the one who signed off on their performance reviews.

The geologist conceded with a careless wave of his paddle-sized hand.

Talia glared at him but held her tongue.

An awkward pause followed until Alex realized that Chen—and the rest of the crew—still expected him to answer the question. He scrambled to find words. "Uh . . . Yeah, I mean, it could be an emergent phenomenon, but . . . that would require a level of self-organization we've only seen among humans or machines."

Idris nodded. "So we're looking at something built by sentient aliens. Got it."

Maybe. But before Alex could express his doubt, Svana, the ship's XO, said in her thick, station-bred accent, "Sir, what do we do now?"

Alex tensed.

Idris leaned forward, rested his elbows on the table, and clasped his hands. He wore a large gold signet ring on his left pinkie, and he started to fiddle with it in an absent manner. "That's the question. Pushkin, you're right—"

"Why, thank you."

"—we have to warn everyone back home. However, the law is clear. Unless we're faced with a clear and present danger, we're not supposed to signal any human-occupied territory until we're at least five light-years away from the xenogenic presence. Not unless we want to spend the next twenty years in prison. So radio silence from now on." He leveled a finger at Yesha. "No more daily messages back to Mars."

She rolled her eyes.

It was a sensible precaution. No one wanted to lead potentially hostile aliens to Earth. An FTL-capable species probably wouldn't have *that* much trouble locating Sol if they really wanted to, but there was no reason to make it easy for them.

Idris continued: "As a precaution, I had Sharah launch a couple of emergency beacons toward the Markov Limit. If anything happens to the *Adamura,* they'll send a tightbeam burst with all our records to Cygni."

61 Cygni had been their point of departure, over three months ago.

"Pity we don't have a packet drone," said Riedemann.

A humorless smile crossed Idris's face. "Blame the accountants." Packet drones were FTL capable, but they cost as much as a small ship.

Korith said, "How long until the company notices we haven't checked in and sends a rescue team after us?"

"Soonest backup could show up is a month, and it could easily be twice that. In any case, we don't have the supplies to keep everyone awake for that long, and I don't know about you, but waiting in cryo isn't exactly appealing. Whatever we're facing here, I'd rather face it on my feet, with my eyes open."

There were nods and murmurs of agreement from the crew.

Idris spread his hands. "We're on our own here, folks. Company guidelines are vague when it comes to first contact. Our main priority is to ensure our safety. After that, we're to pursue the company's interests however we can. Exactly *how* we do that is for me to decide, but I'm open to suggestions. Talia, you're also right; we need to find out as much as we can about this artifact."

The woman gave a sharp nod.

A phlegmy sound of disagreement came from Pushkin. "And what if we attacked?" he said, angry. "*Adamura* not equipped to fight, and—"

"That's a risk I'm willing to take," said Idris.

"Maybe *you* willing," said Pushkin, "but is not risk I want. No."

Idris placed his hands flat on the table. "Until the situation changes, we're staying, and that's final. Is that clear?"

Pushkin grunted, clearly unhappy. "Is clear."

"Good."

Jonah spoke then: "Uh, what about our original mission, Captain? Like Yesha said, what's going to happen to our pay?"

Around the room, the others echoed his questions.

Idris leaned forward, his expression implacable. "Your pay will hold, and all contracts will remain valid. There was always a chance the system would prove unsuitable for a colony. The reason doesn't matter; we still get paid for our time. In fact, if I've read the regs correctly, all of us ought to qualify for full hazard pay. We'll have to check with Corporate once we leave, but I can pretty much guarantee it."

A few excited murmurs sounded. Full hazard pay equaled twice their base salary, and colony survey missions like theirs paid well to start with. Add in overtime and you were looking at the equivalent of a year's salary in a few weeks.

If the money had meant anything to Alex, he would have been impressed.

"Corporate isn't going to be happy about losing a potential colony," said Jonah.

Idris shrugged. "Not our problem." The crew reacted with noticeable approval. Even if the captain's casual dismissal was a put-on, it always went over well when he sided with them over the bosses back home.

Chen said, "How will this affect the timing of the mission, sir?"

"The timing doesn't change. We still hold to the same schedule. Only difference is we'll forgo surveying the rest of the system in order to focus on Talos."

Chen looked mildly relieved, as did several others. Many of them, Alex knew, had plans lined up for when they returned. Vacations, spending time with loved ones, writing research papers, shipping out on another deep-space mission. . . . Not him. For him the future was an unknown land, dark and devoid of promise.

"So, again," said Idris, giving weight to his voice. "How do we proceed? Options, people. I want to hear them."

Yesha said, "Get close to Talos, scan the surface, and image it with every frequency we've got."

Idris nodded. "That was my thought also. What else?"

Korith said, "Could we send drones to look at the hole?"

"They wouldn't be able to get close," said Riedemann. "The EMP will knock 'em out. We could drop them straight down—might get some good intel before the circuits overload—but it's probably a bad idea to start throwing stuff into the hole."

A soft laugh from Sharah. "Well, damn. There goes my plan to lob an asteroid at it."

Everyone but Alex chuckled or smiled. It was easy to forget that ship minds were still human; they didn't often make jokes like normal people.

Jonah hugged himself, as if cold. "What if . . . what if instead of a drone, we drop a crawler by the edge of the hole?"

"It would still get fried by the EMP," said Riedemann.

Idris stroked his chin. "Can you harden a crawler to withstand the pulse?"

"Not sure, Cap'n. I'll look into it, but . . . The amount of lead I'd have to bolt on would probably make the crawler too heavy to move."

"See what you can do and report back to me."

"Sir."

"Anyone else? Chen? Svana?"

Chen raised a hand. "We could try a high-altitude balloon."

Idris nodded. "High-altitude balloon. I like that. Sharah, run some simulations. See if it would work."

"We would still have a problem with the EMP," the ship mind said.

"Noted. What else?"

As the others threw ideas at the captain, Alex stared into the black depths of his coffee. The disk of liquid looked disturbingly like the giant hole. He could see it in his mind: huge, yawning, and deeply *wrong*. And yet, Alex could think of nothing else. The hole remained embedded in his mind . . . a puncture wound in reality, drawing him closer with inexorable force.

He listened to all of the crew's proposals. Some were more reasonable than others, but he knew that none of them would have appealed to Layla. They didn't go far enough. Scans, drones, attempts to communicate . . . half measures at best. The crew seemed to be avoiding the most obvious course of action, as if they were too scared to face it.

It was Talia who finally said: "I have a suggestion."

No one but Alex took notice.

She spoke again, louder this time. "I said, I have a suggestion."

The conversation paused, and Idris swiveled his head to look at the fierce-eyed woman. The captain raised his eyebrows. "And what would that be, Ms. Indelicato?"

"We have a lander. Why don't we use it?"

The room erupted as everyone started to argue. Fear clutched at Alex, and he tried to interrupt, but no one heard him any more than he heard what they were saying. Sharah might have been able to understand everyone's words, but if she did, she didn't bother to translate.

A loud *crack* as Idris slapped the table. The commotion ceased, and he looked them over. "Settle down. We're not going to get anywhere talking all at once." Around the mess hall were a number of sheepish nods. "Now then, Indelicato, why don't you explain." The captain's voice was stern, but there was an approving spark in his expression that confirmed Alex's suspicion—Idris *wanted* this. The reason he kept taking ideas from the crew was because he saw an opportunity here, an opportunity to manage one of the greatest discoveries in human history. And the captain, as Alex had suspected, was nothing if not ambitious.

"We have a lander," Talia repeated. "I say we take it down, land as close as we can to the hole without disrupting the site, and then march over and—"

"No!" Alex cried. The word burst out of him without warning. He hadn't intended to speak, but the thought of going near the hole caused a spike of panic that, for a moment, obliterated all rational thought.

Along with the others, Idris turned to look at him. The captain appeared less than pleased. "You have something to say, Crichton?"

It took a moment for Alex to gather himself enough to respond. He knew that Layla wouldn't have approved, that she would have argued for the opposite position, and that he was betraying her ideals, but he couldn't help it. The fear was overwhelming. "No," he repeated, more softly. "It's too dangerous, and . . . and we shouldn't disturb the site. The Alliance should send a team out to study Talos. A *qualified* team."

"The Alliance might not have that chance," Talia said from between close-set teeth.

Pushkin snorted. "Stuff and nonsense. You've lost your mind. We have no business sticking our noses where—"

Idris stopped him with an upheld hand. The captain frowned, his face as severe as a carved mask. "I'm surprised, Crichton. I would have thought that you, of all people, would leap at an opportunity to study an alien artifact."

Alex swallowed. "I'm a biologist, not an archaeologist. I study microbes. Plants. Animals if there are any."

Idris's frown deepened. "And you're not interested, not even a little bit, in the hole?"

". . . I just think landing is too risky. We don't know if the aliens are friendly or hostile, and again, if we mess up the site, we could destroy priceless information."

"It's a *big* site, Crichton."

Alex stiffened himself against Idris's disapproval. "In my professional opinion, *sir*, landing would be a profound mistake, and I'll submit that opinion as an official recommendation."

"And *my* professional opinion," said Talia, "is that we should land."

Idris glanced around the room, again assessing their mood. "What do the rest of you think? Honest opinions now."

Svana rubbed her arms. "We should leave."

"Land," said Korith.

"Land," said Yesha.

"Leave," said Pushkin. "And you know damn well why."

"Leave," said Alex.

Sharah laughed and softly said, "Land."

When all the votes were tallied, the final count was six *yeas* and six *nays*, with the captain left as the tiebreaker. The crew waited in suspense as Idris sat in silence. Then he said, "Riedemann. Would it even be possible?"

The machine boss chewed on the corner of his mustache. "Could work, Captain. As long as the lander didn't get too close, the electronics should be fine. Our skinsuits are already hardened against solar flares. They'd handle the EMP a lot better than even a shielded crawler, and I might be able to make some improvements."

"You'll do it, then?" said Talia.

"Sir—" Alex said, but Pushkin snorted and overrode him, saying, "You can't seriously consider this, Captain. Is completely mad."

"I'm considering *everything* right now," said Idris. "And I'm not going to rule anything out until we have a better picture of the situation. If trouble pops up, we're running. If Riedemann can't solve the technical problems, landing is a no-go. If for any reason I think the *Adamura* is at risk, I'll abort. We'll do a hard burn to Talos and then reassess." The captain shifted his gaze to the rest of them. "That gives us four days, people. Let's make them count."

4.

For the duration of the 1.25 g burn to Talos VII, they studied the anomaly (and the system as a whole) with every tool at their disposal. Alex did what was expected of him, even though the additional force of the burn made every movement harder, slower, and more dangerous, and he felt increasingly exhausted. Nevertheless, he tried. For Layla, if nothing else.

From a spectral analysis of Talos, he was able to determine that whatever life existed on the planet, it was definitely carbon based. No surprise there. Most of the life found in the Milky Way was carbon based. Just not sentient.

On the second day of the burn, surface imaging actually allowed him to identify two xenoforms. The first was a bloom of yellow-and-blue organisms in one of the salty lakes along the equator, close to an erupting volcano. The organisms were small, microscopic even, although it was hard to be sure of their exact size from so far away. They were motile to a certain degree—they rose and sank in response to sunlight—but nothing about them indicated they were more than simple plants or animals.

The second was a number of low, brown-colored objects that moved about the plains surrounding the hole. Mainly on the eastern side, for some reason. The objects—turtles as he thought of them—were between one and three meters wide. Their motion seemed entirely random: corkscrews and slanting lines and strange wiggles that Alex couldn't make sense of. Whatever they were, they displayed no obvious signs of intelligence. Nor did they seem to interact with the hole.

Of course, appearances could be deceiving.

Aside from that, Alex found nothing of interest. The rest of the crew met with even less success. Except for the hole, there appeared to be no other artificial structures on Talos or in the system. Nor were Talia and Sharah able to tease any more meaning out of the bursts of fractal noise emanating from the hole.

Analyzing the incoming data kept Alex busy enough that he rarely thought of Layla, even though she was the reason he worked. He didn't dwell on the fact. The more he did, the more he knew he was likely to slip back into despair and apathy. For him, forgetfulness was a gift more valuable than any memory.

Every night, he fell asleep within minutes of collapsing into his bunk, and only once did he end up curled around his pillow, crying for things lost and broken.

Mostly he thought about the void that sat waiting for them on Talos. He thought of it, and he dreamed of it too—a great black circle that dominated his nightly visions. Sometimes he imagined he was flying down into the hole, flying toward the mysterious bottom, and then he would wake with a strange feeling in his chest, as if his heart had skipped a beat.

5.

In the evenings, the crew gathered in the mess hall to swap information and suppositions. There were four main topics of discussion: the physical structure of the hole, the various ways they could investigate the hole, the meaning of the hole, and the unknown aliens who had made it.

Normally Alex would have avoided the conversation, but now he lingered to hear what the others were thinking. Besides, although he was reluctant to admit it, the sound and warmth and human company were preferable to the dreadful emptiness of his cabin.

So he remained in his corner seat and sipped his coffee while the others tossed theories back and forth. Sometimes he even contributed.

"What I want to know," said Riedemann one night, "is what's powering those bursts of EM. Fifty-eight point seven terajoules is as much energy as a small nuke."

Jonah frowned. "No ionizing radiation."

"No, but you wouldn't get any from a shielded reactor. It couldn't be too far down in the hole, though, or you'd have to deal with geothermal heat."

"Could do it, even at the bottom."

Riedemann snorted. "Yeah, but you'd have to be crazy. Why would—"

"Who knows why they did anything?" said Pushkin, brandishing a tumbler full of liquor. Like the rest of them, he had taken to referring to the makers of the hole as *they*. The unknown *they*. He pointed at an image of the hole floating over a screen. "That's not handiwork of race scared of challenge."

Talia turned from where she sat eating, her back stiff and perfectly upright. "The turtles are what I'm curious about. What are they? Plants? Animals? *Machines?*" She raised her eyebrows. "They could be caretakers for the hole. They could even be the ones who made the hole."

"It doesn't seem very likely," said Alex.

"But we don't know, do we? That's the point."

"We know one thing," said Chen. He looked up from the soup he'd been spooning into his mouth. "No one would go to all the trouble of building something like this if they didn't have a good reason."

A sly, trollish expression enlivened Pushkin's heavy features. "Now why you assume that, my narrow-minded friend? Hmm?"

Chen put down his spoon and turned his colorless eyes on the geologist. "It just makes sense. No one would devote so many resources to building a structure that size unless it did something."

"We know what it does," said Pushkin, grinning. "It emits blast of electromagnetic energy every ten point six seconds."

Chen didn't seem convinced. "Yes, but why? Why would they need a beacon or a transmitter that big?"

Riedemann smoothed his mustache with the back of a knuckle. "If that thing is a transmitter, it's the most inefficient, ass-backwards one I can think of."

"Problem with you," Pushkin said, extending a meaty hand toward Chen with insulting elegance, "is you can't imagine something built for non-practical purpose. Hole might be nothing more than piece of art."

"Or a church," said Talia.

"A *church*?!" Pushkin's eyes widened with mock astonishment. "So you think *they* have souls? Hmm? And if they do, were they all damned from moment of creation, since Lord's word never reached this space corner? Or do you imagine savior was reincarnated here, there, and everywhere to rescue souls of sentient species throughout universe? Will we find writings of space Jesus at bottom of hole? Hmm?"

If anything, Talia's back grew straighter and her eyes colder, harder. Alex had an uncomfortable sense of violence coiled within her, as if she would happily stab or shoot anyone foolish enough to cross her. If Pushkin noticed, it didn't seem to bother him.

"Heathens are always damned," Talia said, her tone as unforgiving as the sentiment. Then: "Unless they can be converted. There is only one Lord and Savior, and only one chosen people, and *we* are the chosen."

A spark of sadistic glee twinkled beneath Pushkin's heavy brows. "Is so? Does that really seem like actions of kind and loving god? Hmm? Damning those who never had chance for salvation?"

Talia gave him such a flat, empty look, that for a moment, even Alex's grief shrank before it. "What makes you think *He* is kind and loving? What possible evidence do you have that this universe is anything but cruel and heartless?"

Pushkin seemed caught flat-footed. He took a slug from his glass. "Why worship such horrible deity then? That seems height of self-delusion."

"Because He exists," said Talia. "He *is*. And it is His presence and His plan that give purpose to existence."

"Sounds like propaganda. And what *is* purpose to existence, if—as you tell—everything is cruel and heartless?"

Alex wanted to know that as well.

Talia lifted her chin. "To serve Him and to be rewarded in the next life in accordance with our virtues." Her stoic expression cracked for a moment, bitterness distorting her face. "Because heaven knows we aren't in this life."

That Alex understood, and he felt a new sense of kinship with Talia. Whatever had hurt her, it must have been as deep and painful as Layla's death was to him.

Pushkin had the decency not to push the astrophysicist any further, which in Alex's opinion was a smart decision.

Then Chen, who had been listening silently along with Riedemann, said, "I still think no species would spend the amount of time and energy needed to build a structure like that unless it was absolutely necessary."

Riedemann scratched the side of his jaw. "Depends on the size of the civilization."

"That's—"

"Not saying you're wrong, Chen. But, just look at all the crazy stuff humans make for no other reason than we want to. Maybe *they* are different. Maybe not. But if their civilization is big enough, building a hole like this might be a weekend project for them. Who the hell knows?"

Chen cocked his head. "If they were that advanced, why haven't we seen any evidence of them before?"

"It's a big galaxy," said Alex.

Pushkin laughed and leaned back in his chair, hands laced behind his head. "Or maybe they all dead. To all things an end, eh? . . . No, no, wait. Moment of genius has struck; I know what hole is." A wide grin split his face. "Is Jacuzzi."

"A what?" said Chen.

"You know, is tub." The geologist gestured. "Fill him with water, and he'll be nice temperature by time heat filters up from bottom. Party time."

Riedemann was the first to laugh—loud and hearty—quickly followed by Pushkin. Chen smiled faintly, as if he didn't really see the humor. Even Alex snorted at the ridiculousness of it all. Only Talia remained stone-faced and unaffected by the thought.

6.

On the afternoon of the third day, Alex was walking back to the lab after visiting the head when he bumped into Korith and Yesha heading the opposite direction. The two were deep in conversation and didn't see him.

"Hey, watch it, knucklehead," said Yesha. Then, without pause, she said to Korith: "It depends. Are you putting your name in?"

Alex muttered an excuse and detoured around them.

"Of course," said Korith. "As long as Idris—"

"Yeah, yeah. He won't send more than three, four people, I guess."

Alex paused. He looked back. "What?"

The doctor glanced at him. "Didn't you hear? Idris green-lit the landing. It's a go."

"... No, I didn't."

Yesha shrugged. "Guess the captain didn't get around to telling you." And then they walked off, leaving him standing alone in the bare corridor.

Cold crept up Alex's spine. He tried to shake it off. Why was he worried? Just because Idris had jumped the gun and ... The captain couldn't force him or anyone else to go down to Talos. There was nothing for Alex to fear, so why did he feel so bad?

Brooding, he continued back to the lab.

For once, Alex finished his work ahead of schedule. His heart wasn't in it, but he moved without thinking, eyes and hands operating on auto. His brain, though, remained fixated upon the hole and the prospect of a landing party.

He couldn't stop thinking about it.

"Why?" he whispered. Across the lab, Jonah glanced at him and then returned to staring at his own display.

Alex's stomach knotted and gurgled. When he tried eating a midafternoon ration bar, it gave him horrible indigestion. So much so that he had to rush back to the head.

He was just finishing in the lab when a message popped up on his overlays. It was, he saw, copied to everyone on the ship.

> *Ground mission is authorized. Volunteers only. Message me directly
> if you want to participate. Four-member team is required or mission
> will be scrubbed. – Captain Idris*

The mess hall was a buzz of tense conversation by the time Alex arrived for dinner. Everyone kept asking, "Did you see?" and "So? You put your name in or what?" but no one would answer that last question except for Talia, who, with characteristic bluntness, said, *"Yes."*

Even Pushkin was coy about his answer. "Time will show to all." He said this while eating a platter of food equal to Alex's entire daily calorie count.

He wondered how much cargo space Zarian ships had to devote to food. If Pushkin was anything to go by, everyone from their planet ate like starving gorillas.

Alex endured as much of the talk as he could, but after a quarter of an hour, he was a knotted ball of tension and every word grated, so he dumped his half-finished dinner and started for the door.

Halfway there, Pushkin cleared his throat and said, "Ha! No guess what you choose, Crichton."

Alex paused. He looked back to see Pushkin watching him with an expression of cruel amusement in his hooded eyes. Across the mess hall table, Talia regarded him with cold contempt. They both seemed to hate him, if for different reasons.

He left without responding.

Back in his cabin, Alex sat on the edge of the cot. Prickles of sweat popped up on his forehead, and he felt mildly feverish, his whole body going hot and cold.

He shivered.

"Why?" he whispered again.

He clenched his fists and rocked back and forth, an image of the hole burning in his mind. His pulse quickened, his chest tightened, and he squeezed his eyes shut.

If Talia or Jonah or anyone else from the crew landed on Talos, Alex feared what would happen. They had training, but not as xenobiologists. It would be all too easy for them to disrupt or contaminate the site, and thus make it impossible for humanity to study what had originally been there. Not out of malice, but ignorance. And that was without considering the possibility that the landing party might make first contact with the hole's makers.

He took a breath and tightened his fists even further.

Idris was going to send a team to the surface no matter what Alex did or said. That much was clear. The question was, could Alex stand by and watch them go without him?

Before, the answer would have been easy. But now . . . Now he could hear Layla's voice whispering in his ear, and he knew what she would have wanted, what she would have asked for. And he could not bear to betray her.

The pain in his palms eased as he unknotted his fists.

He stood with a swift motion and crossed to the desk opposite the bed. He tapped on the holo-display for a moment and then stabbed his index finger down and sent the message he'd written to Idris:

If you have to send a team to Talos, I want in. – Alex

He let out his breath and let his head fall back. The knot of tension in his gut remained as tight as ever, but with it, he felt a gathering of determination. Some things were easier once you just . . . decided.

It was what Layla would have done. For her sake, he would land on Talos VII. For her sake, he would study the hole and risk whatever was left of himself to learn more about the artifact and the aliens who had made it. For her. If it cost his life . . . so be it. Whatever hardships awaited them on the ground, he was willing to endure. Suffering was its own form of absolution.

He also felt an obscure hope that perhaps—just perhaps—he would find some sort of answer while investigating the hole. Surely the aliens had built it with purpose, and surely they must know more about the workings of the universe than did humans. If he could understand their purpose, maybe it would help pull back the veil of existence and let him glimpse what lay beneath.

Alex knew it was an irrational hope, and he buried it in the depths of his mind, but the idea lingered, weak and fitful.

He shut down the console, turned off the lights, and fell into bed. He was even more exhausted than normal. All he'd done was talk and stare at a screen all day, but the emotional strain of the situation had emptied whatever reserves of energy he had left.

Tired though he was, he couldn't stop thinking about the hole, and the thoughts filled him with nervous anxiety.

He didn't fight the mental excitement. It was a welcome relief from his normal round of morbid obsessions, even if he was so . . . damn . . . tired. . . .

7.

Morning came all too soon, bright and harsh and with no promise of improvement. His neck and the small of his back ached from their ongoing burn, and the mattress had left a deep imprint on his left cheek. Alex tried to calculate how much he weighed at the moment, but he couldn't do the math in his head, and he didn't care enough to use a calculator. Either way, 1.25 of a g was enough to make a man feel older than he was.

With an effort, he dragged himself out of bed and started to pull on his jumpsuit. A text popped up in the corner of his overlays:

<My office. Five minutes. – Idris>

Trust the captain to already be up and working. . . . Alex fought back a flutter of uncertainty. How would Idris respond to his request?

He took a moment to comb his hair and then hurried out of the cabin. His bum knee throbbed with every step; it always did until it warmed up, and the extra .25 g was doing nothing to help.

Alex followed the curve of the ship's hull around to the captain's office. It was the only room that might be considered spare space on the *Adamura,* but even in his more cynical moments, Alex had to admit that it served a useful purpose. Having personnel meetings in Idris's cabin wouldn't have been the best way to maintain the chain of command.

He knocked.

"Enter," said Idris from inside.

The locking mechanism of the pressure door made a loud *clank* as Alex opened it.

The office was a small, spare room—an off-white box with a row of transparent shelves along the left-hand wall. Mounted on the shelves were models of different ships: tugs, freighters, even a planetary defense fighter from Sol. Alex wasn't sure, but he thought they were the ships Idris had served on previously.

For a moment, he imagined tiny people on the tiny ships, each of them living in their own version of reality, as if each person—each being—was locked in a personalized Markov Bubble, forever unable to reach out and touch those around them.

"Crichton," said Idris, jolting Alex from his reverie.

"Sir."

The captain sat on the other side of a thin composite desk. It looked almost comically small compared with the width of his shoulders. Mass was always at a premium on a spaceship, which meant the furniture was usually half the size it should be.

Idris motioned at one of the two chairs bolted to the deck.

Alex sat.

The captain rolled the signet ring around his finger. "Why do you want to go down to Talos, Crichton?"

The question shouldn't have caught Alex off guard, and yet he still felt unprepared to answer it. "I'm the survey xenobiologist. I think I ought to be there. . . . Don't you?"

Idris fixed him with a hard gaze. "What I think isn't the point. Three days ago you were dead set against landing. What changed?"

Uncomfortable, Alex studied the top of the table. "I needed some time to get used to the idea."

"Really. You haven't exactly covered yourself in glory the past few weeks, Crichton. You've been late on half your assignments, and I have a list of complaints as long as my arm from the rest of the crew about your, shall we say, lack of team spirit."

"Sir. That w—"

"Why should I think you're not going to fuck things up if I put you on a landing team? Why would this be any different than before? Help me do my job, Crichton. Tell me why I should take a risk on you."

Alex swallowed hard. For the first time since signing up to the expedition, he felt a sense of shame. He'd always done well at school and work, always prided himself on taking care of the things that needed doing. But that had been *before*, and he knew Idris was right; he—Alex—hadn't acquitted himself with any sort of distinction on the *Adamura*.

But that could change.

"Because," he said, "I want this. It's important to me . . . sir. For personal reasons."

Idris shook his head and laughed in a disbelieving way. "Goddammit. Every time."

"Sir?"

The captain leaned forward and rested his forearms on the desk. "You're not the first fuckup to come through this office, Crichton, and you won't be the last. The company isn't too picky about who they send on these expeditions. I don't know what's going on in that head of yours, and I don't care. But I *do* care about this landing mission. So. I'm asking you, Crichton: Can you keep it together?"

Alex lifted his chin, feeling the sting to his pride. "Yessir."

Idris stabbed a finger at him. "Prove it to me, then. Stay on top of your work from now on. Be the best damn xenobiologist I've ever served with. Because if you can't, if you slip up even once, then that's it. I'll send Yesha in your place."

Knee-jerk outrage caused Alex to say, "Yesha? She's a glorified meteorologist—"

"Climatologist."

"Whatever. She's not a biologist or even an ecologist. She doesn't know the first thing about cataloging an alien biome."

"Exactly," said Idris. "But she's reliable, and that matters."

Alex tried not to take it personally, but it *was* personal, and Idris wasn't wrong. So he clenched his jaw and held his tongue.

"Oh, and one other thing, Crichton. I want you to draft a proposal for the landing party. Best practices, quarantine protocol, how you think we should investigate the site. That sort of thing. Have it on my desk by oh-eight-hundred tonight."

"Yessir."

Idris nodded. "We clear?"

"Yessir. Clear as space."

"Alright. Get out of here."

8.

All that day, Alex slaved over his screens. After spending the usual amount of time going over the latest images and readouts from Talos, he worked on the landing proposal Idris had asked for. It wasn't easy—nothing was—but he managed to recruit enough brain cells to write something halfway coherent, and he sent it off after a late lunch.

The whole ship was a hum of activity as the crew prepared for their arrival at Talos. The machine deck in particular was a source of noises loud and small as Riedemann worked to ready equipment for the mission to the surface.

Four days of work. Four days of study and toil, building and arguing, sweating and swearing. Four days of uncertainty while they raced toward the strange black hole where it sat, pulsing like a great empty heart.

And early in the morning of the fifth day, they arrived.

TALOS VII: 45°30'47.77''N 110°36'3.23''W ELEV: 124M ALT: 549.85KM

CHAPTER III

* * * * * * *

ARRIVAL

1.

Alex hung floating in the astrodome, holding one of the straps bolted next to the *Adamura*'s observation port. With his free hand, he rubbed his knee. Even in weightlessness, it continued to ache.

Through the sapphire window, he could see Talos turning below them. Or above, depending on how you viewed it. The planet was a great sandy-colored ball strewn with craters and volcanoes and rust-red plains. There were no seas; only large lakes stained with sulfur and arsenic. Clouds were rare, and in the northern hemisphere, they lay in long, thin bands—stretched out by the winds that tore across the hole. Sharah had run the numbers; the energy output from the hole was driving the seemingly ceaseless wind, heating a strip of ever-moving air that circulated Talos from west to east.

The hole was visible from space. Barely. A dark pinprick that never changed appearance, regardless of the angle of the sun. With magnification it grew in size to the monstrosity Alex was used to, but without, it seemed unimportant. Innocuous even. *Still big enough to swallow Plinth.* He remembered his last glimpse of Eidolon's capital, shrinking below him as the shuttle arched toward the transport waiting in orbit. . . .

In his overlays, Alex superimposed the map Jonah had created: a series of seven concentric rings radiating from the hole, each one of increasing width. The zones were labeled. Starting from the farthest one out, they were: *Alpha, Beta, Gamma,* and so forth until arriving at the seventh, smallest band, which was *Eta.* As Jonah had explained, the zones corresponded to the different features of the plain surrounding the hole. Near the abyss, in Eta Zone, the ground was worn flat, ablated by the wind and what Alex assumed was the force of the EMP blast (*could electrostatic charges alter the behavior of dust in the air?*). Farther out, Zeta Zone marked a change in texture—a slight irregularity—in the still generally flat ground. There were other changes in each zone thereafter until, at the far border of Alpha Zone, the landscape seemed entirely unaffected by the presence of the hole (although the winds continued to exert their erosive influence on every stone, mound, and prominence).

The map was a useful way to visualize the hole's effect on its surroundings, even if the details were vague. As for the turtles, they seemed to range mostly from Delta to Eta, but Alex knew that some of them had been spotted all the way out in Beta Zone: lone specks on the otherwise empty land, meandering along their seemingly random paths.

The smell of processed algae and pickled radishes wafted past with obnoxious intensity. Alex wrinkled his nose. Weightlessness didn't particularly bother his stomach, but the container of green-and-red mush Pushkin had just cracked open was another matter.

"You mind?" he said.

The geologist hung upside down relative to Alex, floating there like a huge, flabby blimp, the fringe of his beard waving about his face. He slurped up a mouthful of the disgusting pickled dish. "No, I not. Haven't you had shipkraut? Is good for digestion. Mmm-hmm."

Alex frowned and went back to staring at the hole.

2.

Once the *Adamura* stabilized its orbit around Talos and cut its engine, Captain Idris authorized Sharah to bounce a laser off the hole. Jonah protested, saying, "If someone's down there, they might view it as an attack."

Captain Idris's lips thinned. "I'm willing to take that chance. We're not flying into this blind, Masterson."

"I'll make the laser as weak and diffuse as I can," said Sharah. "I doubt anyone will take it as an attack, if they even notice."

From the laser, they learned several things. First, that the air over the hole was blowing from west to east at about four hundred klicks per hour. In the upper atmosphere, that was; lower down the wind was slower, although not *that* much slower.

Second, that the burst of EM every ten point six seconds was causing the atmosphere to vibrate like a giant drum. At the center of the pit, it resulted in the creation of a shockwave similar to what a bomb might produce, and by the edge, a blast of sound about 180 dBs (Talos's atmosphere was similar in density to Earth standard, so the power level of the decibels was fairly comparable).

Riedemann frowned. "That complicates matters. Protecting folks from an EMP is one thing. Protecting them from that amount of sound is actually a lot harder. Even with a helmet, a hundred and eighty decibels is liable to put a serious dent in your hearing."

Third, that the circumference of the hole varied by less than half a millimeter, and the hole extended into the earth for at least thirty kilometers. As best they could tell, the walls of the hole were perfectly smooth for the first twenty-six of those kilometers. Past that, the atmospheric turbulence was too strong to get a reliable reading.

No natural hole could be that deep. The sides would collapse or subside without support. That alone was impressive. But it was the smoothness of the hole that made the aliens' technological prowess seem even more formidable to Alex. He shivered. The creatures had to be hundreds, if not thousands of years more advanced than the Alliance.

"What's it made of?" Yesha asked.

Pushkin was the one to answer. "Around hole? Sandstone. Is bottom of old lake or sea dried out at least million years. Nothing special. Right at hole? Metamorphic quartzite."

"The sandstone got melted?" asked Riedemann.

Pushkin shrugged. "Not just heat make quartzite. Need pressure too."

"Now what, Captain?" Chen asked.

Idris templed his fingers. "Now? We wait a few days and see what happens. If nothing jumps out and starts shooting, we'll send the lander down."

A long sigh came from Pushkin, and he shook his massive head. "Is still too dangerous. Far, far too dangerous."

"No," said Idris. "It's a carefully calibrated risk. The profit potential here is astronomical. I shouldn't have to tell you what that would mean for this crew."

Alex didn't care about the bits. What was the point of riches and fame if you didn't have the answers? Or *an* answer? Without it, the center could not hold.

Pushkin made no attempt to hide his irritation. "Royalties do us no good if dead," he muttered.

"Besides," said Idris, ignoring him, "if the aliens are still on Talos, and if they're paying attention, then they already know we're here. It would be rude to turn back now without going down to introduce ourselves."

3.

They waited in orbit for three days. Three days of watching and measuring. Three days of broadcasting greetings and mathematical theorems that went unacknowledged and unanswered.... Three days of ever-increasing boredom, tension, and excitement. Round and round the *Adamura* went, falling at 27,685.7 kilometers per hour, falling and falling and never hitting. An orbit every one and a half hours. Fifteen point seven two orbits per day, ship time, and with each orbit, Alex felt as if he was being twisted up even tighter.

On the morning of the fourth, another message popped up on Alex's overlays while he was eating breakfast:

<My office. Ten minutes. – Captain Idris>

Alex hurriedly finished eating, trying not to let any crumbs or drops float free of his mouth (eating in zero-g was always an exercise in containment). Despite his efforts, a few bits of his ration bar drifted off toward the galley's intake vent.

Then he used the handholds embedded in the walls to pull himself up the main shaft of the ship and through the curved corridor to the captain's office.

The door was already open, and voices drifted out.

He entered to see Talia and Pushkin standing in front of Idris's desk, anchored by the gecko pads on their boots.

Pushkin rolled his eyes as he saw Alex. "Not *him*. You joke with us."

Alex bit back a response. *The feeling's mutual.*

"Close the door," said Idris, serious.

It took Alex a few moments of maneuvering. Gecko pads helped, but moving objects in weightlessness was still difficult.

He took the spot to Talia's left. She gave him a flat, evaluating look. He returned it. *What the hell have I gotten myself into?* The person he'd been *before* would have been more careful. He wouldn't have jumped into this sort of situation, with these sorts of people. But now . . . he didn't care.

Behind the desk, Idris crossed his arms and let a long moment pass before saying, "Right. I asked for volunteers. Well, I've got them. Everyone but two people put their names up. But I can't send them all. The ship needs its crew, and there's no point in sending, say, Riedemann. This mission has to be lean and mean. We get in, we take a look, and we get out with the minimal amount of disruption."

Alex found himself nodding. The captain was ambitious, but he wasn't stupid. If they ruined the site for future researchers, they'd earn nothing but condemnation from everyone in the Alliance.

"Quantify what exactly means *take a look*, Captain," said Pushkin, nibbling at a fingernail on his left hand. "Do we poke dirt around lander for few days, pretend we know what dirt means, then leave?"

Idris shook his head, his expression as fierce and determined as Alex had ever seen. "There wouldn't be much point in that. No, Talia had the right idea. The landing team will put down as close to the hole as the EMP will allow and then continue toward it on foot."

On foot! Alex had expected as much, but the thought was still daunting.

The captain continued: "The goal is to perform an in-depth survey of the hole and its surroundings." Pushkin looked as if he were about to interrupt, but Idris stopped him with a look. "We can go over the details later. Right now, I have to decide who is going." Idris leveled an index finger at them. "The three of you are the obvious choices. Astrophysics. Geology. Xenobiology. Everyone else is optional. What I need to know is, can you actually work together on an away mission?"

Alex glanced over to give Pushkin an appraising look and caught the geologist eyeing him in a similar manner. Talia never broke her pose.

"Wait," said Alex. "Are you telling me *he*"—and he pointed at Pushkin—"volunteered for this mission?"

The geologist stroked his oiled beard. "You are correct in assumption. I submitted name at first possibility."

"I'm sorry, but what? Why?"

Idris interlaced his fingers. "Since you brought it up, I'd like to know as well."

The smugness emanating from Pushkin was nearly enough to cause Alex to reconsider and march out of the office. "No green-skinned aliens try to shoot us out of sky, so I think it good to investigate while we can. I prefer to avoid risk, but landing on Talos is biggest possibility for learn new information, and I am always eager for *gratification*."

Idris's upper lip curled slightly. "Great. How about you, Talia? Since it seems we're doing confessionals."

The astrophysicist stood even straighter, if possible. "Sir, I think it's worth the risk *because* of the danger. Whether or not the aliens are hostile, they are much more advanced. We have to learn everything we can from them, for the betterment of humanity."

"... *the betterment of humanity,*" said Idris. "Everyone's a politician today. Okay, Crichton, what's your excuse now?"

"Same as before."

The captain snorted and shook his head. "Shit. . . ." He leaned back in his chair and looked them over. "If this weren't so important, I'd be tempted to call this whole thing off."

Maybe you should, Alex thought. But he kept the thought to himself.

"Okay, I'll ask again. Can you three assholes work together? You're going to have to rely on each other down there. If something goes wrong, won't be much we can do to help from orbit."

A tense silence; the hum of the life-support fans was the only sound. Then Talia said, "Sir, yessir."

With an expansive smile and spread of his arms, Pushkin added, "Under circumstances, I believe we become most friendly teammates."

"Yes," said Alex.

Idris didn't seem convinced. "Uh-huh. I'm g—"

"But," said Pushkin, and the captain acquired a wary expression, "it seems that in mission like this, it important, *no,* necessary, to outline clear chain of command. Who has charge of expedition?"

"Me," said Idris. "I'm in charge. As for operational command, that depends on how well the three of you impress me between now and departure. . . . Sharah will be announcing the final team roster later today. Until then, you're dismissed."

With a chorus of *yes sirs* they left the office. In the hallway outside, they paused and looked at one another. For a moment, a sense of shared uncertainty seemed to join them: a realization of what they were about to face together.

"Well," said Pushkin with insincere cheer, "this seems like most grand outing, no?"

"Just don't get in my way," said Talia. She stalked off.

Alex grunted and headed toward the survey lab. Behind him, Pushkin cackled, and the geologist's voice boomed after him with intimidating volume: "Oh, ho, yes! Most grand!"

4.

The final personnel list arrived in Alex's inbox exactly fifteen minutes later. Skimming it, he felt no surprise. The choice of whom to send was obvious.

Lt. Svana Fridasdottir
Alex Crichton, Xenobiology
Tao Chen, Chemistry
Talia Indelicato, Astrophysics
Volya Pushkin, Geology
Jonah Masterson, Cartography

Please report to Riedemann on the machine deck to familiarize your-
self with your new equipment. Departure is set for 0900 tomorrow.
– Sharah

The lander held only six people. One of those needed to be a trained pi-
lot—in case the computer guidance failed—which explained Lt. Fridasdottir's
presence. Also, Alex suspected Idris was sending her to act as a proxy. If anyone got out of line, she'd be there to herd them back. *That answers the question*
of who's in charge.

As Alex headed toward the machine deck, he passed the mess hall. Korith
was there, chest puffed out, arms waving, as he argued with the captain. "—why
you wouldn't send me. Jonah doesn't need to go. He's a cartographer, for fuck's
sake!"

Idris stood with his weight on one foot, glancing at the steaming kettle at the
back of the mess hall. "You're too important to send. Sorry, but that's how it is.
Same with Riedemann. I'm not sending the *Adamura*'s machine boss off-ship,
and I'm sure as hell not sending her doctor."

"But if I'm going to be needed, it's down *there*," said Korith, pleading. He
sounded very young.

Idris sighed. "We can't afford to lose you, Korith. Simple as that. If something happens to the team on Talos, we'll get them to you as fast as possible, but
I'm *not* sending you down there. Am I clear?"

"Yessir." Korith crossed his arms and stood staring at the deck as Idris strode
past him to the kettle. Then Korith noticed Alex lurking in the hallway, and he
scowled and turned away.

Alex continued on, thinking. In earlier days, *before*, he would have spoken
up, argued with Idris. But it didn't seem as important now, and the thought
of arguing with the captain was itself exhausting. Besides, Idris wasn't wrong.
The ship and the people on it had to take priority. Alex and the five others
heading to Talos were, in the end . . . expendable.

Knowing that didn't bother Alex. Perhaps it should have. *Cracked in the head. Sure are.*

The machine deck was a narrow, cross-sectional disk of the *Adamura,* sandwiched between the cargo hold above and the shadow shield below (behind which sat the Markov Drive that allowed them to travel faster than light, and the fusion drive that allowed them to travel much, much slower than light when jetting between planets). It was a warm, somewhat stuffy room, with walls painted flat grey, 3D printers and other machines slotted into alcoves, and a tangled skein of conduits overhead.

Riedemann was busy clipping a set of skinsuits to a workbench when Alex arrived. "There you are!" the machine boss said, glancing over his shoulder. "Come try this on."

The rest of the landing team trailed in as Alex struggled into the skinsuit Riedemann handed him. Putting on a skinsuit while in zero-g was never easy, and the difficulty was compounded by the fact that this particular skinsuit was stiffer than normal, and there was a black metal plate mounted over the power pack on the back.

"EMP shielding," Riedemann explained. "And it's woven throughout the suit. Adds a couple hundred grams, so not too bad."

Once all six of them—including Lt. Fridasdottir—had donned their skinsuits, Riedemann had them stand anchored to the deck with their arms outstretched while he pulled, poked, and took various measurements Alex didn't understand.

Moving about Talia, the machine boss said, "The suit'll keep you alive, but it won't do much more than that. Anywhere closer than ten, fifteen kilometers to the hole and you'll lose wireless, radio, lasers. Everything but oxygen."

Pushkin tapped the plate. "What make this work?"

"PFM." At the geologist's odd look, Riedemann laughed. "Pure fucking magic. That's how. Look, do you really want me to go into the intricacies of electrical engineering?"

"No, that not necessary."

"Yeah, thought so."

Then Chen asked, "What about protection from the sound?"

Riedemann shook his head. "There's not much I can do about that. Active dampening will only help so much when your whole body is getting hammered." He tapped the helmets. "I added some extra insulation on the inside.

On the outside, I put some coatings that should make your helmets acoustically invisible to the frequencies near the hole, only . . ."

The machine boss's pause seemed to trigger Chen's nervousness. He wet his lips. "Only what?"

"Only, the coatings aren't very durable. They'll erode pretty fast with all the dirt and dust flying through the air."

"At least you try," said Pushkin.

After showing them the suits, the machine boss brought them over to the cargo hold. "Ta-da!" he exclaimed, gesturing at what looked to Alex like four large sledges, similar to the ones he and his friends had used on Stewart's World when they hiked up to the best skiing spots.

The sledges were almost three meters long, with streamlined fairings that transformed them into elongated silver bullets. There was hardly any clearance between the upturned noses of the sledges and the honeycombed deck.

"Why do I have unpleasant feeling," said Pushkin, "that you expect us become beast of burden?"

Riedemann smirked. "'Cause you've got a suspicious mind, that's why. Here, look at this." And the machine boss opened the fairing on the near sledge to reveal a flat-bottomed (and otherwise airtight) storage compartment. A hatch by the nose opened to a lower compartment packed with fuel cells, supercapacitors, and an electrical drive train. "Be kinda stupid to make you drag the sledges all the way to the hole, wouldn't it?" said Riedemann. He tapped the lip of the lower compartment. "There's enough room in here for a mini-reactor, like in an exo, but *a* we don't have a printer capable of making one, and *b* rigging those up is tricky work. Not the sort of thing you want to be doing haphazard-like, if you know what I mean."

"Would it explode?" Svana asked.

Riedemann bared his teeth in a somewhat unpleasant smile. "Sure could, among several other unpleasant outcomes. Anyway, power goes down to here—" And he leaned over to point a middle finger at the underside of the sledge's upturned nose. Squatting, Alex saw a wide tank tread along the bottom of the sledge.

The idea, as the machine boss explained it, was for the motorized sledges to carry their portable hab-domes, food, water, medical supplies, and other equipment, including the various pieces of scientific apparatus they would need. However, Alex and the rest of the team would still have to walk on foot all the way to the abyss.

"It seem to myself," said Pushkin, "that if you bolt chair in sledges, we could ride with style and comfort whole way and save us lot of trouble."

Riedemann shook his head. "Thought about it, but that would up the wind resistance, which would be a major problem. Also, the treads take more power to run than wheels, so . . . Put it this way, these babies—" he patted the side of the sledge, "have enough juice to get your gear to the hole, but not much more. And that's even with photovoltaics embedded in the skin of the hull."

"So how are we supposed to bring everything back?" said Alex. They couldn't be leaving junk at the edge of the hole.

"Land yachts," Riedemann said, grinning like an excited kid.

Talia raised an eyebrow. "What?"

"Land yachts! We used to have them back on Mars. Take a sledge, slap a sail and some wheels on it, and whoosh!" He motioned with his hand. "Away you go."

"You can't be serious."

But he was. Packed within each sledge was a carbon-fiber mast, rigging, a spar, a sail, and four small wheels (one a spare). As soon as the team was ready to head back to the lander, they'd convert the sledges—it only took about five minutes—hop in, and let the wind carry them over the plain.

"Just you watch," said Riedemann. "These babies will run fast, real fast. As long as you do your job, they'll take you from the hole to the lander in under a day. Hell, you could probably do it in an hour, hour and a half, if the ground is flat enough."

Which, ultimately, was why they would be landing downwind of the hole. That and because *upwind* the air would constantly be trying to push them into the abyss. Not a problem when they were at a distance, but up close . . . an unexpected gust could easily shove them over the edge. Also, they would be tired on the return trip. It was better to face the wind on the way in rather than the way out. Besides, if they had to flee, they'd want the wind helping, not hindering them.

Even if none of those things mattered, there was still the question of proximity. Spending any length of time close to the hole would be physically dangerous. Fatal even. The EMP wasn't so bad. It was the bursts of sound. Riedemann had been able to shield their suits against some of the noise by coating them with metamaterials that rendered them sonically invisible within certain wavelengths. But he couldn't block all of the wavelengths. And the sheer power of the sound emanating from the hole was enough to shake a person apart. Even in short doses it would cause intense discomfort.

Therefore, once they made it to the hole, they'd have to do their work and then get away as fast as possible.

And to get there, they'd still have to walk. How far exactly, Alex didn't yet know, but his knee twinged just thinking about it.

As Riedemann explained more about the sledges, Alex began to feel as if the amount of equipment and supplies had been miscalculated. No matter how he divided them, there didn't seem to be enough for everyone on the team.

When he mentioned the problem, Jonah snorted and crossed his bony arms. "You didn't hear? The lieutenant is staying with the lander. An' since Captain doesn't want anyone to be alone on the surface, guess who's the lucky guy who gets to run diagnostics while you're out exploring? Yeah, that's right. Me."

"Sorry," said Alex. *So who's going to head up the mission then?* They wouldn't be able to stay in touch with the lander for very long, which meant he, Chen, Pushkin, and Talia would be on their own for the bulk of the journey.

Jonah's shoulders rose and fell. "You just better bring back a metric fuckload of data for me to study, that's all I'm going to say."

After showing them several times how to assemble and disassemble the mast and sails on the sledges—"You'll have to practice this in gravity, if you're really going to get it."—Riedemann spent another hour training them with the rest of the equipment they'd be using on Talos VII. In some ways, it reminded Alex more of preparing for a mountain-climbing expedition than an xenoarchaeological expedition.

Xenoarchaeology . . . Up until then, no such field had existed. There'd been no need. He was the first person to ever put into practice what had been dreamed, feared, and theorized about for generations.

It was a sobering thought.

5.

That night, Alex had a strange, restless sleep that culminated in a dream so vivid, he thought it was real:

He saw himself at home on Eidolon. The sun was low, close to setting. Gold light streamed through the windows of their house and gilded the yaccamé *totem poles on the opposite wall. Teeth, eyes, snarling lips—all glowed bright and beautiful, as if made not of wood but of burnished steel.*

The table was set. A spray of flowers decorated it; a simple luxury. A pork roast, his favorite, waited to be carved among dishes of various hothouse vegetables, cooked and seasoned so they laced the air with a savory aroma.

Layla stood at the far end of the table, waiting for him. There, bathed in the light of a dying sun, she seemed perfect to him, perfect and happy. She smiled, and his heart broke as he looked at her. He stepped forward, but they grew no closer, and he tried to speak, but his mouth formed no words.

A sense of wrongness grew within him. Something was off, something deep within the fabric of the world. The sun kept shining and Layla kept smiling, but reality felt strange. Displaced.

Outside the house, he heard the yowls of approaching tigermauls, and his spine tingled and the hair on the nape of his neck stood on end. The creatures' claws scrabbled against the barrier wall outside their house, and through the windows, he saw the tops of the native plants sway as the beasts stalked back and forth, scrabbling, scraping, trying to break in.

And still Layla kept smiling, as if nothing was amiss.

Dread seized him, immense and unrelenting. The barrier wall crackled as the tigermauls battered it, shorting out the current, and he knew they would soon break through and tear Layla to pieces.

He knew, and yet there was nothing he could do about it.

And still Layla smiled, and still the sun shone, and still the food smelled so good his mouth watered . . . and all the while, his sense of helplessness and of impending doom grew stronger and stronger, until he felt as if he were going to die.

. . .

Alex woke.

Hot. Sweaty. His heart pounding so fast it hurt. Fear shot through him, and he clutched his chest. Was he having a heart attack? That shouldn't be possible.

He tore at the straps that held him against the bed. After a frantic few seconds, his fingers found the quick-release buckles, and he pulled the straps off.

His chest heaved as he shoved himself away from the bed, taking the sheet with him. It wrapped around his limbs, and helpless, he floated across the room and banged into the lockers mounted over the desk.

He grabbed the edge of the desk and hung there, gasping. Globs of tears clung to his eyes. Sweat beaded his face. Tremors racked his body, and his back and abs started to cramp.

He kept breathing. In and out. In and out.

His body was slow to respond; it took over ten minutes before his pulse began to drop.

He carefully untangled himself from the sheet, weak, unsteady. "Lights," he muttered.

The strips overhead flickered to life.

He squinted in pain and turned away so he floated with his back to the light. His shirt was drenched with sweat, and his throat was parched. A chill crept into him as the surge of panic receded, and he felt as if he were sliding down a long steep slope.

A query from Sharah appeared flashing on his overlays. He worked his tongue over his teeth and palate, trying to scrape the gunk off them, and then accepted the query.

Sharah's voice sounded in his head: "Alex, are you alright?"

"Just dandy."

"Your biometric readings are—"

"I had a bad dream, 'K?"

"Alex, regulations—"

"Sharah, I'm fine. Leave it."

". . . I'll only leave it if you let Korith give you a once-over tomorrow."

"*Again?*"

"Either that or I tell Captain Idris you're unfit for duty."

"Fuck you."

"That would be rather hard in my current circumstances. . . . The well-being of this ship and its crew is my primary responsibility, Alex. I can't let you compromise that."

He closed his eyes for a moment, fighting the urge to continue arguing. It wouldn't do any good, though, and they both knew it.

"Fine," he said.

"Very well." Then Sharah hesitated, something she rarely did. "Do you want to talk about it? Your dream, that is?"

"No."

Sharah sounded almost relieved. "As you wish. Would you like something to help you relax? Magnesium, melatonin, the like?"

"Sure. Why not?"

There was a faint clatter in the dispensary drawer by his desk.

"Good night, Alex. I hope you sleep well."

"Yeah. Me too."

The line went dead, leaving him alone in silence.

He pulled himself over to the bed and began to secure the blanket and straps about his legs. When it came to the final strap, the one meant for his torso, he hesitated.

He glanced toward the drawer by the bed, where he kept the holocube of Layla. A hot ache formed in his chest. He reached toward the drawer and then checked himself.

No. He didn't want the pain. But he did.

His hand closed around the strap's buckle, squeezing it. Squeezing it. The holocube wasn't all he had of Layla. No, it wasn't. She'd willed him—

The cabin swam before his filmed eyes, and his throat grew tight. His breath came with a shudder.

Unlike so many couples, she had willed him the contents of her implants. All of her saved material. All of her documents. But most important, all of the audiovisual data the implants had recorded throughout her life. Every private moment. Every joy and sorrow and frustration. Plenty of people refused to share the recordings with even their closest loved ones. *Especially* their loved ones. Too many uncomfortable truths might come to light. That Layla had been okay with him seeing the records was a depth of trust that had staggered him.

Alex had transferred the recordings onto his own hardware before leaving Eidolon. He'd even looked at a few snippets of it, all that he could bear. Just enough to hear her voice, to know that the recordings were intact.

But he didn't dare view more.

The file sat like a dead stone in his directory. Heavy. Grim. Omnipresent. No matter how he tried to ignore it, he couldn't forget its presence, as if it were a magnet constantly tugging him closer.

For the end of the file marked the end of *her.* Her last moments, recorded in perfect detail—every agonized second preserved with the highest resolution modern technology allowed. Alex couldn't bear to see it. And yet, he couldn't stop thinking about the file and wondering how it had been for her in those final, fatal minutes.

A sob burst from him, and he curled in on himself, like a dry leaf before a flame.

6.

Alex clenched his jaw, gripped the arms of the seat, and fixed his eyes on the front of the cockpit as the lander shook around them. Panels and switches rattled, and an angry roar filled the air.

Outside the diamond windshield, a flickering wall of red-and-yellow flame filled the view. The lander's mag-shield parted the superheated plasma a decimeter or so in front of the nose of the vehicle, allowing the plasma to flow over the lander without cooking everything inside. Atmospheric entry was as safe as science (and engineering) could make it, but it sure didn't *look* safe. Alex always felt as if they were a single malfunction away from catastrophe. Which was probably true, although accidents were exceedingly rare.

"Yee-haw!" shouted Lt. Fridasdottir over the intercom.

Alex swallowed and gripped his seat tighter. If nothing else, he was glad to have some weight again.

<*At least no one's shot us down yet. – Jonah*>

<*You just bundle of laughs, aren't you? – Pushkin*>

<*They have to be tracking us. – Chen*>

<*Do they? – Talia*>

The shaking began to subside, as did the roar. Outside, the plasma grew streaky and inconsistent. Then it vanished altogether.

Half of Talos lay before them. Barren. Scabrous. Pocked with craters, sulfurous lakes, and the occasional volcano, dormant or otherwise. Close to the horizon the land was smooth and nearly featureless; there the ferocious wind that raced across the northern hemisphere had worn down the land to a flat, empty plain.

The lander dropped suddenly, causing Alex to bang his head against the back of the seat.

"What was that?!" he shouted into his mic.

"Turbulence!" said Lt. Fridasdottir. "We just hit the top layer of wind. Everyone hold on. It's going to get worse from here on!"

Alex closed his eyes and clenched his teeth as the lander jinked to the side and the straps of his harness dug into his chest.

For twenty minutes the shaking continued. Then the lander angled nose up, bleeding speed so fast it nearly stalled, and the attitude jets cut in with a dull *whomp.*

Alex looked at the others strapped into their seats in the back of the lander.

They exchanged grins, and Chen gave an enthusiastic thumbs-up. Alex couldn't help but smile in return.

"Struts out. Brace for impact," said Lt. Fridasdottir. "Touchdown in six . . .

"Five . . .

"Four . . .

"Three . . .

"Two . . ."

. . .

A jolt ran through the lander, and it listed a few centimeters to the right before coming to a standstill. The jets cut, and for the first time since they had left the *Adamura,* the inside of the craft was silent.

Alex released a breath he hadn't realized he was holding.

They'd done it. They'd made it to Talos.

BETA ZONE

ALPHA ZONE

TALOS VII: 45°30'47.77''N 110°36'3.23''W ELEV: 124M ALT: 4.65KM

CONFUSION

*   *   *   *   *   *   *

To have his path made clear for him is the aspiration of every human being in our beclouded and tempestuous existence.

—JOSEPH CONRAD

CHAPTER I

* ★ * ★ * ★ * ★ * ★ * ★ *

ALPHA ZONE

1.

The door to the airlock popped open with a *hiss*.

Alex pulled it inward. A blast of wind and yellow dirt struck him, forcing him to grab the edge of the airlock to keep his balance. He squinted out of reflex, even though his visor protected him.

A ladder led from the airlock to the ground. He paused at the top for a moment, surveying the view.

The land in Alpha Zone was flat and empty, save for a few rocks worn into sinuous ribbons by the unceasing wind. Complementing the shape of the rocks was the drifting dirt; it ran across the crusted earth like a swarm of seeking snakes.

The sun—where it peeked through the threadbare clouds—had a greenish tint to it, courtesy of the alien atmosphere.

Over the radio, Talia said, "Hurry up, Crichton. Daylight's wasting." Static spattered her voice; the first evidence of the hole's EM bursts.

"Yes, *ma'am*," Alex muttered in the privacy of his helmet. Talia seemed to be taking to the role of team leader with ruthless efficiency. Idris had announced the choice right before their departure from the *Adamura*. Pushkin had kicked up a fuss, of course, saying, "She have no imaginations! She lack vision to understand mind of sentient aliens. Her and Chen. I disagree, sir. I disagree most strongly."

"Objection overruled," Idris replied without a moment's hesitation.

Talia was the right choice, of course. Chen was too much of a nobody, Pushkin was too *pushy*, and Alex knew himself well enough to recognize that he shouldn't be in charge of anything. Not at the moment.

But that didn't mean he liked being bossed around.

He closed the airlock behind himself and climbed down to where Talia was shooting eye bolts into the ground: anchor points for their safety lines. As he stepped off the ladder, he felt relief at having a sense of weight again. Even if Talos's gravity well *was* slightly less than the standard 1 g of thrust on the *Adamura*.

He stood behind Talia while he secured himself to the nearest bolt, letting her body break the wind. It was blowing at a sustained speed of a hundred and twenty-four klicks per hour, with gusts up to a hundred and sixty, enough to knock a grown man off his feet.

Close to the hole, it would be even stronger.

After only a minute, Alex realized how difficult it was to move in the never-ending gale. The air was constantly fighting him. Shoving him back. Pulling at his limbs. Kicking up dust and dirt that obscured his sight.

Frustrated, he switched his overlays to infrared.

Sky and ground reversed contrast, the sky going dark while the ground went pale. Ahead of him, Talia became a glowing white figure, a slim marble statue under a spotlight.

A gust staggered Alex. He grabbed one of the lander's struts until the wind subsided to its usual level and he was able to stand unsupported.

He sucked in his breath as his knee throbbed.

It was going to be a hell of a long walk to the hole.

He moved after Talia and nearly bumped into her as she stopped abruptly. Her comm channel clicked on. "You hear that?" she asked.

"What?"

He concentrated, but at first the only sound outside his own breathing was the constant white noise of the wind.

Then . . .

thud

It might have been his imagination, but it almost seemed as if he felt the sound in his feet as much as he heard it; a faint vibration that passed from the depths of Talos into the marrow of his bones.

His scalp prickled as he realized what it was.

"That."

"Yeah."

Talia looked at him. Through her half-mirrored faceplate, he could see her eyes: a pair of ghostly circles that in infrared glowed as if lit from within.

thud

"It's calling to us," she said.

2.

Once the team ran safety lines around the rest of the lander, they opened the cargo hatch in the side of the vessel. A puff of condensation escaped the seals and streamed away in the wind.

With Jonah, Alex hauled out one of the sledges. It wasn't easy. The sledges had been loaded with food and equipment, packed tightly under the hard shell, and moving them by muscle alone was a challenge.

Next to them, Pushkin grabbed the nose of the second sledge and—one-handed—dragged the sledge out as if it weighed no more than a bag of laundry.

"Thule," Jonah muttered.

"The wonders of gene-hacking," said Alex.

They arranged the sledges in a row, noses pointed into the wind. The undersides of the sledges had a sharkskin-like pattern that allowed them to slide forward but gripped the ground and made it difficult for them to move backward.

Once the sledges were in place, Alex and the others watched to see how the makeshift vehicles withstood the gale. Stronger gusts rocked the sledges and pushed them back a few centimeters, but otherwise, they held.

"Not bad," said Pushkin.

Talia walked over and unfolded small hinged struts that lay embedded within the fronts and backs of the sledges. With the heel of her boot, she drove the sharp, pointed struts several centimeters into the dirt.

Then she pushed on the nose of each sledge.

Even with the wind helping her and even with all of her strength, she wasn't able to move the sledges.

"That should do," she said, straightening.

As an extra precaution, they staked the sledges to the ground. Then Jonah and Pushkin began to assemble a drilling machine to extract core samples from the planet's crust. Chen collected a dozen or so scoops of dirt, which he analyzed in his portable lab while sitting in the lee side of the lander. Alex and Talia practiced setting up and tearing down the hab-domes they'd be using on the trip, as well as the masts and spars needed to turn the sledges into land yachts. Gravity helped, but the wind made both tasks even more difficult than on the *Adamura*. And Lt. Fridasdottir spent her time crawling over the lander, making sure it hadn't suffered any damage on the way down. (A few scratches on the undercarriage, but that was it.)

Later, Pushkin and Chen also took turns assembling and disassembling the masts and shelters.

As they worked, Alex was hyperaware of the

thud

that marked off every ten point six seconds. Sometimes audible, sometimes not. But always he felt it through his soles and in his bones, as if the entire planet were a great vibrating clock. Pulsing, pulsing, never pausing, chipping apart eternity piece by piece, dividing it into a seemingly endless sequence of bits, and each bit ten point six seconds long.

Perhaps that was the point of the hole, he thought. To sunder time itself. To digitize it into manageable chunks and provide an artificial framework against which the universe could be measured. Perhaps it existed only to stand in contrast with the whole of nature, as if to say, "We were here."

Alex wasn't sure if the thought was morbid or inspiring.

3.

They'd been outside for a full eight hours when the lieutenant said over the comm: "Cap'n says that's enough for now. He wants us to grab some chow and then call in. Don't know about you, but I'm starving."

Alex's spine cracked as he straightened from the sledge he'd been repacking.

"Good," said Pushkin. "I have enough of wind."

Like dutiful children, they trooped back to the lander, tired and dusty.

Inside the airlock, Alex held his arms out while the decontamination spray buffeted him. Afterward, the ship's computer pumped the air out of the chamber, leaving him in near vacuum. His faceplate went black, and he knew that a steady stream of UV was irradiating every part of his suit. Even the bottoms of his boots.

He had to stand in the UV for a full twenty minutes for it to be effective. He put on an old spacer chant that always reminded him of the emptiness between the stars and spent the time reviewing Pushkin's and Chen's reports.

Pushkin's findings matched the readings he had taken from orbit; the plain was mainly sandstone. A variant of quartz arenite, to be specific. Alex skimmed the list of constituent minerals. Nothing surprising there. Depth to bedrock was 121.3 meters. Bedrock was igneous, mainly tholeiitic basalt with veins of high-magnesium boninite on the western, hole-side of the samples.

The most interesting point, for Alex, was Pushkin's final comment:

Given (a) hole's outbursts are source of wind, (b) wind is persistent and unchanging, and (c) observed patterns of erosion, age of hole estimated at minimum of 16,000 years. This is highly speculative, though, and need more data to confirm.

Chen's report overlapped somewhat with Pushkin's. He had examined the chemical makeup of the dirt and rocks, breaking them down to their atomic building blocks. Unlike Pushkin, he'd found unusually high traces of heavy metals threaded through the sandstone: manganese, tungsten, cadmium, and a few others.

More important, he'd found organic material in every one of his samples. Most of it looked like bacteria, but a not-insignificant fraction seemed closer to fungus or algae. Standard chirality: left-handed for amino acids, right-handed for sugars. Although, as Chen noted:

Talos VII possesses insufficient water to explain the development and widespread distribution of life. Consider possibility that it was introduced from elsewhere.

The bulk of the report consisted of a long list of molecular diagrams, chemical analyses, and so forth. Alex read all of it. Technically, study of the microbes fell to him, although he was happy to let Chen figure out their chemical composition. It would save time when he started to examine the organisms in detail.

Even if the giant hole hadn't been there, the presence of life on Talos VII wasn't much of a surprise. As humans had ventured out among the stars, they'd discovered that life was fairly common in the Milky Way. It just tended to be basic. Microbes were everywhere. Animals, plants, and other forms of complex life, not so much. Which was one reason why Eidolon with its swarming jungles and seething oceans was such a precious and interesting location. In that, it was the equal of Earth, lacking only a fully sentient species to be its perfect pair.

So the microbes weren't a huge surprise. And although studying them would no doubt turn up one or more interesting points, Alex couldn't muster much enthusiasm. Not when the hole lay before them, a monument in absentia to questions far larger and more interesting than those related to the metabolic pathways of a bacteria-like organism.

Hell, he wouldn't even get to *name* the tiny little buggers. Company policy was to use standard UTF taxonomy, which meant assigning each organism in a biosphere a unique numerical designation. Which was boring as fuck and nearly impossible to remember. The alternative was to use the more archaic Latinate conventions, which usually involved sticking the name of the host planet onto the end of each designation, to differentiate similar (or even identical) names from one planet to another. However, Talos VII wasn't settled, and it was the central colony commission and/or the planetary government that oversaw and authorized those sorts of names. If he named one of the microbes something like . . . like *L. Spicata Talosii,* after the spikes on its outer sheath, he'd just be jerking himself off for no good reason. At the most, some later, official body *might* consider the name as a well-intentioned suggestion, and nothing more.

It was unfair, Alex thought, that you no longer got to name your own discoveries. Not if you were working for a company or government, that was.

Chen ended his report on a rather depressing note:

Unless Xenobiology disagrees, I recommend that we maintain level-three
quarantine and level-four decontamination protocols for the duration
of our stay or until the risk of infection or infestation by the native life is
quantified.

Alex was forced to agree. No matter how small, the danger of contamination was very real and, potentially, deadly. He thought of the first expedition to Blackstone. Twenty-seven of the thirty-four colonists had died inside of a week, killed by the Scourge. He could still see the after-report images from the colony: skin fissured like dried mud, crenulated blood dried black in webs of split flesh, sightless eyeballs sunk and white as opal, limbs kinked in obscene shapes. . . .

He blanked the images from his mind.

Unfortunately, level-three decontamination protocols meant he and the rest of the team would have to devote an hour or two every day to sterilizing their suits and whatever else they brought with them into the shelter, as well as whatever they took *out* of the shelter. (Talos was far too important to risk polluting with their own microbes. And besides, if *they* were still on Talos, *they* might interpret such an infection as a biological attack.)

What a pain in the ass.

Even with those precautions, the realist in Alex told him that—by the end of their trip—they would almost certainly end up breaking quarantine. Humans shed germs and bacteria and cells every moment of every day, and all of those tiny bits of biological material had to be contained (or at least 99.999-some percent). Which was almost impossible. And the reverse was true as well. Talos's air and dirt were full of microbes. A fleck of dirt or a puff of air could all too easily find a way into their systems.

Just one of the many dangers he and the rest of the team would have to face.

Alex's faceplate cleared, marking the end of the UV. He stripped and hung his skinsuit in a locker. Warm water sprayed from the ceiling. He grabbed the soap from a drawer in the wall and scrubbed every centimeter of himself. Then he pulled on his jumpsuit, and the inner door to the airlock popped open, letting him back into the lander.

The first thing he noticed was that he could no longer hear or feel the

thud

within the main part of the ship. In a way, he missed it. Time felt oddly . . . unstructured without it.

He joined Talia, Pushkin, and Lt. Fridasdottir in the crew compartment. While they waited for the others to cycle through decontamination, Alex ate and wrote up his own report. Then he dozed off, letting his tired muscles relax.

As always, his mind turned to Layla. He could just imagine how excited she would have been to study Talos. It was a xenobiologist's dream. Or rather, it was *her* dream. In his mind, he could see how she would have bustled around the lander—both inside and outside—gathering samples, analyzing them, discussing the results. . . . A dull sense of guilt bothered him that he wasn't living up to her standards, but he had neither the energy nor the motivation to stir. Still, he felt a sense of closeness to Layla, knowing that he was where she would have chosen to be, and that closeness was more precious than any gem, even if it were a broken, razor-edged stone that cut him as he held it.

. . .

Once everyone was in the lander, they reported back to the *Adamura*.

Captain Idris listened as they summarized their findings. Afterward, he was silent for several long moments. Then: "Are you willing to proceed under the current circumstances? If there's anything you're uncomfortable with, now's the time to speak up. I don't care how small it is, you speak up. Your ass itches in your suit. You don't like how your feeding tube sits. There's something a bit off with your equipment. You speak up. You can't count on being able to fix anything once you leave."

There was an uncomfortable pause as everyone waited to see who would reply first. Then Pushkin said, "The wind is real bitch. Sir."

Svana, Jonah, and the others laughed. Even Talia smiled.

"Duly noted," Idris said dryly.

No one had any major objections, so they agreed—they would continue as planned.

At the end of the call, Idris said, "Alright. Tomorrow it is. Get some food and rest up. You're going to have an early morning."

4.

Thunk! A rock struck the side of Alex's helmet. His head snapped back, and a veil of crimson stars appeared before his eyes.

He staggered, flailing, and managed to grab his safety line as he dropped to one knee—his left one, of course. A dull pain shot up his leg, his head throbbed, and a film of blood coated his tongue where he'd bitten it.

Grimacing, Alex pushed himself back to his feet. He swallowed the blood and glanced at the readouts from his suit. Everything still nominal.

"Hey!" he said over the comm. "Hey! Watch it!"

Ahead of him, Talia looked back from where she was helping Chen attach his safety line to one of the sledges.

"What?" said Talia.

"You kicked up a rock, and it hit my head. That's what!"

"Are you hurt? Is your helmet damaged?"

"No, not really, but—"

The woman shrugged. "Then why are you complaining?"

"I—" But Talia had already turned back to Chen.

Annoyed, Alex focused on his own sledge and double-checked that the fairing was securely fastened. His tongue and knee continued to throb, and his head also, and the damn wind just Would. Not. Stop.

"Careful what you wish for," he muttered. He'd asked to land on Talos, and by god, he'd landed on Talos.

Finished with his final checklist, he raised a hand, toggled the radio, and said, "All green."

A click in his ear. "Copy that," said Talia.

All four of them were tethered to the sledges. The motorized vehicles would take the lead, serving to break the wind and provide a partial shield against dirt and rocks, while the safety lines would help keep them on their feet and together in the event of a storm or a sudden gust.

When they were ready, Talia held a clenched fist over her head and said, "On my mark. . . . *Mark.*"

Alex tapped the green power button on the back of his sledge, and with a grinding sound, the wide tread on the bottom started to turn, and the sledge pulled forward. It had a semi-autonomous guidance system that would keep the vehicle a constant meter and a half in front of him, no matter how fast he walked.

To his left, Pushkin started forward behind his own sledge. His sloping shoulders were hunched against the wind, and he put his feet down with a heavy slowness that reminded Alex of an elephant: ponderous and inexorable, with the potential for bursts of incredible speed.

At the front of their small train, Talia looked back and raised one of her two walking sticks above her head.

Alex did the same in reply, as did the others.

The comm switched on with a faint crackle. "Remember, check-in calls every two hours," said Lt. Fridasdottir. "Sooner if you see anything interesting or concerning. I want to know what's going on every step of the way."

"Roger that," said Talia.

"And watch yourselves, yeah?" said Jonah, chiming in. "Don't do anything stupid out there."

Alex turned to look at the lander. Fridasdottir and Jonah were standing in the cockpit, watching them. Jonah waved, and Chen waved back.

"Don't worry about us," said Chen. "We'll be okay."

Pushkin's voice boomed over the line. "Soon we return with large harvest of datas: enough to feed even hungriest mind. Prepare for amazement at fruits of reckless but necessary expedition."

The lieutenant wasn't amused. "Just keep those reports coming."

"Good luck!" said Jonah.

Then Alex tucked his chin against his chest, dug his sticks into the soft ground, and leaned into the wind.

Forward. The soil sank and slipped between his feet, half sand and half dirt. Each step took more effort than it should have. Slowed them down. Caused them to fight with the ground nearly as much as they did the wind.

As the dust streaming toward them thickened, Alex switched his view to infrared, turned on a spacer chant, and switched off his brain.

thud

It was going to be a long walk.

They'd landed as close as they dared to the hole, which meant far enough away that the shuttle was safe from the EMP while also being outside the turtles' range (after all, they didn't know if the creatures were hostile or not). *Close,* then, was just over a hundred and six klicks east of the hole, partway into Alpha Zone.

Downwind, of course.

Originally they'd hoped to cover at least twenty-five klicks a day, but between the wind and the sand, Alex was beginning to wonder if they'd be able to manage even fifteen.

Pushkin could do it. Of that Alex was sure. The geologist plowed forward like a tank, never slowing, never faltering, seemingly impervious to the gale raging around them. Left to his own devices, Alex guessed Pushkin would have reached the hole in under three days.

Chen, on the other hand, already seemed tired. *Not good.*

Alex had known from the start that the trek was going to be uncomfortable. There was no way around it. He'd resigned himself to the fact back on the *Adamura,* and now that it was reality, he buried all of his pain, mental and physical, deep within himself and concentrated on one thing and one thing only: taking the next step.

5.

They rested every ten minutes. A brief pause to stretch their backs, readjust their skinsuits and tethers, take a sip of water, and so on. Every thirty minutes they stopped for slightly longer: enough time to take the weight off their feet, eat a bite or two, and shake out their legs.

Every other hour they gave themselves an extra five minutes' downtime, during which they reported back to Lt. Fridasdottir at the lander. And after the first five hours, they took a whole thirty minutes to rest and recover.

Bathroom breaks were handled within their suits. Liquid waste was purified and recycled. Solid waste was desiccated and coated with an inert polymer before being deposited in a pouch on their thigh. The technical term for the polymer-coated nodules was DERPs, or dehydrated excretory recycling pellets.

Or as everyone called them: shit balls.

From their pouches, they took the shit balls and dumped them into a sealed container within the sledges. Everything they brought with them had to be taken back. Even if that meant the digested remains of a preprocessed protein bar.

The system worked well enough. Alex just hated feeling as if he was soiling himself.

As he walked, his mind stilled and widened—becoming more of an observer than a participant—and he let his thoughts wander. Sometimes he watched the sand streaming past his boots and imagined it was water, or else he tried to find meaning in the semi-legible shapes it seemed to form. The attenuated clouds provided similar, if more slow-moving, fascination.

The sound of his breath in the helmet . . . the feel of the skinsuit hugging his torso and limbs . . . the sticks in his hand and the pressure of the wind . . . the steady crunch of the sledge's tread advancing ahead of him . . . Those were the whole of his existence. He could have used his overlays for entertainment—for music or videos or games—but he wasn't interested. That wasn't why he'd come to Talos.

But he did use his overlays to review the microbes and other organic material Chen had sampled yesterday. The results were more ordinary than Alex had expected (or perhaps hoped for). The microbes themselves were extremely basic: amino acids, lipids, RNA, and DNA (no surprise there; DNA had been present on nearly every planet with native life). Some of the microbes were prokaryotes, others eukaryotes: primitive life that had never progressed further and was unlikely to given local conditions.

A speck of dust irritated the corner of Alex's right eye. Tears welled up, and he blinked the dust away, wishing he could rub his eye.

Despite their numerous breaks, the walking still wore them down. Even Pushkin. Alex felt a perverse sense of satisfaction when he noticed the geologist's steps slowing. So he was human after all.

6.

<Did you see that? – Chen>

It took a moment for the text to register with Alex and rouse him from his walking-induced trance. His breathing quickened as he forced himself back to a semblance of alertness and glanced around. The sun was descending ahead of them, and pencil-thin shadows picked out every little rock, pebble, and speck of dirt on the surface of the blasted plain—an expanse of textured nothingness.

<What? – Alex>

thud

<Off to the north. I thought I saw lights in the sky. – Chen>

He frowned and looked up. The sky was black and the ground was lambent. He flicked off the infrared and they reversed. Nothing seemed out of the ordinary.

<Aurora? – Alex>

<No. They were too localized and moving too fast. Hold on, let me check my recordings. – Chen>

thud

For a few minutes, they walked in silence. As with all of them, Chen's implants were recording everything he saw and heard. Maybe also what he felt. Higher-end systems allowed for full sensory capture, including scent. You could turn off the recording, of course, but it was mandatory on company missions—for liability reasons if nothing else—and in any case, Alex never understood why anyone would want to trust their memories to weak, fallible human brains.

Not that he'd had the courage to watch any of his memories from *before,* but it was important to him that they existed. Losing them would have been like a second death.

Again his mind turned to the file sitting in his system. He could feel its weight dragging him down, like a stone in a sack, pulling him toward the crushing depths of the planet. *Layla.* Perhaps it had been a mistake to bring her recordings with him, but the thought of leaving them behind on Eidolon was abhorrent. He would have sooner cut off his own hand. Whatever remained of Layla's unique consciousness lived in his heart and his brain and in the data from her implants. To leave the recordings would have been to abandon her, and he couldn't. He just couldn't.

He started as a new text popped up in his overlays: <*Okay, this is what I have. It's too blurry to make anything out, though. – Chen*>

A video file appeared after the text. Alex watched it. . . . Chen was right. The chemist had been turning his head while also moving his eyes, and the few seconds of video were an indistinguishable blur.

<*What about your helmet cam? – Alex*>

<*It's no better. – Chen*>

<*Did the others see anything? – Alex*>

<*I don't think so. I'll ask. Maybe my eyes are playing tricks on me. I'm not sure. – Chen*>

Alex tugged at the carabiner joining him to the safety line, straightening it out. <*Better ping the lieutenant and let her know. She can check with Sharah. Maybe the* Adamura *picked up something from orbit. – Alex*>

<*Okay. – Chen*>

Alex listened in on their group voice chat as Chen explained the situation to Talia and Pushkin and then—a minute later—over the radio to Lt. Fridas-dottir. The lieutenant responded with crisp seriousness to Chen's account and, the instant he stopped talking, she put them on hold in order to message the *Adamura*.

The group stopped while they waited.

thud

"Maybe turtles throw party for us, eh?" said Pushkin, stretching his arms.

Talia snorted. "That's about as likely as you staying silent for more than a few minutes."

"Why, I no idea what you mean," said Pushkin with a mocking smile. "I purest form of brevity."

The tips of Talia's walking sticks crunched into the dirt as she stabbed them down with slightly more force than necessary. "You have an awfully large vo-cabulary for someone so bad at English. Don't your overlays help you?"

Pushkin's smile curved into a sneer. "I read much, thank you. And overlays for weaklings who can't use brain."

"Maybe you should become a ship mind, then. You'd be nothing *but* brain."

"Maybe will, but I think it long time before I tire of body."

thud

The radio crackled back to life. "Away team, do you copy?" said Lt. Fridas-dottir.

"We copy," said Talia.

"The *Adamura* was on the other side of Talos when Chen saw whatever he saw. Sharah checked, and nothing of that description shows up in the scans they've taken. We even looked through the commsat's records, but no luck there either."

The commsat was a small, fist-sized piece of equipment that orbited Talos directly opposite the *Adamura*. It allowed the ship to bounce signals over the curve of the horizon and down to the lander.

The lieutenant continued: "Captain says to continue as planned, but everyone should watch for the lights, as well as anything else that seems unusual."

"Will do, Control," said Talia.

The line clicked off, and Pushkin sniffed. "As if lights not figment of imagination." He tapped the side of his helmet in a knowing way.

Chen looked down, shoulders hunched inward. For a moment Alex thought he would utter a retort, but instead the chemist readjusted his harness and looked off to the side, toward the horizon.

thud

"Let's go," Talia said, and started forward again.

The wind intensified, and Alex lowered his head and dug his walking sticks into the ground.

7.

At 1800 they made camp. Twenty-one klicks from the lander, and nearly to the edge of Beta Zone. Better than Alex expected.

Together they secured the sledges and inflated the dome that would serve as their living quarters for the duration of the trip. The shelter was supposed to be so simple a child could assemble it. Fat chance. Whoever had designed it was a real asshole; three Reinhart Scholars—including a physicist—and two technical IPDs on their team, and they still couldn't manage to get the dome up in less than twenty minutes.

And even then they weren't done.

The shelter had an airlock with decon equipment inside. The airlock could hold all four of them in an emergency, but in order to ensure full sterilization, only two people were supposed to use it at a time. Otherwise the system would need more than the standard half hour of decon to be 100 percent effective (or as close to 100 percent as they were likely to get). Spread over four people, that meant another hour before everyone could get inside.

Pushkin and Talia went first while Alex helped Chen take core samples at various points in a fifty-meter radius around the shelter. The samples contained the same assortment of microbes as by the lander.

When the airlocks were free, Alex was still wrangling with the core sampler; the drill was hung up about a meter below the ground. "Go on," he said to Chen, who was already by the hab-dome, packing samples. "This is going to take a few minutes."

Mission guidelines said they were supposed to stay buddied up while out on the surface of Talos, but guidelines like that weren't very practical when it came right down to it. Alex hadn't expected to follow them. Nor did the others, he thought.

"Thanks," said Chen.

As the chemist disappeared into the airlock, Alex wrenched on the core sampler, trying to shake it loose. It took several more shakes and drilling back down and then reversing the bit again before he was able to free the machine.

Scowling, Alex dragged the sampler back to the sledges, fighting the wind the whole time. The effort was exhausting after an already exhausting day.

It took even more effort to crack open the sledge fairing (which caught the wind with a hungry howl) and wrestle the sampler back inside. Afterward, Alex had to use his whole body to press the fairing back down again long enough to latch it shut.

Panting, he braced himself against the sledge and stared westward, toward the hole.

thud

The sun hung before him, close to the horizon. It was small and weak, and its pale light had a sickly cast, a greenish-orange that gave the plain below a ghastly hue. The land itself was stark and desolate, devoid of anything familiar, save for their tiny camp. It was the widest, emptiest place he had seen; the sky was so huge, it seemed oppressive, and he and the others no more than ants crawling upon the surface of the windswept earth.

Alex had never felt so alone. Not even in the days after he'd gotten that dreadful call, after . . . He could feel the distance that separated him from Eidolon—from the too-heavy urn at the back of Layla's closet—as if there were a thread stretching from his chest all the way to the home they'd shared. A thread so thin, he feared it would snap if he took even one more step in the op-posite direction, and by snapping, doom him to wander lost and alone, outcast, for the rest of his life.

Talos VII offered no comfort to him or any other human. It was a hostile place, cold and poisonous and touched by aliens. No one, he thought, ought to stay there. Perhaps they shouldn't even visit.

thud

And yet . . . the desolation contained the promise of hidden knowledge, and that promise would have acted as an irresistible lure for Layla. So, he would continue. Despite his despair. Despite the fearful environment and the thread stretching back to his previous life. *Their* life.

He shivered and squatted down and rested his back against the sledge. The howl of the wind grew louder, and he wrapped his arms around his knees.

As darkness settled across the hard-crusted plain, he remembered a quote Layla had once read to him: *"In the land of Od, where the deathbird sings, lies a barren waste. There tall towers once stood, white and gold, now crumbled to ruin, ground flat by time's grim turning. Seek not water among the poisoned thorns but rather a path free of torment."*

8.

"I'm done," said Chen over the radio.

"Roger," said Alex.

His knee made a sharp protest as he stood, and he nearly yelped. *Getting old.* Almost time to look into getting a full joint replacement. Or, if he was feeling particularly extravagant, an entirely new body.

But that was a problem for another time.

He glanced at the straps and struts keeping the sledges anchored in place. According to regulations, he ought to double-check that they were secure, but . . . he was tired, and he knew Talia and Pushkin had been over the sledges front to back. The sledges would be fine.

Alex limped over to the hab-dome entrance. He unhooked both ends of his tether and attached them to the hardpoint next to the access pad. Then, with a final glance at their desolate surroundings, he entered the airlock.

The wind's howl dropped to a muffled roar as the outer door closed behind him. The reduction in sound felt like a weight lifting off him, providing instant relief.

Alex's shoulders sagged as tension bled out of his traps. He hadn't even realized the toll the wind had been taking.

thud

Even inside the shelter, he could still feel the faint blast of the hole, vibrating through his body. There was no getting away from it. Not anymore. The sound would be with them from then on, and with ever-increasing volume.

He wasn't looking forward to that part of the expedition.

Decon took the usual thirty minutes. Except when he had to wash himself, Alex stood staring at the wall, stripped to his skin, and thinking of little more than which ration bar he was going to have for dinner.

At last, decon finished, and the inner airlock door slid open.

Inside the dome, there were four human-sized alcoves set into the walls: built-in shelves that served as their sleeping areas and personal cubbyholes. Pushkin lay crammed into his, broad shoulders pressed against the bulkhead behind him. In contrast, Talia and Chen sat on the floor by the heater in the center of the dome, Chen lost in his overlays (fingers twitching as he manipulated the invisible interface), and Talia folding a tiny origami crane out of the foil wrapper of a ration bar.

"There you are," said Talia, as if she'd expected Alex to somehow appear twenty minutes earlier.

He grunted and made his way to the one alcove that appeared unclaimed.

"What news from outside?" asked Pushkin. "You see more strange phenomena?"

"No." Alex lowered himself onto the shelf he'd be sleeping on.

Chen blinked and refocused his eyes on Alex. "Sharah still hasn't been able to explain what the lights might have been."

"Mmh."

"Maybe because they ocular artifact," said Pushkin with a smirk. Then he raised a broad hand. "Or maybe not. It only idea."

Talia was still eyeing Alex, as if dissecting him from a distance. "What's wrong with your leg? You're walking funny."

"Just sore," said Alex. "I'll be fine."

She raised an eyebrow, unconvinced. "I already checked in with Fridasdottir. Don't forget to send in your own report."

"I won't."

The astrophysicist nodded and returned to pressing folds into the foil wrapper. As she bent her head, a glint of gold appeared in the gap of her collar: a small cross hung about her neck.

It took Alex several minutes to gather the energy to again stand. After walking for so long, sitting was a welcome luxury. Once he was up and moving, he got two ration bars from the bin between Chen and Pushkin's alcoves: a sirloin steak bar and a salmon bar. Or at least, that was what the labels claimed. The bars never tasted the way they were supposed to. Half the ingredients were unpronounceable, and the other half were grown in a petri dish. And while the bars were nutrient dense (just one had 1,500 kcals) they never filled you up the way a normal meal did. Alex had already resigned himself to the fact that he'd feel empty and hungry for the bulk of the trip.

Back in his cubbyhole, he ate, slowly, mechanically, barely tasting the sirloin substitute.

thud

Across the shelter, Pushkin paused whatever he was doing on his overlays. "I wonder," he said, his voice low and resonate, ". . . I wonder what these our aliens valued. Was practicality, or did they—*do they*—possess sense of beauty? Or pleasure?"

"I'm sure it doesn't matter," Talia snapped.

Pushkin cocked his head. "Oh, but does. I struggle to imagine any creature could build such perfect round *hole* if they not possess some sense of ideal. That is, beauty."

Now Chen joined in. "The shape of the hole could have been a side effect of the engineering requirements."

"That's true," said Pushkin, in a surprisingly graceful tone. The day's walking seemed to have left him in a good mood.

Emboldened, Chen continued: "Math can be beautiful, and the whole structure seems to be a mathematical exercise. It's not an accident that it's broadcasting the Mandelbrot set."

"That's also true," said Pushkin. "Does that answer question then? Have we proved that unknown makers had understanding of sublime?"

"Again," said Talia, acid in her voice, "what does it matter?"

A low chuckle from Pushkin, and he levered himself into a more upright position. Debate always seemed to energize him. "Why, because sense of artistic pleasures mean aliens would expend energy on nonessential activities. Makes motives much harder predict. We might find fountain of theirs and not know if he built for thirst or decoration. . . . Alex, what say you?"

Alex didn't want to get pulled into a debate, but he *did* have an opinion on the matter. He wet his mouth and said, "There's a theory among neurobiologists and evolutionary researchers that the reason humans have a sense of beauty is because beauty is functional. At least, at some basic level."

"How so?" asked Chen.

It took Alex a moment to think of an appropriate analogy. "A smooth edge cuts better than a ragged edge." He shrugged. "Most of the time, that is. You get the idea. Symmetry, smooth curves, harmony, all things we're drawn toward. Supposedly functional preferences got carried over to larger aesthetic preferences."

A satisfied smile crossed Pushkin's face. "So, if I understand right, any technologically advanced species should possess at least some sense of beauty."

"That's the theory."

Chen said, "What if the aliens are so different from us we can't tell what they like or don't like?"

"Could happen," said Alex. "But we all exist in the same universe. Convergent evolution suggests there'll be *some* similarity. . . . I don't have a lot in common with a spider, but I could probably agree with a spider on which web is more attractive, or which of the other spiders is largest and most brightly colored. Assuming we see the same part of the spectrum. There are a lot of places for shared ground, no matter how different we are."

Talia snorted. She got up, moved over to her alcove, and placed the tiny foil crane next to her thin pillow. "Beauty is an expression of the divine. It doesn't come from inside us."

"Oh really?" said Pushkin with a sly expression. "Then do you believe *they* can recognize divine? Or do you believe heathens are deaf and blind to all forms of beauty?"

A frown narrowed Talia's face. "Just because an unbeliever can see the divine doesn't mean they can understand or accept it."

"So aliens are damned, then? Every last one of these strange creatures?"

"Yes." Talia's answer came out as a flat statement of irrefutable truth.

Pushkin laced his fingers across his substantial belly. "I feel myself struggle to understand your theology, Ms. Indelicato. The universe, as you describe her, is cruel and uncaring, and god that created universe even more. I agree with you on indifferent nature of reality, but reality you describe same one I see, and I give no weight to existence of supernatural. But you give weight. Much weight. And you claim meaning of life is to follow some form of moral code in hope of uncertain reward in likely imaginary afterlife. Am I correct? Have I described your position?"

Alex held his breath as they waited for Talia's response. He wondered if there was about to be a fight. Talia was ostensibly in charge of the away team, but it didn't feel like it at the moment.

thud

The astrophysicist seemed entirely unrattled by Pushkin's comments, although there was no mistaking the anger in her eyes as she said, "You have."

Pushkin leaned forward, a predatory gleam in his eyes. "Then *why*, dear woman, you insist on keep your faith?"

Talia matched his carnivorous expression with a bare-toothed smile. "Because unlike you, I do have faith, and that faith tells me that everything in this universe was placed here by the Almighty. And because I would be an idiot to *not* believe. Hope . . . hope is what keeps us alive when all else fails."

With the back of his forefinger, Pushkin smoothed his mustache. It needed trimming. "Is that how you survive Bagrev? Hope?"

Talia's head snapped around. Her lips pulled back, and she hissed, "What do you know about Bagrev, *kecharo*?"

If Pushkin was offended by the profanity, it didn't show. "Just that you were unwilling participant in events. I may have glanced at your file before we land to this unlovely orb." Talia started to swear, and as if to excuse his behavior, Pushkin said, "You cannot expect me to risk life and limb without know *something* of my colleagues, can you?"

"That's supposed to be *private*," said Talia, spitting each word out with venom. Pushkin tried to say something, but she talked right over him. "Enough. I don't want to hear it. We're not your playthings. You don't know anything about hope or beauty, and you don't know anything about me, no matter *what* you read in some piece-of-shit corporate psych profile. So keep your nose out of it, and shut up."

With that, she turned away from them and drew the privacy curtain over her alcove.

Alex was inclined to agree with her: Pushkin *was* an asshole. Of the *Adamura*'s crew, no one but the doctor and the captain were supposed to have access to their personnel files. Had Pushkin looked at all of their records?

The geologist chuckled and then, with a placid expression, looked at Chen and said, "You been very quiet. What you tell? Is beauty expression of divine? Is hope our only, ah, *hope*? Is god merciless bastard we have to coddle out of fear of eternal punishment?"

Chen appeared thoroughly lost by the conversation. He blinked, his watery eyes switching between Pushkin and the closed curtain on Talia's alcove. "I . . . I don't know," he said. "I've never really thought about it."

A heavy-lidded wink from Pushkin. "You should, dear man, you should. Every person—man, woman, child, or ship mind—ought to have answer to suit their sense. Otherwise, why, might as well be fleck of dust floating on current of life." He stretched like a great lazy cat. "I say enjoy life while can. Universe is dark and dangerous place—of that Ms. Indelicato and I agree—but is beauty and pleasure too, and pleasure *in* beauty. If nothing matter and everything chance, then only reasonable response is take enjoyments where you can. That includes pleasures of mind as well as body, even if means certain, ah, temporary discomforts." He patted the thin blanket beneath him, as if to drive home his point. Then his bushy eyebrows lowered into a mock scowl. "Or are you disagree?"

"No, I . . . I don't think so," said Chen.

However, Pushkin's philosophy seemed painfully bare to Alex. Pleasure—intellectual or otherwise—was all well and good, but it wasn't *enough*. It couldn't balance out the weight of his grief. For that, Alex needed something more substantial, something more tangible. In that regard, Talia's faith was appealing, but there too, he felt a painful lack. Tempting as it was to lay his problems on an uncaring (or even caring) god, doing so merely transposed the question instead of truly answering it—handing off to another what he was unable to answer for himself. And that didn't sit right with Alex.

In the end, he feared there was no answer. Or none that would ever satisfy him.

"Good," said Pushkin, seeming pleased by Chen's lack of resistance. "You wise to take such *enlightened* view. Now, if you excuse me, I have book to finish read." His lips quirked. "A most pleasant piece of literatures. Perhaps you heard of it. *Captain Ace Savage and the Fiendish Plot of Queen Dragica* by Horus Murgatroyd the Third. If you look for diversion from present circumstances, I recommend."

Pushkin's eyes shifted focus then, and he sank back into his alcove, lips twitching as he read.

thud

Chen looked at Alex, his face round, guileless. The chemist started to speak and then appeared to change his mind. A second later, a text appeared on Alex's overlays:

<That was odd. – Chen>

<Yeah. Pushkin sure likes to hear himself talk. – Alex>

<I don't understand why he and Talia are so . . . obsessed. I just want to study the hole. Why does it have to be a huge philosophical issue? Just let me do my job! – Chen> The chemist's writing contained more energy than anything Alex had heard him say or seen him do. Maybe he wasn't quite as boring as he appeared.

<Same. – Alex> But that wasn't entirely true. Alex understood Pushkin's reasons for asking the questions he did, even if Alex didn't agree with them.

"Going to turn in," Alex said.

Chen nodded. "Night." He got up from by the heater and retreated to his alcove and shut the privacy screen.

Alex did the same. Then he rolled onto his back and closed his eyes. Staring at the glowing icons of his overlays, he opened a document and wrote a quick, rough report of the day, not that there was a lot to convey.

Once the report was off to Fridasdottir, he cleared his throat and, in a low voice, said, "Naru, search for the city of Bagrev." He'd named his system after the old tomcat his grandparents had kept back on Stewart's World. They'd been on their third clone by the time he'd left for Eidolon.

An instant later, a list of search results filled the overlays. He tapped on the first one, expanding it, and read.

Bagrev was a smallish colony city on the planet Ruslan. No surprise there; Talia had joined the expedition at 61 Cygni, Ruslan's home system. The colonization of Ruslan had been a fraught process. Alex had heard occasional stories about turmoil on the planet, but it was a big galaxy, and he hadn't paid much attention to the news.

According to the wiki, there had been a series of clashes between rival ethno-corporate factions on Ruslan. Seven years ago, the clashes had culminated in the orbital bombardment and subsequent occupation of Bagrev by a group known as the Intestate Sarr. They had blockaded the city for four months before the planetary defense force was able to dig them out. In that time, they had, according to widespread reports, inflicted all manner of atrocities upon the resident population. The run-up to and occupation of Bagrev had subsequently been labeled the Unrest by Ruslans, and although no longer an active conflict, the wounds remained fresh and painful.

The more Alex read and saw of Bagrev's occupation, the more horrific it seemed. The Sarr had raped the inhabitants of the city, literally and figuratively, and they'd starved them too, taking the food, water, and air for themselves in a desperate attempt to hold their position long enough to become self-sufficient. Only forty percent of the population had survived.

Alex shied from imagining what Talia might have experienced during the occupation. It made his own tragedy seem smaller, less important (though still no less painful).

He looked at his privacy screen, in the direction of her alcove, thinking.

"We're all fuckups in one way or another," he murmured. In a way, it was a comforting thought. Perfection was daunting, unobtainable, but knowing that he wasn't the only one who struggled helped make the struggle seem more manageable.

Even so, he still felt . . . unsettled. Unsettled and tired.

thud

With his mind full of disturbing images, Alex curled up in his alcove and fell asleep, blanket pulled tight around his shoulders. And as he slept, he dreamed of being chased by faceless, armored militants, and always there was the constant

thud

in the background, an ominous drumbeat driving him forward, faster, deeper, in a frantic attempt to find safety.

Layla . . .

CHAPTER 11

*   *   *   *   *   *   *

BETA ZONE

1.

The next day, the weather was worse. A band of narrow clouds, grey and feathered, streamed past high overhead, while the wind gusted in fitful bursts that kicked up dozens of dust devils nearby. The devils seemed almost alive as they danced across the crusted plain, swaying and swirling with an odd combination of grace and mechanical herks and jerks. And over it all fell the same sickly light from Theta Persei as it rose in the east.

An hour's walking carried them out of Alpha Zone and into Beta Zone. *Only six more to go,* Alex thought. Alpha Zone was thirty-three klicks wide, while Beta was twenty-two, but since they'd landed partway into Alpha, crossing Beta was going to take them the same amount of time. After that, the zones would go by progressively faster. They'd be able to cross more than one per day near the hole, as long as the blasts of sound didn't slow them too much.

Alex failed to notice much of a difference between Alpha and Beta. The ground might have been a bit flatter, a bit paler in Beta, but if so, it was a minor change when seen up close.

He spent the better part of an hour reviewing data from the samples they'd collected at their campsite—the readings were nearly identical to those at the lander—but for the most part, he slogged along behind his sledge, head lowered against the wind, thoughts cycling around the same few, all-too-familiar subjects: *the hole, the walk,* and as always . . . *before.*

The brutal tedium of the howling plain combined with the claustrophobic enclosure of his skinsuit and the monotonous torment of his inescapable thoughts ground away at Alex's mood. He could feel himself getting grimmer by the moment. All he saw before him were mistakes, lost opportunities, and an endless expanse of bitter *if onlys.*

thud

"Please," he'd said, and the word held his heart.

They were walking along the back ridge near their hab-dome, close to the shield wall. The air smelled sweet of fruiting bodies ripened to bursting, and the ground was soft as moss beneath their feet. A high hum of glitterbugs haloed the brush along the trail.

Layla kept walking ahead of him and didn't look back. Her ponytail swung across her back with every quick, light step.

"You're overreacting."

"I'm not. If you'd seen what the char did to Urich . . ."

"I grew up on Eidolon. You don't have to tell me."

"Then you know how dangerous it is. Please."

She hastened up a rocky outcropping, then stopped to wait for him. "Urich didn't follow basic procedure. If he had—"

"No one's perfect. Mistakes happen."

"I'm not going to leave my family."

He made a helpless gesture as he joined her. Sweat dripped down his cheek. "You can always come back. Visit."

"Like you do with your parents?"

He turned away, jaw set. The hum intensified. "We could get an assignment together. On a research station or a survey expedition. It could be interesting."

"You don't really care about that."

"I care about you."

She put her hands on his face and brushed away a lock of hair. "And I love you. But don't ask me to give up my family. Not that. I can't."

"I'm your family too."

Soft regard turned to frustration. "Enough, alright! Just leave it. You keep nagging and nagging and—It's not that bad. Really."

He pulled away only to return a moment later, a planet caught in an elliptical orbit. "It is. And I want you safe."

"I *am* safe. We both are. We just have to be careful. That's all."

thud

A gust of wind jarred Alex from memory. He tried to wet his mouth. It felt as parched as Talos itself.

When he'd arrived on Eidolon, the planet had seemed so beautiful. A new Eden, flourishing with life previously unknown. He'd dismissed the tigermauls and the char and the horn birds as anomalies. Expected risks in an otherwise benign location. The stats on colonists' deaths had been inflated by mistakes among the first wave of settlers. They knew better now.

It had taken time for the lie to become apparent.

Only once he started working in the southern jungles had he begun to appreciate the depths of his mistake. There he'd seen the merciless nature of the planet's overgrown forests, the unrelenting pain and hunger of its teeming inhabitants, and the savage, desperate struggle every plant and animal was engaged in. Eidolon was beguiling at a distance, but in truth, it was a pit of suffering.

He'd lost seven of his colleagues, including Urich: some to the red mold that crept in from the damp ground and infected their lungs. Others to the char or to sheer bad luck. And throughout it all, there were reminders of the ever-present danger—the electrified shield walls. The armored hab-domes. The security bots that patrolled the perimeters. The drones that buzzed overhead at nearly every hour of the day and night. . . .

He'd come to hate it, all of it, and that had spilled over into his relationship with Layla. He didn't understand how she could bear to stay on the planet, amid so much horror. And though he talked and talked with as much eloquence as he could muster, he could not convince her to leave.

thud

A knotted rope seemed to tighten around Alex's head until a dull pain made him squint and frown, and the frowning only worsened the pain. He tried to relax his forehead but couldn't.

He looked over at Chen, who was walking hunched behind his own mechanized sledge.

Alex toggled the chemist's channel. "Hey," he croaked.

Chen grunted. "What?" Even over the radio, his breathing sounded labored.

"You have any family?"

A longer-than-normal pause followed. Alex knew why. It was the first time in the whole trip he had asked Chen or anyone else about their personal lives.

"Parents. Grandparents. Lots of aunts and uncles and cousins."

"What about a partner?"

". . . Yes. A contract partner on the Dibobia Torus, but . . . we don't see each other very much. Too much travel, and too much work."

"No children?"

The light glinted off Chen's helmet as he shook his head. "Haven't had the time. Once we get back, I'll sign up for my first round of STEM shots and then start thinking about a family."

"Ah."

"What about you?"

Alex's throat tightened, cutting off the words. He tried to swallow. It hurt, as if he were trying to force down a chunk of stale bread. "No. No family."

"Not even parents?"

A loose rock caused Alex to stumble. He leaned heavily on his sticks and only barely managed to avoid falling. "Yeah . . . parents, but they're still on Stewart's World." *As if they'd give two shits what I was up to.* He didn't even know if they'd answered the message he'd sent after the funeral, telling them about Layla. He'd left before any response could have reached Eidolon.

For a moment, Alex felt a familiar anger at how they'd ignored him after he'd gone off-world to study xenobiology. But it was an old hurt, and it seemed insignificant compared with what had happened to Layla. . . .

After that, Alex didn't talk, save when necessary. Instead, he focused on walking, and he tried to let the walking fill his mind and push out everything else.

thud

2.

"—Crichton. . . . Crichton!"

Alex started, as if waking from a stupor. He blinked and glanced around. They were still on Talos. Still walking in a staggered line. Still whipped by the wind and sand. The day was more than half done; the uncertain sun was two hands past noon, and their shadows were inching behind them.

Talia was the one talking to him: "Snap out of it, Crichton. You're stumbling all over the place. Take some AcuWake and don't let it happen again."

He mumbled something affirmative and took a sip of water from the nipple in his helmet. The cool liquid helped wash away the tangled cobwebs of his thoughts.

Alex frowned. His sledge seemed closer than it ought to have been, as if it were moving slower than when they had started that morning. Or maybe he was the slow one, and the sledge was keeping pace.

He glanced at the others. *Odd.* The gap between them and their sledges had also decreased. Not a lot, half a meter or less, but enough to notice.

For a few minutes Alex walked and watched the steady progress of the sledges leading the way. He debated saying anything; was there really a problem worth investigating? He didn't want to deal with any extra hassle, but if there *were* a problem with the sledges, then—

Even as he had the thought, Chen's sledge stopped. There was no smoke, no dramatic noise or burst of flame. It just . . . stopped.

Chen didn't see; his head was down. Before Alex could warn him, he walked into the back bumper of the sledge, stumbled, and grabbed the sledge for support.

Talia and Pushkin finally noticed. They paused.

"Ah," said the geologist, for once all joviality absent from his voice. "How delightful."

thud

3.

Half an hour later, they still hadn't resumed their trek. The first thing they'd done was open the fairing on Chen's sledge and run every possible diagnostic on the sledge's systems. When that didn't identify the problem (the supercapacitors, drive train, and electrical system all seemed normal), Talia contacted Lt. Fridasdottir and informed the XO of the situation.

"Let me get Riedemann on the line," the lieutenant said. Crackles of static riddled her words, interference from the hole's EMP. Alex wondered how long it would be before communication with the lander would be impossible.

After a few minutes, the machine boss joined the call and started to talk them through the process of troubleshooting the sledge. After a great deal of frustration—Talia was in a foul mood from the start, insisting that they *had* to get moving again if they were to keep to their schedule, and Riedemann had trouble seeing what they were working on and kept having to repeat his instructions—the reason for the malfunction finally became clear.

"It's the sand," said the machine boss with grim certainty. "I sh--ld have guess-d. Between th- wind and --- pressure waves . . . Pick it up. You'll see."

Chen obediently scooped up a handful of the fine-grained dirt and let it trickle in twisting ribbons between his fingers.

"See?" said Riedemann. "It's not so different from the dust y-- find -n airless moons and plan--s. It jams tre-ds, cuts intern-ls, prevents linkages fr-- moving. Only matter of time before --- ---er sledges lock up."

"Great," said Talia, her voice tight. "What are we supposed to do about it?"

Alex could almost hear the machine boss shaking his head back on the *Adamura*. "There's noth--g you can do. Not down th---. The sledges w---d have t- b- torn apart and rebuilt, --d they'll just jam again unless they're modified t- k--p the sand out. I'm sorry. I should h-ve designed them bet--r. My recommend-tion is to abort now and ret-rn to the lander."

"Ah, finally, advice of reason," said Pushkin.

The thought of turning back so soon opened a pit of sucking tar in Alex's mind. Physically, it would be a relief to abandon Talos, but mentally . . . he wasn't ready to give up so soon, not now that he was finally *doing* something. Even if he was relying on ideals not his own, and even if the whole damn venture was doomed from the start, he had to try. For himself as much for Layla.

Another voice sounded on the line. "Captain Idris here. I've been listen--g in. Indelicato, what's th- status of your team?"

"The team is fine, sir. It's just the sledges."

"Roger that, Inde--cato. In your opinion what—"

thud

"-- th--- the -est w-y t- -------"

Talia frowned. "Can you repeat that, sir? We have some interference."

The captain's voice returned, clearer than before. "You're the ones -n the ground, Indelicato. You tell me. In your opin--n, what's the best course of action?"

Alex could hear Idris's unspoken request: *Is there a way to make this work?*

A glance from Talia toward the rest of the group. "Let me talk with my team, Captain, and I'll get back to you."

"Roger that. We'll be on sta--by. Over."

The line went dead.

"What is to talk?" demanded Pushkin, his voice loud against the wind. "We go back. End of talk."

"Not end of talk," said Talia, sharp. "Can anyone think of a way to keep the sledges running?"

Alex and Chen shook their heads. Pushkin snorted and spread his bucket-like hands. "Not even with week of work."

"Alright," said Talia, fierce as ever. "The sledges are out. That leaves us with two options. Make camp here and study what we can until our supplies run out or turn back now. What's it going to be?"

"I . . . I don't know," said Chen.

Pushkin made a noise of disgust. "Your lack of decision, she is universal constant."

The chemist drew himself up. "You don't have to be so mean. Fine, I say we should turn back. It's the safest option."

"Bah. It offend me to agree, but I agree." The chemist looked as if he were going to comment, but Pushkin barreled on: "Without sledges, is no point to mission. Better we return and use lander for base until leave."

"I disagree," said Talia in a quiet but firm voice. "We're here already. We should make the best of it. I say we set up camp and use the next four days to learn what we can."

"What is learn?" said Pushkin, moving toward Talia until he loomed over her. "Is nothing here but rock and stupid little microbes. Waste of time to stay. Dangerous also. My, myself, that is, *I*, say we go back."

Talia's green-rimmed eyes turned to Alex. "Two votes for leaving. One for staying. What about you?"

The black tar tugged at Alex, causing him to sink deeper into darker, greyer places. He allowed his gaze to scan the empty horizon, taking in the seemingly endless swirl of sand, the bands of racing clouds, the bluish haze of the flat-topped plain as it extended into the distance. . . . His teeth were aching again; he'd been clenching them throughout the discussion.

"Hurry it up, Crichton," said Talia. "Time's wasting."

thud

"I say we keep going," said Alex.

Pushkin snorted and, even through his half-mirrored faceplate, Alex saw him roll his eyes. "And just *how* you think we make pursuit of this shit-for-brains goal? Hmm?"

The desert hardtop crunched under Alex's boots as he walked over to his sledge. He slapped the side. "We drag them."

"Excuse me?"

"We drag them to the hole."

4.

The plan, as Alex explained it, wasn't complicated: strip out the supercapacitors, the drive train, and every other bit of extra mass from the sledges and bury it. Then, take the cargo straps from inside the sledges and use them to rig up harnesses so they could pull the sledges behind them.

Simple enough, but that didn't mean it would be easy.

Chen pushed on the back of his sledge. It barely moved a centimeter. "I can't do this," he said, plaintive. "Not for so many kilometers."

"No," said Alex, "but *you* can." He pointed at Pushkin. "Hell, I bet you could pull all four sledges by yourself, if you had to." It was an exaggeration, but not by much. "If we put the heavier pieces of equipment in your sledge, then—"

"We get it, Crichton," said Talia. She looked between them. "Fine. We'll try. Empty out—"

Pushkin made an exasperated sound. "Indelicato! You can*not* be serious. If—"

"We'll *try*," Talia repeated. "Just to figure out if it works. Then we'll decide. Empty out Chen's sledge and let's see if he can pull it. If not, we'll stop here. That's an order."

thud

For a moment it seemed as if Pushkin wasn't going to budge. Then he grunted and turned to the sledge. Alex joined him.

While they did, Talia called back to the lander. Within moments, she had both Fridasdottir and Idris on the line. "We might have found a possible solution, Captain, but we'll need to test it before we'll know for sure."

"We'll b- here, Indel-cato," said Idris. "Take as long as y-- need."

Removing the supercapacitors wasn't as difficult as Alex had thought. Keeping Chen's supplies from flying out of the sledge as they did so—ripped from their grasp by the wind's invisible fingers—proved far harder. In the end, the solution was to take some of the supplies and divide them up among the other sledges while they experimented on Chen's.

With the supercapacitors removed, and the drive train too, and only the bare minimum of supplies left in the sledge—food, Chen's chip-lab, medical kit, and a few other necessities—they stood back to watch while the chemist slipped on the makeshift harness, leaned into it, and took a step. Then another. And another. And another.

With each step, Alex felt himself rising out of the black tar.

Chen stopped and turned back.

"Well?" Talia said.

The chemist looked uncertain of himself, but he said, "I think I can. It's not going to be easy, but—"

"Of course it isn't," said Talia. "As long as you're not going to collapse, that's what matters."

Pushkin shook his bull-like head. "This scheme is pure foolishness, Ms. Indelicato. Of all half-charged, undercooked—"

"Are you saying you can't keep up with Chen?" asked Talia. Pushkin's piggish eyes narrowed into thin, flat slits. "Because if that's the case—"

"Is not," said Pushkin, the words practically hissing between his teeth.

"Good. Then we keep going. Chen, we'll take turns pulling your sledge until the other ones give out. After that, Pushkin, you'll take as much of the heavy equipment as you can. Crichton and I will divvy up whatever's left. Chen, the rest will be up to you."

Alex heard the unspoken: *and don't let us down.*

Chen nodded. "I'll do my best."

"You better. None of us are getting out of here if we don't."

A hiss of exasperation sounded from inside Pushkin's helmet. "I still say this *bad* idea."

thud

"Noted," said Talia. She toggled the line to the lander back on. "Captain, I was right. We have a way forward," she explained.

"Th-t's excell-nt news, Indelicato," said Idris. He sounded genuinely relieved. "Are you sur- -t won't be t- hard for you and th- team?"

"We'll manage, sir."

"Roger th--. Keep us in th- loop."

"Sir," said Pushkin, and Talia gave him an annoyed glare. "I must register complaints in strongest possible term. This not what I agreed for. Is too dangerous, too difficult."

The captain replied in a stern tone: "If Talia th--ks you c-n do it, th-n s- do I. That's -n order, Pushkin."

The geologist's face darkened with anger, but he merely said, "Yes, sir."

And that was that. Alex could hardly believe it, but the expedition was going to continue. He wasn't happy about the fact, not exactly, but the black tide receded within him, and he felt a sense of satisfaction at having accomplished something.

5.

Before they moved on, they buried Chen's supercapacitors and drive train by the side of their path.

"We'll pick it up on the way back, won't we?" asked Chen.

Alex nodded. "Of course." *Pack it in, pack it out.* The motto of every xenobiologist who landed on a planetary body with alien life. *Do no harm* might have also applied, but that one was more aspirational than not. Too many xenobiologists had, through negligence or stupidity, contaminated the areas they were studying.

Talia helped Pushkin fill the hole and tamp it down. Then the geologist used the team's bolt gun to drive a reflector beacon into a nearby rock, so they could find the spot again.

Chen took first shift on the sledge. His pace dictated the speed the rest of them could walk, so Talia had him move into the lead. After an hour, she took second shift, and Alex took third.

As Alex slid his skinsuit-clad arms through the harness they'd rigged up, he wondered how smart his idea really was. Now that *he* was about to drag the sledge, it seemed almost impossible that they could cross the remaining distance while on foot, facing a headwind, and hitched to a not-inconsiderable weight. A *lot* of kilometers lay between them and the hole.

Don't think about it. All he had to worry about was taking one step at a time. The rest would take care of itself.

That was the hope, at least.

The straps bit into Alex's shoulders as he leaned into them and the sledge's weight settled into his body. *Fuck.* This was going to be harder than he thought.

But it was doable, and that was enough.

The sharkskin pattern on the bottom of the sledge kept the wind from pushing it backward, but it also helped the locked treads glide over the rocks, sand, and dirt. For an object of its mass and volume, the sledge produced far less friction than it might have.

Which didn't mean pulling it was easy.

thud

Around 1600, Pushkin's sledge gave up the ghost. Scowling, Talia stopped. "We don't have time to do this twice more. Let's go ahead and rip out the guts from all the sledges."

So they did.

Once Pushkin was done with his sledge, he dug a coffin-shaped hole, which they filled with the rest of the supercapacitors, drive trains, and every bit of extraneous equipment. Which wasn't much. They were already running lean.

Then they spent some time reorganizing their sledges. Per Talia's plan, the heaviest items went in Pushkin's sledge and the lightest in Chen's.

When everyone was back in their harnesses, Talia raised a walking stick and said, "After me."

thud

From then on, Talia doubled the length of the breaks they took every ten minutes, which helped, but even in the first half hour, Alex could feel fatigue accumulating at a concerning rate. The contents of his sledge were heavier than Chen's, and every extra kilo made a noticeable difference. He could tell he was going to be wrecked by evening.

The same seemed true for Talia, and doubly so for Chen, despite his lighter load. The chemist was trying—Alex would give him that—but he trailed farther and farther behind as the day wore on. At times, Alex glanced back to see him half-lost in the billows of dust behind them: a flat silhouette of a man, like an orange cutout, paper-thin and insubstantial.

6.

The rest of the day was a long, tiring slog that did nothing to brighten Alex's mood. The wind seemed stronger than before, and for some reason, Pushkin kept trying to chat with him with voice and text. Alex didn't want to talk. It took too much energy. And it made the time go by slower. All he wanted was to stare at the ground, his mind blank and empty, and wait for evening to arrive.

Besides, the straps had begun to chafe his shoulders, and the more he thought or talked, the more he noticed the burning sensation. His knee wasn't too happy either.

They continued walking until 1900 in an attempt to make up for the delay with the sledges. Even so, they only ended up covering another fourteen klicks, which wasn't great. Two days into their trip and they were already seven klicks behind schedule, and those seven klicks would have put them within spitting distance of Gamma Zone.

"We'll have to push harder tomorrow," said Talia. A faint crackle of static edged her words. It wasn't enough to interfere with conversation, but that would change as they got closer to the hole.

"We should take fewer breaks," said Chen, shoving the struts of his sledge into the ground. He looked like he was about to keel over.

Alex shook his head. He doubted if Chen could make it through tomorrow without twice the amount of rest.

Pushkin grunted. He was breathing heavier than normal. "Seven klicks not that far. Smart thing is stick to plan. If we burn out, we just fall even more behind. Slow and steady win race. Slow and steady."

"Seven more klicks won't kill us," said Talia. "We push. Otherwise we'll be stuck out here for an extra night. That won't work close to the hole."

Pushkin glared at her but didn't argue the matter.

Once the sledges were secure, Alex worked with Talia and the geologist to set up their shelter. The first step was to bolt the dome to the ground so that it wouldn't blow away. Talia and Pushkin held the collapsed shelter against the dirt and unrolled it a few centimeters at a time while Alex worked his way around the edge, using the bolt gun to fix it in place.

He finished and stood back as Chen and Talia started to prop up the shelter. As he did, he saw . . . *what* he wasn't sure. There was a large, humpbacked shape several hundred meters away, half visible through the sheets of streaming dust. The object looked like a boulder, the first boulder they'd encountered.

And yet, something about it didn't resemble the local rocks. It was a different color. Darker. Rougher. As if the eons of rushing wind and scouring grit hadn't managed to wear away every protruding irregularity.

Alex frowned and took a step forward, raising his hand to block the swirling dirt.

"Alex. Some help if you please," said Chen.

He started to turn back, and the boulder *moved.*

It slid away, swiftly and smoothly, as if the ground were as slick as ice.

"Look! Over there!" said Alex, tabbing his comm.

The others rushed to his side and stood with him, watching as the boulder disappeared into the dusk. Alex switched to infrared: the boulder showed up as a bright, glowing lump receding quickly to the north.

"*Speed and velocity,*" he subvocalized.

A raft of numbers and lines appeared on his overlays. The object was gliding across the ground at exactly ninety-three point four klicks per hour. The highest speed they'd recorded from orbit had been sixty-one klicks.

"Was that one of your 'turtles'?" Talia asked, her voice low and heavy.

"Must be," said Alex. Up until then, none of the turtles had been spotted in Beta Zone, which didn't mean a whole lot, given the short amount of time they'd observed the creatures, but it made him wonder if the turtle had come to investigate their presence. Anything was possible.

The back of his neck prickled.

"They are too huge for liking," said Pushkin. Then he gripped Alex's shoulder and pointed at a spot high overhead. A pair of white-hot lights flitted through a band of clouds, illuminating it from within. Alex turned off the infrared. In visible spectrum, the lights were half as bright and had a greenish-yellow tint that shimmered like an aurora.

The lights appeared to be moving as fast as a drop-shuttle; after a few more seconds they vanished completely. Alex checked his overlays, wanting to know their actual speed. To his surprise, their velocity showed as zero. As far as the program was concerned, it was as if the lights didn't exist, although—and he looked to be sure—his implants *had* recorded video of their flight.

"See, they weren't a figment of my imagination," said Chen.

Talia started toward where the turtle had been. Alex followed with Chen, and Pushkin brought up the rear.

The wind had already partially erased the creature's track, but they could still see a swath of dirt a meter across that had been swept perfectly smooth.

Alex and Chen knelt. They both took samples, and they both dropped some of the dirt from the track into their chip-labs.

"Nothing unusual," Alex said, reading the display. "I think."

"Same," said Chen.

"How does it move?" asked Talia, bending over the track. "It can't be with wheels or treads or feet."

"Why not?" asked Pushkin.

"There aren't any prints. And if it were scraping the ground flat behind itself there would be a ridge of earth on either side, just like you see with a snow-plow."

"We didn't have snow where I live on Shin-Zar."

"Fine, a road grader, or something like that."

Alex stayed silent, thinking. Then he dug his hand into the middle of the track, burrowing into the ground as far as he could.

"What?" said Talia.

Alex felt around in the dirt for a moment and then pulled his hand back. He shook his head. "I thought there might be an induction plate."

"We would have detected the current," said Chen.

"Maybe lights connected to turtles," said Pushkin. "Lasers could provide energy."

"How would the lights produce a laser?" said Talia. "Besides, the heat signatures would have showed up from orbit."

Alex shook his head again. "The turtles are alive. Or they're controlled by something, some*one,* alive. It reacted to me. I'm sure of it."

"I still want to know how it's able to get around," said Talia.

Chen had been slowly turning in a circle, looking in every direction. "I don't see any more of them."

"Did you try—"

"I tried every wavelength my suit can detect. If there are any other turtles around here, they're too well shielded to see."

thud

7.

Talia alerted Lt. Fridasdottir about their encounter with the turtle, as well as the appearance of the lights, and she attempted to forward all of the data their skinsuits and implants had collected during the encounters, but the EM interference from the hole made it impossible to send the full-sized files. The transfers kept stalling out. Even the lieutenant's voice was getting hard to hear.

In the end, Talia resorted to sending text summaries of the data. It was an inelegant solution, but until they returned, it was the only option.

As before, the *Adamura* hadn't detected the lights from orbit. Either they were too small, too dim, or somehow shielded from detection. Sharah seemed frustrated by the failure of the ship's sensors, from what little Alex heard of her over the comms (he was barely able to make out one word in three when the ship mind spoke).

Captain Idris wanted them to do more to investigate the area where the turtle had been, but Talia put her foot down and insisted they raise the dome and get inside. They were already running late, decon would be as lengthy as ever, and none of them wanted to be outside in the dark with one and possibly more turtles nearby. The captain tried to argue, but Talia insisted. In that, Alex appreciated her leadership, and—for once—he thought Pushkin felt the same.

"No need make us easy prey," the geologist grumbled as the captain signed off.

"Agreed," said Talia.

thud

8.

Again Alex found himself waiting to go through decon, this time with Push-kin. Talia and Chen had gone first; Alex suspected Talia wanted to get Chen inside as soon as possible. The chemist looked like he'd hit the wall . . . and the wall had hit back.

While the two of them cycled through the dome's airlock, Alex took ground samples in a grid pattern around their camp. Pushkin followed, doing the same with his own specialized equipment. They were looking for different things— Alex for microbes and other life-forms, Pushkin for the composition of the rocks and soil—but their methods were essentially the same.

Neither of them spoke while they worked.

When he finished, Alex stood in the lee side of the dome, arms crossed, bolt gun in hand, while he scanned the darkening plain for more turtles.

He felt an uncomfortable itch at the base of his skull. There was something deeply unsettling about knowing that unseen and possibly hostile creatures were patrolling the land around you. It reminded him of Eidolon, when the tigermauls would come stalking close to the electrified shield wall, or when they'd been out hiking and . . .

A mire of grief threatened to drown him. He squeezed his eyes shut, trying to deny the reality of the universe. Everything within him felt sick and hollow.

thud

Alex opened his eyes to see Pushkin standing some distance from the hab-dome, hands planted on his prodigious hips, swaying to a tune only he could hear. Alex wondered what he was thinking.

He didn't need to ask. The geologist said, "Entire planet keeping time with metronome size of city." His helmet swiveled as he looked back at Alex. "Maybe unknown makers were lovers of music, dancers to fractal beat."

"Maybe." It seemed unlikely to Alex, but he had nothing by which to judge the hole on Talos VII. It was outside any human experience, and thus, im-possible to judge without further context. *Exogenesis.* The word rose to the forefront of his mind. *Life from the outside.* That was the rough translation, anyway. The term had come up more than once in his xenobiology classes. It was a theoretical concept that, as of yet, had no practical examples. The idea was that life could have evolved in other dimensions or realms of existence (superluminal space was a common area of speculation), ones either unknown to modern physics or inaccessible to ordinary, three-dimensional beings made of baryonic matter. Life without antecedent amid the normal causal chain of the universe. And were that life to intrude on the universe in an *exogenic* event, the consequences had the potential to be unimaginably devastating.

There were layers to the strangeness of living beings, and exogenesis represented the far depths. One of the scariest things Alex had ever heard a professor say was that the technology of a *truly* advanced species might be indistinguishable from the natural forces of the universe, even as the acts and works of humans might appear to an ant or a worm.

He tightened his grip on the bolt gun and pressed closer to the hab-dome.

The next twenty minutes passed in silence, aside from the wind and the steady

thuds

of the planet's beating heart.

Alex felt irritated with himself. He was getting poetic, maudlin even, and that was always a sign he'd reached the limits of his physical and mental stamina. The day had overstayed its welcome, and he still had to get through decon. Food, a wet cloth on his feet, and shelter from the wind were his only real desires at the moment. Everything else—the sheer impossibility of the hole, the turtles, and his own grand existential questions—all of it would have to wait.

A text popped up on his overlays: <*Clear. – Talia*>

Pushkin was already moving toward the dome. "Be good and make double-check of sledges, would you? Wonderful. I wait in airlock."

Alex let his breath hiss between his teeth. He didn't even have the energy to curse, but right then, he felt nothing good toward the geologist. It was always like that on expeditions. Patience wore thin, tempers frayed . . . getting along with others in less-than-ideal circumstances was a challenge, and Talos VII was perhaps the most challenging environment any of them had faced.

Leaning heavily on his sticks, he stumped over to the sledges and gave them a cursory glance. The struts were secure enough. The straps too. He didn't need to physically check each and every one of them, regs be damned. It was a waste of time, and he was full out of fucks.

Shoulders hunched, he made his way back to the hab, deposited his samples in the clean box embedded within the dome's outer shell, and entered the airlock. Pushkin was sitting on the bench along the right-hand wall, fingers laced behind his helmet, eyes half-lidded. "That was fast," he said, hardly stirring.

Alex grunted and closed the outer airlock door.

He set a timer on his overlays and then closed his eyes while the decon gases sprayed the outside of their skinsuits. Fifteen minutes later, the timer sounded, and he snapped out of his somewhat nap.

Off came the skinsuits. In the UV light, he noticed a glowing band tattooed around Pushkin's left ring finger. *Married?* Maybe not. There were a lot of strange traditions throughout human-settled space.

Alex rubbed his own hand, missing the familiar weight. The gold-and-blue ring he'd worn for so long was back on Eidolon, sitting next to the urn he'd abandoned. Sitting alone in the dark closet, cold, empty, a promise that could no longer be fulfilled.

A dark veil seemed to close in on his vision, and everything around him grew grey and distant, unimportant and unreal. He forced himself to speak in an attempt to regain a sense of solidity. "Pair-bonded partner?" He pointed at the band.

Pushkin lifted his hand, looked at the tattoo as if he'd just noticed it. "Nothing so ordinary. Any canker with low enough standards can find partner. Harder to find is bond of brotherhood. When you risk life with someone, and that person saves you, and you them, you forge unbreakable chain." His deep-set eyes were black voids in the UV light. "How many people in universe, Crichton, who come help if you call? Parents excluded, of course."

"I . . ." The question left him off-balance. Talking with Pushkin often had that effect. "None, I suppose." It wasn't an answer Alex wanted to give, but lying would take more energy than he had.

The geologist assumed a smug expression. "Exactly. This ring represent just such bond. *Thun* is his name, and if I need, I can call on him just as he can call on me."

Alex wasn't buying it. "Uh-huh. And how'd you ever convince anyone your ass was worth saving?"

"Cloud dive accident," Pushkin replied blithely. "Are you familiar with sport of cloud dive, Crichton?"

"I've seen clips."

"Then you know how dangerous can be in high-g planet. But, ah, what glories you see! Why—"

As Pushkin droned on, Alex tuned him out. So many words came from the man's mouth, and Alex wasn't sure he believed any of them. *Cloud diving. As if he'd risk his life on something like that.*

At long last, the lights switched back to normal full spectrum, and the welcome *ding* sounded, marking the end of the decon.

"Finally," Alex muttered. He limped over to the inner airlock, favoring his left foot, which had developed a set of unpleasant blisters.

9.

The mood inside the hab-dome was tense.

Alex sat on the floor of the shelter with his hands inside the gloves of the clean box. The box allowed him to continue working on his samples without contaminating their living space.

Right then, he was using the manipulators on the chip-lab to tease apart the nucleus of a single-celled organism he'd isolated from the soil. Technically he ought to have been asleep, but neither he nor the others felt like turning in yet, despite their exhaustion. Not when they knew what was lurking outside.

If one of the turtles rammed the shelter . . . There wouldn't be much left. Just smears of blood and meat.

He glanced at the upper right corner of his overlays, where he'd placed the feed from the security cameras outside. Nothing but dust and darkness.

Somewhere out there were the turtles. Hiding? Watching? Gathering? It was impossible to tell. But they *were* out there. On the *Adamura*, Alex had estimated their numbers to be in the hundreds of thousands.

Not for the first time, he wondered what they ate. The area surrounding the hole didn't seem to contain enough biomass to sustain the turtles' population. Assuming they were living. If they weren't, that raised a host of other questions.

I should put the bolt gun in the clean box, he thought. That way he could get at it from inside the shelter. It wouldn't do much against creatures as large as the turtles, but at least it would be something.

For all the technology he and his companions had brought with them, Alex felt as if they were still no different than primitives crouching around a fire while some hungry, fanged monster roamed the darkness beyond, waiting for the perfect moment to pounce and drag them away.

First contact with an alien species was always a tricky business, even if the aliens weren't sentient. First contact where they *knew* sentience was involved was exponentially more difficult. It was hard enough to figure out what another human was going to do. An alien? Forget it. Some things could be taken for granted, of course. All living things needed energy to live and procreate. And they all possessed the drive to survive. Other than that, anything was possible.

Alex remembered reading about a polyp-like creature that lived in the arctic region of Eidolon. Every solar eclipse, it detached from the rock it was growing on and hopped, *hopped,* up and down fourteen times. And no one knew why. And that was in a biosphere that had been thoroughly studied.

During his initial training as a xenobiologist, he'd sat through a course on what they should and shouldn't do in the unlikely case they encountered intelligent life somewhere in the universe. Most of what he recalled from the course could be summed up by the phrase "Don't make the situation worse." And: "We don't know." Which wasn't particularly helpful.

Contact between two intelligent species could easily be a disaster for both sides. He wouldn't be surprised if aliens actively avoided other intelligent species. If *he* didn't always want to spend time with humans, why would an alien?

Maybe they could console each other in their existential angst. His mouth twisted into an approximation of a smile.

Talia made a sound of disgust and bounced to her feet and started to pace. Alex didn't know how she still had the energy.

From his alcove, Chen looked at her with his watery eyes, seeming too exhausted to do much more.

"My dear commander," Pushkin said in an uncharacteristically gentle voice, "your paces are rather distracting."

"Tough," said Talia. "There's nowhere else to go."

"Technically—"

"Technically can bite my ass."

She paced, Alex worked, and outside, the wind's howl acquired a choppy rhythm.

thud

Talia flopped down on her mattress, threw an arm over her eyes. Her foot twitched, tapping the side of the dome.

Pushkin let out a huff of disapproval, and she said, "Still reading that nonsense you seem to enjoy?"

"*Captain Ace Savage* is one of finest literary works in settled space."

"Bah!"

"If you cannot appreciate such simple pleasures, maybe is *you* at fault, not book."

Talia eyed him from under the crook of her arm. "I prefer stories with actual literary merit. Not that dreck."

"Then your opinion need recalibration," said Pushkin, seemingly unruffled by the criticism. "Is surprising you even read fiction."

"Movies are better."

"I rest case."

Alex tried to tune them out as he scanned the chip-lab's results. His brow furrowed as he tallied the numbers.

"Is something wrong?" Chen asked from his alcove. His voice was soft so as not to disturb the others.

"No. Just weird."

Talia lowered her arm. "What sort of weird?"

"There's, uh, a microbe here, with a really high concentration of heavy metals. Haven't seen anything like it before."

Pushkin cleared his invisible overlays with a swipe of his hand. "Could he feast on metals we found in ground?"

"Not sure. Maybe. I don't know which direction the reaction is going. The metabolic process is—" Alex shrugged. "I need the lab back on the *Adamura* to really make sense of it."

Chen swung his legs over the edge of his alcove. "Can you send me the data?"

Without taking his eyes off the chip-lab, Alex forwarded his results to the chemist.

"How common is the microbe?" Talia asked. "What sort of population density are we looking at?"

"Same densities we've seen before. It's there, but you're not going to find large masses of it."

"Do we have to worry about it affecting our equipment?"

Alex tore his gaze away from the chip-lab. "Unknown."

Her face tightened. "You better make it known, Crichton, before we end up with an unplanned pressure leak."

"Yes, ma'am."

10.

That night, Alex slept badly. He often did, but that night was worse than usual. The constant

thud

kept intruding on his thoughts, disrupting his dreams, ruining any chance of proper rest. At times, he opened his eyes to stare at the dark curve of the dome. Outside, the wind chorused with ravenous intensity, as if desperate to get inside. Desperate to rip and tear at the soft contents within.

He plugged his ears, which helped with the wind but did nothing to block the metronomic

thuds

that paced out the black and empty hours.

Sleep came at him sideways, in uncertain fits. Hallucinatory bursts that blurred the boundaries of perception.

It was after. *No longer* before. *He'd received the call as he was leaving the Commission with their new seed stock. The call seemed like an eternity ago. Time had dilated beyond all reason since.*

He'd driven straight to the hospital. Half out of his mind, he'd disabled the automatic steering, forced the armored buggy to race at twice the legal speed across the muddy track that served as a road.

The building was a block of icy whiteness. Black slashes for windows. Laser turrets swiveling along the electrified outer walls. A citadel under siege, even there in the heart of the capital. And outside, the relentless growth of jungle, dense and dark, aching with hunger.

A nurse met him. Refused to answer his questions. Led him through bright-lit corridors that stank of antiseptic. The doctor with a shock of red hair and words that couldn't mean what they meant.

The morgue was cold as fear. He stood there, trembling. On the slab of copper-clad steel, he saw her lying. Petals of skin hung wide, weeping lymph fluid as a pointless balm to brutalized flesh. The indifferent cruelty of the tigermaul's work laid bare.

He identified. He witnessed. The sheet ascended, covering what was left of the face he knew so well.

The doctor was saying things. Things that didn't matter. Then: "—couldn't revive. There was too much tissue damage. I'm deeply sorry. If there was anything I could—"

Tissue damage. That was the technical term for the butchery he had seen. The softness of human bodies was no match for the teeth and claws of the tigermaul. The damage done precluded cryo, precluded saving what made her her. *A brain could not be transferred into a construct if the brain itself was mashed and mangled, cracked like a melon.*

The doctor pressed something cold and hard into his hand. A piece of manufactured crystal, the memory core of her implants, extracted, cleaned, preserved even as she hadn't been. "—next of kin . . . beneficiary . . . power of attorney . . ." Words without meaning that passed him by as he stared at the crystal, mesmerized by the horrific beauty of the shifting sparkles.

The core was there.

She was not.

And he alone.

CHAPTER III

*   *   *   *   *   *   *

GAMMA ZONE

1.

When Alex woke, he lay for a while, contemplating genocide. Or more accurate, theriocide: the intentional eradication of a group of animals.

With a properly designed retroviral, it ought to be possible to wipe out the entire population of tigermauls. He wouldn't even have to kill them; just sterilize them, and they'd all be dead in a generation. That wasn't so bad, was it? The kindest form of extinction. . . .

It was an evil thought, and he knew it. With a sigh, he put it aside. Taking revenge on the tigermauls made no more sense than raging against the wind. They—*it*—had been pursuing their nature, same as every other creature. Hating them was no different than hating himself. . . . But he did, and the reality of their nature inexorably led him back to the same damn questions that continued to bedevil him. If nature itself was to blame, then where was he to look for answers? Should he stand on the plains of Talos and shout himself raw at an uncaring universe in the futile hope that the universe might answer?

Alex thought he was beginning to understand why so many religions started in the desert. The emptiness of the land did something to a person's brain, focused it on the strangeness of one's inner life.

And of course, on Talos, there was the never-ending
thud
to contend with, beating away at their bodies and brains like a hydraulic spike, unrelenting and merciless.

He blinked and blinked again, seeing the curved ceiling swim before him. A wake-me-up pill was starting to seem like a necessity, but the stubborn part of Alex still refused to give in and resort to drugs. It felt like surrender, and he'd be damned if he was going to give the universe the satisfaction. Not that the universe cared.

Because it didn't.

He thought of the tigermauls again and screwed his eyes shut. He might be damned anyway.

With a word, he activated his overlays. They were uncomfortably bright behind his closed eyelids. A few quick selections were enough to burrow through layers of folders until he found himself looking at the file titled *Layla*. It sat alone and forlorn at the base level of his personal documents. Only the file wasn't his. Or rather, it didn't feel like it. He was an impostor caretaker, given hold of a precious object that should never have left the possession of its original owner.

He raised his hand and held it trembling before the projected image. Only a few virtual inches separated his finger from the glowing file.

He nearly tapped on it. To see. To know. To share in her suffering as a form of penance. The urge was horribly tempting.

But he couldn't bring himself to do it. Fear overcame desire, and he lowered his hand and croaked, *"Display off,"* in a rough, tight-throated voice.

The overlays vanished, leaving him alone in his self-imposed darkness, and he cursed himself for his cowardice.

2.

It was cold that day. Colder than before, in any case, at minus thirty-four Celsius, and the wind had a mournful note to it, as if lamenting past sins. Tenuous streamers of morning mist fled before the gale and suicided against the uncertain rays that crept outward from the rising sun.

No turtles were visible. For that Alex was grateful, although it made him nervous. Where *were* they?

From camp to Gamma Zone was a bit more than seven klicks. He was curious what they would find when they arrived. Orbital imaging had revealed some interesting surface coloration in Gamma. *Exposed rock or biological matter?*

Alex helped Talia deflate the hab-dome while Pushkin and Chen packed up the rest of their equipment and secured it in the sledges.

The dome was just beginning to sag when an enormous gust of wind struck.

Alex and Talia staggered, and the dome caved inward, as if punched by an invisible giant. The force of the wind caused Chen's sledge—the lightest sledge—to break free, struts ripping loose from the packed ground. The sledge skidded sideways and slammed into Chen's left knee.

The chemist's leg buckled, and he fell. The comms crackled, and a high-pitched scream blasted Alex's ears.

Alex dropped the dome's pressure pump and ran toward Chen. Talia was two steps ahead of him. Moving with startling speed, Pushkin grabbed the wayward sledge and pulled it away from Chen.

"How bad is it?" Talia asked, dropping to the ground.

Chen shook his head, face twisted with pain. Dismay filled Alex as he saw Chen's knee. The joint bent at an unnatural angle; Alex wasn't sure, but it looked as if the end of a bone was protruding, pressing outward against the underside of Chen's skinsuit.

Ice water flooded Alex's gut. Had he fucked up? If he'd taken the time to properly check the sledges . . . *No.* Couldn't be. He was overreacting. There was no way to know for sure that he could have made any difference. The wind might have been strong enough to push the sledge loose no matter what.

No way to be sure.

But he couldn't help but feel responsible. And it was horrible.

"Let me see," Talia said.

"*Ahhh!* Don't touch it!"

"I'll be careful."

Pushkin secured the struts on the sledge, and then came to stand by Alex as Talia gently felt Chen's leg.

"His knee is dislocated," she said in a calm, almost clinical tone. "Tendons might be torn. Hard to say, I'm not a doctor."

"Shit," said Alex. Breaks were bad enough, but tearing a tendon or ligament was really nasty. It could be four to six months before Chen would be able to walk normally again.

The yawning void opened up within him again. *That's it. We failed.* How could the expedition possibly continue now?

Another horrible gust of wind made them hunch against the onslaught.

Chen groaned. His eyes were squeezed shut, and his chest moved up and down at a frantic pace.

"Breathe slower," said Talia. "Your pulse is too high."

He didn't answer.

Talia looked at Alex and Pushkin. "We have to get him inside."

Neither of them hesitated; they hurried back to the hab-dome and started to reinflate it.

The sight of Chen's twisted knee continued to dominate Alex's mind. *There's no way to know for sure,* he thought as he manhandled the pressure pump.

But he didn't believe it.

thud

Working together, he and Pushkin managed to get the hab-dome back up and functional in record time.

Once it was ready, Talia helped Chen stand. His eyes were glassy from painkillers, but he seemed otherwise lucid. With Talia supporting him, the two of them made their way into the airlock, Chen hopping on his one good leg.

The airlock door closed, and Pushkin turned to Alex. "Hmph. Unfortunate. Is no choice now but turn back, I think."

"Yeah."

"We best say news to our benevolent overseers."

Alex nodded, mute. His mind raced as he tried to think of any possible way they could continue toward the hole. At the same time, he questioned his own level of commitment. Just how hard was he willing to push? How much was he willing to endure? And for what? . . . That *was* the question. For what?

If he'd known, he thought he might have been willing to stop right then and there. But strangely enough, having no idea if investigating the hole was worth it made him all the more determined to see the task through. He'd made his decision back on the *Adamura*—accepted the challenge, sunk his teeth in—and he wasn't about to give up. Not until he saw the hole with his own eyes. There was nothing for him outside of the expedition. Nothing but grey oblivion and the husk of a life with no good end.

If he stopped, he *would* stop.

Guilt and bitter regret threatened to drown him. If only he'd realized sooner. If only he'd done the responsible thing and checked the sledges as he was supposed to. But he hadn't, and now the expedition was about to end because of his own selfish shortsightedness.

His inner self rebelled against the knowledge. Surely there had to be a solution to the problem. Something.

I could go on alone, he thought. But he recoiled from the idea. Determined as he was, the thought of trekking across Talos's blasted landscape all by himself seemed not only impractical but foolhardy in the extreme. Events seemed to be pushing them to extremes, though, and he feared that reasonable measures would no longer suffice in the situation they now found themselves in.

thud

"What i- it?" asked Lt. Fridasdottir, sharp and worried when Pushkin called the lander. "An---er turtle?" Her voice hissed and popped with the static, forcing Alex to strain his ears to pick out the words.

"Is worse," said Pushkin. He explained, and Alex provided corroboration.

The lieutenant swore. "I'll let th- capt--n kn-w. Hold o-."

Alex and Pushkin remained huddled around the transmitter while they waited, forming a pocket of relatively still air between themselves.

In his mind, Alex again saw the sledges as they'd been last night. He clenched his hands, wishing he could go back in time just a few hours. It would have been so easy to check the sledges: a few moments of inconvenience in exchange for an entire future, not to mention his own peace of mind. . . . In retrospect, it was a more-than-fair exchange.

The worst thing was, he knew he would have happily traded his peace of mind—and Chen's knee, for that matter—in order to guarantee that the expedition would continue. It wasn't something Alex was proud of, but his pride had died the same day as Layla. Now all that remained was mere existence, shabby, painful, and undignified.

"I don't want to go back," said Alex.

Pushkin looked at him. The geologist's faceplate was half-mirrored against the glare of the morning sun, which gave his head a bulbous, insectile appearance, made all the more unsettling by the ghost of his eyes partially visible within. Alex knew he looked the same; he could see himself reflected, strangely distorted, on the gilded surface of their visors.

"You most strangely set on this, Crichton. We should never come here in first place. Our sledges break, and now this accident . . ." He *tsked*. "Fate, she seems to send us message, and never am I one to ignore warning sign."

"Maybe not, but I already have blisters on both my heels, and turning around now won't make them hurt any less."

The reflections on Pushkin's visor swung from side to side. "You are optimist, I see. A dreamer. I like, but universe, she has other ideas."

Then the radio crackled again, and Fridasdottir said, "Korith -s t-lking w--h T-lia. Call back once y-- have - --tter idea of Chen's cond-tion. We'll b- on standby."

"Roger that, lander," said Pushkin.

thud

<We're through. Airlock is free. – Talia>

3.

Twenty minutes later, the inner airlock popped open, and Alex and Pushkin hurried into the hab-dome.

"Well?" Pushkin demanded.

Chen was lying in his alcove, eyes closed, face coated with sweat. His skinsuit lay in a crumpled heap on the floor. A white-and-blue pressure cuff was strapped around his right knee, which was already swollen to twice its normal size and purplish-red from subdermal bleeding.

Alex's left knee twinged with sympathetic pain.

Talia motioned for them to keep their voices down. "I reset the joint and bandaged him up as best I could," she said. "His knee is wrecked. I'm pretty sure the ACL ruptured, and maybe some of his quad tendons. It's hard to tell with all the swelling."

"What did Korith say?" Alex asked.

Talia's slim shoulders rose and fell. "About the same. Without a scan of—"

A small noise from Chen made her pause. He stirred slightly, finding a more comfortable position, and then lay still again, save for his breathing.

She continued in a quieter voice: "Without a scan of Chen's leg, we won't know for sure how bad the damage is."

"But is too bad for him go on," said Pushkin.

"Yes." Talia drew the back of her sleeve across her forehead; she looked about as tired and stressed as Alex had ever seen her. "I already updated Fridasdottir, but the captain wants to talk with us as soon as possible." She didn't seem to be looking forward to the prospect.

"We regrouped now," said Pushkin. "What is to wait?"

"Nothing. Nothing is to wait," said Talia.

"Hold on," said Alex, and they looked at him. He wet his mouth. The whole time in decon, he'd been thinking and thinking, running through the various options. "Even if Chen can't walk, maybe there's a way to—"

Pushkin snorted. "What? You expect him crawl to hole?"

"No," said Alex, forcing his voice to stay low. "But . . . what if we left him in the spare hab-dome? He could wait for us here." The spare was half the size of the main one but had all of the same amenities, just compacted. "As long as he can feed and clean himself—"

Talia shook her head. "We need the spare. If something happened to this dome, we'd be in serious trouble. I do *not* want to live in my skinsuit until we get back to the lander." She crossed her arms, a deep frown forming between her eyebrows.

Alex felt himself frowning as well. "That rules out one of us taking him back to the lander."

"We stick together no matter what. If one of us goes back, we all go back."

"Is no choice then," said Pushkin, exasperation coloring his voice. "We abort and return. This whole expedition clusterfuck of galactic proportions. We tried, we failed, now end. Unfortunate, but attempt minor footnote in history of humanity. Perhaps is for best. Better-equipped team should examine artifact, no matter what egos say. You know this. I know this. Chen know this."

No. Alex wasn't willing to give up. Not yet. *Not like this.* "What if we shift things around in the sledges and put Chen in one of them?" He pointed at Pushkin. "You could pull him."

"Ridiculous," said Pushkin. "Preposterous. Delusional."

Talia glanced between them. "That's . . . I'm inclined to agree. Sorry, Crichton. We'd have to divvy up everything in Chen's sledge and—"

"There's not that much."

"—and *still* find room for Chen to sit somewhere. The sledges aren't that big, and it's not like we brought a lot of extra equipment we can dump."

Alex wasn't deterred. "There's a lot more room in the sledges now that we removed the supercapacitors and drive trains."

She eyed him as if trying to make sense of him. "How much more weight do you really think we can pull?"

"Enough. And we wouldn't have to bring the mast or the sail or the wheels from Chen's sledge. All that could stay. You and I can handle a few extra kilos, and Pushkin, you're more than strong enough to handle Chen. He's not that big." Alex was bluffing now, making assumptions reason told him were unreasonable, but he wasn't going to admit as much.

The geologist rolled his deep-set eyes enough to show his yellowish, bloodshot sclera, and he muttered something in Russian that sounded incredibly profane. Then: "And what of capacitors? And drive trains? And fucking mast and sail and fucking wheels? Is important we bring back with us, no?"

"No, we don't have to."

Talia blinked. "That's not what I expect to hear from a xenobiologist. I thought that you of all people would insist on packing out all our gear."

Alex refused to back down. "It would be nice if we could, but if we can't, we can't. The next expedition can pick it up for us."

thud

Pushkin shook his shaggy, bull-like head. "This utter waste of time."

Before Alex could respond, Chen startled them by saying, "I can do it." His eyes were still closed, and the sweat was dripping off his cheeks, but he continued speaking. "I-I can go on half rations. That would save us . . . save us some weight, and we have plenty of-of Ebutrophene. It won't be too hard. Don't . . . don't stop because of me. . . . Don't." His voice faded out, and he licked his lips, breathing still fast.

"Why?" Talia asked, the word hard, direct, singular.

The chemist licked his lips again. "Because I want to know. I don't know why, but I want to know."

"We all do," said Alex.

"Alright then," said Talia. "We'll try."

Pushkin stared at her, aghast. "No! Madness. Tell me you not serious, Ms. Indelicato."

"I am, and you better get used to it, Volya."

The Zarian drew up his posture, chest swelling, a vein in his neck pulsing. "Bah! Self-serving arrogance! I not agree to this."

"Tough," said Talia, her tone uncompromising. "It's my call, and I say it's worth a shot."

Pushkin's lips drew back from his teeth in an unpleasantly aggressive smile. "Is not dictatorship. You cannot force me. You have not authority."

"No?" Talia stepped forward until she was standing toe-to-toe with Pushkin. He looked as if he could break her with a single hand, but that was only if one took their bodies into consideration. When it came to their minds, Alex knew whom he would bet on. "Let's see about that. Line three. Lieutenant Fridasdottir, do you read?"

"I r--d you."

"Put on the captain, if you would."

Pushkin's grin became a snarl.

"Roger."

thud

"Idr-s here. St--us report."

Talia kept her gaze fixed on Pushkin as she spoke. "Chen is stable, Captain. No change in his condition. I think we might have found a way to continue, but there's a problem."

"Oh? Wh-- pr--lem?"

"One of our team doesn't think—"

While she spoke, Pushkin had started to fidget, as if fit to burst with words desperate to escape, and at last, they broke free in a loud torrent. "Is stupid idea, Captain. Foolishness. They want to torture themselves, good, good, but not me. Not I."

Even through the static, Alex heard the captain's voice sharpen: "Ind-lic-t-, expl--n." Talia quickly outlined Alex's proposal, after which, Idris said, "Alright. Wh-t's th- probl-m, Pushkin?"

"As said, is foolishness! Enough with this! Time is come that we—"

"So the pr-blem is y-- dis-gree. G-t it. Noted. Indelic-to is still -n ch-rge -f the expedit--n. If sh- says you go, y-- go. Th-t's -n order."

Pushkin released his breath in a long hiss between the flat line of his clenched teeth. His teeth, unlike Alex's, met perfectly edge to edge, like a ceramic vise. "And what if I not go . . . *Captain*?"

The answer was quick to come: "Th-n you're -n dereliction -f duty, --d y--r contr-ct is null and void. You forf--t all wages, bonuses, an- rig-ts, and the com--ny will pr-bably cut all ties w-th you."

"Roger that, *Captain*."

"Indelicato, cont-ct me -f th-re a any other iss s. In the meantime, y cont---e to have my faith as th- head -f this miss--n. Idris --t."

The line went dead, and Talia tilted her head upward to better face Pushkin. The pause that followed made Alex's skin prickle. Then, she said, "The calculus hasn't changed, Pushkin. We'll drag the sledges, same as before, just with a little more weight."

"*Hmph.*"

"Besides, if we give up, we lose any chance of being the first ones to examine the hole. A few more days, and we get our names in the history books for good. Think about that."

Pushkin scratched his beard, fingers digging deep among the hairs. "I suppose is some merit in that, if look at from certain point of view."

"Then look at it from that point of view," said Talia in a clipped tone. "What's it going to be, Pushkin?"

thud

The geologist grimaced. "I not like to operate with such narrow edge of safety. If we suffer another misfortune—"

"We'll deal with it, just as we've dealt with everything else," said Talia firmly.

A grunt from Pushkin. Then, finally, he sniffed and said, "Fine, have your way, Indelicato. But you understand I won't put up with more nonsense. One more thing go wrong—one more thing!—and you see my backside, and no person or alien in galaxy can get me to turn around."

"Oh, I understand," said Talia, her voice deadly quiet.

Pushkin sniffed again and went to look at Chen. Talia mouthed *coward* in his direction before joining them.

Alex was relieved that the expedition would continue, but he couldn't help but feel a sense of creeping dread at the situation. Pushkin wasn't wrong, things were growing precarious. It would only take one more accident and they would be in serious trouble. Chen already was.

The void within him narrowed but didn't close, not entirely. The universe was unbalanced, and Alex wasn't sure if it would ever regain its equilibrium, or if it would spin itself apart, stars and planets and gases flying out into the frozen depths.

4.

Two more hours passed as they reallocated their supplies, bolted down Chen's now spare sledge, disassembled and stored the hab-dome, and installed Chen in Pushkin's sledge.

The chemist was lucid enough, but he kept dozing off, even when buffeted by the violent wind. A common side effect of Ebutrophene. *No operating heavy machinery,* Alex recalled. *No piloting spaceships, shuttles, or other flying vehicles. No use of weapons.*

Once they harnessed themselves to the sledges, Pushkin stomped a foot against the ground, raising a cloud of dust. Then he leaned forward and began to trudge into the wind, toward the hole.

The straps bit into Alex's chest and shoulders as he and Talia followed, step-by-painful-step, their heads lowered against the constant gale, their safety lines flapping with annoying regularity. The added weight in Alex's sledge was noticeable but not unbearable, although he knew that the extra kilos would accumulate with every step, piling in a mountain of crushing fatigue.

But that was a concern for future him. Present him only had to worry about taking the next step.

Alex looked back once. He saw where the hab-dome had been anchored, the marks already scoured clean. Next to it, Chen's abandoned sledge was a slug of matte-grey metal; a pewter teardrop arched against the wind. Beyond that, the horizon was a hazy line. Then the sand rose up and drew a thick veil across their past, hiding it entirely.

5.

The border to Gamma Zone came and went with seemingly no change to the surface of the plain. Whatever color variation was present wasn't visible from the ground, especially not with the sand blowing into their visors at all times.

Gamma Zone was nineteen klicks wide, too wide to cross in a single day, even if they'd started at the outer edge of the zone that morning. In any case, Alex was doubtful of their ability to cover any great distance. Between the sledges they dragged and the delay Chen's accident had caused, he thought it unlikely they would come close to matching the fourteen klicks they'd covered yesterday. It was worrying.

thud

The sound made Alex's teeth buzz. It was noticeably louder than before. He could actually *hear* the output from the hole now, not just feel it. The sensation was annoying, and it was only going to get worse. The hardest part was that it interfered with his ability to concentrate. Every ten point six seconds a

thud

arrived and disrupted his thoughts. And just as he recovered and began to focus again, another

thud

He found himself clenching his jaw during the pulses to keep his teeth from buzzing and in an attempt to contain his growing anger. The hole may have been one of the great wonders of the universe, but he was beginning to wish it would just *shut up* for a few minutes.

With their increasing power, the

thuds

made contact with the lander progressively more tenuous. By early afternoon, they could no longer communicate with Lt. Fridasdottir via audio, and they had to resort to written messages, and even those began to show corruption. How long until the

thuds

cut them off entirely, Alex wasn't sure, but it wouldn't be long now. And he feared the isolation that would follow, the hermetic sealing-in of their little group, wrapped as it was by dirt, desolation, and despair.

The wind was stronger as well. Not hugely, but enough that each step took added effort and the torrent of dust streaming toward them was thicker and more turbulent. Staring into the dust was like racing down an endless tunnel at over a hundred klicks per hour.

He could only look at it for a few minutes at a time. Then he began to feel strange and had to switch his gaze to the ground.

The comm snapped on with a crackle of static.

"A m-ment, Alex," said Pushkin.

Alex grimaced to himself. "What?"

thud

It was still early in the day, and their shadows stretched out in front of them: strange spidery figures leading the way deeper into the wasteland. He saw Pushkin's head turn as he looked back.

"I wond--. Why did you sign w--- *Adamura*?"

Alex bit the inside of his cheek until he nearly bled. Then he forced his jaw to relax. "If you read our personnel files then you know damn well why."

"Come n-w, th-t's no answ--. Was it pain of l-st rel-----ship or guilt of her ---th gn-- at you?"

Alex kept his eyes fixed on the ground and remained silent. *Fuck you,* he mouthed. He didn't say it, though, as much as he wanted to.

The comm clicked as Pushkin switched to the group channel. "Talia," he said. "Ms. Indelicato. Pl--se say. Why did y-- go on survey mission --r Company?"

Next to Alex, the slow cadence of her steps never faltered. "That's n-ne of your busi-ess. Why did y--?"

"Me? I signed on --cause - ------ t- -----tigate --- ----al --------- -f --- ----by quasars."

thud

Pushkin continued: "So again, Ms. --delicato, I ask: Wh-- prompted you sign up for th-- del---tful *excursion*?"

"Th- pursuit of God's glor---s tr-th," she said. It was an honest enough answer, but Alex couldn't help feel that her true motivation was something else, something deeper, more visceral.

"Bah," said Pushkin. Still, he seemed to have satisfied whatever misplaced, busybody curiosity he had, because he said nothing more over the common line. But every time Alex happened to see him through his visor, the geologist's fleshy lips were moving, and Alex noticed that Chen seemed to be nodding in response and—occasionally—answering.

Alex was just glad he wasn't on the receiving end of Pushkin's logorrhea.

His gaze slid to Chen's braced and bandaged knee. Again a twinge of guilt afflicted him.

6.

A chime sounded in Alex's right ear, marking the end of the hour. Time to rest. He stopped, as did Talia and Pushkin.

It was 1500. They'd already been walking for seven hours, and they still had another six hours to go until sunset. Even Pushkin seemed tired; he moved with unusual slowness.

Alex turned in a circle, scanning their surroundings. Dirt and dust and not much else. Same as it had been since they broke camp.

The emptiness worried him. They ought to have seen another turtle by now. In fact, they ought to have seen more than one. Were the creatures avoiding them? Or had Alex and his companions just chanced upon an uninhabited area of the plain?

Either possibility raised questions.

He helped Talia secure their sledges. Then he went to the rear of his and opened a small hatch. He dug into the pouch on his thigh, pulled out three shit balls, and dropped them into the container in the sledge.

He looked over at Pushkin and pointed at the open hatch.

Pushkin shook his head.

So he *was* full of shit. Didn't surprise Alex. Not after the past few days.

He reached for the lid of the hatch, intending to close it. A sharp pain stabbed the front of his right shoulder. He winced and sucked in his breath.

"Dammit."

He blinked back tears. Both of his shoulders ached from the harness, but the right one . . . He cautiously rotated his arm side to side. It felt like he had a blister. A *big* one. Now that he was concentrating on it, he was aware of a warm wetness spreading underneath his suit, moving from his shoulder toward his ribs.

"Dammit."

He called up his medical readings. Everything within expected norms. Slight dehydration, rising heart rate, but that was all. He selected a mild pain-killer, a liquid form of Norodon, and sucked it down his feeding tube.

That was all he could do for the moment. He'd have to wait until they stopped for the night before he could get out of his suit, disinfect the wound, and spray it with artificial skin. Twelve hours' rest and he'd be good as new. Until then, he just had to keep going and hope the harness didn't cause too much damage.

He shut the hatch. Then he set his alarm for ten minutes and sat against the sledge with his knees pulled up against his chest and his head resting in the crook of his left arm.

Within seconds of closing his eyes, he was asleep.

7.

"Alex! Wa-- up! Wake up!"

A jolt of adrenaline coursed through him. He sucked in air and struggled to stand, even though he was off-balance. Light—harsh, too bright—filled his eyes. He squinted and blinked, trying to figure out what was going on.

Pushkin grabbed him by the arm, steadying him.

Alex stared at Pushkin's half-mirrored face, confused, nearly ready to sock him.

One of Pushkin's massive hands gripped Alex's shoulder. His left shoulder, fortunately. The geologist pointed behind them with his other hand. "L--k. East," he rumbled.

Alex looked.

Several kilometers away, a turtle glided across the plain. The dust alternately hid and revealed the creature, which made it hard to guess its path, as it kept changing direction. It didn't seem to be heading toward them, though. If any-thing, Alex guessed it was moving off to the southwest.

He checked the time. Only seven minutes since he'd sat down.

"How long has it been there?" he said.

Pushkin shook his head. "That I don-- kn--. I just saw."

"It seems t- be alone," said Talia, joining them. Chen was still sitting in Pushkin's sledge, seemingly sound asleep.

Alex switched to infrared and looked around. Talia was right. He wished they could get a view from orbit. Find out if any of the turtles were hanging out beyond the edge of the horizon.

He glanced at the sky. In theory they ought to be able to spot the *Adamura* at times, but so far the dust and the clouds had kept it hidden. Sharah and Captain Idris would be watching their progress, though. Watching and wondering.

The turtle turned again. Now it was angling somewhat parallel to their own path, meandering along in a cursive, discursive manner.

Alex tagged the turtle on his overlays so he wouldn't have to keep an eye on it every single moment. No doubt the others had done the same. However, he was careful to use pattern recognition only. No range finding or the like. He didn't know what would happen if he bounced a laser off the turtle, and he wasn't particularly eager to find out.

On their main line to the lander, Talia wrote:

<Just spotted another turtle a few klicks away. So far, no indication of hostilities. Will update as needed. – Talia>

A few moments later: *<Rog#r th@t, aw✳y team. Keep your distờ#ce, if possible. – Svana>*

"We sho--- start move," said Pushkin.

8.

Before they resumed walking, Talia insisted on swapping sledges with Pushkin. For whatever reason the geologist objected, but Talia refused to budge, and she took over the responsibility of pulling Chen. As she leaned into her harness, Alex saw her talking to the chemist, who—for his part—looked groggy and bewildered, as if unsure of his surroundings.

Aren't we all? Alex thought.

9.

The turtle, or one very much like it, kept pace with them until evening. It never wandered very close, nor very far away, but always remained within a few klicks of them, even in the thickest clouds of dust and sand. Alex considered its actions definitive proof that the creatures were either intelligent or designed/controlled by intelligence. The odds of the turtle's seemingly random movements just *happening* to keep it alongside their party hour after hour were too high.

He had to take two more doses of Norodon in order to tamp down the pain in his shoulder. As always, the drug gave him an uncomfortably dry throat. But at least it allowed him to keep pulling the sledge.

He just tried not to think of what the harness was doing to his shoulder.

All things considered, they made good time that day. Sixteen klicks in total— and nine of them in Gamma Zone—which was more than Alex expected. Talia pushed them late into the evening, until the sun was below the horizon and the post-sunset light was fading from the vast bowl of the sky.

By the time they stopped, the throbbing in his shoulder had gotten so bad, he was contemplating a dose of Ebutrophene, same as Chen. He decided to wait, though. He figured the pain would go down once he could get his suit off and patch up the blister.

The turtle wandered off and vanished into the dusk while they were setting up the shelter. Alex suspected it hadn't gone too far. That or another turtle, one they hadn't seen yet, had taken over sentry duties. The thought made his scalp crawl.

"Fi--lly," said Talia. Her lips continued to move in silent dialogue within her helmet and, a moment later, Alex saw the message she sent to the lander:

<*The turtle is no longer within visual range. No other turtles visible. We're going to stop here, make camp, and take our readings. Will report in again before night. – Talia*>

The expected response was slow to arrive, and when it did:

<^^$Å^V//□òÉ□òü° 4«-°wûÿö(μbù ̄Δ°o□òèô2UΔʃÿp* GÇ□S2□£tf ̄ôÈ/f†H‡ □π□$4ˇ>

Talia pressed her lips together. "Damm-t." She tried again, with the same results.

"This is end," said Pushkin. "We are alone --d fors-ken, cut off fr-- lieutenant and *Adam-ra*."

"We knew this was coming," said Alex.

"Ex--tly," said Talia. "We keep going, s-me as before. I'm still -n charge -f this exp-dition. N-th-ng's changed."

A sly, disconcerting smile formed on Pushkin's lips as he regarded her. "Of course."

"Nothing's ch-nged," she repeated.

thud

10.

Alex sat in the lee side of the shelter until Talia, Pushkin, and Chen were all inside. Decon was going to take him longer than usual, and he didn't want to hold them up.

"Right, then," he muttered to himself once Talia sent him the all-clear.

He double- and triple-checked the sledges to make sure they were secure before climbing into the airlock and sealing the outer door. Then he took his place in the center of the chamber and raised his arms to either side.

With a soft *hiss* the decon spray covered him in a fine mist of grey droplets.

He closed his eyes, imagining he was lying in his cabin, back on the *Adamura*.

After that, depressurization, followed by the twenty minutes of UV.

thud

The odd calmness of the wait reminded him of long evenings spent driving and flying back from work, when he'd zone out in the back of a car or shuttle, exhausted from his hours (and often days) in the lab. The return trips had been interstitials—twilight moments that divided his existence into discrete segments.

There had been so much travel. . . . He could have stayed near Plinth, near Layla, but the best postings were out past the edge of settled territory, out in the depths of the wilderness. He kept accepting assignments farther and farther away. The pay had been good, but the time away from home, from Layla, had been hard, and the travel itself was exhausting.

He told himself the work was worth it. For both of them. They had loans to pay off; savings to accrue; property to—hopefully—buy; a hab-dome of their own to build. But maybe it had been selfishness. The work kept him from having to deal with questions and conversations that he saw no way to resolve.

So he'd pushed himself. It helped him feel useful. And always there were the twilight trips, underscored by the hum of tires or the rumble of rockets, and the first stars poked cold holes in the darkening sky.

thud

The UV ended. Then repressurization, which he could feel, like soft hands pressing against every part of his body.

He unlocked his helmet and pulled it off. "Hold scrub shower until further notification," he said. "Authorization Bravo-Delta-Delta-six-eight-five-six."

"Affirmative," answered the shelter's pseudo-intelligence.

With a feeling of dread, he reached for the seam at the top of his collar. He tugged down, and the suit peeled open like the skin of a fruit.

Cold air struck the front of his bare torso. He shivered, first from the change in temperature and then because he saw streaks of dried blood and lymph fluid along his ribs. A moist, rotting stench made him gag.

"Shit," he mumbled.

He carefully worked his left arm free. Next his legs. Last of all, he grasped the suit above his right shoulder.

He took a breath, steeling himself.

Then he began to roll down the sleeve. The first few centimeters went fine. After that—

"Aggh!"

A hot blade cut through his shoulder. He bent over, grimacing. He stayed there, eyes screwed shut, until he could bring himself to straighten up.

For a moment, he stood there, staring at the floor and still holding the sleeve. He knew removing the whole thing was going to hurt even more. And he knew waiting wouldn't help. But even so, he hesitated, same as he would if he had to grab a piece of red-hot metal.

He set his teeth and pulled.

His vision went red and black, and he fell forward onto one knee, uttering a soundless scream.

A fan of blood sprayed the floor as the front of his shoulder tore open. The touch of the air caused the wound to sting, as if he'd dumped salt onto it. He clapped his hand over his shoulder and held it there, panting, while blood welled between his fingers.

With a groan, he got to his feet and staggered over to the first-aid kit built into the wall. He had to let go of his shoulder in order to open the kit and grab a can of disinfectant spray. He took the opportunity to actually look at the wound for the first time.

A red slit ran from the top, outer part of his shoulder down to the corner of his armpit. Around it, the flesh was inflamed, and the skin was scraped, ripped, and bruised. Yellowish lymph fluid wept from the abrasions and mixed with blood streaming from the slit.

The disinfectant hurt almost as much as removing the suit. He bit his tongue and counted to ten while he waited for it to take effect. Then he took a sterile wipe and tried to clean his shoulder.

It didn't do much good. The blood kept pulsing out, soaking the wipe and making a mess.

Finally he gave up. He grabbed a tube of Celludox—a clotting agent/growth matrix—and squirted it directly into the wound. It burned at first, but the green goop had a topical anesthetic in it, and within a few seconds, the throbbing in his shoulder began to subside.

He let out a breath he hadn't realized he was holding. Better. Much better.

He wiped off the excess Celludox. Next, he took one of the syringes of surgical glue and carefully squeezed out a thin line along the edge of the goop-filled slit. He spread the glue flat with the included plastic applicator, and then pressed the edges of the wound together (careful to keep his fingers out of the glue) for the recommended thirty seconds.

When he let go, the edges remained firmly stuck to one another.

Another sterile wipe, and this time he was able to get all the blood and fluid off his skin, as well as the remnants of Celludox.

Last of all, the TruSkin.

He sprayed a thick layer of the artificial skin over the front of his shoulder. It wasn't as strong as real skin, but it would prevent scarring, and it would help protect the area from further damage.

Finished, Alex closed the first aid kit.

He stood there, his back hunched and his chin resting on his chest. Tired. He was so tired. Dragging the sledges and fighting the wind was hard enough without having to deal with something like his shoulder. The pain had chewed up his last reserves of strength. Left him feeling weak and hollow. Old. His hands and feet were cold and growing colder: onset symptoms of shock. Food would help, but right then, he found even the thought of moving overwhelming.

Chen has it worse, he told himself, but it didn't help.

<What are you, make shit in there? What keeps you? – Pushkin>

<Is everything alright? – Talia>

Alex sighed and lifted his head.

<I'm fine. Be out in a minute. – Alex>

He picked up his suit and turned it over in his hands. *There.* On the inside. The lining of the suit had folded, forming a sharp-edged crease that had been pressing against his shoulder, cutting into it with every motion of his body. The weight of the sledge on his harness must have caused the liner to fold.

He frowned, thinking.

First things first.

"Initiate scrub shower," he said. "Authorization Bravo-Delta-Delta-six-eight-five-six."

"Initiating," said the pseudo-intelligence. The voice was female. Simulated or prerecorded he couldn't tell, but she sounded like a Loony. Made sense. The shelter had probably been made on or around Earth's moon.

Needles of steaming water erupted from the center of the ceiling. He tensed as they struck his injured shoulder, but the TruSkin shed the water with ease, and the anesthetic masked the pain he was sure the pummeling caused.

He washed himself thoroughly and then rinsed the suit, inside and outside. When he was satisfied that the suit was clean, he said, "Shower off," and the water stopped.

A few quick shakes, and the last remaining droplets fell off the suit. Not for the first time he blessed the anonymous scientists who had invented hydrophobic coatings.

He wiped his hands dry. Then he opened one of the pouches on the belt of the suit and pulled out a roll of vacuum tape. Riedemann called it FTL tape. The joke being that the tape was so strong, you could patch the hull with it and still survive the jump to superluminal space. Which was nonsense, of course. But not by much.

He cut two sections of tape, each ten centimeters long. With one hand he smoothed the lining in the shoulder of the suit. With the other, he placed the pieces of tape in an X configuration.

He nodded. There. That would hold it.

He'd have to be careful, though. The split on his shoulder was too deep to heal overnight, and TruSkin wasn't *that* strong. Even without the crease in the lining, his harness might still pull the wound open again. The best option, he decided, would be to cover it with several layers of medical tape and bandages. The extra padding would help keep the suit from rubbing.

<You come or what? – Pushkin>

<YES! – Alex>

He stowed his suit and dressed in his regulation jumpsuit.

thud

His teeth buzzed. Even within the shelter, there was no escaping the sound of the hole. For a short time he'd forgotten about it—distracted by his shoulder—

but now the noise seemed twice as loud, and it felt rough and harsh, like sand-paper scraping across his nerves.

Another symptom of shock, he thought in a detached manner.

Right then, he just wanted to be somewhere very still and very quiet. Fat chance. Until they turned back, he was stuck with the relentless beat of the hole and stuck with the miserable company of Pushkin, Talia, and Chen. At least the roar of the wind was no longer quite so loud, and he didn't have to worry about it throwing him into the air if he put his feet wrong.

thud

He lifted his chin, preparing himself. Then he unlocked the inner door and went to join the others.

"I'm fine," he said. "Just had some trouble with my suit. . . ."

11.

The three of them rested not in silence—the wind precluded that—but silent all the same. Alex sat crosswise on the plastic slab that served as his bed, crosswise so he faced the heating element that glowed in the center of the floor. He pulled his thermal blanket tight around himself and took another bite of an energy bar: his fifth one that evening. Chocolate-flavored, fat-fortified algae protein. Disgusting stuff, but less so than the other flavors. Worst one was the licorice/lamb-flavored bar. Whoever had invented it ought to be forced to eat that and nothing else for an entire year.

Pushkin lay on his own slab, eyes twitching as he stared blankly at the wall of the shelter. The tips of his fingers twitched as well—small, spasmodic move-ments that reminded Alex of the death throes of a squashed spider. Reading a book or playing a game, that was Alex's guess.

Talia sat on the floor with her legs crossed. She was folding one of the foil wrappers from their meal packs. Folding and refolding, lips pursed as her thin fingers moved with impressive nimbleness. The crinkle of the foil sounded un-pleasantly sharp to him, but he didn't complain. It would take more energy than he had, and it would just stir things up.

Still, every crinkle made him tense. It was a stupid response, but he couldn't help it. He was too wound up. Too anxious. They all were.

As usual, Chen was hunched over his chip-lab, eyes buried in the viewfinder.

His injured leg was propped up on a folded blanket, and his skin had an unhealthy sheen. He'd only said a few words the whole evening; even with the Ebutrophene he still seemed to be in pain, and he had the pinched look of a migraine sufferer.

Alex again reviewed the samples he'd taken from around their latest campsite. The amount of metal in the soil was continuing to increase, as were the number of microbes, although their population was unusually uniform. A single tablespoon of soil on Eidolon (or on Earth, if one wanted the Ur example), held around fifty billion microbes, with a hundred thousand or more individual species of bacteria, fungi, protozoa (or the alien equivalent), and so forth. On Talos, by comparison, he had only found a few dozen species, although their numbers were still in the billions.

He zeroed in on one bacteria-like microbe that appeared to be new. It had the same basic structure as the other Talos-native bacteria—same amino acids, same DNA equivalent, same lipids in the cell membrane—but the microbe was producing a large amount of a chemical that Alex didn't recognize. The chemical seemed to be a waste by-product, but there was enough of it, he thought, that there was a chance the microbe had been engineered to make it.

The foil again crinkled beneath Talia's fingers.

Alex shed the thermal blanket, put down his energy bar, and went over to crouch by Chen. "Hey, what do you think of this?" he asked in a hushed tone and held out his chip-lab.

Chen pulled his face out from the viewfinder and frowned. "That's . . ." His eyes darted back and forth as he scanned the chip-lab screen. "That's a photovoltaic dye."

"What do you mean? It can absorb UV and convert it into electricity?"

"Exactly. Look at this."

A file popped up on Alex's overlays. He opened it and saw a comparison between the chemical he'd been examining and some sort of industrial molecule. It was, he read, used in various applications to generate a weak electrical current sufficient to power certain small devices.

"Huh." He started to stand, then said, "You doing okay? Can I get you anything?"

More foil crinkled.

Chen shook his head. His eyes darted between Pushkin and Talia, and his voice dropped to a low whisper: "Do you think that the aliens . . . I mean, do you think that the hole . . . that it . . ."

"What?"

"Never mind. It doesn't matter."

Alex hesitated, and then patted Chen on the shoulder and retreated to his alcove. He picked up his half-finished energy bar and pulled the thermal blanket back around his shoulders.

How much electricity could the photovoltaic dye generate in large amounts? If the microbe was widespread, there could be literal tons of it in the soil. But to what end? The dye was of no use on its own. It needed to be coupled with other materials before it was of any use.

The turtles? he wondered. Maybe they ingested it, and—

Pushkin stood and padded across the shelter to the food bin, his bare feet slapping against the floor. Alex wrinkled his nose; the rest of them were wearing socks. It was only polite.

The lid of the bin banged against the wall as Pushkin flipped it open.

Another crinkle as Talia turned the foil in her hands. It was assuming a definite shape under the guidance of her slow, deliberate fingers. An angular *something*.

thud

Pushkin sucked in his breath between his teeth. Packaging rustled as he rummaged through the bin. Then he slammed the lid down.

The noise made Alex jolt. He scowled and burrowed deeper into his blanket. *Sweaty bastard can't leave us—*

The air around him grew colder as Pushkin stalked over with three heavy steps and planted himself directly in front of him, blocking the warmth from the heating element.

Alex looked up to see Pushkin giving him a flat, unpleasant stare.

"You ate last chocolate bar," said Pushkin.

Alex swallowed his latest bite. "So?"

"I wanted bar."

"Go get another one, then." They had plenty of the bars in the sledges.

"You already ate three of bars. *Three.* And then you eat last one also, like pig at trough."

Pig? Speak for yourself. "Licorice-lamb won't kill you."

Talia placed the foil on the floor in front of her. Somehow she'd managed to fold it into a bird with a head, beak, legs, and a pair of outstretched wings, feathers included. The bird—a raptor of some kind—looked as if it was pouncing on some poor small animal. Every sharp shiny plane in its body screamed cruelty. Ferocity. It could have been made of a hundred paper-thin knives, each one polished to mirror smoothness.

A dark flush climbed Pushkin's cheeks. "We spend whole day stuck in foul suits, drink pasty snot they call food. When stop, I want to have nice solid meal with bit of something sweet. If best I can get is chocolate-flavored algae bar, then I sure as *fuck* want chocolate-flavored algae bar! Is so much to ask?! Just because you not feel so good, oh poor you, as if we didn't walk every single fucking meter here with you, doesn't mean you get to pick and choose and eat only bars you want and stick us with lamb/licorice/ball-sack/monkey-excrement leftovers!"

Pushkin's voice was a hammer pounding in Alex's skull. He fought the urge to cover his ears and retreat under the blanket. That or hit Pushkin. Anything to stop the excess noise.

He squinted with discomfort.

Pushkin snarled and slapped what remained of the bar from Alex's hand. It flew across the shelter and bounced against the side of the food bin.

thud

For the first time Alex realized how dangerous it could be to be trapped with Pushkin in close quarters. He eyed the distance between his bunk and the clean box where he'd stashed the bolt gun. Could he reach it in time?

Pushkin turned and took two steps toward his bunk. On the second step, there was a small metallic *crinkle*.

The sound caught Alex's attention.

Pushkin froze with one foot on Talia's folded bird, now a disk of crumpled foil, flat and ruined. Then he snorted, shook his massive head, and continued to his alcove.

Talia didn't speak, didn't move. She just sat with her gaze fixed on the remnants of the bird, and her delicate hands spread wide on her thighs.

After an interminable length, she stirred. She took a short breath and touched the crumpled plat of foil with the tip of her middle finger.

A low sound came from her. At first Alex thought she was speaking, but then he realized she was actually singing. A slow, sad song that he didn't recognize. Her voice was rough and had a weariness to it that gave him gooseflesh up

and down his arms. And yet, in spite of that, there was a sweetness to her voice
as well, a drop of honey in a cup of chell.

And she sang:

Ai!

*Wake and watch what fortune brings, upon the backs of silent
wings. Waves of fire and waves of lightning, blasts of thunder,
breaking, crashing.*

Ai! Ai! Ai!

*Hear the walls of iron groan. Hear the children
scream and moan. We cannot flee. We cannot fight,
nor hope for rescue from our plight.*

Ai! Ai! Ai!

*Now the Sarr, that hated foe, has seized our home and laid us low.
Bite your tongue and bow your head;
It will not help to join the dead.*

Ai! Ai! Ai!

*Children of Unrest, remember! Remember!
Where'er you may wander, remember! Remember!
Remember what was lost.
Remember what was lost.*

"So we sang after Bagrev fell," said Talia. Then she picked up the plat of
foil and crumpled it into a ball. With the foil still tucked inside her fist, she
turned to her bunk and lay on her side, facing the wall. She pulled her blanket over herself and from then on was silent, save for the slow pattern of her
breathing.

Alex relaxed his grip on the edge of his own bunk. He wasn't sure what he
had been expecting, but that wasn't it. He glanced at Pushkin; the geologist had

an expression of puzzled contempt. Then he sneered and went back to looking at his overlays.

Alex shook his head. Strange doings in strange places. He was just glad that Talia hadn't lost her temper. Again he wondered at what she had endured during the Unrest.

Perhaps, he realized, he wasn't the only one who needed to visit the hole.

12.

The four of them said little for the rest of the evening. Alex continued working, and Talia and Pushkin ignored each other with an almost physical intensity. Chen, for his part, remained hunched over his chip-lab, eyes fixed on the viewfinder, his face lit from the side by the dull orange glow of the electric heater.

Right then, Alex hated both Pushkin and Talia for making the expedition harder than it had to be. And it wasn't easy to begin with.

If only Layla had been there. She would have brightened the whole trip. It still would have been difficult, but the two of them would have comforted each other, and that would have made all the hurts and pains far more bearable. . . . That companionship was what Alex so often missed. Knowing that someone else was with you, someone who cared for you, and whom you cared for in turn, was worth more than any amount of bits.

A hand seemed to clutch at Alex's heart. Of all of them, Layla would have enjoyed the visit to Talos VII the most. And unlike Chen, she'd always excelled at hiking and camping and . . . and . . .

And all it did was get her killed.

Alex pulled out the alcove's privacy screen and leaned back against the curved wall, grateful the others could no longer see him.

He took a shuddery breath. It was hard to get enough air.

Everyone said you never got over your first love. Maybe that was true. He'd been lucky enough to marry his, and for a time, he thought he'd cheated fate. Only, fate had been saving up, tallying the cost of all the good times while he/she/it/whatever waited for the right moment to collect. And boy had it ever. Old fate had ambushed him and beat him until Alex thought he'd never recover. Beat him until nothing remained but grief and the sick pangs of regret.

A pair of tears spilled from his eyes, hot splashes of remembrance.

He thought of the file sitting on his system, thought of hearing her voice again, seeing what she saw. But he shied from the prospect, though he ached for her presence, even if only as a digital ghost. He knew the experience would be so real, so immediate, it would destroy him.

If he'd had the holocube with him, he might have looked at it, but he feared the effect would have been much the same.

He wiped his cheeks on his arms and kept working. It was the only thing he could do. Sometimes he thought that was the scariest fact of all.

Tired though they were, the four of them went to sleep far, far too late. If Sharah had a link to the shelter, Alex knew she would have berated them for being irresponsible. Still, they couldn't help it; they were too wound up to rest. Instead, they sat in silence, each of them pursuing their own activity, and each of them watching and listening for any sign of the turtles until deep into the night.

When he finally slept, Alex dreamed.

Music spilled from the battered storage container the citizens of Plinth used as a bar and general meeting hall. He recognized the pounding song: another creepy, over-the-top ballad of death and monsters from Todash and the Boys.

It was evening, he'd finished his work assignments, and he and the three guys he was bunking with were walking through the crowd toward the storage container. Every day they gathered there to down a shot or two of whatever rotgut Hamish was serving, cop a nice buzz, and eye the same half-dozen women their own age. Four of the women already had partners, but hey, you never knew. You might get lucky all the same.

Only that night was different. That was the night she had been there.

He seemed to float through the crowd as he and his buddies made their way toward the only empty stools. Dread and anticipation coursed through him; he knew what was about to happen, and he wasn't sure he wanted to live through it again. Wasn't sure he could. The memory had once been sweet, but now it hurt and hurt bad.

He couldn't stop the dream, though. It pulled him along, as inexorable as fate.

Bodies shifted, and the crowd parted, and people faded from existence as they moved to the edges of his vision. Overhead Todash was howling, "—to fleeee. And there's nothing at the door. Hey, there's nothing at the door. Babe, what's that knocking at the door?" and her voice was climbing to a wavering, saw-blade crescendo that sounded as if her vocal cords were about to snap, and . . .

. . . and then he saw her.

Layla.

Slim, dark-haired, animated—she stood at the bar with several friends, none of whom he'd seen in Plinth before. They wore the sort of scuffed jumpsuits that were common among the locals, and their skin had the deep tan that only came from growing up beneath the Eidolonian sun. Small white scars stood out like lash marks on their hands—evidence of all-too-frequent encounters with the thorned bellberry shrubs that clogged the gaps between the trunks of the yaccamé trees.

At first he thought she was angry. Then he realized it was just the angle of her eyebrows, and her mood was actually light and quick.

Entirely by chance, she happened to glance at him and see him watching. A longer look followed the glance. Her eyes were dark and liquid, pools of oil, and they had a merry twinkle to them.

It wasn't love at first sight. Hell, it wasn't even lust at first sight. But it was something. She was the first new woman he'd seen in over a month, and that alone was enough to arouse his interest.

"Hey there, rocketboy," she said. "Why don't you and your friends come join us? You can tell us all the interesting bits about space that they failed to mention in school."

The wave of jealousy that passed through the room was palpable. Alex remembered how, in real life, he had strode over to the bar, buoyed forward on a swell of unexpected confidence.

Not now. Now, he felt a sense of sickness and foreboding. Todash was screaming about something squirming in the darkness, and everything he saw seemed to be painted onto a pane of glass—glass that was cracked and scarred and close to shattering.

He floated forward and took his seat by the bar. His buddies had vanished.

"I'm a xenobiologist, actually," he said, accepting a shot of greenish-brown liquor from Hamish. "Not ship crew."

Layla raised an eyebrow. "How about that! So am I."

"A xenobiologist?

"Mmm-hmm. For the Central Commission. You?"

"Company man. Hasthoth Conglomerate."

Layla smiled and clinked glasses with him. She smiled, and his sickness intensified. Because he knew. He knew what lay in wait for her: the pain, the tears, and that final deadly outing.

He tried to warn her. More than anything, he wanted to warn her. Even though he knew it was a dream, he felt if he could just make her understand, everything would turn out differently. They could have done better from the start, been kinder, more attentive to each other. Together, they could have found a healthier balance. And then she would never have gone off on her trip. Not alone, at least.

The words wouldn't leave his mouth, though. All he could do was smile and mumble along with the pre-established script, a slave to causality like the rest of creation. It terrified him. It infuriated him. But he couldn't break free. He couldn't warn her. And he couldn't save her.

The only thing he could do was endure.

It was the worst punishment he could imagine.

"So what's your specialty?" she asked, leaning closer so he could hear over Todash's strained vocals. Todash and the Boys, five bits on a Friday night, bring your loved one, listen to songs that make you shout and shake and forget your debts to Central Commission, dontcha know, baaaby, baby, and the night is cold and whose hand is that caressing your neck. . . .

"Microbes, mostly. What's yours?"

"Macrobes." She laughed, a delightful chime. "Plants and such, although sometimes it's hard to know the difference between plant and animal on Eidolon."

"I know, right?!"

Then the conversation became fuzzy and indistinct, as so often happened in dreams. He knew in general what they were saying, but he couldn't pick out individual words, only the hum of the crowd and the emotions behind his discussion with Layla.

They talked for what seemed like hours. The whole while he strove to tell her what he wanted but without success.

At last, everything grew sharp again, as if a pair of lenses had been dropped in front of his eyes. The wail of the music was louder than ever—too loud for him to make out what Todash was singing and far, far too loud to understand whatever Layla was saying.

"What?!" he shouted.

The corners of her eyes crinkled. She scooted closer to him, grabbed his arm, and pulled him down until his ear was level with her mouth. Her breath was warm against his skin, and he could smell her. It was a good smell. The best smell.

"I said, let's get out of here!"

He pulled back to look at her, to make sure she was serious. She tilted her head, a mischievous expression on her face. Her cheeks were flushed. Whether from the alcohol or something else, he wasn't sure.

What he did know—both in the present of his dreaming mind and when he had first seen her like that—was that she owned him. That was the moment he had fallen for her. It wasn't love at first sight. Hell, it wasn't even lust at first sight. But it was close enough. From then on, he belonged to her, body and soul.

"Sure! That sounds—" he started to say.

And then the dream shattered and her face exploded in a thousand shards and the storage container vanished, leaving him floating alone in darkness while Todash and the Boys wailed around him and somewhere in the void he heard something wet and massive move toward him on hundreds of tiny feet, and he screamed and screamed, but no one heard. . . .

CHAPTER IV

* * * * * * *

DELTA ZONE

1.

They were all sleep-deprived the next morning. The others took their AcuWake so they'd be functional. Alex didn't. He hated the stuff, and besides, if he felt bad enough to avoid sleep, why would he want to take a pill to feel better? All the wake-me-ups did was clear your mind, and he didn't want that. Not really. It was like the guys he knew who would pop a hangover pill after a night of drinking. What was the point? Make your choices and pay the piper. There was no other way to live. Not in the end. The universe saw to that. It always did.

thud

He gritted his teeth. The sound was an insistent burr forcing its way into his body and brain. With each pulse, his vision distorted slightly, a slight blur of shape and color, like a screen experiencing a momentary power surge.

The distortion messed with his sense of balance, made him take extra care with his steps, as if he'd had too many shots of rotgut.

As before, Talia and Pushkin took turns pulling Chen. Alex knew if he volunteered they would have refused; they seemed intent on monopolizing the chemist's attention, talking to him as they dragged his sledge, although Alex never heard what they were saying in the privacy of their helmets.

He wouldn't have volunteered in any case. His shoulder was already hurting. The pain frightened him; he shied from imagining what the split in his skin would look like that evening.

Maybe he'd have to get a shoulder replacement to go along with his knee. That and his teeth. His whole jaw ached from clenching. *Knee, shoulder, teeth.* It felt as if he were falling apart. Not from old age—that wasn't really a problem if you got your STEM shots—but from accumulated experience. Alex believed that it didn't matter how youthful you were (or seemed); the years and sorrows took their toll no matter what. And in some cases, in *his* case, you paid the price in flesh.

He looked at the pale, cloud-streaked sky, searching for answers somewhere in the depthless bound, but the stars were hidden—masked behind the atmosphere—and all he saw was a momentary flicker that might have been the *Adamura* passing overhead, like a meteorite that flared and burned out.

He dropped his gaze to the ground and hunched in on himself. One more step. That was all that mattered. One more step, and then the next and the next and the . . .

thud

2.

No turtles were visible when they started walking, but within half an hour, one of the alien creatures appeared along the northern horizon. The dark, boulder-like lump kept pace with them from then on, although its path remained erratic, and it maintained a distance of at least ten klicks at all times.

When they stopped for their hourly break at 1000, Pushkin—who seemed to have more energy than the rest of them combined—took his core sampler and made several test drills around the rock where they'd anchored the sledges.

The comm clicked on. "The r------s --- -ff."

Alex checked the channel tag. Pushkin. "What?" he said.

"I s---, --- ----ings --- -ff."

<I can't hear a thing you're saying. – Alex>

<Shits. – Pushkin>

<It's texts from here on out. – Alex>

<Yes, thank you for point out obvious, Crichton. How would I manage without your help? What I **try** to say is readings are off. – Pushkin>

He held up a core sample, turned it back and forth in the light.

<Threads of trace metals get thicker. Much thicker. They look like cables woven through ground. – Pushkin>

Talia joined Alex as he walked over to the geologist.

<How deep do they go? – Talia>

<As deep as drill. – Pushkin>

<Are they carrying any current? – Alex>

<EMP induces some, but I see no outgo flow. – Pushkin>

Alex looked at the darkened plain. <*You think the threads surround the entire hole? – Alex*>

Pushkin shrugged. <*No way to say from here, but I guess yes. Land seems isotropic in every direction. I doubt we happen to find unique area. – Pushkin*>

<*Unless they assumed visitors would choose to walk straight into the wind. – Talia*>

To that, none of them had a response.

3.

Alex stumped forward, eyes half-closed. His legs were burning. His shoulder was on fire. The blisters on his feet had rubbed raw again. Blood moistened his boots.

thud

The one good thing about the discomfort was that it kept him focused on the *now*. Any time his thoughts wandered, painful reality dragged them back, forced him to be present. It was a gift, but a horrible one.

The radio crackled in his ear, but no intelligible words came. Then: <*Did you see the lights? – Chen*>

<*No. Same as before? – Alex*>

<*Just two this time, and they only appeared for a few seconds. – Talia*>

Alex scanned the sky. Empty but for the banded clouds. Then he looked for the turtle that had been shadowing them. It wasn't anywhere on the horizon, but he knew it—or one like it—must be close.

He switched to infrared, just to be sure. The thermal imaging gave the dust streaming past them a peculiar beauty; it reminded him of the sand beaches that lined the Seven Rivers on Eidolon. They'd gone kayaking on the rivers several times, at the height of summer, but—

thud

A throb in his shoulder made him wince, screw his eyes shut. He dismissed the lights from his mind and returned his gaze to the ground. One step at a time. . . .

4.

The day seemed endless.

Talia was relentless. She urged them on with sharp commands, cut their breaks short, and refused to let them stop when the sun neared setting. They walked late into the evening and only stopped when it became too hard to see, even with headlamps.

As much as Alex hated it, Talia's single-minded persistence paid off. They covered a full eighteen klicks: ten to the inner edge of Gamma Zone, and another eight into Delta. Over halfway to the hole, and only six more klicks until they reached Epsilon Zone.

Six more klicks. That's not so far. But it would have to wait until tomorrow. None of them had the energy to keep walking.

Alex felt delirious with pain, exhaustion, and the dizzying pulse of the hole. He knew the others were downing stims, even Pushkin; it was the only way they could keep going and going and . . . and he knew he was going to have to start taking the drugs also. He wouldn't be able to keep up otherwise.

The walking, the motion of the ground past his feet, the constant stream of dust and the distortion of the never-ending

thuds

meant that when they finally stopped, everything seemed to keep moving, pulling away from him toward the horizon, and he kept seeing the same fine-grained texture across his vision—a flickering overlay that seemed to pulse and swirl at times, as if he were seeing the pixels that made up reality itself.

He shook his head, which was a mistake, because he had to grab the back of his sledge for balance. His headlamps formed pale cones in the dust, cones that lent the world shape and substance. Sometimes he felt as if they were magic. As if the only things in the universe that really existed were those within the scope of his lights. And when he turned his head, they ceased to exist.

He wasn't sure if the idea was comforting or terrifying, although the illusion of control appealed to him.

Talia glanced over. Sparkling horns emanated from her helmet; her own lights giving shape to the world around them.

When she saw he didn't need help, she went with Pushkin to set up the hab-dome, leaving Alex to watch Chen.

<Everything's so very strange. – Chen>

Alex looked into his helmet. The chemist was staring at the hidden stars, a dreamy expression on his face.

5.

Once the hab-dome was ready, Alex did his usual rounds. He checked and double-checked the sledges to ensure they were properly secured. He took his soil samples and stashed them in the clean box on the outside of the dome. And then, he faced his fear and headed into the airlock.

As usual, he was the last to go through decon, which meant he had the airlock to himself. It wasn't a situation he would be able to arrange for the rest of the trip, but as long as he could, he would. Alex didn't want Pushkin or Talia to know about his shoulder. Not if it was avoidable. Pushkin might decide to quit the expedition once and for all if another problem arose, and even if that weren't the case . . . Alex didn't want either of them to see his weakness. It didn't feel safe, there on the empty plains of Talos VII.

Realizing that, he knew then he didn't trust Pushkin or Talia to help him in an emergency. Which was *not* how things ought to be on an away mission— every man and woman for themselves, and no guarantee of teamwork along the way.

You're getting paranoid, Alex told himself. They were helping Chen, after all. What was he so afraid of? And yet, he still didn't want the others knowing about his injury, just in case.

In case of what? What? . . . What?

He screwed his eyes shut and then opened and closed them several times, hard, wishing that he could rub them. The world was a staticky screen before him; every solid surface alive with jittery motion.

thud

Removing his skinsuit was as painful as he'd feared; he fell to the floor, mouth open in a soundless scream, his whole body rigid with agony.

When he could move, he saw that the blister on his shoulder had reopened, and the sore was even deeper.

As before, he cleaned it, packed it with Celludox, and glued the red and inflamed skin back together. He wasn't hopeful it would hold, even though the crease in the skinsuit was still taped flat.

The important thing now was to avoid infection. He really didn't want to take systemic antibiotics while having to exert himself as much as he was. That was a recipe for more injuries.

From the first-aid station on the wall, he fetched a couple of iron pills and downed them. He figured they would help with all the blood he was losing.

At least the biofilters in the hab-dome wouldn't have any trouble removing the blood from the decon water. . . . He just hoped Talia and Pushkin wouldn't look at the decon records; they'd know at once that something was wrong.

As jets of air dried him, he let his head fall back and stared at the ceiling. He'd expected the trip to be hard. But not *this* hard. What if they didn't learn anything meaningful about the hole or its makers? What if their time, pain, and effort were all for nothing?

It didn't matter. Layla would have tried, so he was trying. But it hurt. If meaning was this hard to find, no wonder so few tried or succeeded.

6.

Behind him, voices rose in anger. Alex scowled. Pushkin and Talia had been arguing for over an hour, and it was getting distracting. He glared at them from under his blanket.

"—and you build nonsense word castles," said Pushkin. As usual, he was reclining in his alcove, picking crumbs out of his beard. "First you claim unknown makers cannot perceive divine."

"I—"

"That is, they are heathens condemned to fiery pit because of birth. Okay, if that your position, then stick with! You can't now say they must have belief in higher power or—"

Talia sprang to her feet. "Their belief may be wrong, but—"

"Ah-hah!"

"But belief must still exist! Even ship minds often have faith. Not always, but some."

Pushkin waved a hand dismissively. "Pshaw. Example of extremes. Ship minds crazy as spacebirds, every last one."

"Even if they are, it still proves my point. No matter the shape of intelligence, we look for understanding."

Pushkin slapped a hand against the curved side of the dome. "Humans do, Ms. Indelicato. *Humans,* and humans are *not* rule, as far as we know."

"We know nothing else."

"Precisely!"

Talia turned to Chen, who was watching them from his alcove, like a child stuck between two parents battling for his affection. "What do you think,

Chen? Yes or no? Would aliens believe in a higher power? Would they have faith of some form?"

thud

The chemist was slow to answer, but at last he said, "Why does it matter?"

Talia threw up her hands and paced twice around the dome. "Because," she said, "belief is a basic part of what it means to be human. The need to trust in something bigger than yourself. The desire to understand. It's something I think any sentient, self-aware species would have to have. If not, where would they get their hope? What would drive them to greater and greater heights? Nothing, that's what."

"Ah-hah," said Pushkin, raising a finger. "Plenty of humans not believe in supernatural, and we get along just fine, thank-you-very-much."

"History would disagree," said Talia. "Besides, you believe in powers beyond yourself. You're just too arrogant to acknowledge that what you're talking about is *God* and not a unified field theory. And because of your arrogance, you assume knowledge you don't actually possess."

Pushkin heaved his bulk into a more upright position, his eyes bright and sharp. "What I *believe* is we have one life—one life only—and she is often short, painful, and unpleasant, so we should enjoy how we can. That's what I believe."

"That's hardly a philosophy," scoffed Talia. "Selfishness just leads to sloth and cruelty."

A deep frown creased Pushkin's face. "Faith led to just as much cruelty, Ms. Indelicato. I work hard because I *enjoy* it. On occasion I am nice to people, because I *enjoy*. And yes, I make habit of indulge every type of pleasure because, again, I *enjoy* them. Beauty in all things, Ms. Indelicato, even in villainy."

Disgust contorted Talia's face. "See," she said, turning on Chen. "That's what happens when man puts himself above the rest of creation."

"I . . . I don't know," said Chen.

"That smartest thing you said tonight," rumbled Pushkin. "Desire to understand, yes. I think that basic requirement for any sentient species. But does not mean she results in desire to believe in something greater than yourself."

Talia stood with her hands on her hips, shaking her head. Her hair swept back and forth like a tasseled pendulum. "Science alone can't answer the biggest questions. It can't tell us *why*."

"Of course it can," said Pushkin. "We know perfectly well how something come from nothing, and we known since twenty-first century. You're—"

"But it still doesn't explain *why*." Talia resumed pacing, her steps crisp and abbreviated. "It doesn't give us any sense of meaning. You can't tell people they're nothing more than random collections of atoms and expect them to behave as they should."

"I didn't—"

"Without a belief in a higher purpose, we can't be fully developed as self-aware beings. Nor could any aliens."

Pushkin drained the water pouch that had been sitting by his knee. "Okay. I play. Say *they* do make faith of sort. We not even call her religion. So how is believing in random supernatural element proof of anything? It not. And sure as hell not mean they better for it. Maybe their belief systems demand blood sacrifice every Thursday. Ever think of that?"

"The specifics aren't important," said Talia, stiff.

"And devil is in details. . . . If specifics not matter, then you should not mind convert to another religion, Ms. Indelicato. Perhaps you like to, oh, pray to Zeus or Odin or Reginald Pig-Headed God of Khoiso?"

"Now you're just being offensive."

"No, I am realistic, unlike you, my dear." And he leered at her in a manner that Alex thought was explicitly offensive.

Talia laughed, a short, choppy sound devoid of mirth. "Then I feel sorry for you, because you have nothing to comfort you when tragedy strikes."

A vein throbbed on the side of Pushkin's temple, and his head swelled like a purple balloon ready to pop. "You smug-ass bitch, you have no idea what I endure in life. You survive occupation of Bagrev. Whoop-dee-fucking-do. Good for you. You not only one familiar with *tragedy*. I courted her. I bedded her more times than I remember. So you can go fuck off with your sermons."

His outburst didn't seem to surprise Talia. She tilted her head back with an expression of such condescending pity, Alex felt a flicker of defensiveness himself. "Of course. Why should I have expected anything else from you?" A snarl distorted Pushkin's face, but before he could respond, Talia shifted her attention back to Chen. "Do you really agree with this man?"

Chen shook his head. A sheen of sweat gleamed on his forehead. Being put on the spot seemed to be making him intensely uncomfortable. "I don't know. I never thought about it much. I just want things to work," he said.

"And when they don't?" she said. "That's the question."

"Then we fix them."

"Some things can't be fixed." Alex froze as Talia's raptor-like gaze settled upon him. "What about you, Crichton? Where do you stand on all this? You must have an opinion."

"Yes, do tell," said Pushkin. "Share your wisdom, yes, please. Do you think aliens who made hole are true believers like dear Talia here? Do you think faith is indispensable for sentient race to achieve anything great? Do tell, Crichton. I can't wait to hear."

thud

Alex blinked as he tried to sort through his thoughts. The grainy, sand-like texture still distorted his vision, making things seem vague and intangible, as if they'd been fuzzed so far he could pass his hand through solid objects.

He swallowed. "I'm not sure . . ." He paused and started again, louder this time. "I'm not sure if anything really matters."

Pushkin snorted. "Bah. How useless are you? Of all philosophical positions, apathy—*nihilism*—is worst."

Talia let out a sharp laugh. "You're no different, Pushkin. You don't believe in anything but your own selfish—"

Pushkin interrupted her, and then they were back at it again, spitting venom-laced arguments back and forth, and neither really listening to the other except to find more ammunition for attack. It was draining to listen to. Alex didn't know how they found the energy. . . . No, that wasn't right. He knew how. It was the stims.

He took another look at their faces. Eyes that were too quick, too bright, pupils dilated wide as the hole, cheeks flushed, skin shiny with sweat and grease, jerky marionette movements. *Yeah.* . . . They were overcranked, jacked up like hard-core wireheads ready to rip out the throats of anyone who got on their nerves.

Alex could sympathize, but not really. Right then he half hated both Pushkin and Talia for making him think about things he didn't want to. The presence of the hole raised enough existential questions without adding in the supernatural.

thud

7.

The noise of the hole disrupted Alex's dreams, kept them from forming coherent images or narratives. He'd get quick impressions of people, places, or emotions, and then the inevitable

thud

would disperse his imaginings, and they'd evaporate like mist in the morning.

Partway through the night, he woke and lay staring at the dark ceiling, listening to the others' breathing. Pushkin's chest rose and fell like heavy bellows, filling and emptying the geologist's massive, gene-hacked lungs with a steady, heavy, animal-like rumble. Talia's breaths came quick and shallow, as if she were dreaming of running a frantic race, and when Alex looked at her in her alcove, there was a frown on her face. Chen's breathing was slower, calmer than either of theirs, but every few minutes, he started and a mumble or whimper escaped his lips, as if he were pleading for respite.

Alex tried to ignore the sounds, tried to ignore the

thuds

Instead, he found himself thinking of Pushkin and Talia's argument. He turned it over in his mind like a precious object, searching for flaws, searching for new angles and flashes of revelation.

It was exhausting, unrewarding work.

His parents had never talked with him about philosophy or religion or any sort of existential questions. Nor had anyone else in his family. Like so many on Stewart's World, their life had been consumed with the hard, technical work of surviving in the hostile environment. Nothing about the colony was natural. Everything was artifice—metal and machine and composites, all designed to protect them from the lethal rays and harsh temperatures that constantly assaulted the planetary surface. His parents were well educated (they each had their IPDs), as were most of the people on Stewart's World. You couldn't survive otherwise. Unskilled labor simply wasn't a thing on Stewart's, and there was something about the relentless intellectual grind of their technological bootstrapping that seemed to crush the imagination.

At least, in his family.

Even through the bulk of his schooling, the coursework hadn't exposed Alex to the sorts of questions he'd been grappling with ever since . . . since *before* became *after.* All of the subjects had been focused toward educating the next generation of scientists and engineers that the colony needed to function, with no thought given for the how, the why, or the rightness and wrongness of things.

It hadn't been until he'd started formal training as a xenobiologist that he'd heard anyone discuss such topics, and only when considering the possibility of encountering sentient aliens.

He'd listened with dutiful interest, but so much of the material had bounced off him, as he didn't understand the importance, and it hadn't seemed of any practical use.

thud

Layla and her family had been different. They had *cared,* and they'd been willing to talk about their beliefs. Especially Layla. Their openness—their *earnestness*—had required a readjustment on his part, one he hadn't really made, and the longer he and she were together, the more conflict it had caused. . . .

The curved ceiling swam above him, and he turned on his side, blinking. His shoulder throbbed with a hot pulse.

Maybe Talia was right. Faith was important. *Belief* was important. It gave you a reason to endure. But belief in what? The supernatural didn't appeal to Alex; in that he agreed with Pushkin. He could also see Pushkin's point about the importance of enjoying himself. Humans were hedonistic at heart; Alex firmly believed that. If you didn't derive *some* sense of reward from your life, why continue on? But pleasure for pleasure's sake wasn't enough.

Which left Alex back where he started. What could he believe in—or what could he *do*—that he would find rewarding and meaningful enough to put up with the sorrows of life?

thud

He closed his eyes. In front of him hung the titanium urn, bright against a black backdrop. He reached for it, and the metal was cold against his fingers. And then he was falling, falling, falling into the spinning void, and he lost his grip on the urn, and there was nothing to grab on to. Nothing to hold. Nothing to love.

CHAPTER V

* * * * * * *

EPSILON ZONE

1.

Pop!

A gunshot-like report went off in Alex's face. His eyes flew open, and he jerked upright as a white-hot lance stabbed through his lower jaw.

"Ahh!"

He clapped a hand to the side of his face while he scrabbled for something he could use as a mirror. *There.* The corner of his thermal blanket, where it wasn't so wrinkled.

He hadn't been shot. In fact, nothing appeared wrong from the outside; his face looked the same as ever. If it weren't for the bolt of pain burrowing into his jawbone, he wouldn't have known there was a problem.

He cautiously used his tongue to probe the side of his mouth. As his tongue touched the lower molar second from the back, he felt loose pieces of tooth move against the gums.

Fuck!

"What's wrong?" Talia demanded, groggy as she tumbled out of her alcove.

Pushkin pulled back his privacy screen and peered out with wary interest.

"Crked a tth," Alex mumbled.

"What?"

"Crked a tooth!"

The corners of Talia's eyes tightened, and Pushkin sucked in his breath, clucked his tongue, and said, "No, no, no. I did not want hear that, no, I did not. Good morning." And he pulled the screen closed again.

Talia went for the first aid kit, but Alex waved her off. He hunched over the sink set in the side of the wall and spit out the pieces of tooth. They stuck in the composite bowl, gleaming white amid the stringers of blood that fell from his mouth. He coughed and spit again. Another piece of bone *clinked* as it hit.

It was bound to happen, he told himself, but it wasn't much comfort.

Mouthwash, more Norodon, a topical anesthetic, and several swigs of water later, Alex had cleaned up and was getting into his skinsuit. The right side of his jaw was swollen, and he could feel a migraine incoming, even through the haze of painkillers.

Despite himself, he tabbed a dose of AcuWake. Within minutes, he felt a jittery sense of clarity, like cold water splashed across his face.

Chen watched the whole while, his round eyes unblinking.

thud

2.

The wind was stronger that day.

Alex leaned into his harness, feeling every muscle in his body protesting. At least the Norodon helped with his tooth and his shoulder and the blisters on his feet. *Small mercies.*

They'd been walking for four days. Only four days. The fact felt incredible, impossible. Everything before Talos seemed hazy and insubstantial, as if it had been a strange, half-muted dream. And yet Talos didn't feel any more real. Brighter, yes. Louder, yes. More intense, yes, but there was a surreality to the dust-scoured plain that left Alex unmoored and uncertain, without a proper sense of place.

He wet his tongue. *Dry. So dry.* The AcuWake had that effect.

Don't think. Just walk. Just walk.

3.

Reddish patches began to appear on the crusted soil. When Alex tested them, he found concentrated amounts of the photovoltaic dye he'd discovered earlier. But as usual, he had no idea what its ultimate purpose was.

This day, a pair of turtles appeared, one by the northern horizon, one by the southern. The southern turtle ventured closer than the northern; at times it was only two or three kilometers away.

For the most part Alex ignored them. Unless (or until) they came closer, he wasn't going to worry about the creatures. He'd study the video of them later, when he wasn't so damn tired. . . .

Talia took first shift pulling Chen. When they stopped for their hourly break at 0900, Pushkin moved to take over, but Talia refused, and they got into a heated argument that began with texts and then devolved into them shouting at each other through their helmets. Talia tried to pull rank, but Pushkin just sat on the harness attached to Chen's sledge and refused to budge until Talia gave up.

While they were screaming at each other, Alex crawled over to the side of the sledge and touched visors with Chen. The chemist didn't look too good. His eyes were hollow, bruised, and there was a greenish cast to his skin.

"Hey, you doing okay?" Alex asked.

"I'm . . . I'm doing my best."

"Can I get you anything?"

"No. But . . . thank you."

Alex glanced at Talia and Pushkin, who were nearly butting heads themselves. "What's Talia been saying to you? Seems like the two of them have been talking your ears off."

Chen shrugged in his suit. "It's . . . She's been explaining Adysópitos Orthodoxy to me."

"Is that what she believes?"

A nod from Chen. "Yeah. It's—" Pushkin boomed something loud enough to be heard through his helmet and over the wind. Chen continued, "It's interesting, I suppose."

"What about *him*?" Alex pushed his chin toward the geologist.

Chen's eyes darted from side to side, as if he was trying to escape the conversation. "Just . . . more stuff. You know how he . . . how he likes to talk. There's so much I've never thought of. So many years I just didn't . . . think."

Something about Chen's tone didn't sit right with Alex. "You want me to take a turn pulling you? Give you a break? I can, if you want."

Chen shook his head with an almost frantic look. "No, I'm fine," he mumbled. "Thank you. I'm fine."

"Uh-huh." Alex wasn't convinced, but he wasn't going to force the issue, not if he didn't have to. Putting himself between Talia and Pushkin was an unappealing prospect right then. But he couldn't bring himself to leave Chen. Not yet. He eyed the chemist's skin. It seemed greener than before, and the man kept swallowing as if he were about to throw up.

"Hey," said Alex, "what are you going to do when you get home?"

The question caught Chen by surprise. "Home? Have my knee fixed and then write some papers."

"No, not that. Not work."

"You mean like a hobby?"

"Yeah. What do you do in your free time?"

Chen had to think about that. "Walk."

". . . Walk?"

The chemist nodded. "Not like . . . this. My partner and I, we walk around the torus. It's a big one. It takes about two . . . two and a half days, but you can keep going as long as you want. There's a park that runs around the whole middle."

Alex tried to imagine. "And after?"

"After walking?"

"Yeah. You can't walk forever."

Chen shrugged. "Sometimes I volunteer at the . . . local teaching center, help set up the lab . . . oversee experiments with the children."

"Really? Why?"

The chemist's forehead beetled. "Because I like helping. And it's important. The station . . . needs it."

4.

By noon they had passed into Epsilon Zone. There was more bare rock visible in Epsilon—the wind had scraped away most of the surface dirt there—and the sound of the hole was noticeably louder. Now it was a full-bodied

Thud

that shook Alex's bones and muscles and made his teeth buzz and his cheeks vibrate. Whenever it struck, he felt a spike of pressure in his sinuses and in his cheekbones. He wondered if they would get nosebleeds when they were closer.

The static in his vision was more pronounced as well. The grains were the size of rice, and they jittered and swam with a life of their own. He held his hand up and stared at the swirling patterns. The dust racing past their feet was hypnotizing, a continuous stream of fractal patterns that danced to the beat of the hole.

This can't be good for us.

Thinking was becoming harder and harder. Every time he managed to focus on something

Thud

He couldn't even read the results from his soil samples. He tried, but every time he was in the middle of an equation, a

Thud

would drive the words out of his head, leaving him frustrated. So he gave up and just plodded along, shoulder aching, jaw throbbing, mind empty, arms half-numb from the harness.

A sense of grim helplessness grew within him. Each pulse was an assault on his body, one he couldn't avoid. He was trapped. They were all trapped. And despite the vastness of the sickly sky, he felt an almost claustrophobic sense of confinement. His aversion to the sonic blows was so great, he started clenching his muscles in anticipation of every

Thud

as if to ward off the blow he knew was coming.

Distracted as he was, Alex's thoughts started to wander, random memories passing through his mind in the ten point six seconds between bursts.

—sitting at the kitchen table over at the Harrises', playing Scratch Seven with Taurin, Neptune, and Layla. The cards turning over, and Layla laughing as she claimed a straight flush—

—the two of them climbing to the peak of Mt. Adonis as the sun rose over Pantheon Range—

—the first time he and Layla had had sex together. The awkwardness, the excitement . . . how they'd alternated between urgency and shyness. How they'd spent half the night cozied up together, talking about the future—

Thud

—bits and pieces of arguments they'd had about his postings; disparate impressions of words spoken in anger, misunderstandings, uncharitable interpretations . . . all of which consolidated into a single, etched image—

He and she, staring at each other through a video call. He sitting at his desk in bare company work housing near the Arctic Circle; she standing at home, in their greenhouse, glitterbugs buzzing about her head, chips of iridescent metal vibrant with life.

Her face was set in hard lines he had grown far too familiar with. His own was no different. The argument was the same as ever: too much time away from home, the next posting promised to be no better, money versus family, the difference between their priorities. He couldn't seem to make her understand, and he knew she felt the same. So they stared at each other with frustrated helplessness, and the silence was a corrosive poison that ate away at the bonds between them.

Thud

Alex's vision blurred. He blinked away the film of tears that had formed. Where was he? He wasn't sure. On Talos, walking, always walking. *In Purgatory.* That's what the planet was: an in-between place, where reality thinned and bent.

5.

It was evening, and dusk was falling across the barren plain. The sun lay in front of them, half-hidden behind the horizon. The clouds of dust acted like a filter, cutting the glare and allowing Alex to look directly at the greenish-orange disk without his visor darkening. The sun was a paper cutout. Thin. One-dimensional. As if it were a flat prop pasted against the dome of the heavens.

They'd covered thirteen klicks so far. Another two and they'd call it quits for the day. As he'd expected, they hadn't been able to match their performance of the previous day. Even with an extra few minutes' rest every hour, the four of them were just too damn tired. It wasn't only physical exhaustion, either. The constant beating of the hole was wearing them down mentally. Chopping everything into sections exactly ten point six seconds long.

He used his tongue to probe the gap between his teeth. The root of the molar was still embedded in his jaw, but the top was sharp and jagged; he'd cut the side of his tongue and the inside of his cheek several times.

He grimaced and tried to stop worrying the broken tooth. But his tongue returned to it again and again; there was a perverse pleasure in feeling the damage he'd done to himself.

The sun had just dipped below the horizon when they reached fifteen kilometers and Talia called an end to the day's trek. Mind blank and muscles burning, Alex fumbled with his harness, trying to unclip it.

By the far sledge, Talia stumbled and went down on one knee.

Alex blinked and stopped. Beside him, Pushkin did the same. Something was wrong, but Alex wasn't sure what. His thoughts were slow and his movements were slower.

Alex blinked again and worked his tongue in his mouth. It felt dry and fuzzy.

Thud

What had he missed? What was off?

Talia's foot.

It wasn't resting on the ground. It was resting *in* the ground.

The strangeness of the sight helped clear Alex's mind. The dirt around her foot was moving. Rippling. As if it were alive.

Thud

Talia pushed herself upright and pulled her boot out of the ground. Beads of silver metal rolled down the surface of her suit and splashed against the dry earth, molten raindrops that glimmered and gleamed in the ghastly light until the dust covered them in a powdery blanket.

Thud

Alex and Pushkin unhooked their harnesses and went to join Talia. She had already pulled out a chip-lab and was probing the puddle of liquid metal.

Alex squatted next to her. His first urge was to poke the surface of the metal, but he wasn't that stupid.

Thud

The metal rippled in response to the blast.

<Is it mercury? – Alex>

<No, is not dense enough. Gallium, I think. – Pushkin>

<Shouldn't it be solid at this temperature? – Alex>

He switched his overlays to infrared. A twisting vein of glowing metal stretched across the surface of the plain. It wasn't the only one. Thousands of such veins surrounded them, branching and combining with fractal complexity. Ahead of them, closer to the hole, the caul of veins grew denser and increasingly interconnected. Behind them, the veins attenuated away into nothingness.

Thud

Talia motioned them closer. They crowded around her, and she pointed at the edge of the gallium. With the tip of her chip-lab, she pushed the metal back. The gallium was sticky; it clung to its surroundings, almost like hot wax.

Underneath the metal was a trough of . . . something. It looked like grey stone, but Alex knew it could just as easily be ceramic or some sort of exotic composite.

Then the silvery metal flowed around Talia's chip-lab and covered the trough back up.

<Gallium confirmed. It's laced with vanadium and a few other trace metals. There's a ridge or a wire at the bottom of the conduit. I don't know what it's for, but perhaps Riedemann might. – Talia>

<I figured it out. – Chen>

Surprised, they looked back at him, where he sat strapped into his sledge. Even through his visor, Alex could see that Chen appeared sickly. His skin was grey, and there was a yellowish stain around his nostrils and upper lip.

Thud

<Do say. – Pushkin>

<Vanadium. Gallium. It's a superconductor. – Chen>

<It's too hot for that. – Talia>

Thud

<The metal would need to be chilled. That's what the wire is for, but the system is old. Something broke. The magnetic field from the EMP couples with the gallium, heats it up, gallium melts. – Chen>

Thud

<But what's it **for**? – Alex>

<Is not obvious? – Pushkin> His lips curled in the semblance of a smile. <Gallium, threads of metal under ground. Is not obvious? Is antenna. A giant fucking antenna. – Pushkin>

Thud

Chen nodded weakly. <That's what I think. – Chen>

<It probably would have been a phased array then. That would have allowed them *to focus* the EMP, instead of broadcasting it all over the place like a megaphone. – Talia>

Once again, the scale of the hole staggered Alex. Just producing the power required to chill that much gallium would have been a major engineering feat.

Thud

<Why leave it, the metal, exposed to the elements? – Alex>

Talia shrugged. <Why build the hole in the first place? I wouldn't step in the gallium if you can help it. Our suits should protect us, but the current the EMP is inducing is enough to fry you. – Talia>

Alex saw Pushkin laugh, a silent show behind his visor. Then the geologist moved over to the largest vein of gallium and stomped in the liquid metal with one huge boot. Coin-sized drops splashed outward; a silvery spray that the wind ripped away and sent flying eastward, the drops bouncing across the surface of the ground.

<DON'T! STOP THAT! – Alex>

Pushkin laughed again and jumped in the gallium like a kid in a muddy puddle.

Talia started toward him. *<Knock it off! – Talia>*

Alex took a single step forward and—

—a huge black shape rushed past, as fast and silent as a mag-train. It clipped his hip, and the sky and ground flashed around him as he rolled, scrabbling for purchase. He couldn't stop himself; the wind was too strong.

A burst of light filled his eyes as his back struck a rock.

His vision cleared just as the shape smashed aside Talia's sledge—tearing apart the cowling and sending equipment flying everywhere—and rammed into Pushkin. The geologist flew ten meters through the air, spinning and tumbling like a top.

A spark of flame leapt from the muzzle of the bolt gun as Talia fired. The gun could punch through twenty centimeters of solid granite, but Alex saw the bolt bounce off the side of the craggy turtle without even chipping it. The creature looked like rock, but it might as well have been made of tungsten carbide.

The turtle changed direction faster than anything that big and bulky should have and darted away in a straight line, vanishing into the veils of billowing sand.

Talia kept the bolt gun trained in the direction of the turtle as she backstepped to Alex and helped him up.

<You hurt? – Talia>

<Fine. – Alex>

<Pushkin! – Chen> The chemist pointed at the fallen geologist.

A jet of white, condensation-filled air leaked from the back of Pushkin's skinsuit.

Alex broke out in a cold sweat. He ran to Pushkin as fast as the wind allowed, Talia close beside him.

As Alex dropped down next to Pushkin, the geologist flailed at him, trying to grab him. Through his half-mirrored visor, Pushkin's face was strained and contorted with fear.

Alex ducked Pushkin's clumsy bear hug and scooted behind him.

<Hold still, dammit! – Alex>

Pushkin might not have been able to send texts, but he was obviously still receiving them, because he stopped moving.

The back of Pushkin's suit was a mess. The casing of his rebreather unit was bent and scratched. Dials broken. The valve of the oxygen tank crushed; from it streamed the jet of air. There was also air leaking from within the rebreather.

Alex tore open the pouch on his belt and grabbed the roll of vacuum tape. He cut a strip as long as his arm, then handed the roll to Talia. She accepted and tucked the bolt gun under her arm.

<Keep giving me sections. Same length. – Alex>

He wrapped the first strip around the crushed valve. Then he took the strip Talia was offering him and also wrapped it around the valve. The third piece of tape went over the back of the rebreather. The dust in the air made it hard to get the tape to stick, but he thought he got a decent seal.

<Th fk-- -ake --u s- lng? – Pushkin>

<Shut up and don't move. – Alex>

He covered the back of the rebreather with a crosshatched mat of vacuum tape. It bulged in a few places, but it held. When he finished, he stared at the tank's pressure gauge, which fortunately hadn't broken.

His heart sank along with the needle in the dial. He did the math in his head.

Five minutes.

Five minutes until Pushkin ran out of air.

Alex wet his lips, mind racing. More tape wouldn't help; he'd already slapped on most of the roll and it still hadn't stopped the leaks. The hab-dome would take too long to put up. They had the tools and parts to repair the rebreather and replace the tank valve, but that would take time. Time they didn't have. Besides, he'd have to shut down the rebreather when he was working on it, which wouldn't do Pushkin much good.

There *was* a spare suit stored in Talia's sledge. Was it still intact? Changing from one suit to another would take minutes and minutes. Pushkin would pass out before he got more than halfway into the new suit. And Alex knew he and Talia couldn't manhandle the geologist into the outfit if he were unconscious.

What was the alternative? Standing around and watching him asphyxiate?

"Fuck. Fuckity, fuck, fuck, fuck. Fu—"

Alex stopped. There was another option. The other suit. Undamaged rebreather. If he pulled it off, he could try swapping— Might be fast enough. Barely.

He jumped to his feet, grabbed Pushkin by the shoulders, and banged their visors together, keeping them pressed against one another.

"Stay here!" shouted Alex.

Then he bounded toward the sledges.

To Talia: <*Find the spare suit. Now! – Alex*>

He felt the drumming of her footsteps as she followed him.

Thud

Alex unlocked the hatch at the back of his sledge. He dug through the contents, searching for the toolbox.

<*It won't do any good. – Talia*>

<*Gotta try. – Alex*>

His hand closed around the handle of the toolbox. He yanked it out, grabbed an air tank, closed up the sledge, and sprinted back to Pushkin.

Talia kept pace with him. She'd found the spare suit; it flapped in her hand like a flayed skin.

<*I cnt gat in2 tht! – Pushkin*>

<*Shut up. – Alex*>

He dropped to his knees on the ground and jammed the tank between his legs to keep it from rolling away. He pointed, and Talia placed the suit in front of him.

<*Hold it down. – Alex*>

She squatted and pinned the suit's arms and legs to the ground with her legs and feet. Slim as she was, her body helped block the incoming dust, which was important.

They'd all had training on how to repair their suits. It was a basic requirement for survey missions. Alex just hoped he remembered enough of his training.

He popped open the toolbox and took out the variable-speed drill. He picked the right screwdriver head, slipped it onto the drill, and then bent over the suit as he removed the first of the screws that held the rebreather attached.

The screwdriver head was magnetic, but it still wasn't strong enough to keep the loose screw from slipping between his fingers and flying off into the wind.

"Shit."

Didn't matter. He could replace it later.

As he started on the next screw, Alex glanced at the clock on his overlays. Three minutes and forty seconds left.

He had to move faster.

There were seven screws in total. He managed to get the rest of them out without losing any more. Then he swapped the drill for an open-faced wrench. There were four hoses and three straps that had to be detached from the rebreather before it could be pulled free of the spare suit.

He timed himself as he loosened the threaded ring around the end of each hose.

Too slow. Too slow.

The last hose popped free of the suit. Two minutes and twenty-three seconds remaining. It was going to be close.

Alex grabbed the drill again and turned to Pushkin. He ripped off some of the vacuum tape, set the screwdriver head against a screw in Pushkin's re-breather, and pulled the trigger.

The drill vibrated in his hand as the head spun.

He pulled out the first screw and dropped it into the pouch on his belt. Then another. They were going to break quarantine, but there was no way around it. He just hoped none of the microbes in the dust or air would prove dangerous to Pushkin. He didn't think they would, but it was impossible to know for sure.

Screws finished, he started on the hoses.

The first two were easy. Small puffs of condensation escaped the ends of the hoses as he worked them loose. The third one, though, gave him trouble. It was set in a nook along the bottom of the rebreather, which made it hard to reach with the wrench. Plus, it felt as if one of Riedemann's technicians had tightened the threaded ring with a power tool.

The wrench slipped off the ring.

And again.

"Shit-shit-shit-shit."

One minute and six seconds remaining.

<Start hyperventilating. – Alex>

<Waht fr? – Pushkin>

<You're going to have to hold your breath. – Alex>

Pushkin's chest began to expand and contract with frantic speed.

Alex braced the wrench against the side of his wrist. No good. A shadow fell over him as Talia moved next to him. She reached past him and tried to grip the ring between thumb and forefinger. The ring was on too tightly, though; her fingers kept sliding off.

Alex batted her away and tried again with the wrench. He couldn't find a good angle, though. And he couldn't get a good grip on the wrench; his gloves were too thick.

Forty-two seconds.

"Fuck!"

He paused for a moment. Then he grabbed his left glove and, with a savage twist, unlocked it from the arm of his suit. A burst of white air escaped as he broke the seal. His cuff automatically tightened like a tourniquet, preventing the rest of his suit from depressurizing.

Cold struck his hand, bitter and burning, as he peeled off the glove. The streaming dust stung his skin, like thousands of pinpricks.

<What are you doing?! – Talia>

<Take it! – Alex>

He shoved the glove at her until she accepted it. Then he ripped off his other glove as well. The cold hurt, but he wouldn't get frostbite for a few minutes. Long enough.

Thirty seconds.

He winced as his fingers closed around the steel wrench. It was like holding a bar of ice. He might have been optimistic about the frostbite.

He turned sideways, fit the wrench to the threaded ring, and *twisted*. For a moment it felt as if the muscles in his wrist and forearm would tear. Then the ring gave, and he was spinning it off the end of the hose fast as he could.

Twenty seconds.

He placed the wrench on the collar of the last hose. It was the feeder line for Pushkin's helmet. Once he disconnected it, the air would drain from the helmet, exposing Pushkin to the atmosphere of Talos VII.

<Take a deep breath and hold it. Now! – Alex>

Pushkin's chest expanded, and he gave a thumbs-up.

Alex yanked on the freezing wrench. Once. Twice. And then it turned, and he spun the threaded ring off the end of the hose. The hose sprang outward with a spray of air and sparkling ice crystals.

He flipped the latches on the three straps mounted around the rebreather and then pulled the whole assembly, including the air tank with the damaged valve, off the back of Pushkin's suit.

He dropped it on the ground.

Ten seconds gone.

Talia shoved the new rebreather into his hands. It took him several moments of fiddling to fit it onto the mounting plate on Pushkin's suit.

Twenty seconds.

One. Two. Three. He clipped the straps to the rebreather and slapped down the latches, securing them.

He snatched up the drill from by his foot. Then he reached into his pouch and fumbled around for a screw. His fingers were going numb; he had trouble feeling the screws, much less holding them.

Somehow he managed.

The drill juddered as he set the screw.

Then another.

And another.

Forty-seven seconds gone.

He didn't bother with the rest of the screws; he could place them later.

He dropped the drill. It skittered across the dirt for several feet, driven by the wind.

Wrench. Where was the fucking wrench? He looked around, panic filling him. It wasn't on the ground. It wasn't—

Talia rapped him on the shoulder. She pointed at his belt. He'd stuck the wrench there without even realizing it.

The frigid metal felt as if it were branding him when he grasped it. Ignoring the pain, he grabbed the first hose on the rebreather, jammed the end of it into the appropriate socket, and started to tighten the ring that would hold it in place.

Fifty-eight seconds.

Alex had no idea how long Pushkin could hold his breath. Depended on his cardio. Depended on his gene-hacking. Add in the effects of fear, panic— Anything more than a minute was a gamble.

The ever-present dust had gotten into the threads of the ring; it threatened to stop Alex from fully securing the hose. Clenching his jaw, he put his weight behind the wrench and strained.

The ring turned the final half revolution. There. Done.

One minute and nineteen seconds.

The second hose went slightly faster.

. . .

One minute and thirty seconds.

Pushkin swayed. Talia moved next to him and put her hands on his shoulders, holding him in place.

Alex's fingers were so cold, it took him three tries to place the end of the third hose into its socket. He used the pad of his thumb to loosely tighten the ring. Then he fit the wrench to it and wrenched.

One minute and forty-two seconds.

Last hose. As Alex fit it into the socket, Pushkin began to heave, like a cat hacking up a hairball. Alex shouted with frustration and tried to twist the wrench even faster.

The threaded ring locked into place, and Pushkin slumped forward, going limp in Talia's hands. She strained to hold him sitting upright.

Alex reached down, groping for the tank of air.

It wasn't there.

Adrenaline shot through him. He spun around, looking. The tank had slipped out from between his legs and rolled away.

Where? Where? He didn't have time to—

The tank had fetched up against a rock thirty meters away.

Alex jumped toward it, letting the wind carry him as far as possible. Two more jumps, and he slid to a stop on his hands and knees next to the rock. He grabbed the tank, tucked it under one elbow, then put his head down and bulled forward straight into the wind.

Two minutes and five seconds.

Alex staggered up to Pushkin and Talia. He mated the tank with its socket on the rebreather and spun it round and round until it stopped.

He'd hoped to have a few seconds to flush the system, but—

He turned the knob on the valve, opening the valve and flooding the lines with fresh air. A small green light appeared on the back of the rebreather.

Talia shook Pushkin. Then she pushed him onto his back and placed both hands on his chest. She shoved down—hard—and released.

And again.

And again.

Alex peered into Pushkin's helmet. The geologist's face was slack, and his skin had turned red and purple. His lips had a bluish tint.

"Come on," Alex muttered.

The words had barely left his mouth when Pushkin gasped and his eyes fluttered open. He started upright, failed to sit upright, and flopped back down, gaping like a fish.

Relief and weariness swept through Alex. He slumped onto his heels, his mind going blank. Then he felt the cold in his hands again. He reached toward Talia.

She gave him his gloves back, and he clumsily pulled them on. His palms were scratched and bloody from where he'd landed by the tank of air.

Before he rejoined the gloves to his sleeves, he told the suit to keep the cuffs cinched down. It would be easy to decontaminate his hands once they assembled the hab-dome, but it wouldn't be so easy to decon his lungs if he breathed any of Talos's atmosphere, as Pushkin had. The only two ways to decon your lungs were with fire or vacuum.

Still, even though the cuffs remained tight, he could feel warmth seeping back into his hands as the suit heated the gloves.

Pushkin motioned him closer, and Alex leaned over and bumped helmets with him.

Hoarse and faint, he heard Pushkin say, "You crazy bastard."

"You alright?"

Pushkin coughed. "I live."

"What'd it smell like?"

"What?"

Alex gestured at the sky. "The air."

"Like devil's own farts."

Thud

Alex patted Pushkin on the shoulder and got to his feet, feeling out of his mind with exhaustion. His hands tingled, and his jaw throbbed as if someone had punched him.

Talia looked up at him, expression unreadable through her darkened visor.

<*Thanks for the help. – Alex*>

She nodded once.

Alex looked for the turtle that had attacked them. No sign of it remained. Nor were any other turtles visible.

Then he turned his gaze to Talia's crushed sledge. Pieces of equipment lay scattered in a broad swath across the land. A sense of dread settled into his bones. The main hab-dome had been in her sledge, along with a good portion of their food.

He closed his eyes, momentarily overwhelmed. The sun was almost down. They didn't have much time to gather up the scattered supplies. And they still had to secure the remaining sledges, raise the hab-dome—if it was still intact—go through decon . . . It was going to be hours before any of them could rest.

Thud

Don't think about it. One thing at a time. He turned and trudged after the drill he'd dropped. Pushkin's rebreather still needed those four other screws. Talia could work on that while Alex started gathering up the supplies.

Chen started to unstrap himself from his sledge. *<How can I help? – Chen>* *<Stay there. You'll just be in the way. – Talia>*

6.

The main hab-dome was wrecked. The turtle had ripped the walls, making it impossible for it to hold pressure, and the tears were too big to patch. Fortunately, the spare dome—which had been in Alex's sledge—was safe. Assembled and inflated, it was discouragingly small there on the dark plain of Talos.

Of the contents of Talia's sledge, they were able to recover about two-thirds. The rest were lost to the wind, stolen away and sent tumbling across the desert surface like discarded trash.

Because the spare hab-dome was so much smaller, only one person at a time was supposed to go through decon. Talia and Chen managed to squeeze into the airlock together, since Chen still needed help to move around on his injured leg. Pushkin was too large for Alex and him to share the space, so once again, Alex had the airlock to himself.

When it came time to remove his skinsuit, he almost didn't bother. But he knew he had to. And it was no easier than before. He ended up puking from the pain, hacking and heaving onto the floor of the airlock.

At least his hands gave him a reason to take extra time going through decon. The ground had torn patches of skin off his palms, and the points of small rocks had left deep scratches in the meat at the base of his thumbs. The wounds were still raw, and he knew if he let them scab over, they would crack and be miserable for the rest of the trip. His fingers were stiff and swollen from the cold, and he struggled with anything that required fine motor control.

He treated the scrapes same as his shoulder: first with a layer of Celludox (which helped numb the sting), then with a thin application of TruSkin. Afterward, his fingers still felt clumsy, but he could, with care, open and close his hands well enough to function.

Once decon was finished, he reluctantly pulled his skinsuit back on. He and Pushkin had been exposed to the microbes on Talos. There was no knowing what sort of effect, if any, they might have. Until they were sure it was safe, he and Pushkin would have to live in their suits, to avoid contaminating the inside of the dome. That meant no more solid food for the time being.

At last. The airlock opened, and he stumbled across the threshold into the interior.

The four of them sat crowded around the central heater. The spare hab-dome wasn't as well insulated. Alex could feel the cold from the ground leaching the warmth from his ass and legs, even with his skinsuit's internal temperature turned up.

For a long time, none of them moved, too brutalized by the day's events to stir. Pushkin's face was bruised and swollen, as if his head had been inflated until capillaries began to burst.

Talia's voice was a hoarse croak: "This is what's left."

A file appeared on Alex's overlays. He opened it to see a list of supplies: rations, survey equipment, air tanks, water, batteries . . . the list went on. There wasn't much food left. A couple of days on half rations, no more. And that was only if they converted a decent amount of the remaining bars into a slurry so he and Pushkin could eat in their suits (the suits could do the conversion automatically via an input pouch near the side of his ribs, but Alex *hated* the taste of the deliquesced bars; it was like cold snot).

"Do you think the turtles will attack again?" asked Chen.

"I don't think so. Not if we don't aggravate them," said Talia. No one looked at Pushkin. He at least had the good grace to look uncomfortable.

"We can't avoid the gallium," Alex pointed out. His voice sounded tinny coming from the speaker at the front of his helmet. "If we drag the sledges over it—"

"We test that," said Talia, her tone short.

Thud

A long silence followed; the brief conversation had burned through their remaining energy.

Alex picked at the plating between his feet. He hated to think it, hated to say it, but . . . "Don't know about you, but I don't think I'm up for walking tomorrow." He looked around at their pinched faces. "We could stay here for a day, recover some before we head out."

Pushkin snorted. "You still dream we reach hole?"

"How far away are we now?" Chen asked.

"Seventeen kilometers," said Talia.

"*Only* seventeen," said Alex. "One full day and a bit more." Despite his words, the distance seemed enormous. The closer they got to the hole, the slower they'd move, and now that they'd lost a good chunk of their equipment . . .

Talia seemed to read his thoughts. In a quiet, serious voice, she said, "We're running without a safety net now. If something happens to this hab-dome, we'll all have to live in our suits. We barely have enough food for the next few days, we lost your core sampler, Pushkin, and the transmitter array is broken, so even if we *could* punch through the interference, we can't now." She shook her head. "I think you and I—" she looked at Chen, "should wear our suits anyway. If the turtles *do* come back, it'll be our only protection."

Pushkin let out a heavy breath. "If you expect me to live in skinsuit for rest of expedition, you sorely mistaken."

"Regulations—"

"Damn regulations. If Alex and I not show symptoms by end of tomorrow, skinsuit comes off, and there not damn thing you can do about it, Indelicato."

Talia's eyes burned with suppressed hatred. "How safe would it be?" she asked Alex.

"Fairly safe," he said, knowing his instructors would have hated his answer. "But there's no way to be sure."

Talia fixed Pushkin with her implacable glare. "I don't care how uncomfortable it is, Pushkin; you follow the regs. We're all going to be stuck in our skinsuits. You're not being singled out, even if you *were* the one who put us in our current situation."

"We see about that, Indelicato." Pushkin folded his thick arms and shifted his gaze as if he were staring at his overlays. Alex had his doubts.

And not a word of thanks for saving your life. Asshole.

"So are we going to keep going?" Chen asked.

"I don't know," said Talia. "We'll reassess tomorrow, see how we feel. Agreed?"

"Agreed," Alex and Chen answered, while Pushkin went: "Humph."

Thud

7.

Alex had trouble sleeping. He always did, but even more so in a skinsuit. He just couldn't find a comfortable position for his head in the helmet. It was meant to be worn standing up, not lying on his side.

His thoughts were wandering again, random memories passing in and out of his mind like a mixed-up slideshow. No matter how hard he tried to sleep, his brain wouldn't let him. Nor would the

Thud

He debated popping some AcuWake and staying up for the whole night, but it wasn't a great idea. The pills would clear his brain alright, same as a good night's sleep, but they wouldn't help his body repair and recover the way that natural rest would. Besides, too long on the pills tended to mess with people's heads, and the hole was already doing enough of that.

We're going weird, like milk left out in the sun.

He tongued the jagged remains of his molar. Not an easy day. Again he saw the mass of the turtle crashing into Pushkin, and he suppressed a shiver. It was obvious the turtles were there to defend the hole—perhaps even to maintain it—but it was also obvious their capabilities were limited. Otherwise the antenna of gallium would still be chilled and working.

He shook his head. What a crazy design. What sort of creatures would think that exposed superconductors were a good idea? Especially ones that would melt at the slightest chance?

Across the shelter, Pushkin coughed and turned in his alcove.

Alex frowned. He was still surprised they'd been able to save Pushkin. By all rights the geologist should have died. As for *why* saving Pushkin had been so important to him . . . Alex wasn't sure. He didn't like Pushkin. In fact, he often wanted to punch him. But he hadn't hesitated to risk his own life in order to help the man.

Why? If nothing mattered, then why try so hard? Because losing Pushkin would have endangered the expedition? Because helping other humans was an instinctive imperative? His mitochondria and gut bacteria driving him to protect and perpetuate their own?

No, that wasn't it. . . . Rather, Alex knew the cost of death, and he didn't feel it was his place to decide who would pay and who wouldn't. He didn't have the knowledge or authority to determine the worthy or the righteous. Perhaps no one did.

Thud

Life. Death. Two sides to the same tarnished coin. Did the most precious of currencies hold its value over time? Or did it depreciate like all made things? A flashing, spinning span of glory, and then the coin was spent and melted into oblivion, perhaps to be recast, perhaps abandoned or adulterated beyond recovery.

Thud

"What are you afraid of?"

He had bristled at the question. "I'm not afraid."

They were sitting in bed. The dimmable window that faced them was clear. Outside, a roof of purple thunderclouds roiled across the jungle forests of Eidolon while lightning flashed between the pregnant billows and the world growled in response.

"Then why wait?"

"We've gone over that."

"Go over it again."

He cleared the charts from his overlays, focused on her. Electricity reflected in her eyes, blue-white and bright.

"Building a new hab-dome would be too expensive, and this one isn't big enough. Maybe in a few years, if I get promoted to head technician at the lab."

She looked back at the storm. "We could make it work. If we budget."

"Barely. And what kind of life would that be?"

"You just don't want to try."

". . . That's not true."

"There's never a perfect time. You can't wait to become the person you'll be after having children. That only happens by having a child. It's an act of faith."

"That's how you end up with parents who should never have had kids in the first place."

"We're not like that, and you know it."

He didn't answer.

"Just because you don't know what to make of life doesn't mean someone else shouldn't get the chance to figure it out."

"By that logic, everyone ought to have as many children as possible."

"Maybe they should. Maybe we should."

Thud

Alex wrapped his arms around himself and curled into a tight ball, recognizing the inevitability of what was and what had been.

He shouldn't have been so afraid.

He should have said yes, but there had always been more pressing concerns. Work. Money. With STEM shots, waiting wasn't an issue; only the Reform Hutterites still had to worry about pushing out kids in their twenties and thirties, which had always seemed far, far too young to Alex. You were still a kid yourself in your thirties!

Now he knew that way of thinking had been a mistake. Life gave no quarter, had no mercy, and STEM shots were no guarantee of immortality (or even long life). If they'd had a child, something of Layla would have lived on, but instead . . . the darkness had won. She was gone, and he was alone. All because of the cruel randomness of an uncaring universe.

Thud

His tears pooled inside the helmet. And if they'd had a kid, she might not have gone on that final, fatal trip.

The privacy screen swam in front of Alex, and he didn't know if it was a result of the tears or the blurring caused by the inexorable blasts.

8.

Deep in the night, Alex heard a muffled scream. He started and yanked back his privacy screen to see Talia twisting and turning in her alcove, head thrashing from side to side. She was still wearing her skinsuit—same as the rest of them—and a dim, red nightlight in her helmet illuminated the grimace on her thin face.

Shit. Alex was halfway out of his own alcove when Talia's contortions subsided and the lines of her body smoothed, though her hands remained clenched and her breathing short. Her eyelids never lifted.

If she was having a bad dream, it was the worst Alex had ever seen. Worse even than his own.

He glanced at the others. Chen was still asleep, and Pushkin's privacy screen was extended, making it impossible to tell if he was awake or not.

Wary, Alex retreated to the back of his alcove. He continued to watch Talia for the next quarter of an hour, just to make sure nothing happened. The astrophysicist continued to toss about and make low noises, but whatever was tormenting her never seemed to wake her, not even when she banged her head against the inside of the helmet.

At last, Alex turned his back on her and closed his eyes. The world's problems weren't his to fix. He couldn't even fix his own.

9.

In the morning, it became obvious that none of them were ready to break camp, not even Talia. They didn't even discuss whether to turn back or continue; the consensus was *stay* and *do as little as possible.*

The bruising on Pushkin's face had gotten worse. Alex felt a twinge of empathy. His own jaw was still swollen and painful, and it occurred to him that maybe he *should* take some antibiotics. If the root of his molar got infected, he'd be in for a rough ride.

So he did, though he knew the antibiotics would only make him feel even more tired. He also popped his morning AcuWake, which helped, but despite the hard-edge clarity the pill gave him, Alex felt a twisting underneath, as if his mental sharpness were a structure built on rotting foundations. All of it felt off. *He* felt off, and there was no help for it.

He was glad for one thing; their respite would let his shoulder heal some, which it desperately needed. Another few days in the harness would have caused serious harm.

Just past noon, he and Pushkin headed outside and tried to establish a direct laser link with the *Adamura*. It was an exercise in futility. The equipment couldn't lock onto the ship. Every time it came close, the

Thud

would disrupt the targeting software.

Throughout the whole process, Pushkin didn't make a single mention of the previous day's events. Not even to thank Alex. The geologist was uncharacteristically withdrawn, talking only in single words or grunts.

Alex couldn't help tweaking him. It was bad of him, he knew, but Pushkin's refusal to admit wrongdoing and inability to say *thank you* were galling.

"Hey, is that another turtle?" Alex said.

Pushkin flinched and spun to look where Alex was pointing. But there was no turtle, only billows of orange dust.

He glared at Alex while chewing on his fleshy lower lip. "You know we not go to hole," he said. Then he stomped past Alex and went over to the sledges.

Alex stood staring at their laser transmitter. The geologist was probably right, but Alex didn't want to admit it. Not yet. Not until the universe forced him to.

What am I doing? He wished he knew.

After disassembling the transmitter, he took samples from around the habdome as he normally would have done after setting up camp. The amount of microbes in the soil had more than tripled since Delta Zone; they seemed to be clustered around the veins of gallium. Feeding on them or replenishing them, Alex wasn't sure, but there was *some* sort of relationship between the metal and the microbes.

He was packing up his samples when a pair of turtles appeared on the western horizon.

When informed, Talia replied: *<Now's a good time. Go ahead with the sledge. – Talia>*

<No. – Pushkin.> And the geologist walked straight into the airlock and started decon while ignoring everything that Talia and Alex said to him.

Alex waited where he was until Pushkin was inside. There was a chance Talia could force him to come back out, do his job. . . .

But no. After half an hour:

<He's not responding. – Talia>

Thud

Five minutes later, she joined Alex on the windy plain. Together, they dragged her ruined sledge a hundred meters away from the hab-dome. Without a harness to help—the turtle had destroyed the front of the sledge—it was difficult, frustrating work, but they made it in the end.

<Everyone on alert. We're about to try. – Talia> She had the bolt gun by her side, ready to use. It wouldn't do anything against the turtles, but Alex supposed that having it gave her a sense of protection, if however illusionary.

There was no real protection against the dangers of life, he thought. You could try, but there were always unknown forces and events that were so unexpected—and powerful—they would overwhelm any possible defense.

He moved behind the sledge along with Talia, and they placed their hands against the back of it and prepared to push.

Talia gave him a nod, and Alex dug his feet into the ground. Together, they shoved the sledge over the nearest vein of gallium. The nose of the sledge dipped as it went over the conduit full of metal, and the silvery liquid sloshed to either side, heavy waves pushing aside the soft dust.

They stopped then and looked to the turtles. The creatures seemed oblivious, but Alex doubted they hadn't noticed, and that worried him even more.

<That's not good. – Alex.>

<Why? – Talia>

<It means they understand intent. – Alex>

Talia's expression tightened. She understood. *<Try again. – Talia>*

So they pushed the sledge over four more of the veins. And still the turtles failed to react.

<That's that, then. We're clear to continue. – Talia>

<No. – Pushkin>
Thud

10

The four of them faced each other inside the cramped hab-dome. Chen was sitting in his alcove; the rest of them were standing. Pushkin's massive hands opened and closed in a steady rhythm, as if he wanted to crush something . . . or someone.

The geologist was still wearing his skinsuit. He hadn't made good on his threat from last night to remove it, although neither he nor Alex were showing any signs of infection.

"The turtles don't seem to be overtly hostile," said Talia. The bags under her eyes were unusually dark, and the lines around her mouth had deepened. "I think we can keep going."

"No," said Pushkin. "I went along with foolishness long enough, and look where it get us. No. I not take another step west. Not me. Not now. Let others study hole. My part in that *done*."

"This isn't your decision," said Talia. "You keep forgetting *I'm* in charge of this mission, and—"

Pushkin took a shuffling step forward and stood uncomfortably close to her, his bulk threatening. "You can't force me." His voice was low, emotionless, but his words were weighted with unshakable conviction. "You not have authority. Company can fire me when we get back. I don't care. But this isn't military, and none of us has to risk lives just because you say so."

Talia stared up at him, not giving a centimeter. "Fine. Have it your way. This is a democracy and everyone has an equal say. We'll vote on it."

"Uh-uh. That not work, Indelicato," said Pushkin, shaking his head. "*I* decide *I* had enough. I don't care what rest of you do."

"Wrong," said Talia, her voice cracking like a whip. "Shared food, shared equipment. You don't get to make decisions that affect the rest of us all on your own. Can't have it both ways. We *vote*."

Pushkin's heavy lids descended in a measured blink. ". . . Alright. Vote then."

Talia cast a quick glance at Alex. "Crichton?"

"We keep going."

She nodded. "Chen?" When he didn't answer, she looked over at him. "Chen? What's your answer?"

He looked between her and Pushkin. "I'm . . . I'm not sure. I'm sorry. I don't know."

Talia's gaze was implacable. "That won't do, Chen. You have to decide."

"She is right," said Pushkin. "For once in miserable life, you have to decide. Pick, Chen. Pick! What is it? Risk lives to look at fucking hole in ground that we already saw perfectly well from orbit? Risk herd of murderous xenos between us and hole when we could—"

"That's enough," snapped Talia.

Alex spoke up: "It's worth the risk. If we don't—"

"Really," said Pushkin, sneering. "It not feel *worth risk* when I breathe last breaths yesterday. I wished I was safe home, in silk robe, with glass of chilled Venusian scotch to sip while I read scientific papers that *properly equipped and trained team* produced after examine hole as should." He waved his hands. "You should be ashamed of yourself, Crichton. You're xenobiologist! We leave bits and pieces of equipment across whole goddamn planet. Is what we should do? Is right? Hmm?"

"No," Alex mumbled. The argument was exhausting, and he was already tired from their time outside. "But we haven't had a choice. If—"

"*Right,*" said Pushkin, leaning in close. "And now we *make* choice." He turned on Chen with sudden force. "So choose, Chen. For once in spineless life, *choose!*"

Talia kept her gaze fixed on the chemist the whole time. "Choose," she said.

Chen gulped and wet his lips. His mouth worked like a fish's, and then with an apologetic, hangdog expression, he said, "I-I agree with Pushkin. I vote we go back."

For an instant, Alex thought he saw a flare of rage and contempt in Talia's eyes as she stared at the chemist. Then her face went flat again.

Pushkin beamed with triumph. "There you go. That not so hard, now was it?"

Seemingly emotionless, Talia said, "Two votes to leave, and two votes to keep going. Since I'm leading this expedition, I cast the tiebreaker. And I say we keep going."

Pushkin lowered his head, anger darkening his features. "No, no. Is not acceptable, Indelicato. You not get to vote twice. Not how works. Is tie. Stalemate. So we sit and stay until food run out or do right thing and go back now. Is only way. You lose, Indelicato. Accept defeat with good grace."

Talia never blinked, never budged. "Set your alarm. Be ready to leave in the morning."

"I ready . . . ready to head back." And Pushkin sauntered over to his alcove, flopped down on his blanket, and stretched his arms over his head.

Talia remained standing where she was, shoulders rigid, face blank. Then she nodded, as if to herself, and marched to her own alcove.

Chen glanced between them and then looked to Alex with a helpless look. His worry was palpable.

Alex shrugged. The dream was over. Pushkin—or rather the universe—had won. The expedition was a failure.

For a moment he wondered if he could continue on himself. It wasn't *that* far to the hole. If he brought enough ration bars and slept in his skinsuit, he could make it without the hab-dome. . . . But no, that was crazy. He'd have no way of getting back, in any case. Not before he ran out of food.

He sat in his alcove and closed his eyes. The jagged remains of his molar pricked the underside of his tongue.

Thud

11.

Alex lay with his head propped up, thermal blanket wrapped around his skinsuit, eyes half-closed as he stared at the results from his soil samples. The numbers seemed to move of their own accord, and his brain felt dull and sluggish.

Across the cramped hab-dome, Talia was folding and refolding a food wrapper. Without his suit helmet to filter out the noise, the sound would have been unbearably annoying. She swayed as she worked, and through her visor, Alex could see her lips moving in a constant, inaudible murmur—an unusual amount of talkativeness for her.

In the alcove to her left, Chen appeared distracted, and he occasionally said something inaudible in his helmet, always—it seemed to Alex—in response to something Talia had said. Since her confrontation with Pushkin, Talia had been directing a constant stream of conversation at the chemist, which worried Alex. He wished he could hear what she was saying to him.

As for Pushkin, he lounged in his alcove, eyes focused on his overlays, as if he was reading or watching something. But Alex also noticed that sometimes the geologist's mouth would twitch in the manner of subvocalization, and then Chen would invariably react with a blink or a change of expression.

Bunch of teenagers. Drama was inevitable on any expedition, but Alex always tried to steer clear of it. It wasn't appealing when he'd been a kid, and it really wasn't appealing in adults. But even so, he still wondered what Talia and Pushkin were saying to Chen. They seemed to be more interested in him than the hole.

He closed his eyes. Did it really matter? Humans didn't always make sense to him. Layla had; she'd understood him, and he'd understood her, but there were plenty of people who were a mystery. Even if he could logic out their responses, he didn't *feel* them, and that made them hard to predict or explain.

Thud

He pulled the thermal blanket closer around himself, trying to ward off the chill from the ground creeping through his skinsuit.

He didn't think he could sleep. Again. In fact, he didn't think he'd sleep until they left the hole far behind. If Talia prevailed, and they continued on . . . No, he wasn't going to delude himself with false hope. The trip was over; the adventure had failed.

Which left him where? Despair filled him, the void gaped wide, and in the distance, Alex felt the icy presence of existential nightmares reaching with bony fingers for his soul. The oldest fears were the most powerful. If there were gods, he thought for sure that the first and greatest—and evilest—would be the god of darkness. Light required effort. Light was a struggle. But the dark was easy, and it had existed before all else and would be there to envelop the universe in its smothering cloak when the last dim stars guttered out at the end of time.

His heart raced, and the jittery rice-grains crowding his vision jumped in response. A flush crawled up his body, warming his limbs and forcing him to alertness.

He had nothing, nothing . . . nothing. Hope had sunk and left him floundering in a blank and endless sea, and the waves crashed heavy upon him, pushing him down, filling his mouth, making it difficult to breathe.

Thud

His gaze darted across the inside of the dome as he searched for escape. What could he do? Nothing, and that was the most panic-inducing part of it.

An alert appeared on his overlays; his oxygen levels were getting too high. He was hyperventilating. The suit started to compensate, lowering the oxygen concentration in his helmet, but it did nothing to dull the edge of fear scraping across his nerves.

Alex didn't know how he could make it through the night, much less another day.

His despair broke him. He had no ability left to resist temptation, and the fears of the past paled before the fear that tore at him.

Frantic, he dug through his system until he once again saw the file hanging projected before him. *Layla*. He acted without thinking, driven by the sickening surge of adrenaline.

He tapped the file.

It expanded to fill his vision and lists of entries scrolled past. Thousands. Tens of thousands. He blindly stabbed at one near the top and—

A window opened before him. Layla's parents, laughing and talking in their hab-dome while music sounded in the background. Guests moved about: mostly teenagers, dancing, drinking, talking. A banner hung over the main room, and it said: *Happy Solstice!*

And her voice sounded: "—Mom. Mom! What do you want?"

Her mother looked over, happy. "Just some of the sparkling."

The image swung down, disorienting, as Layla poured pale wine into a glass sitting on the banded counter.

Thud

Alex lay where he was, frozen. He watched and watched, drinking down the images like a man dying of thirst. The recording was from years and years ago, long before Layla had completed her training as a xenobiologist. She sounded young and full of bright hope. When she swung past a glass-faced cupboard, he paused the video to study her reflection, distorted though it was. The familiar outline of her face caused him to gasp slightly and fall back against the outer wall of the dome.

It was surreal to see the world as she had. It felt intrusive too, as if he were violating her privacy, even though she had willed him the recordings.

When she left the party for the bathroom, he tabbed out of the memory and selected another, two years later.

This time he saw the main administrative building at Plinth: an ungainly assemblage of storage containers with narrow windows cut at regular intervals. Layla and several friends were walking past the building toward the common ground near the center of the town.

The recordings mesmerized Alex. He barely blinked, barely breathed, and his heart hurt with every beat.

Thud

Now that he had started, he couldn't stop watching. He bounced around from clip to clip, but even the slow, quiet moments kept him fixated. Just listening to the familiar pattern of Layla's breathing or seeing the small motions she made while reading or watching videos—the way she scratched the back of her hand, the way she covered her mouth when sneezing—brought a tidal wave of emotions with them. Several times he even caught a whiff of her scent. Imagined, of course, but the remembrance was powerful enough to send him careening through years of memories.

Hours passed. He wasn't sure; he avoided looking at the time in the top right of his overlays.

For the most part, he kept to the earlier parts of the records, when Layla was in school, when she started working for the Central Commission. Before she'd met him. He didn't want to see himself. But in the end, morbid curiosity got the best of him, and after some searching, he found the exact day and moment he had thought of the previous night:

Their discussion about having children.

Through her eyes, he saw the lightning along the horizon, and he heard with her ears his arguments and evasions. His weakness seemed far more apparent from the outside, more than he'd ever feared, and he found himself hating the thin sound of his voice and the way he kept looking at the bedtop and avoiding her gaze.

The conversation was shorter, more brusque than he remembered. None of the emotions he'd felt at the time seemed to show on his face; he was a stony cipher, seeming far more unfeeling than he'd thought, and every word he said landed like a bruise.

He kept watching past the end of his own recollection, despite the blurring of his vision.

Bad as it was, he could have borne his self-directed anger and loathing if that had been the extent of it. But then Layla rose from the bed and headed down the hallway to the kitchen. There, she leaned against the counter of their tea nook and looked at herself in the strip of mirror mounted above.

The raw pain in her expression shocked him. There were tears gathered at the corners of her eyes, and her face distorted, and she looked down with a small cough and a cry.

"Dammit," she said softly.

Then she dabbed her eyes and set about making herself food.

Thud

Dazed, Alex stopped the recording, closed the window, and cleared his overlays.

He lay staring at the curved ceiling, barely able to breathe. It was late. Too late. And he felt the weight of every misplaced word, every ill-timed action in his life packed on top of his chest, like plates of iron crushing him down.

Action seemed impossible. He had no idea how he was supposed to recover from the welter of grief, guilt, and remorse racking him. The idea that he might one day be a normal functioning human again was too ludicrous to believe. Some things couldn't be fixed.

He had to sleep. Somehow. It was the only escape he could think of.

So he did what he'd never done before; he tabbed a double dose of melatonin and sucked it down with grateful gulps.

Won't take long, he thought, closing his eyes and gripping the handhold in the side of the alcove. He just had to hang on until the melatonin took effect, and then maybe, just maybe, it would knock him out.

If they'd had any alcohol with them, he would have chugged it as fast as he could, and consequences be damned.

Thud

He focused on his breathing, trying to control it. The problem was, the effort felt futile. *Everything* felt futile.

. . .

The melatonin hit like a meteorite. A felted blanket settled across his mind, muffling his thoughts and dulling his senses. He surrendered with willing helplessness. Fighting took too much energy, and he was just so damn tired of fighting. What was the point anymore?

A tunnel closed in around his vision as he fell, fell, fell, and the abyss swallowed him whole.

DESOLATION

*   *   *   *   *   *   *   *   *

To "know thyself" must mean to know the malignancy of one's own instincts and to know, as well, one's power to deflect it.

—KARL A. MENNINGER

CHAPTER 1

* * * * * * *

ZETA ZONE

1.

In the distance, Alex heard his piercing morning alarm, loud and insistent. It dragged him back to an approximation of wakefulness. The melatonin was still in his system. He felt sluggish, thick-headed, and his pulse throbbed with uncomfortable strength.

His eyes opened.

He regretted the choice a half second later. The light stabbed at his eyes like needles. Grimacing, he swung his legs off the side of the bunk and rubbed his face.

He felt twice as heavy as normal.

The others appeared equally out of it, although Talia was already gathering her things and moving toward the airlock.

Alex tabbed a double-strength dose of AcuWake. It gave objects around him a shimmery, hard-edged appearance, but the drug didn't do much to actually clear his head.

"Chen," said Talia. "I'll help you outside." She reached for his arm.

"I carry him, and easier than you," said Pushkin. The bruising on his face wasn't getting any better, Alex noted. Pushkin stomped over to Chen's alcove. "Move."

Talia motioned at Chen again. The chemist hesitated, and before he could say anything, Pushkin scooped him up and held him in the crook of one arm, like an oversized baby. "See? Easy."

"Hey, now—" Chen started to say.

Thud

Expressionless, Talia turned and entered the airlock. The door closed behind her with a loud *click*.

Then Pushkin said to Chen, "You better eat before we—" A heavy, rasping cough interrupted him, and he set Chen down before doubling over and hacking.

Should check his blood levels, Alex thought.

Despite his cough, Pushkin was markedly more cheerful as they prepared to leave. "It be nice to get out of these damned skinsuits and have proper bath," he said.

Alex wanted to argue, but he didn't have the energy. All motivation had left him. He sat on the edge of the alcove until both Pushkin and Chen asked him what was wrong. Explaining would have taken more effort than Alex had in him. So he did his part, silently, sluggishly, mind blank save for the desire to just *stop*.

Thud

What if he did? Alex wondered how the others would react if he sat on the packed ground and stayed there until the wind or the turtles or the lack of food did him in. Problem was, Pushkin would probably just pick him up and put him in a sledge, force him to come back with them.

"Time to go!" said Pushkin as they crowded into the tiny airlock. The geologist supported Chen with an arm around his waist, holding up his weight seemingly without effort.

Outside, the sky was grey and cloud-striped.

Talia stood by what had been Alex's sledge, legs spread wide, torso leaning into the wind. She held the bolt gun in her right hand, the weapon next to her thigh, ready to use.

<I've moved all the food, water, sails, and wheels into this sledge. No one is going back. We keep walking until we reach the hole, and that's that. My decision, and it's final. You can either stay here and risk starving or getting run over by the turtles, or you can come with me. – Talia>

In his befuddled state, Alex at first thought she was talking to him. But then he realized her words were aimed at Pushkin.

The geologist dropped Chen—raising a small cloud of dust—and started toward Talia. Chen grimaced and let out a silent cry and curled around his injured knee.

Talia lifted the heavy bolt gun, pointed it at Pushkin. Even without an aimbot, Alex had no doubt she could hit Pushkin dead-on. A shock of adrenaline coursed through him, and he froze, not knowing whether to run or fight.

<Ah, ah. That's close enough. – Talia>

The geologist's glove-covered hands opened and closed. *<You psycho-crazy bitch. – Pushkin>*

She never wavered. <*Make up your mind. I'm not going to wait. – Talia*>
<*Why?! Why in name of Earth this so important to you? – Pushkin*>
<*You wouldn't understand. – Talia*>

Alex saw the geologist swearing inside his helmet. Then the swearing turned into more coughing, and after a minute: <*Fine, damn you. But you better not sleep, because instant you look away, I grab that sledge, and I go back. – Pushkin*>

<*You take the lead. – Talia*> She motioned with the bolt gun, and with frustration clear on his face, the geologist reluctantly picked up Chen and carried him to the sledge where he'd sit.

Alex watched the whole exchange, with disbelief at Talia's brazen use of force. In all his years in the field, he'd never seen anything like it, and the surprise left him sick and trembling as his body struggled to burn off the unneeded adrenaline.

He funneled the excess energy into breaking camp, and it wasn't until the hab-dome was packed away that his nerves began to settle. He was still on edge, but the situation was no longer quite so alarming. Not in an immediate sense, even if it was, on the whole, fucked.

It wasn't until they took the first few steps toward the hole that he began to believe that maybe, just maybe, Talia's gamble would pay off and the expedition would continue. Selfishly, he was grateful for that, but he didn't see how Talia could keep Pushkin at bay the whole time. And if she couldn't . . . He shied from the thought.

Still, it was only seventeen klicks to the hole. Not *that* far in the grand scheme of things. He'd run that distance more than once. If Layla . . . He shook his head. If *Talia* could keep control of the group for another day or so, they'd be within striking distance of the hole. Even Pushkin wouldn't give up then. His curiosity would be too strong.

Or so Alex hoped. It was hard to be sure of anything at the moment.

2.

The gutters of metal strewn across the ground proved to be a major obstacle. Where possible, Talia had the group detour around them, but in many places the only option was to cross the troughs, splashing gallium alloy to either side as they dragged the sledges over. It wasn't easy. The sledges often caught, and Alex found himself tiring faster than normal. His left knee didn't like the added challenge; the joint was a constant aggravation, the tissue and tendons hot with inflammation.

To distract himself, he returned to Layla's recordings and started to watch again. The dam had been broken, and he made no attempt to hold it back. He *needed* to hear and see her, and he was curious too; he wanted to know more about her life. Even in marriage, there were plenty of private moments, and he yearned to learn more about who she had been when he wasn't around.

So he watched as he walked. In its own way, the viewing was as painful as his knee or shoulder or tooth, but it was a pain he chose and, in a sense, welcomed.

With each snippet he selected, he moved forward in time, sometimes by only a day or two, sometimes by years, and each jump took him another step closer toward the dreaded end. After stumbling across a few memories of Layla with her first few boyfriends, he had skipped ahead and, despite his initial aversion, started to revisit her recordings starting from when the two of them first met.

The memories were distracting, though—he often stumbled when Layla swept her gaze around—and they were emotionally exhausting as well.

In the end, he stopped searching for familiar moments, moments he knew of or remembered, and instead settled on a section of time when Layla was studying while lounging in a window seat at her parents'. It was late afternoon, verging on evening, and rain pattered against the outside of their hab-dome while she read a text on the native flora of Eidolon, one that Alex recognized from his own coursework.

He kept the video playing in the upper left of his overlays, and the sound of the rain, and of Layla moving, breathing, occasionally taking a drink of chell, were a comfort as he continued trudging across the dry, howling waste of Talos VII.

In a way, it felt as if she were there with him, keeping him company.

After three hours of walking, the inner border of Epsilon Zone came and went, and then they were into Zeta, which was only eight kilometers wide.

Thud

The sound grew louder with every klick. They weren't that far from the hole now. Fifteen kilometers in total, and the volume was rising faster than before. When Alex checked, it was ninety-seven decibels, more than enough to cause hearing damage if they were stupid enough to remove their helmets.

The wind continued to increase in ferocity, slowing their progress to little more than a crawl. Literally. At times the gusts were so strong, Alex and Talia had to lean forward until their hands touched the ground. They clawed their way across the ground as if they were pulling themselves along the bottom of a silt-laden ocean.

The wind even managed to stagger Pushkin. Twice his boots slipped and he nearly fell flat on his belly before catching himself. Each time, he pushed back up with exaggerated slowness, coughed, and then continued forward.

Talia kept him at the front of their small procession, and her hand was never far from the grip of the bolt gun.

Around 1500 a turtle appeared to the south. They watched it carefully, but it didn't move toward them, just meandered about in an area roughly a klick in diameter.

Twenty minutes later, they spotted another turtle, this one off to the northwest. Two more emerged from the dust soon afterward, all of them moving in semi-random patterns that somehow never intersected with where the three of them were standing.

There was no point in stopping—the turtles didn't show any sign of leaving—so they continued on, alert for the slightest hint of hostility.

Whenever they dragged the sledges through the gallium, Alex noticed that the turtles would pause, and one of them would often start to move toward the sledges, as if alerted by the activity. But the creatures never did more than that, although there was no question in his mind that they would attack again if they thought the humans were deliberately messing with the veins of metal.

He realized he was starting to think of the turtles as intelligent, decision-making creatures. Tigermauls were certainly at least that smart. But the turtles could also be nothing more than machines, and he reminded himself to not make unwarranted assumptions.

Within half an hour, another six turtles had appeared in the vicinity. The huge creatures slid across the ground at a leisurely pace, sweeping the earth flat behind them. Again Alex had a vision of them propelling themselves around upon a bed of centipede-like legs, each leg reaching and grasping. . . .

Thud

3.

They sat against the lee side of the sledges, resting. Talia faced Pushkin, the bolt gun in her lap.

Alex let his head fall back against the fairing. Shoals of jittering grains swirled across the sky above. The visual static was getting worse. He waved a hand past his face and watched it leave bright trails in the air, like a time-lapse glowstick.

The sight made him queasy.

It reminded him of when he and Layla took some jolt at the summer Grind, in Plinth's central park. They'd ended up lying on their backs, staring at the night sky, finding shapes silly and profound in the patterns of the stars. Layla had gotten scared at one point; she became convinced she wasn't solid, and he'd spent at least half an hour comforting her and showing her that, yes, she was still corporeal. Or maybe it had been only a couple of minutes. Jolt screwed with your sense of time. He was tempted to look up her recording of the experience and check.

Maybe he would. Later.

Chen used both hands to reposition his injured leg.

<Chen, I need a new air filter. Can you hand me one from your sledge? – Talia>

The chemist's sledge also happened to be Pushkin's, and the geologist was quick to interject: <Chen, can you get me that rock over there? I want to sample him. – Pushkin> The stone he indicated was just outside of Chen's reach, meaning the chemist would have to scoot across the ground to reach it.

<Chen. Air filter, now. – Talia>

<The rock, please. Why this delay? It take second to grab, no more. – Pushkin>

The chemist glanced between them, conflicted.

<Chen. – Talia>

At last, Chen gave her an apologetic look and pulled himself over the ground to the rock. Talia's lips tightened, and Alex saw her grip and regrip the bolt gun.

The rock looked like any other rock in that area of the desert. There was nothing special about it, only Pushkin's desire to annoy Talia. They all knew it, but no one said it.

When their break ended, Talia insisted on Alex pulling Chen's sledge for the next segment of their walk. She wouldn't give up her own sledge—the one with the food, water, and other essential supplies—so she had to ask Alex to do it for her.

He didn't argue, but in the privacy of his helmet, Alex cursed her and Pushkin both.

It was like that every time they stopped to rest. Talia and Pushkin kept fighting over Chen in little and large ways. To Alex, it seemed as if Pushkin had the upper hand. He was more eloquent and sweeter-toned (when he wanted to be), but Talia never gave up.

Alex tried to ignore their petty power struggle. It was more drama, and he didn't care. If Chen had asked for help, Alex would have said something, but he wasn't going to intervene where he wasn't welcome and where it probably wouldn't do any good.

Thud

4.

Slightly past noon, one of the turtles diverged from the rest of the group and came sliding with uncanny smoothness through the curtains of dust until it was only a klick or two away.

<Turtle at five o'clock. – Alex> He flipped over to infrared, just to be sure, and then back again.

He stopped as Talia did. Up ahead, Pushkin stabbed one of his walking sticks in the ground and lifted a hand to shield his faceplate from the sand.

As before, the turtle was moving in an erratic fashion. It could have been the same one they'd seen the previous day, or a completely different creature. There was no way to tell. Alex guessed it was a new turtle, though. Something about its motion . . . a certain herky-jerkiness that hadn't been there previously. The turtle would slide forward at a good clip, abruptly change directions, and then stop for a few seconds before resuming its course. And so on and so forth.

<It's coming closer. – Talia>

Alex glanced at the range finder in the corner of his overlays. She was right. And the turtle was making pretty good progress too, for all its stopping and starting. Another five minutes and it would reach them. Assuming it held its course.

But it didn't.

The turtle paused next to a rock striped with bands of red and yellow. The alien was only about half a klick away now. Close enough that, when it moved on, Alex's optics allowed him to spot a patch of disturbed dirt where it had been sitting.

<You see that? – Alex>

<Could it be hunting? Eating? – Talia>

<Eating what? There aren't enough microbes to feed it. – Alex>

<Maintenance, then? – Chen>

<Again, maintaining what? – Alex>

A cloud of dust obscured the turtle, a cloud so thick, the turtle disappeared, even on infrared.

Alex shifted, nervous. He was starting to feel as if they were being stalked. He glanced behind them. Still clear.

He tensed as the turtle reappeared only thirty meters away: a great hulking shape, like a shadow within the dust. *Fuck, it's fast!*

Pushkin crouched and crab-walked around the backside of his sledge.

<No sudden movements. – Talia>

<My ass. If it attack, I run. – Pushkin> He unclipped his harness and safety line.

The turtle paused . . . and then darted forward, leaving behind an oval of upturned earth . . .

. . . paused . . .

. . . and with another burst of speed, was in front of them, no more than six meters away. The noonday sun lit the creature from above, picked out the crevices in its stony shell.

Thud

The turtle slowed to a stop, and Alex thought he felt a faint vibration through the earth, separate from that of the hole. It lasted only a moment, and when it was gone, he wondered if he'd imagined it.

The turtle started off again, only this time, it headed straight toward the sledges. Alex had a panicked moment to wonder if the creature was blind, and then he and Talia were scrambling backwards on hands and feet, trying to move out of its path.

Pushkin's face contorted, and he turned to run, stumbled, and fell onto his hands and knees.

A meter from the sledges, the turtle abruptly changed directions and went sliding off to the south, leaving streamers of light across Alex's vision. A line of dust billowed up behind the alien, marking its passage.

"Dammit!" His heart was pounding twice its normal rate, and he was flushed and hot all over. "Fans up," he said. Cool air washed over his face, providing welcome relief.

Pushkin got to his feet. His bruised face was dark red and covered with sweat, and he was breathing heavily. A coughing fit took him, and he bent over.

<Was clear enough warning for you, Indelicato? They make it painfully obvious they not want us here. Time to admit defeat and LEAVE. – Pushkin>

She aimed the bolt gun at him. *<Not yet. We're too close to turn back. – Talia>*

The geologist gave her the finger. *<Something wrong with you, Indelicato. Something deeply, deeply wrong. – Pushkin>*

As they continued to argue, Alex carefully got back to his feet. He grabbed the top of the sledge, noting in a detached way how shaky his hands were.

The turtle was already sixty or seventy meters away and still moving to the south.

Alex watched until he was sure the creature wasn't about to return. Then he retrieved his chip-lab from the sledge, detached his harness (though he kept his safety line clipped to the sledge), and staggered toward the patch of tousled earth the turtle had left behind.

Without the harness, Alex felt uncomfortably light, as if the wind could blow him away at any moment. He swayed as he walked; the wind and the visual static were ruining his sense of balance.

He knelt next to the patch and ran several quick tests.

Thud

The noise of the wind seemed to fade away as Alex struggled to make out the results. It was hard for his eyes to focus on the words and numbers, but bit by bit, he saw that the temperature of the dirt was 0.3 degrees higher than ambient; spectral analysis of the surface revealed the usual assortment of elements; and chemical sniffers picked up only one new compound—a complex organic chemical that looked like an alcohol of some form.

<Anything? – Chen>

Alex shook his head. He pushed the chip-lab's sampling tube a few centimeters into the dirt. A new set of readings scrolled across his overlays. With some effort he confirmed they were identical to the ones he'd taken at their last camp.

He frowned and sat back on his heels. What he really wanted to do was take a deep core sample. Find out if there was anything buried at that spot that the turtle had been interacting with. But if there *was* something underneath the surface, he was afraid the drill would damage it.

"Let's see," he murmured. With the flat of his hand, he brushed away the top layer of dirt. The wind caught the dust and carried it in twisting streamers to the east.

Alex kept brushing, working his way deeper into the earth. He made swift progress; for once the wind helped. When he hadn't encountered anything after a third of a meter, he started scooping out dirt by the handful.

Another few decimeters, and then his fingers struck something hard.

He stopped.

<There's something here. – Alex>

Talia hurried over and watched as he felt around the edges of the object.

It was . . . smooth on one part and . . . covered with wavy ridges on another, like some sort of scalloped rail. He described it to the others, but none of them could make any sense of it.

<It can't be powering the turtles via induction. Otherwise they'd be locked on set paths. – Talia>

Alex stood and brushed his gloves clean on his thighs. "I don't know," he said to himself. "I just don't . . . know."

5.

At 1743 the wind gusted, and Alex stumbled and fell onto his hands and knees. He landed badly, with more of his weight on his right arm than his left. The angle caused his suit to pull and the harness to dig into his shoulder. A white-hot blade seemed to slice through the front of his deltoid as the muscle tore open again.

He screamed into his helmet and slumped forward, cradling his shoulder as he waited for the pain to subside.

A flood of warmth spread down his side. Blood. Lots of it.

"Ebutrophene," he gasped. "Four hundred milligrams." Norodon wasn't going to cut it. Not this time.

A green light appeared next to his feed tube, and he gratefully sucked down the painkiller.

Thud

He became aware of Talia standing next to him, staring down at him. The astrophysicist held out a hand.

Alex ignored her and struggled to his feet, still cradling his shoulder. He put his head down and started to pull on his sledge. The Ebutrophene was already taking effect; the pressure from the harness was no longer suicide-inducing, just merely agonizing.

After a moment Talia swung back to her own sledge, and they continued onward.

Thud

6.

They only covered eight klicks that day, which was two klicks short of Eta Zone (the final zone), and nine klicks short of the hole.

A half-dozen turtles were loitering nearby when they finally stopped to make camp. The group almost seemed like a herd of animals, gently grazing, but Alex didn't allow the thought to lull him into a sense of security. Whatever the creatures were up to, he doubted it was something as prosaic as eating. As far as he could tell, they *didn't* eat, which raised all sorts of problematic questions.

He told Talia he had a blister to clean, which got him the airlock to himself. After removing his skinsuit, Alex wasn't surprised to see a centimeter-wide gap in his shoulder, red and raw and abraded around the edges. The muscle *had* torn.

He cleaned and disinfected the wound, the same as before, but instead of relying on the surgical glue to hold the skin and muscle together, he used needle and thread to stitch it up.

Under the influence of Ebutrophene, he found the experience more fascinating than painful. The sensation of the thread sliding through his flesh was . . . uniquely unpleasant.

When he finished, he stared at the stitches with a dull sense of accomplishment. *That* ought to keep his shoulder from splitting open again.

He felt as if he were falling apart. Molar, shoulder, knee . . . piece by piece the universe was dismantling him into his component parts.

A defeated sigh escaped him.

He washed out his suit, pulled it back on, and entered the main part of the shelter. The others glanced at him from their alcoves and then returned to eating.

Alex refilled the food pouch in his skinsuit, drank his half-ration dinner, and then—feeling as if he were fragile and might break with any sudden jar—made his way across the two meters of open space to Pushkin's alcove.

The geologist gave him an unfriendly look. The bruises on his heavy jowls were turning a dark purple, verging on black. The discoloration made Alex think of plague and putrefaction.

He held up the dome's medilab. "I need to run some tests."

Pushkin's glare didn't soften, but he lifted his right arm, turning it so Alex could reach the access port on his skinsuit.

Alex hooked up the medilab to the port and started taking samples and analyzing the data.

It didn't take long.

Disconnecting the medilab, he said, "You have microbes from Talos in your lungs and under your skin."

Thud

"So? We know that," said Pushkin, covering his right arm with the left.

Alex shook his head as he returned the medilab to its slot on the wall. "You don't get it. They're growing."

Even with the bruises, Pushkin's face paled. "How much danger?"

Alex shrugged. "Don't know, but I'd take some antibiotics, if I were you. Probably won't help, but . . . maybe they will."

"What about the rest of us?" Chen asked.

"You should still be safe."

Pushkin struggled to his feet. "Hell with your safety! I'm one eaten alive here!"

Ignoring him, Talia said, "Are you infected as well?"

"Maybe," said Alex. "Bloodwork is still normal."

Pushkin jabbed a finger at Talia. "This bullshit. We go back! I need medical treatment *now*!"

"No."

His face twisted. He bellowed and charged Talia, a solid mass of muscle, bone, and sinew bearing down on her.

She sidestepped him and—

BANG!

. . .

A shocking silence followed.

The head of an eye bolt protruded from the back of Pushkin's left shoulder. The arm hung limp and useless. Blood started to well up around the bolt.

Pushkin turned around. His mouth formed an *O* as he slumped to the floor and clutched his injured shoulder. Then he hunched over and an animalistic howl overloaded his suit's speakers.

"You shot me! You fuck shot me! Ahhh!"

Thud

7.

Talia edged back along the wall of the hab-dome, keeping the bolt gun trained on Pushkin. Alex watched, too shocked to move, and uncertain of what he should do in any case.

"Take some Ebutrophene," she said. "That's an order."

"Ahh! Fuck you! Fuck, fuck, fuck." Pushkin continued to swear as he rocked back and forth. But Alex saw the tension in the geologist's body ease slightly after a few seconds, and he guessed it was from the painkiller.

"Crichton, go help him."

"Me? I—"

Pushkin looked up at Talia. "You bitch! I relieve you on basis of incompetence and take control of—"

"You have no say here," she said, cold and calm.

He spat at her, and his spittle coated the inside of his visor. "You insane! I'm not move one step from here. Good luck reach hole without me. I'm done, and expedition is done."

Talia readjusted her grip on the bolt gun. "Stay, then. But we're taking the hab-dome with us, and you can't sail back to the lander with one hand. You want to sit out here, all alone, with the turtles? Be my guest."

Alex watched conflicting emotions distort Pushkin's bearded face: anger, fear, hate, pain. In the end, he thought the fear won out. Pushkin swore again and looked back down, his left hand still clamped around the bolt sticking out of his shoulder.

"Chen," said Talia. "Grab the medkit." The first-aid box was on the wall next to Chen's alcove.

"Yes, Chen, grab medkit," Pushkin said from between clenched teeth. "Go on, make what she tells you. Lick her boots and kiss her ass, and maybe she not shoot you."

Thud

The chemist didn't move; he seemed petrified by the situation.

Alex took the initiative. He retrieved the medkit and knelt by Pushkin while being careful not to cross Talia's line of sight. Pushkin turned his head to the side so he couldn't see his shoulder. "Do what you must," he said.

Alex did.

It wasn't pretty. He cut the skinsuit away from Pushkin's shoulder—thinking all the while about how they were contaminating the inside of the hab-dome—disinfected the skin, and then used a pair of pliers to pull out the bolt. Fortunately for Pushkin, the bolts weren't threaded, and the metal rod came free easily enough.

Alex was surprised the bolt hadn't gone straight through the man's shoulder. If it had struck anyone else on the team, it would have. But Pushkin's delt was so thick, and his bones were so hard, the bolt had skated across his humerus and stopped against the inside surface of his scapula, and neither bone had broken.

Alex commented on it, and Pushkin grunted. "Our bones are two, three times denser than you one-g humans. Minimum. First Alliance doctor I saw said . . . ah . . . said my bones harder than marble."

"That explains it," said Alex. He dropped the bloody bolt into a sample bag and used more sanitary wipes to clean Pushkin's shoulder. He sprayed Cellu-dox in the wound, covered it with a large adhesive bandage, and then helped Pushkin extract his arm from the damaged skinsuit. Alex used a repair kit to patch the bolt holes in the suit before guiding Pushkin's arm back into the sleeve and sealing him up again.

Talia watched the whole time, bolt gun at the ready. A few times Alex thought he saw her tremble, but it was a slight movement and barely visible.

Finished, Alex limped to his alcove.

Pushkin sat on the edge of his bed, injured arm hanging limp and useless by his side. He sat and stared at Talia with undisguised hatred.

Talia stared back.

"Great," Alex muttered, wrapping his thermal blanket around himself.

Thud

He suspected none of them were going to sleep. Not that they could have with the blasts from the hole.

After a good ten minutes of silence, Pushkin scratched under his chin with his good hand. He seemed to have mastered the pain from being shot; there was a focused intensity to him now that had been absent previously.

"You never get posted to another survey mission," he said in a matter-of-fact tone. "I see to that. Trust me."

Talia shrugged. "I'm not the one who tried to attack a teammate."

He bared his broad teeth. "I'm not one who forced teammate to walk against their will."

"Some things are more important than any one person."

"That's sort of reasoning that leads to death camps."

Talia stiffened and didn't reply.

An evil grin flickered about Pushkin's mouth. "Is true. And doesn't your religion say something about every life is sacred? Not even sparrow will fall but Lord will see it? Something like that? You're hypocrite, Indelicato."

"You'd sacrifice us all if it would get you what you wanted," she said, her tone biting.

"So what if I would? Is that how you are? You want to be like me? Is that it? You think I'm right to act like this?"

"*No.*" Pushkin tried to say something else, but Talia raised the bolt gun again, cutting him off. "Enough talking."

Thud

8.

Talia and Pushkin continued to sit facing each other, neither of them willing to move or break eye contact.

Even through his helmet, Alex could hear Talia humming in a constant wavering drone—the same song she'd sung before, cycled on a constant loop. She swayed as she hummed, and her eyes were glazed and empty.

In contrast, Pushkin appeared relaxed, almost dangerously so. At first Alex thought the Ebutrophene might be responsible, but the longer he watched, the more he became convinced the geologist was biding his time, waiting for the perfect moment to act.

Thud

A text popped up on his overlays:

<Should we do anything? – Chen>

<I don't think there's much we can do against Pushkin, and if you want to try to take the bolt gun from Talia, be my guest. – Alex>

The chemist shifted in his alcove and never replied.

It was 1049. Alex was so tired, he felt drunk, and yet with Talia and Pushkin in a standoff, he didn't feel as if he could sleep. Not that sleep was really an option with the volume of the

Thuds

that kept interrupting reality. He could have tried the melatonin again, but all things considered, it made him feel worse the next morning than if he'd just downed more AcuWake.

Still, he closed his eyes anyway, hoping for some rest. With everything that had happened that day—and the days before—he had little to no reserves of strength left.

Thud

He shifted positions to relieve the pressure on his injured shoulder. He relaxed his limbs and slowed his breathing . . . willed himself to sink into the comforting depths of oblivion.

Thud

His eyes flew open. *Dammit.* He couldn't even rest, not with the constant blasts of sound. . . . For the first time since they left the lander, Alex felt that time was running out. The pulses were getting so strong, he doubted it was possible to endure them for any extended length. The aural assaults were breaking down their bodies, and the only solution was to leave. Between that, the equipment they'd lost, injuries, and now Pushkin and Talia's fight . . . the expedition was operating on borrowed time.

You better know what you're doing, he thought, meaning Talia. But also himself. He'd been willing to risk everything to reach the hole, and now Alex was realizing just how large a risk that actually was. The expedition had turned into one of the nightmare experiences you read about in school—read about and wondered how any of the people involved had survived.

Was he still okay with dying on that plain, there on Talos? . . . He thought so, but only if he could get to the hole first.

Thud

On the other side of the shelter, Pushkin coughed, a long, racking cough that sounded unpleasantly wet and stringy.

Alex frowned. If the alien microbes continued to multiply at the same swift rate in Pushkin, the geologist would be in real danger in a day or two. *What if Talia gets him killed?* Alex picked a flake of dried blood off the palm of his left glove. Did he really want Pushkin's death on his conscience?

No.

He grimaced. Layla would have wanted to keep going, but not at the cost of Pushkin's life. Alex knew that. If turning back would save the geologist, then . . . then there was no choice, and Alex would have to accept that the expedition had failed. Oh, they'd collected loads of useful data, but there was still so much to learn about the hole.

Bitter disappointment coated his tongue, and the ground seemed to tilt and spin beneath him. He clutched the edge of his alcove. It didn't help.

Thud

With no other sanctuary, he retreated to Layla's recordings and blindly picked a day and time.

The inside of a greenhouse filled his overlays. He could nearly smell the moist, heated air and the rich, fungal odor of composted soil. Layla sat amid rows of planted squash and beets and carrots, and tomato vines hung like tangled hair from long trestles along the underside of the milky, semi-transparent ceiling. Layers of leaves dimmed the light, and it felt as if she sat in a small green grotto hidden somewhere in a great jungle.

She was repotting a miniature bellberry, each pendulous fruiting body a riot of splattered colors. Around her several glitterbugs darted and hummed, their articulated appendages laden with clumps of soot-soft sporidesm collected from the Eidolonian plant. Even in the depths of the green shadows, the glitterbugs glowed like pieces of burnished metal, bright and magical.

Alex watched as Layla placed the bellberry into a new pot. A thorn caught the back of her left hand and a pinprick of blood raised. She poured handfuls of dirt around the plant's tuberous bottom half and pressed down with gentle firmness.

"There," she said. "Now you can grow."

And then she stood and left the cave of leaves.

Thud

He stopped the video, but the remembered scent of the greenhouse and the low thrum of the glitterbug wings lingered with him.

The hab-dome no longer spun around him.

He blinked and went to wipe his eyes. *Tink*. His gloved hand bumped against his helmet faceplate.

He blinked again and let out a long breath.

Alright. He'd do what was necessary, but he still resented that events had made it impossible to investigate the hole on Layla's behalf. Yet he couldn't betray her memory by letting Pushkin die any more than he could have stayed on the *Adamura* and passed up the opportunity to land on Talos VII.

It seemed ironic that her ideals restrained him as much as they had initially impelled him.

He snorted, feeling suddenly cynical. What could the hole tell them, in any case? A bunch of numbers? Physical parameters that held no significance beyond the hole's engineering requirements? Just because the structure had been made by aliens didn't automatically mean it could tell them anything unique or profound about the universe. It *was* important, of course. But a source of philosophical wisdom? He doubted it.

Thud

Whatever. Maybe he didn't have any answers, but he had a responsibility. He'd talk with Talia tomorrow, convince her to take Pushkin back. If nothing else . . . if nothing else, Alex could do it himself and let Talia and Chen continue on to the hole.

And then what? Once he arrived at the lander, was he going to take up his life from before? Would he be content studying the hole at a distance? How could he sit and work and try to pretend everything was alright when it most definitely *wasn't*?

The thought was crushing.

Thud

Pushkin coughed again.

"Fuck," Alex muttered, and he turned on his helmet's noise-canceling function. He probably should have used it sooner, but he hated the slight feeling of pressure it created in his ears.

Thud

The sound was softer, but the vibrations that swept through his body were as strong as ever. He suppressed a groan and bunched his pillow under his helmet, hoping that more padding would reduce the shaking.

Thud

It was going to be a long night.

As he lay there, he drifted into a strange twilight state, halfway between slumber and wakefulness. His mind felt unmoored from his body, and at times he imagined he was lying on a raft that rose and fell with the surge of the sea.

In that timeless neverwhere, the pounding of the hole grew in significance until it dominated his every thought and vision, like a towering monolith, black and pulsing. He couldn't hide from it, nor did he want to, for it fascinated him . . . drew him closer with a siren-like attraction. Perhaps it was his exhaustion. Perhaps it was the Ebutrophene. But he began to think he could detect a fine-grained structure buried within each

Thud

—a physical manifestation of the fractal pattern the blasts of energy contained. More, he could *feel* the difference from one pulse to the next: a subtle shift of the grain, determined by mathematical principles as old as the universe itself.

There was a greater meaning to it, greater even than the underlying math. He felt sure of it. But he couldn't grasp the truth, whatever it was. He could only catch hints of it, like a blind man groping along the edges of a giant polyhedron.

That bothered him. Frustrated him. It felt as if he had a piece of sand lodged in his innermost recesses, a sharp-edged particle that never ceased to irritate and inflame him.

He *wanted* to understand. Without understanding, what was the point?

Thud

In the end, the hole's emanations battered him into submission, and he fell to dreaming. But it was no easy sleep. His disquiet over ending the expedition was a constant torment, and it undermined his visions, darkened them, filled them with shadowed figures and shrieking sounds. In the end, the visions dragged him—twisting and protesting, pleading for mercy—dragged him down dark and troubled paths to the place he did his best to avoid:

He saw her in their kitchen, and he shrank from the memory. Light streamed in through the windows at a low angle, and the air had the fresh chill of morning. There was fruit on the counter: sliced apples. He remembered them with particular vividness. Layla had cut an apple for him every morning they were together. It had been part of their morning ritual.

Her long, dark hair was unbound and hung freely between her shoulders. There was a frown on her face, and angry words flew between them, each one an acrid bullet chewing away at their faith in one another.

They were arguing about work again. What else? About his postings to the south—four weeks of separation and only video calls for company. About the long hours the lab had her working, and the way her mother would visit unannounced, and—and—

And then he brought up Kohren, the asshole at Layla's lab who kept hanging around her at every opportunity. Mentioning him was a low blow, born more out of frustration with other issues than any real suspicion, but it struck home, and for a second, Layla stood stunned and speechless.

The crinkle of pain that tightened the papery skin around her eyes hurt him more than any physical wound. But then anger masked her pain, and his own anger flared anew, and the words flew faster than ever.

. . .

None of the things he'd been so upset about mattered. Not in the grand scheme of things. Only he hadn't understood that. The lesson was yet untaught and unlearned, and his two teachers—grief and regret—yet waited for him.

He wept as he relived the moment, wishing he could break the chain of causality, to step out of time and hug her and tell her he loved her and that the angst and anger were just a mistake. Too much stress, too much work, not enough sleep.

But he couldn't. Events unfolded as they always had, and causality condemned him to relive his sins.

In the end, Layla stormed out, as she always did, leaving him with the lingering scent of her perfume and slices of apple uneaten on the counter.

She'd gone to her parents then, and later that day, she messaged him to say she was joining a couple of her friends on a day trip to the Salk Barrens for some hiking.

He hadn't answered. Not to tell her he loved her, not to make up, not even to wish her a safe trip. Still angry, he'd archived the text, thinking he'd talk with her when she got back, when they'd both had a chance to cool down.

If only he hadn't been so damn stubborn. Maybe she wouldn't have gone. Maybe she would still be alive. . . .

The Salk Barrens should have been safe. They were bare of the dense yaccamé *forests, which proved so treacherous for the settlers and scientists, and the char lived in wetter climes, as did the red mold.*

It should have been safe.

Layla's group brought overwatch drones with them—standard procedure for any group venturing beyond the shield walls. But the winds were strong that day, and somehow . . . somehow . . . the drones missed a lone tigermaul creeping through the chintz grass. The animal was far outside its normal range; a rogue female seeking to claim new territory for the litter incubating in its bladders. Only it happened to scent Layla's group, and it had done what tigermauls always did; it went for the kill.

Alex had imagined the moment a thousand times: the fear and pain Layla must have felt. The shock of the tigermaul charge, the evil gleam of its yellow eyes, the sense of helplessness as the barbed creature set its teeth and claws in her flesh. . . .

He was in their kitchen again, with the crystalline light streaming in from the west, and the slices of apple weeping beads of juice. And the most horrible sense of emptiness pervaded the house, an absence so profound, it felt as if a piece of him had been physically removed.

And yet he could not move. He was frozen in place, same as the apple, same as the light, condemned to spend eternity staring in place, regretting his mistakes.

Words couldn't express what he felt. All fell short before the enormity of what had happened and the irrevocable progression of time.

If only . . . But that was the most useless of prayers when applied to what had been *instead of* what could be.

And he saw no hope in what could be.

CHAPTER II

* * * * * * *

ETA ZONE

1.

Late during the night, movement in the darkly lit hab-dome caught Alex's attention, roused him from his stupor. He forced his eyes open to see Talia sidestep past his alcove and crouch next to Chen. She pressed her helmet against the chemist's, obviously speaking to him, though no one else could hear. Talia still held the bolt gun aimed in Pushkin's direction, and the geologist still sat stiff-backed and awake—waiting to seize the slightest opportunity.

For what seemed like an endless while, Talia and Chen spoke. Then, when Alex began to think they would stay like that for the rest of the night, Talia carefully stood and made her way back to her own alcove.

Alex lay staring at the curve of the wall for some time, remembering. His heart felt cold within him: a chilled husk that moved without meaning.

2.

When the morning alarm sounded, Alex clenched his fists. He felt like a turtle had run him over, and even a double dose of AcuWake wasn't enough to return any sense of normalcy.

The others were in no better shape, and Pushkin looked even worse. He coughed, twice—hard—and Alex saw traces of blood at the corners of his lips. When Pushkin stood, he swayed, as if drunk.

Talia and the geologist kept to the sides of the shelter and always opposite one another, as if particle and antiparticle repulsed by the presence of their mirrored self. As for Chen, Alex noticed he seemed somewhat more open with Talia, but it was a skittish affinity, brittle and uncertain.

Alex examined Pushkin again, much to the geologist's annoyance. "Leave be," he rumbled, shoving Alex away. "No more poke and prod. I know what say machines."

Alex had his doubts, but in any case, the readings he got off Pushkin were only getting worse. The amount of alien microbes in his blood was skyrocketing, his temperature was rising, and fluid seemed to be accumulating in the Zarian's enormous lungs.

After putting away the medilab, Alex made his way around the dome to where Talia was packing up her kit one-handed. She still held the bolt gun in her right hand. He gestured at her, and she reluctantly touched helmets with him.

"I'm worried about Pushkin," he said. "If he can't fight off this infection, he's going to get sepsis, go into shock. We'd have to put him under until we got back to the lander, and it wouldn't be easy trying to move him around if he's unconscious."

"What's your point?"

"I think we should turn back."

Thud

Talia eyed him for a long moment. Her pupils quivered with micro-tremors, and they weren't a visual artifact induced by the hole's blasts. She was wired to the gills. *Too much AcuWake,* he thought.

"One more day," she said.

He shook his head inside his helmet. "I don't think Pushkin will make it. Maybe I'm wrong, but do you want to take that chance?"

"You're the last one I expected to give up."

"It's not—We don't have a choice. Pushkin's life is on the line."

"*Everyone's* life is on the line," she said with a sudden snarl. "Do you know what will happen if *they* attack us? We'll lose. Humanity will lose. All gone. Dead. Planets blasted bare. Men, women, children, and the screaming, the *screaming.*" Her eyes went round and white-rimmed, as if she'd seen a horror. "We can't let it happen. Not again."

"Not ag—Nothing's happened. You're imagining things. We have to—"

"No!" She raised the bolt gun, placing the weapon between them. Then, with the speaker on her skinsuit, she said, "Everyone outside! Now!"

Thud

Alex's mind whirled as he and Chen proceeded through the airlock. *She's lost it,* he thought. Could he grab the bolt gun from her? Would she let him get close enough?

Talia wasn't taking any chances, though. She was the last to leave the hab-dome, and she kept a wide gap between herself and the rest of the group.

She gestured at the sledges. *<Harnesses on. Let's go. – Talia>*

"Nine klicks," Alex said to himself. They could do this.

They had to.

3.

When they took their half-hour and hourly breaks, Alex watched Pushkin closer than ever. The geologist was holding the same steady pace with his sledge, but there was a slowness to his motions that hadn't been there before. Several times, he glimpsed Pushkin coughing in his suit. But only a glimpse, as Pushkin always turned away when he saw Alex looking.

Alex kept waiting for an opportunity to grab the bolt gun from Talia, but she was far too careful for him. Finally, Alex sent a private text to Pushkin:

<If you distract Talia, I can grab the bolt gun. – Alex>

<Fuck you. – Pushkin>

<What's wrong with you? If you don't get medical attention, you're going to be screwed. – Alex>

The geologist glanced with hate-filled eyes back over his shoulder. *<Now you care? Fuck off. I not need your sympathy, asshole. – Pushkin>*

Thud

Not long after, a notification appeared in the corner of Alex's overlays. A message from . . . He frowned. From both Chen and Pushkin. Were they coordinating against Talia, despite what Pushkin had said? Curious, Alex tapped on the alert.

A group chat appeared. It wasn't a new thread; it looked as if Chen and Pushkin had been talking for hours. Maybe longer. Alex's frown deepened as he scrolled back through their conversation, and the more he read, the more concerned he became.

The conversation was unbalanced in the extreme: Pushkin directing a torrent of words at Chen, and Chen answering with only single words or short sentences. The bulk of Pushkin's texts centered on the same few topics he and Talia had been arguing about night after night. Questions of belief and beauty and morality, all wrapped in a philosophy of selfish sensuality.

Worst yet, Pushkin's ramblings showed clear signs of deterioration. Even over the course of a few hours, Alex could see the Zarian growing increasingly

incoherent, words and phrases becoming disjointed, unhinged, free of causality. Something seemed deeply wrong with the man's brain.

The most recent texts concerned Talia, which Alex had expected. Angry
rants about her presumption and supposed false authority. But there were also
lines about Alex as well, and the hairs on the back of his neck prickled as he
read paragraph after paragraph of Pushkin arguing not for violence, but for the
utter *wrongness* of what the geologist took to be Alex's beliefs.

Most disturbing of all, Chen seemed to be agreeing with Pushkin more and
more. Somehow Pushkin's incoherence was proving persuasive, though Alex
couldn't fathom how or why. Perhaps the sheer number of words was enough
to sway Chen's opinion. Either way, he seemed entranced by the stumbling
artifice of Pushkin's verbal gymnastics.

Thud

Deeply unsettled, Alex took screenshots of the conversation. Then he quit
the group chat, hoping that Pushkin hadn't noticed his presence.

Had Chen added him to the chat on purpose? Alex wondered. But if so, the
chemist showed no outward sign.

Alex wanted nothing to do with Talia right then, but he saw no other choice,
so he sent her a private message that simply said *Read this,* followed by the
screenshots.

Her attenuated shadow—which stretched out next to him; an odd, inky
companion—slowed as she received the material. After a few minutes with no
other reaction, he glanced back and raised his eyebrows in a questioning manner.

Talia's face had the grim set of a zealot whose every belief had been confirmed. He might as well have sought a response from a granite statue. Without
so much as a flicker of emotion, she motioned forward with the bolt gun.

<Keep walking. – Talia>

4.

THUD

Pain. Pain in his shoulder. And pain everywhere else. Alex was beginning to
think the hole was going to batter him to pieces. He barely had time to recover
from one blast before

THUD

Even the force of the wind seemed minor by comparison. The others were faring no better; when he saw their faces, they were locked into expressions of grim discomfort.

The sound of the hole had exceeded sound. It was beyond anything Alex's ears could handle, even with the suit's noise-canceling system. Each blast had become a physical blow that shook him as if he were standing upon the surface of a giant speaker.

THUD

He couldn't hear the pattern in the blast anymore. Maybe it had been just a figment of his sleep-addled mind. But he kept trying to catch hold of it again. If he could, he felt it would make the noise somewhat more bearable.

THUD

The suit wouldn't let him have another dose of Ebutrophene. Eight hundred milligrams a day was the limit; any more and he risked liver failure, heart failure, twitchy muscles, jaundice, and purple toenails, among other side effects. Right then, he would have happily risked liver and/or heart failure in order to reduce the pain, but he couldn't bypass the suit's hardwired safety controls.

THUD

He tabbed a dose of Norodon, his second in the past ten minutes. It didn't seem to be doing anything, but he figured another slug of it couldn't hurt. . . . Well, it could, but any damage it caused was long term and easily fixed back in the Alliance. He'd already had one set of kidneys replaced. What was another?

THUD

His vision fuzzed out. The optical distortions the blasts caused were getting stronger. Everything he looked at seemed to squirm as if alive, and the shifting grains had started to form fractal patterns that grew more and more distinct the longer he stared at them. The fractals felt like a patterned veil draped over reality—a veil that separated the known from the unknown. He could almost see what lay on the other side, shimmering and shifting, summoning him with liquid singing. . . .

He'd tried watching more of Layla's memories, but the interference from each

THUD

was too distracting. And besides, he found himself drawn to every painful moment, every recording of every little dispute and argument they'd had. Like picking at a scab, he couldn't stop reliving the mistakes in their relationship, his and hers, but his seemed far worse when viewed from the outside. And in each hurt they dealt, he could see the foundation being laid for future sorrow, and bitter regret filled his mouth.

5.

Groups of turtles continued to pass in and out of sight as the day progressed. At the most, Alex counted thirty-four scattered across the plain. At the least, only seven. They never barred the way or showed aggression, but he still found the sight of their hulking shapes ominous.

THUD

The lights in his helmet flickered, and a haze of static crossed his visor HUD. (Not his overlays. Those were safe. At least for the time.) The hole's EMP was starting to overwhelm the suit's electrical system.

Alex just hoped Riedemann's pure fucking magic would be enough to keep them alive.

THUD

By midafternoon, it was obvious that they weren't going to reach the hole that day. No one said it, but the math was undeniable. They just weren't going fast enough. The wind was too strong, the sledges too heavy, and the gutters of gallium too deep.

When they paused to rest, they didn't talk and they didn't look at each other. They just sat and stared at the ground, devoid of energy.

Talia was humming to herself again, her head moving to a private rhythm. Sitting in his sledge, Chen was hunched over his chip-lab, seemingly oblivious to the world around them.

Pushkin pinched his forearms with obsessive regularity, eyes half-closed, shoulders slumped. Pinch and twist. Pinch and twist. Almost as if he were trying to pull off pieces of his skin, like chunks of moldy bread. Alex's gorge rose and he looked away.

6.

The sun sat two hands above the horizon, glowing behind a scrim of sparkling dust, when Talia stumbled over a vein of gallium and went down on one knee.

Pushkin whirled and threw a fist-sized rock at her. The rock left twisting streaks across Alex's vision.

THUD

Talia jerked to the side faster than should have been possible, kicking up dirt and gallium.

The rock missed and bounced across the desert crust.

She got to her feet, bolt gun aimed at Pushkin's head. *<Y$&'re 01101110 01101111 01110100 00001101 00001010 the only one w✳&# augments. Keep going. – T✳(ia>*

Pushkin silently snarled at her and then resumed trudging eastward.

Alex was slow to follow. Talia's augments . . . heightened reflexes like hers were normally only gene-hacked into athletes or military personnel. *Just what did you do in Bagrev?* he wondered.

7.

They covered five klicks that day. An impressive amount considering the challenges they faced, but still not enough. Four klicks remained. Four klicks of wind and dirt and pounding blasts. Four klicks of grey troughs filled with liquid metal.

Four klicks too many.

At least his shoulder hadn't ripped open again. *Small mercies.*

As they were setting up camp—Alex had to do most of the work himself while Talia supervised—a turtle slid over and idled nearby, no more than twenty or thirty meters away.

On the outside, the creature seemed motionless, but Alex wondered about its underside. Was it repairing or altering another scalloped rail, of the sort he'd found before? He imagined thousands of tiny manipulators sifting like cilia through the dirt, placing and replacing individual atoms of metal.

No one in the group was comfortable making camp near a turtle, but it was too late to move, and the alien wasn't overtly hostile, so they chanced it.

When the hab-dome was up, a wild urge came over Alex. He retrieved his chip-lab from his sledge and started walking toward the turtle.

Talia shouted at him, but he couldn't hear anything from inside her suit. In the corner of his overlays, he saw: *<St&$!! – T@(✳$>* but he ignored it.

Up close, the turtle seemed even larger: a flat-bottomed boulder bigger than all their sledges combined. It shifted a miniscule amount, and Alex stopped a meter away.

Staying there, he took as many readings as he could of the turtle. With all the EM interference, he didn't know if the chip-lab would be reliable, but the opportunity was too good to pass up. Spectrographic analysis, chemical sniffer, density, radioactivity, refraction index . . . dozens of words and figures streamed past his eyes: chromium, terbium, carbon, a whole slew of organic chemicals, corundum, basalt-like rock, and more, so much more.

When the lab was finished, he lowered it, feeling as if he ought to do something more. "Hello?" he said through the speaker on the front of his skinsuit. "We come in peace."

The turtle didn't react in any obvious way.

THUD

Alex tried flashing the emergency light on his suit, first in binary and then in trinary (each time following the standard mathematical first-contact procedure that xenobiologists had developed decades ago). He even tried stomping the ground in the same pattern but without success.

He was both relieved and disappointed when the turtle failed to respond.

The two methods of communication he *didn't* attempt were (a) tapping on the turtle's rocky carapace—he wasn't that foolish—and (b) a scent-based communication. Since he had no idea what, if any, chemicals would be appropriate, Alex figured it was better to do nothing than to risk emitting what could easily be a mortal insult.

THUD

Talia gave him an ugly look as he made his way back to the sledges. Alex didn't care. Learning more about the turtles—a potentially intelligent alien species— was part of why he'd come to Talos, and that goal, that *need,* was more important than any order or company reg or even the bolt gun Talia was holding.

Besides, Layla would have gone up to the turtle. So how could he not?

8.

Once they were inside the hab-dome, Alex drank his liquid half-ration dinner, then fetched the medilab and again went to Pushkin. Neither of them spoke, and after a moment, the geologist grudgingly extended his arm.

Alex fumbled with the medilab probe as he struggled to insert it into the skinsuit access port. Such a simple task shouldn't have been so difficult, but even simple actions had become challenging.

Alex struggled to read the feed from the medilab. He blinked and blinked again and worked his tongue in his mouth. It felt dry and fuzzy.

THUD

The numbers were still heading in the wrong direction, but they weren't as bad as Alex had feared based on the results from that morning. Pushkin's immune system was still managing to hold off the alien microbes. But only just.

When Alex explained as much, Pushkin grunted and said, "Us Zarians harder to kill than you Terrans."

"I was born on Stewart's World."

"Unimportant difference."

9.

As the previous night, Pushkin and Talia sat facing each other, while Alex and Chen lay in their alcoves (Chen with his injured leg supported by an empty sample container).

Talia kept one hand on the bolt gun in her lap, while with the other, she folded and refolded the foil top to a meal pack. She seemed obsessed with it. First she folded a flower. Then, a sword. Then a ship. Then an abstract design that curled upon itself in ever smaller iterations. And all the while she kept humming the same maddening song to herself.

THUD

When she finished a shape, she would stare at it for a second or two and then flatten it and start anew. Alex could tell she'd taken more AcuWake; her movements were overly quick, birdlike, and she had a hyperaware look, as if she could see and comprehend a thousand frantic stimuli every passing moment.

Pushkin moved less, but he had the same hopped-up edge, as if his whole body were vibrating at an ultrasonic frequency.

THUD

The possibility of violence pressed upon them with stifling anticipation. Even so, Alex dosed himself with an extra helping of melatonin and closed his eyes. Whatever was going to happen between Talia and Pushkin, he wanted no part in it. But he *was* desperately, desperately tired, and he needed all the rest he could get.

Four kilometers. It wasn't so far.

THUD

True sleep proved impossible. He drifted in and out of dreams, and yet he was always aware of his body lying in the alcove, and of the dim red glow that suffused the nighttime dome, like the dull gleam of a dying star.

And always he could hear and feel the dreaded
THUD
At one point, he felt as if he were swirling down a drain, sinking and sinking and the universe a sideways blur around him, and then his vision changed, and he saw—

Plinth, in the haze of afternoon, windblown pollen giving the sky a surreal purple hue. The warmth of summer radiated from the living earth, and the cries of distant horn birds sounded across the shield wall.

The domed church had opened its doors, and the guests in their finery stood before folding chairs set in ordered rows. Friends, family—mostly her friends, none of his family. His buddies from work were there out of politeness. They didn't really know each other.

But the day was beautiful, and so was Layla, and his heart sang at the sight. Her dress was blue as sapphire, simple and elegant. His jacket was red as a robin's breast. Together they flared with contrasted vibrance matched only by the strength of their feeling.

Words were spoken, sentiments expressed, promises made.

Then: "Will you?" asked the officiant, ponderous in his dignity. And the question was repeated in variation, but always at its core: *Will you?*

"Yes."

In its simplicity, the most powerful of words. A pledge of sincerity, a hope for the future. An expression of faith.

"Yes."

And the church music swelled high, though it paled before his inner melody, and a glitterbug landed on Layla's coiled hair, and she laughed to see it, and he laughed with her.

And in that moment, all seemed right and well with the universe, and the cries of the horn birds faded to silence.
THUD
Alex twisted in the alcove, tormented by grief and recrimination. His jaw hurt, his shoulder throbbed, and everything seemed pointless. He dug his fingernails into his thigh, trying to hurt himself through the skinsuit, trying to distract himself. He was tempted to rip off the suit and scratch himself raw. *Anything* to force himself out of his head and stop him from thinking.

A rustle and an odd bump caught his attention.

He froze, listening. An image of the shelter surrounded by turtles flashed through his mind.

THUD

Another bump, accompanied by a subdued murmur.

He looked around his privacy screen. Pushkin was still sitting on the edge of his alcove, but his head was slumped forward, and his chest barely moved.

Across from the geologist, in Chen's alcove, Alex saw a strange, mounded shape, barely visible in the dome's sullen glow. An upright group of lumps and curves that failed to resolve into a recognizable object.

THUD

It took Alex a moment to realize what he was seeing, and even then, he didn't understand.

The shape was Talia and Chen—Chen kneeling, Talia standing over him, her hands on either side of his helmetless face. She too was helmetless, skinsuit unseamed to expose pale, sunstarved flesh, and her lips moved in an unceasing murmur.

The chemist stared up at her with a dazed, dumbstruck expression, as if gazing at a noonday sun, mesmerized by the beauty of its deadly shine. His mouth hung open, and a wordless noise emanated from deep within his throat: a begging whine bereft of any human quality.

Bewilderment took Alex. Why would either of them . . . ? What were they doing? *Why?*

THUD

A deep sense of unease formed within Alex. Out of concern, he turned up the volume on his helmet headphones, and from Talia, he heard a soft yet fierce chant, a recitation of conviction:

> "—the fires of retribution dare not overstep the boundary set for them but must await the decision of Thy Will; and for Whom all creation sighs with great sighs awaiting deliverance; by Whom all adverse natures have been put to flight and the legion of the enemy has been subdued, the devil is affrighted, the serpent trampled underfoot, and the dragon slain; Thou Who—"

Alex felt as if he had chanced upon a forbidden ritual, one not meant for prying eyes. He shrank behind his privacy screen, fearful that Talia might notice and loose her fury upon him, for at that moment, he had no idea what she was capable of.

THUD

He wondered if Chen wanted what was happening, or if Talia had insisted. It was hard to say *no* to a bolt gun.

Bile coated his tongue.

It wasn't his business. He didn't know the whys behind their behavior; there was no reason to think anything was wrong, except for his instinct that insisted something was.

He listened again to Talia's ongoing recitation:

> ". . . Cast away from his soul every malady, all disbelief, spare him from the furious attacks of unclean, infernal, fiery, evil-serving, lustful spirits, the love of gold and silver, conceit, fornication, every shameless, unseemly, dark, and profane demon. Indeed, O God, expel from Thy servant, Chen, every energy of the devil, every enchantment and delusion; all idolatry, lunacy, astrology, necromancy, every bird of omen, the love of luxury and the flesh, all greed, drunkenness, carnality, adultery, licentiousness, shamelessness, anger—"

She went on, and Chen continued to kneel before her and listen with an open mouth and a stupefied expression.

THUD

It's an exorcism, Alex realized. He'd never seen one, nor heard the associated prayers, but Talia's invocations seemed clear enough. She was trying to drive what she saw as evil from Chen. And he was letting her. And neither of them seemed worried about having opened their skinsuits and exposed themselves to contamination.

Perturbed, Alex closed the screen, turned down his headphones, pulled the blanket over his head, and wrapped it around his helmet. Even with that, he still heard the occasional rustle or murmur from the other side of the shelter. That didn't bother him so much as the fact that, after a while, he noticed that Talia's chanting had fallen into sync with the slow tempo of the hole's

THUD

What made it all the more disturbing was that he didn't think she was doing it on purpose. It had just happened.

And when she finished, with a final appeal to the Lord her God, and Chen grunted, as if struck, the sounds perfectly coincided with the latest

THUD

CONSUMMATION

★　　★　　★　　★　　★　　★　　★

'Tis a human thing, love,
a holy thing,
to love
what death has touched.

—CHAIM STERN

CHAPTER 1

*   *   *   *   *   *   *

BREAKING POINT

1.

Morning arrived all too soon.

They rolled out of their bunks and stood staring at each other, eyes bloodshot, faces dumb and slack. The melatonin was still in Alex's system; he felt as if his head were packed with wool and he were deep underwater. When Talia spoke to him, it took him long seconds to figure out how to reply.

"What?" he said. His tongue seemed twice its normal size.

THUD

She shoved her way past him and grabbed the food bin from the storage rack on the wall. She was wearing her skinsuit again, as was Chen, the two of them covered from head to toe as if nothing had happened. Everything seemed the same between them, which puzzled Alex. Was Chen really okay with Talia performing an exorcism on him? For her part, Talia appeared no more out of sorts than before.

Alex nearly asked Chen, just for the hell of it, but decided it might make things worse. Instead he said, <*You okay? – Alex*>

Chen gave him an odd look, as if he didn't understand the question. <*My knee still hurts, but the Norodon keeps it under control. Thanks for asking. – Chen*>

THUD

Pushkin leaned against the wall by his alcove, coughing. And coughing. His shoulders shook as if he were having a seizure. Then he hacked and spit, and Alex saw a gob of something purple hit the inside of his helmet.

When Alex tried to check on him, the geologist refused with a hateful glare, and Alex again thought of the deranged ramblings he'd seen in the man's messages.

THUD

Alex took a triple dose of AcuWake—one more than the maximum recommended dose—and tried to eat, but he couldn't stomach even the liquid rations. The vibrations from the hole were making him nauseous. He assumed the same was true for the others.

The blisters on his feet were worse than ever, and his shoulder still throbbed with a deep pain. He tabbed another dose of Ebutrophene and closed his eyes while he waited for it to take effect.

THUD

2.

Outside, a pack of turtles was milling about the shelter. Two to the north. Five to the southeast. One glided past no more than six meters away: a rocky dreadnought that gleamed red and yellow in the banded rays of the rising sun.

Alex tagged them on his overlays, although he wasn't confident the system would keep functioning.

He looked to the west. He ought to have been able to see the hole—it was only four klicks away, after all—but the dirt and the dust in the air were too thick. In one place, where the haze thinned, he thought he caught a glimpse of something long and dark streaked across the horizon. Then the wind gusted, and all he could see were the billows of yellow dust, swirling and streaming.

THUD

He staggered over to the sledges and started to unclip the lines strung between them and the bolts shot into the ground. When he finished, he had to remove each bolt with a device that fit over them and pulled all sixteen centimeters of tempered steel out of the ground. The device was somewhat like a mechanical corkscrew one of his bunkmates back on Eidolon used to have.

The wind made it hard work. He jammed his feet into the ground, hunched over, and strained over every bolt. Pulling the bolt out of Pushkin had been far easier. He was just glad they weren't buried in solid stone.

THUD

He was breathing hard by the time he got the last piece of metal out. He opened the back of Talia's sledge and dropped them into the box they came from. Then he folded the extractor in half and wedged it into the corner of the sledge.

He frowned. For some reason it wouldn't fit properly. He pulled it out and tried again.

<Ahg00100001 – Chen>

THUD

Alex glanced back at the shelter. Pushkin was supposed to be taking down the dome—under Talia's direction—while Alex freed up the sledges. He didn't see them, but he guessed they were on the other side of the shelter, along with Chen.

He eyed a turtle that had approached somewhat closer than normal. It moved on, and he bent over the sledge again. Why *wouldn't* the extractor fit? He reached inside the sledge, trying to feel what was blocking it.

THUD

< .'. – 0101000001110101011100110110100000kin >

Alex stopped and frowned. He looked at the shelter. He still couldn't see Pushkin, Talia, or Chen.

A dull sense of worry percolated through him. He shoved the extractor into the sledge—forcing it to fit—and closed the hatch. Then he picked up the line that led to the shelter and followed it back, stepping over the veins of molten metal that laced the ground.

THUD

A thick cloud of reddish dust obscured Alex's vision as he rounded the shelter.

"Fuck," he muttered, and switched to infrared, hoping it would still work.

It did. The ground glowed with radiant heat, while the sky went black and cold, save for the lines of crooked clouds that streamed west to east. The dust sparkled with a dark brilliance, alternating eddies and folds of soft effulgence with yawning voids that collapsed and expanded at irregular intervals.

Through the racing dust, he saw three figures, bright and glowing. Talia and Pushkin, standing with their arms wrapped around each other, close to the side of the shelter, swaying back and forth in the rushing wind. A few meters away, Chen lay on the ground, his injured leg stretched out behind him.

Alarm shot through Alex, clearing his mind to a degree. Where was the bolt gun?

He hurried toward them, keeping one hand against the shelter to support himself.

THUD

Talia twisted in Pushkin's arms. Then she wormed an arm free and dug her thumb into the geologist's injured shoulder. He jerked and tossed her aside like a rag doll.

She rolled across the ground—the wind pushing her along—and slid to a stop on all fours.

"Stop it!" Alex shouted, although he knew it wouldn't help.

THUD

Then he saw the bolt gun. It was on the ground close to Chen; the chemist was crawling crab-like toward it.

Pushkin started forward even as Talia got to her feet and—

Chen's hand closed around the gun. He lifted it, the barrel weaving loops as the wind caught the weapon.

Both Talia and Pushkin were shouting, their faces reddened masks of anger inside their helmets. They gestured toward Chen, urging him to toss the gun to them.

THUD

White showed around Chen's eyes. He wavered, buffeted by the wind.

Pushkin bellowed so loudly Alex actually heard him say, *"GIVE ME GUN!"* Then he took a step toward Chen.

Talia did the same, and again.

Alex remained frozen, not knowing what to do. If he tackled Talia or Pushkin, the other would take over, and if Chen panicked . . . His own heart rate was dangerously high; his vision darkened around the edges, and his hands and feet went cold.

THUD

Pushkin took one more step and—

Chen swung the barrel toward him, then back toward Talia as she edged forward. . . .

Then the chemist turned and tossed the bolt gun toward Alex, and Alex glimpsed pure desperation in his expression.

THUD

Startled, Alex caught the gun, fumbled, dropped it by his feet. He threw himself down and pinned the gun against the ground before the wind could tear it away.

The dirt vibrated as Pushkin and Talia charged him.

He rolled onto his back, scrabbling to bring the gun to bear. His fingers felt like frozen lumps.

Talia swerved sideways and slammed into Pushkin's legs. He stumbled, and the two of them fell onto Alex.

THUD

The weight of their bodies knocked the breath out of Alex, and he felt a lightning pain in his left knee as something *popped* and gave way. His diaphragm locked up, making it impossible to get air as he struggled to move. Alarms flashed inside his helmet. He couldn't see anything; bodies obscured his view.

He wriggled an arm free and then the weight vanished as Pushkin rolled off him.

Alex gasped, about to pass out from lack of oxygen. Sparkles and tracers and glowing lines obscured his vision. Where was the gun? The gun!

Through the shifting haze, he saw Pushkin sitting upright, holding Talia down by her throat. Her arms and legs flailed, kicking up plumes of milky dirt that half obscured her as they flowed eastward.

THUD

Chen appeared, hobbling forward on one leg. He threw himself at Pushkin, grabbed his arms, tried to pull him off Talia.

The Zarian was too strong. Chen might as well have been yanking on a block of iron.

Pushkin let go of Talia with one hand and backhanded Chen. The force of the blow knocked Chen across the ground.

With his free hand, Pushkin pried up a rock as big as a dinner plate. On the ground, Talia thrashed with frantic energy.

Alex's searching hands collided with the bolt gun. He grabbed it, struggled to wrap his fingers around the grip. *Safety!* Where was the safety?

Before he could find it, Pushkin lifted the rock over his head. Talia raised an arm to protect herself just as Pushkin brought the rock down onto the top of her helmet with all of his titanic strength.

THUD

Talia's visor shattered. Frosted blood sprayed in every direction, along with jets of escaping air. Shards of the visor tumbled across the ground, like tiny sparkling pinwheels.

Pushkin lifted the rock over his head and smashed it into Talia's helmet again.

And again.

And then he slammed the rock into the center of her sternum. Her chest caved in, lungs collapsing, ribs breaking. A gout of teeth and blood erupted from Talia's ruined face and splattered Pushkin with gore.

Her legs twitched, and she went limp.

THUD

Alex gaped, unable to process what had happened. He belatedly remembered to lift the bolt gun and—

Pushkin scrabbled over, ape-like on hands and feet, and slapped the gun away. Alex yelled as his middle finger snapped.

The geologist lifted the rock over him—

Layla.

Chen hopped over and shoulder-dove into the back of Pushkin's left knee. The geologist's knee buckled, knocking him off-balance, causing him to drop the rock.

It landed next to Alex's head.

He scooted backwards, twisting around, looking for the gun.

THUD

There it was. Past the dome and the sledges, wedged against a rock.

Without thinking, Alex jumped toward it.

His left knee buckled, but the wind still caught him and sent him flying.

He spun through the air and landed on his back twenty meters away. A rock dug into his spine, causing him to cry out. He rolled onto one knee and staggered upright.

Pushkin was walking toward him. The front of his suit was painted with shining blood. And through his visor, his eyes gleamed with an eerie sheen, bright and mad and hot as coals.

Chen lay on the ground behind the geologist, motionless.

"Wait!" Alex shouted as Pushkin moved toward him with the smooth pace of a stalking tigermaul.

The Zarian didn't react.

Alex knew he couldn't fight him. Pushkin was too strong. Too fast. There was no outrunning him, not on a destroyed knee. And Alex couldn't hide. Not outside, not inside; the airlock wouldn't do anything to stop Pushkin.

THUD

Alex gathered himself up and started toward the fallen bolt gun, heading diagonally into the wind, trying to move as fast as he could. Running was impossible, but a quick scramble—

It wasn't fast enough.

Pushkin jumped at him. Alex swerved, and he felt more than saw the mass of the Zarian's body sail past.

He shouted as something closed around his right ankle and pulled his legs out from under him. He landed hard on his stomach and his helmet bounced against the ground, dazing him.

He twisted around, kicking with his free leg.

Pushkin lay on the ground behind him, one of the Zarian's massive hands wrapped around his ankle. He stared up at Alex, a snarl on his face.

THUD

Alex kicked again, and nailed Pushkin on the top of his thumb. The man's grip loosened, and Alex managed to pull free with a wrench and a yank. He struggled to his feet, panting, sweat coursing down his face.

Without looking back, he staggered toward the gun.

Ten steps away, he stepped in a vein of gallium. He pitched forward and rammed his shin against the edge of the trough, spilling molten metal across the crusted earth.

THUD

Pain shot through his leg. He grunted and dragged himself forward, limping.

He was only five steps away from the gun.

Three.

Two.

His hand closed around the grip of the weapon.

Over a hundred and fifty kilos of bone and muscle slammed into him from the side, driving him into Talia's sledge.

THUD

Alex felt his right shoulder pop and dislocate as Pushkin's weight crushed him against the fairing, and his delt tore open for a third time, flooding the inside of his suit with blood.

He screamed.

He fought to stay on his feet; if he fell, he was dead. But then what felt like an iron weight struck the side of his head.

The sky tilted, and he lost all sense of up and down.

THUD

The wind drove him across the ground, bouncing and tumbling. He rolled to a stop on his belly and blinked as he stared at the chapped earth.

He started to push himself onto all fours, and his right shoulder gave out. He screamed again.

He looked up.

Pushkin was moving toward him from the sledge, fifteen meters away. Three meters away, lying on the ground, was the bolt gun.

Pushkin spotted the gun at the same time he did.

The Zarian jumped.

THUD

Alex lunged forward, pulling himself across the ground with his good arm. He gasped for breath and lunged again.

Pushkin landed in a puff of dust not four meters away. He sprang forward, his legs pulled up on either side of his torso, like a monkey leaping from a branch.

THUD

The wind gusted just as Alex reached the bolt gun. It carried Pushkin farther than he'd intended, and the Zarian landed a half meter behind Alex, sending up ribbons of coiling dust from around his boots.

Alex grabbed the gun with his left hand and flipped onto his back.

Pushkin's mounded bulk blotted out the sun as he charged him.

Alex pulled the trigger as fast as he could.

The gun bucked in his hand six times, and Pushkin stumbled and crashed onto him and smothered him under his weight.

THUD

Pushkin's visor clanked against Alex's. The geologist stared at him, eyes still wide and crazed. There was red froth at the corners of his mouth, and a strange, purplish crust around his eyes.

"Why?!" Alex shouted.

A horrible grin split Pushkin's mouth, and he laughed in such a ghoulish manner, Alex recoiled within his helmet. "You not understand? None of us get off planet. I'm infected. *You're* infected. We all infected. The walls fell, and shadows walk, and we all—" His mouth continued to move, but his voice faded until it was too soft to hear.

And then his massive neck went limp, and Alex knew he was dead.

THUD

Panic gripped Alex. He had to get free; he couldn't breathe. He thrashed from side to side and shoved at Pushkin's shoulder. His body was like a sack of wet cement: heavy and almost impossible to move.

It took all of Alex's remaining strength, but at last he succeeded in rolling the Zarian off him.

He lay where he was, panting. Shaking. He felt so hot he thought he was going to pass out, even though his suit fans were on the max. He realized he was crying; tears were streaming down the sides of his face, and he couldn't seem to fill his lungs with air.

His suit felt too hot, too tight. He gripped the sides of his helmet and wished he could pull it off. Pull it all off and dive into a pool of water that would wash him clean.

THUD

"Ebutrophene," he said. "Four hundred milligrams."

He swallowed the drug and, holding his dislocated arm, slowly, painfully, got to his feet.

Pushkin's blood slicked the front of his suit. More blood was splattered on the ground around him, like torn petals pressed flat against the dry earth.

Pushkin lay on his back, eyes still open, bright and baleful, as if he could burn a hole in the heavens through sheer willpower. Dead or not, his gaze was so unpleasant, Alex considered removing the geologist's helmet just to pull down his lids and put an end to whatever dire vision he seemed to see.

But he didn't.

Because he wasn't crazy. Not like Pushkin.

Not like him.

THUD

When Alex lifted his gaze, he froze. A ring of turtles sat around him and Pushkin. Fourteen of them. Still and silent as megaliths raised about an ancient burial mound.

His heart lurched in his chest.

There was no way to escape.

THUD

CHAPTER II

* * * * * * *

APOTHEOSIS

1.

Alex wet his lips. He could *feel* the turtles watching him. Watching and judging. Their presence weighed on him from every direction, pressing on him with palpable intensity. The air in his helmet was thick and syrupy; each breath was a challenge.

He glanced at the bolt gun on the ground.

One shot left. Not that it would do him any good.

THUD

He decided he'd rather meet his fate than wait to be crushed or immolated or whatever it was the turtles could do.

He took a step forward and then stopped.

The turtles didn't react.

He moved forward again, this time with greater confidence.

THUD

He paused after every step, but the turtles never budged. Never reacted to him. He passed between the two in front of him, not half a meter from either creature. In the morning light, the bumps on their shells had a certain translucency, an amber color that reminded him of the shell of the lion clam on Eidolon.

The moment he was outside the ring of turtles, they began to move.

Alex started, frightened, and backed away.

The turtles slid inward until they met in the center of their ring, hiding Pushkin's body from sight.

THUD

Alex stared. He wondered what the turtles wanted with Pushkin. Were they eating him? Analyzing him? Praying over him? Or were they just maintenance staff whose only task was to keep the hole's antenna in good working order?

Whatever the answer, he doubted he would find out.

He turned his back on the turtles, Pushkin, and the bolt gun, and limped back toward the dome.

THUD

2.

Alex stopped by the airlock. He pressed the elbow of his dislocated arm against his side, lifted his forearm so it was level with the ground, and used the airlock frame to push his forearm out and around, like a sailboat boom swinging in an arc.

His humerus shifted back into place with an audible *pop* and a sickening sensation of bone sliding over bone. The spike of pain made him stagger and his vision flash white.

He opened and closed his right hand. Usable, if barely, and the bleeding from his left shoulder seemed to have stopped, which was good.

As fast as he could, he hobbled back around the shelter. His knee felt loose, unstable. ACL was torn again.

THUD

Talia was a lost cause. He barely glanced at her; the sight was too gruesome.

But as he approached Chen's crumpled form, Alex saw the man's chest move. *Still breathing.* A faint sense of relief passed through Alex.

The chemist was unconscious, eyes rolled back, and there was a leak in his faceplate. A needle of white vapor hissing out of a hairline crack. And there was another leak along his abdomen, near the crest of his hip bone.

From his belt, Alex managed to extract his roll of FTL tape. He slapped a piece onto Chen's visor and another onto his abdomen.

THUD

The chemist's suit pressure stabilized within seconds. His eyelids fluttered, and then he jerked awake and took a panicked breath.

Alex bumped helmets with him. "Chen! Can you hear me? You okay?"

Chen's eyes rolled as if to escape his skull. "Red, red, red—said I couldn't didn't understand but I did, got it got it. Wrong, wrong, wrong—"

"What's wrong? What'd you get?"

"Asking right. Answer wrong. No such thing as nothing. Choose the path or path chooses you, knife cuts, blood spills. Run, run, run, impossible to escape."

He kept babbling, and nothing Alex said would snap him out of it. Delirium, or something like it.

THUD

Alex felt along Chen's arms, legs, and chest. The chemist yelped when Alex pressed against his left side, though he never stopped spouting nonsense. *Cracked rib.* Maybe more than one.

Alex tried to help Chen up, but the man was completely uncooperative. Worse, he kept twitching and thrashing in a way that made it impossible for Alex to move him, especially with his own injuries.

Out of desperation, Alex punched in the emergency override on the control panel at the back of Chen's skinsuit and administered a heavy dose of sedatives.

Thirty seconds later, Chen went limp and his breathing slowed as he slipped into a semi-comatose state.

THUD

Alex used the FTL tape to wrap his injured knee. He hoped it would be enough to keep the joint stable while walking. The area was already swelling; from experience, he knew it would be too stiff to bend in a few hours.

He looked back.

The fourteen turtles still sat nose to nose in a circle over Pushkin's remains. From a distance, they resembled a rocky floret, rayed out from a single point.

They didn't stir as Alex dragged Talia's body to the hab-dome and shoved it through the airlock and inside.

Biocontainment was completely broken by now, but Alex couldn't leave a corpse to rot outside. Not if he could help it. As long as the dome remained intact, it would keep Talia's remains isolated from Talos's ecosystem.

Back to Chen, and he hauled the chemist to the sledges.

THUD

Alex leaned on his knees as he caught his breath. Chen needed help. *He* needed help, and sailing one of the sledges back to the lander with both of his arms injured would be dicey at best.

But it would only take a couple of hours to reach the lander.

That's what he should do. That was the smart choice.

He looked at the hazy horizon in front of him.

Four klicks. Not so far. To turn back now, after everything that had happened . . . If he chugged AcuWake and Ebutrophene and ate caffeine pills, and if he didn't worry about the damage he was doing to his knee . . . Dump the equipment. Take only what was needed to return to the lander.

It could be done. Four klicks was barely anything.

Barely anything . . .

THUD

He used Talia's sledge. Out went the core sampler. Out went the chip-lab, spare skinsuit, bio samples, storage units, communication gear, and everything else that wasn't essential. The few remaining rations stayed.

When the sledge was stripped, he heaved Chen's limp form into the fairing—hard, painful work that took him almost a quarter of an hour.

THUD

He looked over, expecting to see the fourteen turtles again.

Gone.

The plain was empty. Desolate. As if he and Chen were the only living things on the planet. Where Pushkin had been, nothing remained. Only a patch of overturned earth that the turtles' undersides had scoured flat.

THUD

Alex retrieved his chip-lab and trudged over to the overturned earth. The machine hummed in his hands as he sampled the soil, sending the probe down to its farthest extent: thirty-four centimeters below the surface.

He hated to think what the probe might encounter, but he had to know if Pushkin was still there.

With some trepidation, he extracted the probe from the ground. Relief to see it free of blood, and the results on the screen were the same as always: stone, dirt, and the usual Talos microbes.

THUD

He took samples in two other places. Both times the results were the same.

No sign remained of Pushkin. Whatever the turtles had done to him, he had vanished. Even with the chip-lab, Alex wasn't able to detect a single fragment of DNA in the soil. It was as if Pushkin had never existed.

Another mystery he knew he'd never solve.

THUD

3.

THUD

Alex dug his walking sticks into the desert hardtop and pushed down as he took a step forward.

Then another.

Even with all the Ebutrophene he'd taken, his shoulders burned where the harness bit into them, and his knee pulsed with hot pain, and his broken finger was swollen tight within the skinsuit glove, and his broken tooth still throbbed.

Not doing too well, he thought. Acknowledging the fact gave him a sense of calm, as if the unknown was no longer so frightening.

The ground had a swirling, fractal pattern to it; everything did now. The sky swarmed with the jittering grains, and nothing seemed stationary. His own body appeared to shift and shimmer on the surface, as if he were growing insubstantial.

THUD

He still felt shocked by the fight. That it had happened didn't surprise him as it once would have. Not really. But the reality of it, the uncompromising finality, and the obscenity of bodies broken, smashed, exposed . . . He couldn't help thinking of what had happened to Layla, how the tigermaul had done as much or worse to her.

THUD

One kilometer down.

The network of gallium was getting thicker; he couldn't walk more than a few meters without having to splash through a trough or two. Sometimes he stepped in one without realizing and fell to his knees. Once he banged his shin again. He ended up lying on his back, clutching his leg until the pain subsided.

No turtles were within sight, but for whatever reason, dust devils kept forming on the plain. They never lasted very long; each blast from the hole disrupted them, tore them apart, and sent their tattered remains flying eastward. They kept popping into existence, though, like spirits doomed to an unfairly quick lifespan.

THUD

Two kilometers down.

His mind had begun to wander. One moment he was on the surface of Talos. The next he was—

—fourteen again and running through the access tunnels on Stewart's World, chasing Horus and the other boys on their way to break into the complex that housed the settlement's air scrubbers. The thrill of the forbidden, the lure of the unknown.

The complex had the best view in the settlement; they could see all the way to the northern mountains, and the sight when Proxima Centauri rose gleaming and glittering over the horizon filled them with starstruck awe. They sat and watched—cracked jokes, sipped rotgut, and boasted about their imagined futures. The experience was more than worth the punishments they earned.

THUD

He didn't know if it was the pain or the painkillers (or just the unholy thunder that kept crashing down upon him), but he'd started seeing . . . seeing *what* he wasn't sure. Strange artifacts in the fractal fuzz; distortions of the pattern that shimmered like prismatic refractions. But they never appeared for longer than ten point six seconds. That unforgiving, unyielding subdivision that ruled his life and, it seemed, the rest of the universe as well.

Pulling the sledge had become too hard. The troughs of gallium were deepening, the wind was strengthening, he was tiring, and the day was aging. He stopped and stood leaning forward, allowing the wind to support and cushion him.

Keep going or turn back?

Keep going or . . .

Keep going.

THUD

He shoved the sledge's struts into the ground, stomping on them extra hard to make sure they held. If he'd had the bolt gun, he would have used it.

Then he popped the fairing and checked on Chen. Still breathing, still mumbling to himself and unaware of his surroundings.

Alex stared at the chemist for longer than he should have. Then he closed the fairing, unclipped his harness from the sledge, and left the sledge behind as he continued westward. Alone and lonesome. Fractured and pain-ridden, nearly delirious.

THUD

Without the sledge, he should have been faster, but his pace hardly changed. The terrain was still challenging, the resistance from the wind was continuing to increase, and his knee was giving him ever more difficulty. The combination limited him to a heavy-footed tread that was barely faster than a crawl.

Four klicks. At normal walking speed, it would have taken him less than an hour. As it was, five hours (including breaks) seemed more likely.

The walk back to the sledge wouldn't take nearly as long. Not with the wind at his back. The biggest challenge on the return would be to avoid being blown off his feet. The best technique might be a low-gravity-style hop that let the wind do part of the work.

He wasn't sure his knee was up for it.

He'd have to experiment.

THUD

The distortions were everywhere now, hovering about him like rainbow warpings of the spacetime fabric. They had an involuted appearance, as if reality was folding in on itself at different points, and he had an inexplicable feeling that they were *real* and that they were watching him . . . and had always been watching him. Only now the substance of existence had thinned enough for him to become aware of their presence.

He spoke to the distortions, and he thought they heard, but they didn't respond. The fractal light that flared from them reminded him of relativistic jets from a pulsar—beautiful plumes that swirled and dissolved along their edges.

When he saw a turtle, he saw several of the distortions hovering above the creature's shell. *Angels,* he thought. He wasn't religious, but it was the only word that fit.

THUD

He saw Layla on the trail by their house, laughing as she batted at a glitterbug. She had a bandage along her left arm; it was the day after her operation, and they were both giddy with joy that it was over and done with and that she would retain full use of her arm. The spine the doctor had dug out had been no bigger than a splinter, but it could have killed her.

The price of living in paradise.

THUD

The winter solstice; the mountains were cold and moody, the forest dark and silent. He'd taken his flier out and raced over the landscape until he found an open-topped hill to land on, far from Plinth.

He'd gotten out, keeping his blaster rifle with him. The tigermauls were scarce at that time of year, but that was no reason to take chances.

From the hill he looked out over hundreds of kilometers of overgrown wilderness. Eidolon was his adopted home, but at that moment, it had struck him how far he was from Stewart's World, and from Earth, the origin of their species. *He* was the alien on Eidolon, and most everything on the planet wanted him dead.

He'd shivered then, and for the first time in his life, he'd felt truly lost. Lost and alone.

What *were* they doing there?

THUD

Three kilometers down.

One to go.

Alex lipped his feed tube and took a gulp of water. Every part of his body screamed at him to turn around. To escape the punishing blows that kept pounding through him. To escape from the vastness that lay before him.

But he couldn't.

He wouldn't.

THUD

With each blast, the top few centimeters of earth blurred, growing soft and pollen-like. He stumbled and braced himself against the ground. Before he could get up, the next

THUD

struck. He felt the soil vibrate and dissolve around his gloves, becoming brown foam. The sensation filled him with inexplicable revulsion.

He snatched his hands back and scrambled to his feet.

The wind stripped the loose dirt away, adding it to the torrents of dust already streaming through the air.

He wondered why the ground hadn't eroded away entirely. After sixteen thousand years, there ought to be nothing but bedrock left.

Did the wind ever stop? Did it ever reverse course? Had all of the dirt come from the other side of the—

THUD

—they were arguing about work again. About children. About things that didn't matter. The anger on her face hurt him to see, but he didn't stop, didn't back down—

—he sat alone on their bed. It was dark. The sheets were a knotted mess. No time to clean since the call to the hospital, since . . . since . . . He curled over, sobbing.

—the bright interior of the remembrance center, the Memorialist droning on and on and on and none of it mattered. None of it—

—folding her clothes, because she never would again. Ignoring the urn that sat on the shelf at the back of the closet—

THUD

—the urn hung before him, brushed steel dull and cold, heavy with the unbearable weight of oblivion, a dreadful talisman of death. He reached for it but could not touch it. He cried out, but she did not answer.

He wept, and there was no comfort.

The urn. The file. One beside the other. In one her body. In the other, all that remained of her mind, though every thought and feeling was lost to the void, to the inexorable march of entropy.

Gone. Gone. *Gone.*

The wind staggered him, and he gasped, crying as he had that first day, when he'd realized there was no changing or fixing what had happened.

He screamed into his helmet.

THUD

He had to know. He had come so far, endured so much, and now all of reality seemed to be tearing itself apart and the end was near.

He had to know.

His overlays were a flickering mess, but he could still see. Still use them. Down through his folders to the file. *Layla.* He clicked on it and jumped to the final entry. He skimmed past her readying for the hike, past her turbulent skimmer flight, past the first hour of her and her friends picking their way through the fields of windswept chintz grass, heading toward the exposed promontories to the north.

The multicolored grass swung before Layla, the brittle, sharp-edged stalks clattering against each other like pieces of bone china. She couldn't see more than a few meters along the beaten game trail the group was following.

The wind then was blowing even as it was blowing on Talos.

Alex glanced at the timestamp at the bottom of the recording. Three minutes and forty seconds remaining.

His heart lurched.

THUD

Every twitch and bend of the chintz grass made Alex flinch. He felt disembodied; despite the pain of his injuries, his mind was wholly on Eidolon, with Layla.

He studied the jagged sky for the overwatch drones. *Where were they?* But none showed, and the wind gusted harder than ever, and the grass rattled like a field of flensed ribs.

When it came, it came so fast he could barely see. A flash of muscled legs red and orange, hooked claws reaching forward, a frill of raised barbs, and a toothed maw opening wide. Then the tigermaul struck, and the world spun sideways.

"Ahh!"

Teeth snapping. Metallic snarls. Dirt and wet gasps and patches of sky. He couldn't see. He didn't want to see.

Then a drone swooped past, and it was over.

THUD

Layla was lying on her side. Blood or dirt blocked the vision from her groundside eye. With the other, she looked up at the clusters of patterned chintz grass, and above them, the pale morning sky.

Her breathing was short and shallow, and it crackled from liquid in her lungs.

Alex stood leaning into the wind, one hand against the ground, eyes fixed on his staticky overlays, ears straining for the faintest sound.

Layla shifted slightly, as if to push herself upright, but then she went slack again. The gaps between her breaths grew longer, and the breaths diminished in depth.

Blades of chintz grass swayed, white sky streaked with feathered clouds, silence but for wind.

"It's all so beautiful," she said softly.

And the recording went dark.

THUD

Alex stared at the horizon. Another of the involuted angels drifted past near a turtle thirty or so meters away.

His mind was blank. He didn't know what to think or feel. Ever since she died, he'd imagined her final moments a thousand thousand times. Every day he died with her. And he'd imagined how she might have cursed or pleaded, how she might have screamed for help.

But never in all his imaginings did he think that she had reacted with anything but fear, pain, or anger.

THUD

He forced himself to continue forward. It was the only thing he could do.

4.

Half a klick to go.

Not far at all. Not far at . . .

The blast was unimaginable. When it hit, his vision went black, and for a moment, oblivion swallowed him. His overlays were useless; distortion lines ran across his field of vision, making it impossible to see the projections clearly.

"Off," he said, and the lines vanished. His implants were fried; they'd have to be replaced. A bit more and his nervous system would be fried too. The suit was acting as a Faraday cage, but no Faraday cage was perfect. His skin itched and crawled as the high-potential fields washed over him.

Without his suit, any one of the blasts would have killed him. That close to the hole, the EMP would couple with the iron in his body and induce a current in it, same as with the gallium. The resulting flow of energy would be so intense, it would vaporize him on the spot.

Riedemann had derived entirely too much pleasure from telling them *that* particular fact.

Alex fell onto his hands and knees for the second time in as many steps.

He decided to stay there. It was too hard to balance on his feet. Only three hundred meters remained. He could cover them on all fours. It wouldn't be easy, but he could do it.

He glanced up. He still couldn't see anything other than the clouds of abrasive dust racing toward him and the half-dozen or so angels gleaming and glittering amid the fractal static.

He put his head down. He hoped the air would clear. If he got to the edge of the hole only to find that the haze hid everything out past a kilometer or so . . . he didn't know what he would do.

Another slice of oblivion.

He crawled forward. Slowly. Painfully. He tried to keep his injured knee off the ground, but it was a failing attempt. He bit his tongue to distract himself. Also to keep his teeth from rattling together with each detonation.

His shoulder wouldn't let him put much weight on his right arm. He tried once and cried out as a pulse of warm blood soaked the inside of his suit.

Every meter or so he had to lift his hands and legs to move over a trough of gallium. The veins of molten metal were hard to see; dirt covered them, and he often plunged a hand into the slick, dense liquid. When he did, the unsettling warmth of the metal seeped through his glove, he felt a faint buzz in the air, and he tasted the sharp tang of ozone.

Thirty meters from the hole, he noticed that the dirt under his hands and knees was firmer than before. When the blast struck, his gloves didn't sink into the vibrating earth quite so far and less dust seemed to sweep past underneath him.

He looked up, forcing his head against the wind. The effort was almost more than his neck could maintain.

In front of him, the wall of dust had thinned and in places . . . parted.

He couldn't make out much. Just a darkness that weighted the land before him, but it was enough to encourage him.

He bowed his neck and crawled forward with renewed speed.

Nearly there. . . .

The ground grew harder and harder until he found himself crawling across what looked and felt like glazed ceramic. The material was grey, and the top centimeter was transparent. The surface was smoother than it had any right to be after however many thousands of years. After the comparative softness of the dirt, the flat, unforgiving surface was painful against his injured knee and made him wish he had a pad for it.

The net of gallium stopped at the ceramic. *Good.* He was sick of having to deal with it.

He kept crawling.

As much as he wanted to, he resisted the urge to look up again. Not yet. Not until he reached his destination. He didn't want to see parts of the hole. He wanted to see the entirety, all at once. Otherwise, what was the point?

5.

A drop-off appeared beneath the tips of Alex's leading hand. He stopped and stared.

The ceramic ended in a perfect right angle. The corner looked atomically sharp. So sharp that he was afraid to touch it, for fear it would slice through his suit. He imagined he could hear a high, keening whistle as the edge sheared through the wind.

He pulled his hand back to a safer position.

His breathing quickened, and his heart fluttered as it skipped three, four beats.

He'd made it. He'd finally made it.

He steeled himself and then lifted his head.

The force of the blast shoved him back onto his heels.

He blinked and shook his head as he tried to clear his vision. It took a few seconds before his eyes would focus.

In front of him gaped an abyss, black and bottomless. The far side was lost in the distance; hidden by the curve of the planet and the thickness of the atmosphere. The same was true to his left and right. The precipice seemed to stretch out to infinity, the bend in it so slight as to be imperceptible.

It felt as if he were sitting on the lip of a cliff at the end of creation, as if there were nothing on the other side of the hole. Nothing but blackness and eternity.

The air over the hole was relatively clear. High above, the bands of clouds arced around the center of the hole, shoved aside by the enormous pulses of energy from below. The blasts had torn apart one cloud, leaving behind nothing but tattered pennants of mist.

In several places along the rim of the hole, colored lights flitted from cloud to cloud, like shards of aurora emancipated from the ionosphere.

Alex grimaced and leaned into the wind, allowing it to support most of his weight as he peered over the edge of the hole.

The inner wall was a dark grey, darker than the ceramic he was sitting on. It was perfectly smooth, but not reflective, and it fell away in a straight line, angling inward only slightly. There were no markings on the wall, no hatches or access points, nor even signs of ordinary wear. A complete absence of anything that might convey information, if even about the ordinary passage of time.

A few kilometers down, he saw several streamers of dust, trapped in vortexes of air along the side of the gigantic maw.

The depths of the chasm lay hidden beneath a thick, viscous shadow. And in the center of that blackness, at the very heart of the void, he saw . . . no, he *felt* a twisting of reality itself. A fractal inversion that made his head spin and his stomach heave—an angel-like convolution writ large.

There was *something* down there. Something heaving and quivering and straining against the confines of the world. A conscious force that was so far beyond anything Alex had imagined, his sense of self shrank before it. He was a speck of sand caught in the fringe of a giant whirlpool. A maelstrom that threatened to tear apart the planet and the surrounding space, ripping shreds in the velvet backdrop of the vacuum so that a malevolent light might shine through. . . .

It took him longer than before to recover from oblivion. His neck hurt; he thought the blast might have given him whiplash, as he'd had his head over the edge of the hole.

He edged back, frightened, unable to make sense of what lay below.

Several of the angels hung before him in a shifting arc. They seemed even more tangible, and he imagined he saw structures within them: patterns within patterns, jeweled gears interlocking and turning, facets of incomprehensible engines.

Alex thought he was starting to go mad. Maybe he already was.

He sat where he was, hands on his knees, and gazed out at the barren emptiness.

What could he hope to learn about the hole now? Without proper equipment, he was limited to his distortion-riddled senses. The *something* at the bottom of the hole, and the angels, were personal anecdote, and unreliable ones at that. How could he convince anyone to trust his feelings when he didn't trust them himself?

Whatever the ultimate purpose of the hole, he wasn't going to figure it out. Not then. Perhaps no one ever would. The only beings who knew for certain were the aliens who made it, and they weren't talking. At least, not in any way he could understand.

A sour taste filled his mouth. He'd failed. He couldn't study the hole the way he'd wanted—the way *Layla* would have wanted. *Fool!* He should have known better. Only he'd hoped . . . he'd hoped so badly—

He'd been so convinced that the expedition was worth the effort. For her sake. Perhaps it had been, but now it was at an end. *He* was at an end. It would be decades or longer before anyone would be able to tease information out of the hole. Too long for him. He wasn't sure how he could survive the next few minutes, much less the next year.

Layla would have been willing to wait. But he wasn't her, and she wasn't there.

His face crumpled, and he hunched over, pressing his helmet against the ceramic ground as he sobbed in desperate gasping hiccups.

"I don't know how to do this," he moaned. "I don't . . . I don't—"

He shook his head, eyes still clenched shut. His nose was clogged, and his breath came in short gasps between his sobs.

When his frazzled brain recovered, he opened his eyes, lifted his gaze.

It seemed only fitting that he'd come so far just to see a hole. After all, it was a nullity, a void, a *lack,* and that was what he'd found. A lack. A fissure in the fabric of reality, a fissure that he couldn't plaster over. Not with any amount of rationalizing.

Tears coursed down his face as he stared into the hateful abyss.

A terrible urge welled up inside him then—an insidious, snake-tongued whisper from the darkest part of his mind, and it said, *"Jump."* He'd heard it before, whenever standing atop a bridge or a skyscraper or other high point, but never so strong or so loud. The urge was dangerously compelling; he twitched forward, an aborted lunge that would have carried him over the edge.

He froze, staring into the darkness below. It would be so easy. One more step, and his torment would end. And maybe he would learn something as he fell. A revelation that he could never otherwise be privy to. Secret knowledge that required the ultimate sacrifice to access.

Layla's face floated before him, like an image on his overlays. She seemed sad for him, and her sadness deepened his. He reached toward her, but his arm wasn't long enough. Her lips moved, but he couldn't hear what she said, and that more than anything upset him.

She vanished, and he collapsed forward, groaning his agony. Why? Why? *Why?*

What was the point of their suffering? And why should he endure it? Selfishness wasn't the answer, and God or gods hadn't touched him. Which left him with nothing to hold on to, nothing to keep him from giving up and stepping away from the game.

"Jump."

He staggered upright, ready to do it. The fall wouldn't be so bad. A minute or so of free fall, and then he would either hit or the EMP would tear him apart.

He spread his arms and leaned over the edge of the hole, allowing the wind to support him. Below him was nothing but the matte plane of the wall and, past that, the black emptiness of the twisting void.

He wobbled as he struggled to maintain his balance. He had to get the timing just right or he'd end up hitting the wall and . . .

Even at that final moment, he couldn't let go of his fear and pain, couldn't stop his mind from racing at a frantic pace.

He looked to the sky.

High above, a spark of light inched across the dome of the heavens. He squinted, wondering what it was.

A moment later he realized: the light was the *Adamura,* carving its curving path around Talos VII.

Had he really been up there, on board that celestial visitor? Had he once flown instead of crawled? He barely remembered what it was like on the *Adamura*—it felt as if years had passed—but for the first time, he missed it.

A painful sense of wonder filled him as he stared at the shining star of a spaceship, and his heart ached at the fullness of existence.

It's all so beautiful.

He thought of Chen, still lying in the sledge, wounded, alone, waiting for him to return.

And Alex hesitated.

If he jumped, Chen would die.

Was that what he wanted? To commit murder by inaction? To remove someone else's chance to live and find meaning in the universe?

Alex's breath caught as he struggled in an agony of indecision. It seemed monstrously unfair that *he* was the only one who could help Chen. Why couldn't he just let go, for once, and be free of the horrors that had tormented him from the moment he'd received the fateful call that marked the end of *before* and the beginning of the joyless *now*?

Why?

He lifted his head and howled into his helmet, releasing all of his pain and anger in a primal blast of his own.

In an abstract sense, he didn't care what happened to *anyone*. As far as he was concerned, humanity could go extinct, and the universe would be neither better nor worse than before.

But when the abstract became concrete, when it was a man struggling to breathe in front of you . . . then it was different. Alex wasn't sure why, but it was, and he knew he couldn't consign a helpless soul to the void.

Despite his resentment, the realization was freeing, for it removed—for a time—the burden of decision. He had no choice. Not if he was going to save Chen. If he wanted to end himself later, once they arrived at the lander, he always could. But in the meantime, Chen's need overrode Alex's desire.

And if they *were* going to return, then there were still tests and observations that he could make on the way back. Things to learn, data to record. All of which would be useful.

Alex's thoughts expanded. If he made it to the lander, he would want to organize the information they'd collected. So that others would understand. So that *he* could understand.

The expedition had given him a goal, and the goal had given him a reason to keep moving. He recognized that now. As long as he had a destination in mind, he could keep putting one foot in front of the other. It didn't mean life would be easy or pleasant, but maybe it could be bearable.

Maybe.

He could continue to study the hole, for himself and for Layla. And if the hole ultimately proved to be uninteresting, there was an entire galaxy waiting to be explored. If he'd learned one thing on Talos, it was that there were still deep mysteries in the universe—unexpected truths that could rewrite their understanding of reality itself.

Wasn't that worth staying around for?

He didn't know. But perhaps it was worth finding out.

Either way, he couldn't bring himself to kill Chen.

The urge to jump had passed, and in its absence, Alex felt a sense of almost unbearable lightness. His tears were no longer born of sorrow but of release.

"Forgive me," he whispered, edging back from the hole. He thought Layla would understand. She always had.

He watched the *Adamura* arc toward the dust-hazed horizon, and for the first time since *before,* he felt a sense of hope. He laughed then, and blinked back the tears.

The time between bursts seemed to be getting shorter. No . . . that couldn't be right. The gaps in his memory were getting longer.

He shivered. He didn't have much more time. He had to leave soon or he'd end up swallowed by one of the slices of oblivion, never to wake again.

Besides, there was someone relying on him now. He couldn't afford to fail.

It was a new feeling. He liked it.

The fractal angels still hung before him. He raised a hand, and they flared brighter than ever. Then he turned his back on the glittering creatures—visual artifacts or living beings, he still couldn't tell—and on the vastness of the hole and its seething depths.

Behind him, he saw seven turtles sitting in a half circle ten meters away.

He wondered how long they had been watching.

Please, Alex thought, and he was surprised by the strength of his desire. Please let him pass. The thought of dying now filled him with more fear than the thought of jumping.

He took a step and then another.

The turtles silently moved aside.

As he trudged away from the hole, Alex thought of what lay before him. Of the trek back to the sledge and of everything he'd have to do before he could start east for the lander. He'd have to pull Chen out of the sledge, attach the wheels, raise the mast and sail, somehow wrangle Chen back into the converted vehicle . . . and he was already so tired, and his body hurt so damn *much*.

And he thought of having to deal with Idris and Jonah again, and Lt. Fridasdottir, and everyone back on the *Adamura*. He thought of the endless questions. The forms. The wire scans. The investigations, and how tedious the whole process would be.

Despite it all, Alex smiled. That was okay. He was willing to put up with the discomfort and inconvenience.

He was willing to try.

"I conclude that all is well," says Edipus, *and that remark is sacred.*

—ALBERT CAMUS

ADDENDUM

* * * * * * *

APPENDIX I

*   *   *   *   *   *   *

TERMINOLOGY

"May your path always lead to knowledge."
"Knowledge to freedom."

—ENTROPIC LITANY

"Eat the path."

—INARË

A

ACUWAKE: *see* StimWare.

ADYSÓPITOS ORTHODOXY: heretical Roman Catholic sect that emphasizes the inescapable suffering of material life and rejects the concept of a compassionate god, instead believing that Christ's travails on the cross led the deity to become fierce and unforgiving. In this view, one's purpose in life is to praise and elevate God with no expectation of further reward (but with every fear of damnation). Sect formed among the asteroid miners of Sol following a series of catastrophic equipment failures, famines, and pandemics.

B

BEANSTALK: *see* Space Elevator.

BELLBERRY: plantlike organism native to Eidolon, named after its proportionally large, bell-shaped fruiting bodies, noted for the wide variety of colors they exhibit. Reproduction is accomplished via sporidesm, which serves as a major food source for local insectile fauna.

BERYL NUT: edible nut with gemlike shell used in certain brands of meal packs. Gene-hacked species native to Eidolon.

BITS: cryptocurrency dated to Galactic Standard Time (GST). Most widely accepted form of legal tender across interstellar space. Official currency of the Solar Alliance.

BLASTER: laser that fires a pulse instead of a continuous beam.

BOSS: generic Hutterite term for a person in charge of any sort of project or organization. Adopted into general usage with numerous variations following the Hutterite Expansion.

C

CAPTAIN ACE SAVAGE: popular series of science-fiction novels authored by Horus Murgatroyd III during the late twenty-first and early twenty-second century. Originally appeared as a weekly serial in the *Pluto Daily*. Typified by over-the-top plots, extravagant characters, complete disregard for scientific accuracy, and a general tone of good-hearted glee. Considered lowbrow fiction by most critics, series has been hugely successful throughout settled space. Adapted into several films, games, and various spin-off properties.

CELLUDOX: clotting/growth matrix used to stop bleeding and foster tissue repair. Standard part of any well-equipped first aid kit. Often applied to deep wounds prior to suturing. Primary component of medifoam, which quickly supplanted Celludox in popularity.

CHAR: Medium-sized reptilian animal native to Eidolon. Covered in bony spines, and possessing the ability to deliver substantial electrical discharges via specialized organs in its mouth. Charges are strong enough to incapacitate and even kill prey while—as name indicates—charring flesh, hide, and other organic material. Attacks on humans are the exception, not the rule, but several fatalities have been recorded (all by electrocution-induced heart attack).

CHELL: tea derived from the leaves of the Sheva palm on Eidolon. A mild stimulant used throughout human-settled space, second in popularity only to coffee. More common among colonists than Terrans.

CHINTZ GRASS: grassy symbiote native to Eidolon, named for the colors on its stalks that—when seen in aggregate—form chintz-like patterns. Sharp-edged, triangular stalks; glabrous leaves; and fragrant, tuberous roots are notable features. Composite organism that arises from an amoebozoan similar to Terran slime molds, which live among the filaments of multiple fungoid species in a mutualistic relationship.

CRYO: cryogenic sleep; suspended animation induced via a cocktail of drugs prior to FTL travel.

CRYO SICKNESS: generalized digestive, metabolic, and hormonal distress caused by spending too long in cryo (or too many back-to-back trips). Unpleasant to deadly with side effects scaling to length of time in cryo and/or number of trips. Some individuals are more prone than others.

D

DERPs: dehydrated excretory recycling pellets. Sterile, polymer-coated feces as processed by appropriately equipped skinsuits.

E

EARTH CENTRAL: main Solar Alliance headquarters. Built around the base of the Honolulu beanstalk. (*See also* Beanstalk.)

EBUTROPHENE: fast-acting liquid analgesic suitable for severe to extreme pain. Contraindicated for long-term use.

EIDOLON: planet in orbit around Epsilon Eridani. An Earth-like garden planet teeming with native life, none sentient and most either poisonous or hostile. The colony has the highest mortality rate of any settled planet.

ENTROPIC PRINCIPIA: central text of Entropism. Originated as a statement of intent, later expanded to a philosophical treatise containing a summary of all known scientific knowledge, with primary emphasis on astronomy, physics, and mathematics. (*See also* Entropism.)

ENTROPISM: stateless, pseudo-religion driven by a belief in the heat death of the universe and a desire to escape or postpone said death. Founded by mathematician Jalal Sunyaev-Zel'dovich in the mid-twenty-first century. Entropists devote considerable resources to scientific research and have contributed—directly or indirectly—to numerous important discoveries. Open adherents are noted for their gradient robes. As an organization, Entropists have proven difficult to control, as they pledge loyalty to no one government, only to the rigors of their pursuit. Their technology consistently runs several decades ahead of the main of human society, if not more. "By our actions we increase the entropy of the Universe. By our entropy, we seek salvation from the coming dark." (*See also* Nova Energium.)

EXOSKELETON: (EXO in common parlance) a powered frame used for combat, freight, mining, and mobility. Exos vary widely in design and function, with some being open to the elements and others hardened for vacuum or the depths of oceans. Armored exos are standard equipment for Solar Alliance combat troops.

EXPEDITION BOSS: *see* Boss.

F

FTL: faster than light. The primary mode of transportation between stars. (*See also* Markov Drive.)

FTL TAPE: slang for vacuum tape, a type of incredibly tough, pressure-sensitive tape. Strong enough to patch breaches in outer hull. Despite popular belief, not suitable for repairs intended to last the duration of FTL trips.

FULL SWEEP: highest hand in Scratch Seven, consisting of four sevens, two kings, and a nine, for a count of ninety-one and a score of thirteen.

G

GECKO PADS: adhesive pads on the bottom of skinsuits and boots intended for climbing or maneuvering in zero-g. As name implies, pads (which are covered with bristles around 5 μm in diameter) depend on van der Waals force for adhesion. Shear force is limiting factor for maximal load, but also provides mechanism for release.

GLITTERBUG: small, insectile animal native to Eidolon. Noted for their brilliant, metallic exoskeletons.

GREAT BEACON: first alien artifact found by humans. Located at Talos VII (Theta Persei 2). The Beacon is a hole fifty kilometers wide and thirty deep. It emits an EMP at 304 MHz every ten point six seconds, along with a burst of structured sound that is a representation of the Mandelbrot set in trinary code. Surrounded by a net of vanadium-laced gallium that may have once acted as a superconductor. Giant turtle-like creatures (without heads or legs) roam the plain surrounding the hole. As of yet, no one has discovered their relationship with the artifact. Intended purpose of the Great Beacon remains a mystery.

GST: Galactic Standard Time. Universal chronology as determined by emissions of TEQs from the galactic core. Causality may appear to be broken but only appear; a must always cause b.

H

HASTHOTH CONGLOMERATE: interstellar corporation that began as a shipping interest specializing in interplanetary cargo deliveries before expanding into the development of pseudo-intelligences, construction of terraforming equipment, and funding of extra-solar surveys with an eye toward commercial exploitation.

HIVE MIND: psycho-mechanical joining of two or more brains. Usually accomplished by continual-beam synchronization of subject implants, ensuring agreement between intero-, extero-, and proprioceptive stimuli. Total exchange of prior sense memory is a common (though not required) part of establishing a hive mind. Effective range depends on signal bandwidth and tolerance for lag. Breakdown tends to occur when physical proximity exceeds tolerance. Largest recorded hive mind was forty-nine, but experiment was short-lived as participants experienced debilitating sensory overload. (*See also* Implants.)

HORN BIRDS: carnivorous flying animals native to Eidolon. Migratory, with leathery quad-wings and backwards-swept horns on their heads. Intensely social, their vocalizations are a constant source of annoyance for any who live close to their nesting grounds. Although not large enough to physically overpower a human (mass rarely exceeds 7 kg), their bite is highly acidic and will cause serious injuries and/or death.

HUTTERITE EXPANSION: series of intensive colonization efforts by Reform Hutterites, starting in the Solar System and expanding outward following the discovery of FTL. The period is said to begin shortly after the construction of Earth's first space elevator and end with the settlement of Eidolon. (*See also* Reform Hutterites.)

I

IMPLANTS: the melding of the organic and inorganic. Sophisticated computational electronics embedded in human brains and which interface via direct neural input. Common throughout settled space, implants provide such a profound advantage to users, few groups or individuals refuse them. Varying levels of integration are available, from basic audiovisual to the full array of senses, including scent, touch, internal psychosomatic stimuli (i.e., "emotions"), and to a limited degree, mental activity (i.e., "thoughts"). Widespread adoption led to equally widespread change in attitude toward memories, virtual spaces, and means of interaction among individuals. Invention also resulted in creation of hive minds (*See also* Hive Mind.)

INARË: [[**Invalid Input: Entry Not Found**]]

IPD: interplanetary diploma. Only educational degree accepted throughout all of settled space. Accreditation is overseen by Bao University on Stewart's World in cooperation with several schools in Sol. IPDs cover most relevant subjects, including law, medicine, and all the major sciences.

L

LION CLAM: animal native to Eidolon. Noted for its amber shell. Used in the manufacture of a sepia-colored ink.

M

MACHINE BOSS: *see* Boss.

MAG-SHIELD: either the magnetospheric dipolar torus of ionized plasma used to protect spaceships from solar radiation during interplanetary trips *or* the magneto-hydrodynamic system used for braking and thermal protection during reentry.

MARKOV BUBBLE: sphere of subluminal space permeated with a conditioned EM field that allows for tardyonic matter to transition through the membrane of fluidic spacetime into superluminal space.

MARKOV DRIVE: antimatter-fueled machine that allows for FTL travel. (*See also* Unified Field Theory.)

MARKOV, ILYA: engineer and physicist who outlined the unified field theory in 2107, thus allowing for modern FTL travel.

MARKOV LIMIT: distance from a gravitational mass at which it becomes possible to sustain a Markov Bubble and thus transition to FTL travel.

MEDIBOT: robotic assistant capable of diagnosis and treatment for all but the most difficult cases. Doctors rely on medibots for the majority of surgeries. Many ships forgo a doctor entirely, prioritizing cost savings over the relatively small risk of needing a human physician.

MEMORIALIST: one who leads services at a remembrance center. A nondenominational (and ostensibly secular) grief guide/counselor. Traditional uniform is a plain grey smock.

MT. ADONIS: *see* Pantheon Range.

N

NOMATI: polyp-like animals native to the arctic regions of Eidolon. Every solar eclipse, they detach from their anchor point (usually a rock) and hop fourteen times. Reason as yet unknown.

NORODON: fast-acting liquid analgesic suitable for mid-level to severe pain.

NOVA ENERGIUM: the headquarters and prime research lab of the Entropists. Located near Shin-Zar.

O

ORBITAL RING: large, artificial ring placed around a planet. Can be built at nearly any distance, but first ring is usually built in low orbit. Basic concept is simple: rotating cable orbits equator. A non-orbiting, superconducting shell encases said cable. The shell is used to accelerate/decelerate cable as needed. Solar panels and structures can be constructed on outer shell, including stationary space elevators. Gravity on outer surface of shell/ring is near planetary levels. A cheap and practical way to move large amounts of mass in and out of orbit.

OROS FERN: plant native to Eidolon. Green-black, with leaves that grow from a coiled shape similar to fiddleheads (thus the name).

P

PACKET: small, unmanned, FTL-capable messenger drone.

PANTHEON RANGE: large volcanic mountain range on Eidolon with individual peaks named after Greek and Roman gods. Popular climbing destination for Eidolons and tourists.

PRISONER: anyone not an Entropist. One imprisoned within the dying universe by their lack of knowledge.

PSEUDO-INTELLIGENCE: convincing simulacrum of sentience. True artificial intelligence has thus far proven more difficult (and dangerous) to create than anticipated. Pseudo-intelligences are programs capable of limited executive function but lack self-awareness, creativity, and introspection. Despite their limitations, they've proven immensely helpful in nearly every realm of human endeavor, from piloting ships to managing cities. (*See also* Ship Mind.)

Q

QUESTANT: an Entropist. One who quests for a way to save humanity from the heat death of the universe.

R

RED MOLD: opportunistic plasmodial syncytium native to Eidolon. Major driver in biological decay in large portions of Eidolon's biosphere. Toxic to humans; deadly if inhaled and grows in lungs (mortality approaches 100% after seven days). Once red mold passes blood/brain barrier, no treatment is possible.

REFORM HUTTERITES: heretical offshoot of traditional ethnoreligious Hutteritism, now far outnumbering their forebears. Reform Hutterites (RHs) accept the use of modern technology where it allows them to further pursue the spread of humanity and establish their claim over God's creation, but they frown on any use of tech, such as STEM shots, for what they deem selfish, individual needs. Where possible, they hew to communal-based life. They have proven highly successful everywhere they've settled. Unlike traditional Hutterites, RHs are known to serve in the military, although this is still frowned upon by the majority of their society.

REGINALD THE PIG-HEADED GOD: local cult leader in the city of Khoiso. Gene-hacked human with a head in the shape of a pig's. Believed by his followers to be a deity in flesh and possessed of supernatural powers.

REMEMBRANCE CENTER: nondenominational location that serves as funeral home (usually a crematorium), columbarium, and memorial center. Ostensibly secular, but in practice most Memorialists are either Reform Hutterites or lapsed Unitarians. Practice began on Stewart's World and soon spread to other settled worlds outside of Sol. (*See also* Memorialist.)

RUSLAN: rocky planet in orbit around 61 Cygni A. Second-newest colony in the League, behind Weyland. Primarily settled by Russian interests. Extensive mining takes place in the asteroid belts around A's binary partner, Cygni B.

S

SALK BARRENS: area north of Plinth, on Eidolon. A dry expanse bare of *yaccamé* trees but dense with chintz grass. (*See also* Chintz Grass.)

SCOURGE: microbe that killed twenty-seven of thirty-four humans sent to survey the rocky planetoid Blackstone.

SCRATCH SEVEN: traditional spacer card game. Goal is to accumulate as many sevens or multiples of seven as possible by adding values of cards (face cards go by their numerical value).

SHADOW SHIELD: a plug of radiation shielding that sits between a reactor and the main body of a spaceship. Comprising two layers: neutron shielding (usually lithium hydroxide) and gamma-ray shielding (either tungsten or mercury). In order to keep stations and crew within the "shadow" cast by the shield, spaceships usually dock nose-first.

SHEVA PALM: perennial woody plant of no more than three meters high, native to Eidolon. Named for the seven leaves that top its monotrunk (*sheva* being the pronunciation of *seven* in Hebrew). The dried leaves are used to make chell. Eidolon's largest agricultural export. (*See also* Chell.)

SHIN-ZAR: high-g planet in orbit around Tau Ceti. Fiercely independent, the colony often has a fractious relationship with the Solar Alliance. Notable for the high number of settlers of Korean descent.
Also notable for population-wide gene-hacking in order to help the inhabitants adapt to the stronger-than-Earth gravity. Main alterations being: significantly thicker skeletal structure, increased lung capacity (to compensate for low oxygen levels), increased hemoglobin, increased muscular mass via myostatin inhibition, doubled tendons, and generally larger organs. Divergent genetic population. (*See also* Entropism.)

SHIP MIND: the somatic transcendence of humanity. Brains removed from bodies, placed in a growth matrix, and bathed with nutrients to induce tissue expansion and synaptic formation. Ship minds are the result of a confluence of factors: human desire to push their intellect to the limit, the failure to develop true AI, the increasing size of spaceships, and the destructive potential of any space-faring vessel. Having a single person, a single *mind,* to oversee the many operations of a ship was appealing. However, no unaugmented brain was capable of handling the amount of sensory information a full-sized spaceship produced. The larger the vessel, the larger the brain needed. Ship minds are some of the most brilliant individuals humanity has produced. Also, in cases, some of the most disturbed. The growth process is difficult, and severe psychiatric side effects have been noted.

It is theorized that ship minds—both on and off ships—are responsible for directing far more of the daily affairs of humans than any but the most paranoid suspect. But while their means and methods may sometimes be opaque, their desires are no different than those of any other living creature: to live long and prosper.

SKINSUIT: general-purpose, skintight protective clothing that—with a helmet—can act as a spacesuit, diving equipment, and cold-weather gear. Standard equipment for anyone in a hostile environment.

SLV: superluminal vehicle. League designation for a civilian vessel capable of FTL.

SOLAR ALLIANCE: Sol-based government consisting of three primary members: Earth, Mars, and Venus, with Earth being the largest and most powerful faction. Originally formed prior to the discovery of FTL. Shin-Zar and many of the interstellar colonies retain a high degree of independence, with stronger ties to individual countries and companies than the Solar Alliance itself.

SPACE ELEVATOR: carbon-fiber ribbon that extends from the surface of a planet all the way to an anchor point (usually an asteroid) out past geostationary orbit. Crawlers transport mass up and down the ribbon.

SPACER'S TAN: inevitable result of spending days and months under the full-spectrum lights used in spaceships to avoid seasonal affective disorder, vitamin D deficiency, and a host of other ailments. Especially notable in native station dwellers and lifelong ship inhabitants.

STEM SHOTS: series of anti-senescent injections that revitalize cellular processes, suppress mutagenic factors, restore telomere length, and generally return the body to a state equivalent to mid-twenties biological age. Usually repeated every twenty years thereafter. Doesn't stop age-induced cartilage growth in ears, nose, etc.

STEWART'S WORLD: rocky planet in orbit around Alpha Centauri. First settled world outside of Sol. Discovered and named by Ort Stewart. Not a hospitable place, and as a result, the settlers produce a higher than normal proportion of scientists, their expertise being needed to survive the harsh environment. Also why so many spacers come from Stewart's World; they're eager to find somewhere more temperate.

STIMWARE: one of several brands of a popular sleep-replacement medication. The drug contains two different compounds: one to reset the body's circadian rhythm, and one to clear the brain of metabolites such as β-amyloid.

When sleep-deprived, dosage prevents neurodegeneration and maintains high-level mental/physical functioning. Anabolic state of sleep is not replicated, so normal rest is still needed for secretion of growth hormone and proper recovery from daily stresses.

STRAIGHT SWEEP: highest natural hand in Scratch Seven, consisting of four kings, two queens, and an eight, for a count of eighty-four and a score of twelve.

T

TEQ: *see* Transluminal Energy Quantum.

THRESH: hardcore smasher metal that originated in the farming communities of Eidolon. Noted for use of agricultural implements as instruments.

THULE: aka the Lord of Empty Spaces. Pronounced *THOOL*. God of the spacers. Derived from *ultima Thule*, Latin phrase used to mean "a place beyond the borders of all maps." Originally applied to a trans-Neptunian planetesimal in Sol, the term came to be applied to the "unknown" in general, and from there gained personification. Extensive superstitions surround Thule among the asteroid miners in Sol and elsewhere.

TIGERMAUL: large, felinesque predator native to Eidolon. Noted for the barbs on its back, yellow eyes, and high intelligence.

TRANSLUMINAL ENERGY QUANTUM (TEQ): the most fundamental building block of reality. A quantized entity of Planck length 1, Planck energy 1, and zero mass. Occupies every point of space, both sub- and superluminal as well as within the luminal membrane that divides the two.

TRUSKIN: artificial spray-on skin used to form a flexible bandage, encourage proper tissue regeneration, and prevent scarring. Via bioelectrical signals, the body is induced to grow skin with proper collagen structure, vasculature, and innervation. Spray provides scaffolding and nutrients to accelerate process, which results in substantially reduced healing times.

U

UNIFIED FIELD THEORY: theory outlined by Ilya Markov in 2107 that provides the underpinnings for FTL travel (as well as numerous other technologies).

UTF: United Taxonomical Foundation. Non-profit, non-governmental organization that oversees the naming conventions and cataloguing of all known life-forms. Their numerical designations supplanted earlier binomial nomenclature systems. Headquartered on Earth, but with substantial facilities on Eidolon.

W

WIREHEAD: pejorative term for person who becomes addicted to their implants, either via obsession with virtual content or—more dangerously—via direct stimulation of the pleasure centers of their brain. Such stimulation is illegal throughout the Solar Alliance and also on Shin-Zar, but addiction remains all too common, and those so afflicted often neglect themselves to the point of death.

WIRE SCAN: an in-depth, invasive review of all the data gathered by a person's implants. Often damaging to the physical and mental health of the subject, given the strength of the electrical signals used as well as the intimate nature of the probe. Sometimes results in loss of brain function.

Y

YACCAMÉ TREE: tree-like species native to Eidolon. Technically sessile animals, *yaccamé* trees are noted for the multicolored "wood" of their trunks. (The wood in this case actually being a fibrous horn that carries nutrients from the fleshy body underground to the fronds overhead.) Tough and beautiful, *yaccamé* wood is used for numerous building applications, including the rainbow totem poles the Eidolon colony is noted for. By law, only deceased *yaccamé* trees are legal to harvest, but high demand for the wood elsewhere in human-settled space has led to large amounts of poaching and a substantial black market. Etymology of *yaccamé* is unclear, with linguists arguing it originates from Avestan (and thus has its roots in the Zoroastrian tradition), Tamil, and Turkish. A definitive answer has proven elusive.

APPENDIX II

*   *   *   *   *   *   *

TIMELINE

1700–1800 (EST.):

- The Sundering

2025–2054:

- Development and construction of Earth's first space elevator. Quickly followed by increased exploration and economic development within the Solar System (Sol). First humans land on Mars. Moon base built, as well as several space stations throughout Sol. Asteroid mining starts.

2054–2104:

- With the space elevator up, colonization of the Solar System accelerates. Hutterite Expansion begins. First floating city on Venus established. Permanent (although not self-sustaining) outposts on Mars. Many more habitats and stations built throughout the system. Construction begins on an orbital ring around Earth.

- Fission-powered, nuclear-thermal rockets are primary mode of transportation in Solar System.

- Mathematician Jalal Sunyaev-Zel'dovich publishes founding precepts of Entropism.

- Law enforcement becomes increasingly difficult throughout the Solar System. Clashes start between the outer settlements and the inner planets. International space law is increased and further developed by the UN and individual governments. Militias spring up on Mars and among the asteroid miners. Space-based corporations use private security firms to safeguard their investments. Space is fully militarized at this point.

- Venus and Mars remain tightly tied to Earth, politically and resource-wise, but independence movements begin to form.

- Giant solar arrays built in space provide cheap power throughout Sol. Overlays, implants, and genetic modification are common among those who can afford them.

- Powerful fusion drives replace older fission rockets, drastically reducing travel times within the Solar System.

2104–2154:

- Fink-Nottle's Pious Newt Emporium established.

- Earth consolidates its power by forming the Solar Alliance, a system-wide government headed by Earth but including the planetary governments of Mars and Venus as well as numerous stations, outposts, and territories.

- STEM shots are invented, effectively rendering humans biologically immortal. This leads to the launch of several self-sustaining, sublight colony ships to Alpha Centauri.

- Soon after, Ilya Markov codifies the unified field theory (UFT). Working prototype of an FTL drive constructed in 2114. Experimental vessel *Daedalus* makes first FTL flight.

- FTL ships depart for Alpha Centauri, overtaking sublight colony ships. First extra-solar colony is founded on Stewart's World at Alpha Centauri.

- Oelert (2122) confirms that the majority of local superluminal matter exists in a vast halo around the Milky Way.

- Several more extra-solar colonies follow. First on Shin-Zar. Then on Eidolon. Some of the cities/outposts are funded by corporations. Some by nations back on Earth. Either way, colonies are highly dependent on supplies from Sol to begin with, and most of the colonists end up deep in debt after buying the needed equipment.

2154–2230:

- Weyland colonized.

- Numenism founded on Mars by Sal Horker II circa 2165–2179 (est.).

- Reginald the Pig-Headed God begins his ministry in Khoiso.

- As they grow, colonies begin to assert their independence from Earth and Sol. Clashes between local factions (e.g., the Unrest on Ruslan). Relations with Earth grow fractious. Venus tries and fails to win its independence in the Zahn Offensive.

- Alex Crichton born in 2197.

- Ruslan colonized.

2234

- Discovery of the Great Beacon on Talos VII by the crew of the SLV *Adamura,* and subsequent events.

*   *   *   *

AFTERWORD & ACKNOWLEDGMENTS

1.

I wrote this story because of a bad dream.

Back in 2011, when I was finishing *Inheritance* (the fourth and final book in the Inheritance Cycle), I had a night of dreams that, for various reasons, were incredibly vivid, both visually and emotionally.

The dreams were divided into two halves. In the first, I found myself walking through a dark, grim forest full of trees that were tall and twisted and just felt *wrong*. On the branches perched owls with barbed crests around their heads. The birds were two-dimensional and pitch black, save for their eyes, which glowed white. On the ground, by ponds, were frogs with bioluminescent stalks that sprouted from their heads, like angler fish, and on the moss under the trees were white, maggoty grubs that hopped around and went *skree-skree* and *skree-skro*. And when the grubs landed, they burst into five or six centipedes that burrowed into the moss and disappeared.

The trees and the creatures made such an impression on me I worked them into *Inheritance,* and I believe they made the book richer and stranger than it would have otherwise been. Especially the burrow grubs, which seem to have thoroughly horrified some of my readers.

During the second half of the night, my dreams changed, and I dreamt of a planet. A bare and rocky planet, turning endlessly in the depths of space. And on the planet, I saw a massive hole. And I heard it pulse, like a massive speaker, and in the sound it produced, I sensed the structure of the Mandelbrot set, a fractal pattern that wound deeper and deeper within itself. An infinity of detail from a finite beginning. And along with all that, I saw a group of three people on the edge of the plain surrounding the hole, and I saw them walking toward it—walking and walking in a slow, unhappy quest.

2.

As you can tell, those dreams had an outsized impact on me.

I spent a fair amount of time over the past decade writing about what I saw that night, both as a form of exorcism and as a means of trying to convey the emotions I experienced. Now that I'm done . . . I suppose I'm ready for my sleeping brain to serve up another chunk of weirdness as writing inspiration, although this time, I would prefer something a bit more cheery!

In 2013, I started my research for the Fractalverse and *To Sleep in a Sea of Stars*. It was a task that consumed the entire year, but during that time, I thought it a good idea to attempt a prequel short story for *TSiaSoS* as a way of getting some experience in this new setting before attempting a story as large as *TSiaSoS*'s. Keep in mind, I had been writing fantasy from the age of fifteen until the age of twenty-eight, and the experience left a number of linguistic habits imprinted on my brain. Habits that I needed to purge if I were to write the sort of science fiction I wanted to.

Originally I thought *Fractal Noise* would be ten or fifteen pages long, max. As with so many of my projects, it ballooned to many times that size. Still, compared with the Inheritance Cycle and *TSiaSoS*, I suppose it *is* a short story.

I finished the first draft of *Fractal Noise* on October 8, 2013. That version of the story was half the size of the book you now hold and—I was dismayed to realize—didn't really work. It was a much more depressing, misanthropic, and nihilistic work, and after some introspection, I realized that (a) I didn't want to publish anything so dark and (b) I wanted to move on and write *TSiaSoS* instead of spending another few months revising *Fractal Noise*.

(A point regarding (a): life is hard for everyone. It seems to me the height of authorial misconduct to publish anything that might make people's lives worse. If a book can inspire someone, if it can help them when depressed or down, then it can also do the opposite. Which is why you'll never catch me writing anything that's ultimately nihilistic or defeatist.)

So that's what I did. *TSiaSoS* took me until 2020 to write and edit (far longer than expected). And by the way, if you enjoyed *Fractal Noise*, be sure to check out *To Sleep in a Sea of Stars*. It follows and builds on many of the events in *Fractal Noise*, while also telling a *much* bigger story.

Once *TSiaSoS* was out of my hair, I sat down and reread *Fractal Noise* and realized that, yes, this was a story I still wanted to tell. With a much clearer vision for the book, I jumped into revisions and—to my delight—they went smoothly and quickly.

3.

As with all of my books, I was fortunate enough to have an enormous amount of help from my friends, family, and colleagues. They are:

At Home

My parents, for their unwavering support throughout what has been a time of great changes. Huge thanks to my father, Kenneth, for keeping a hundred different wheels turning while I've been writing/editing. And equally big thanks to my mother, Talita, for reading, rereading, and helping edit various versions of *Fractal Noise* over the years.

Also a special note of appreciation to my wife, Ash, for her advice, help, and love during this process. Knowing you has made this book all the more important to me.

My awesome assistants, Immanuela and Holly, who have done an amazing job with websites, social media, promotions, art, writing, content management and creation, and so much more. Thank you both! These books wouldn't be possible without you.

My friend Martin Clemons, for providing some much-needed technical expertise re: radios, conductors, and electricity. It was his suggestion that the net of gallium should be an antenna, which also gave me some interesting ideas about the nature of the hole itself.

At Writers House

My one-and-only agent, Simon Lipskar, who helped shepherd *Fractal Noise* to publication, as he has done so well with my other novels. It's been a long road with this one, eh, Simon? Thanks as always, and here's to future books!

At Tor

Will Hinton, my editor, who helped me finalize the process of converting *Fractal Noise* from a short story into a full-sized novel. Among other incredibly helpful suggestions, he helped me add an important (and needed!) emotional through line between Alex and Layla.

Also in editorial: Assistant editor Oliver Dougherty for helping coordinate this whole project. Copyeditor Christina MacDonald, whose attention to hyphens (along with many other grammatical details) is greatly appreciated.

In publicity/marketing: Lucille Rettino, Eileen Lawrence, Caroline Perny, Sarah Reidy, and Renata Sweeney. As usual, they've done a bang-up job of getting the word out about this book.

In design/production: Rafal Gibek, Jim Kapp, Heather Saunders, Greg Collins, and Peter Lutjen, who are responsible for typesetting, designing, and generally making *Fractal Noise* look so good. (Can I rave about the cover for a second, because *yowza!*)

And thanks to everyone else at Tor who worked on this book.

4.

And of course, the biggest thanks of all go to you, the reader. Without your support, none of this would be possible.

As for me . . . After so many years spent writing about spaceships, lasers, and aliens, I feel a hankering to write something with swords and dragons instead. There's a certain character from the Inheritance Cycle who I think needs his own book. (Perhaps you can guess.)

In the meantime, remember to be kind to those you love. They're all we really have.

Christopher Paolini
July 13, 2022

ABOUT THE AUTHOR

Lo Hunter

CHRISTOPHER PAOLINI, firstborn of Kenneth and Talita. Creator of the World of Eragon and the Fractalverse. Holder of the Guinness World Record for youngest author of a bestselling series. Qualified for marksman in the Australian army. Scottish laird. Dodged gunfire . . . more than once. As a child, was chased by a moose in Alaska. Has his name inscribed on Mars. Husband. Father. Asker of questions and teller of stories.

fractalverse.net
paolini.net
Facebook.com/PaoliniOfficial
Goodreads: Christopher Paolini
Instagram: @christopher_paolini
Twitter: @paolini

Discover More
at
Fractalverse.net

- Meet the *Wallfish* crew.

- See the Jellies, nightmares, and spaceships . . . in full color!

- Listen to "Sea of Stars" and other Fractalverse songs by actress Jennifer Hale.

- Watch exciting RTC broadcasts.

- Find up-to-date news on the latest happenings.

- Visit the shop and get your own piece of the Fractalverse.

- See awesome fan art!

- And much, much more . . .

EAT THE PATH